JENNIFER WILLCOCK

Contents

To Ian and Ben

AURORA HIGHLANDS
LUPINE MEADOWS
WOLF CITY
ALPHA RIVER
LAKE SIDARA
WOLF KINGDOM
CLIFFS OF VULPES
TO THE LAKE DISTRICT

TO THE AURORA DISTRICT
THE FOREST
URSA HIGHLANDS
PAVO RIVER
FALLS DISTRICT
PHASIA RIVER

Chapter One
Teo

I'*D GIVE ANYTHING TO play hooky right now.*

The sun streaming through the floor-to-ceiling windows warmed the throne room, teasing Teo like a flirt. Dust particles danced in the sunbeams as he stuffed the desire to stand and stretch his arms. Listening to people from his clan, the Wolves, complain about the new policies he'd put in place was one of the least favorite parts of his new role as king of Wolf Kingdom. A role he'd been preparing for his whole life yet still felt unprepared to assume. Granted, Teo had barely been an adult when his father, the king, passed away two months ago from the Lupine Flu—the illness that had killed hundreds of people from his clan. Even so, Teo, the heir to the throne, hadn't had any choice but to step into the role.

He shifted his weight slightly, leaning on the forearm he rested on the arm of the chair. These days the palace held court the old-fashioned way—Teo sitting on a large chair with leather upholstery framed by ornately carved armrests. Behind him, above his head, a carving of a wolf print let everyone know who sat there.

Surrounding King Teowulf, was his advisory council, three members to his right and three to his left, in chairs not nearly so ornate as his own. The men and women listened to the people's viewpoints, suggestions, but mostly complaints, in a town hall meeting once a week. They and his mother encouraged Teo to be accessible to his people. Although he knew the advice was wise, the continuous grumblings of the Wolf clan made his head hurt. He blew out a silent breath.

The Wolf Pack guards, made up of his people's strongest, fiercest men and women, stood spaced around the room, watchful in their stillness. Thankfully, their services hadn't been needed thus far.

Stifling a yawn, Teo's gaze wandered to the sunbeams. A mild snap had melted the little snow that had fallen, and the warm air beckoned him outside. Was Jenna getting one last bike ride in? His lips lifted slightly as the girl with the emerald eyes and dark curls hijacked his mind, not for the first time that day. Although he'd seen her last week, it felt like a year. He mentally sifted through the rest of his day. Perhaps he could find time right after he finished here.

His mother wouldn't be happy, but he was his own man now. He ruled the kingdom, didn't he? Her worries about him being romantically linked with a girl from the Forest clan—nicknamed Foresters because they resided in the forest outside Wolf City—were silly. The Wolf Clan's hatred of the Foresters had to stop, and Teo was determined it would happen during his reign.

His shoulders hiked up at the thought. Although the Wolves had been respectful of Dr. Hood and his daughter, whom everyone called Rider, after they saved the clan from the Lupine Flu, it was a different matter entirely for their king to date someone other than a Wolf. Every romantic interest was viewed through the filter of marriage by the press and, apparently, his mother. Tapping the toe of his shoe, Teo stared at the windows. Their relationship felt long-distance, even though she lived only a few kilometres away.

A cough interrupted his thoughts, bringing him back to the warm throne room. His Uncle Alarick's attention was glued to the lord speaking loudly, about what, Teo had no idea. *Focus.* The gentleman smacked his fist into his palm. In his peripheral vision, Teo noticed the Wolf Pack step closer.

His uncle cleared his throat once more. *Pay attention.* "Lord Burr, I hear what you're saying, but it is impossible for us to control the number of Foresters in your shop at one time. Don't you want their business? From what you're saying, they aren't being a nuisance." His uncle's tone was mild.

Lord Burr's top lip curled as he eyed Teo, directing his comments to him, not the king's right-hand man. "Your Majesty, with all due respect, I don't think you understand how challenging it is to deal with a crowd of Foresters."

"Then enlighten me." Each of Teo's words crackled with frost.

The man spluttered, "Uh, they touch everything. I can't keep my eyes on all of them at the same time."

Teo templed his fingers as if he were about to pray. "Obviously." He locked eyes with the lord. "Have they stolen anything?"

"No." The man dropped his gaze.

"Please understand, Lord Burr. We don't police Foresters anymore. They will be welcomed in your shop, or it will be closed." Teo tugged his jacket sleeve over his wrist. "Who's next, Alarick?"

Lord Burr's lips thinned. "Your Majesty, as you've seen I'm not the only one to complain about the Foresters. You've allowed them to waltz in and take over."

"They've been given access to places they've been denied before. That's not taking over." Teo motioned for the Wolf Pack to escort the man out, signalling the end of the discussion. He'd heard the lord's complaint, but Teo was in no mood to argue with someone who wasn't ready to listen.

"Maybe we should find the Haan family—give them back their rightful position in the palace," the man growled as the Wolf Pack practically carried him out of the room.

Teo's brow furrowed as Alarick wrote furiously on a pad of paper. He leaned sideways to hiss at his uncle, "What was that about? I haven't heard that name mentioned since I was a kid." A knot formed in Teo's gut. The Haans had been rivals of the Howells several decades ago, claiming Joseph Haan was the rightful heir to the throne because he was the firstborn son of Teo's great-uncle, who abdicated the throne for love, then regretted his decision when the affair failed. Joseph had challenged Teo's great-grandfather for the throne, but the king had laughed him off, saying Joseph had no grounds for the challenge. He'd willingly given up the throne. Joseph then allegedly hired an assassin, whose attempt to kill the king was unsuccessful. Because the evidence against Joseph was only circumstantial, he was freed. Still, Teo's great-grandfather had banished Joseph and every living relative from Wolf Kingdom.

Alarick laid his pen on the pad. "Not your concern, Teo. It's people grumbling and making idle threats. Nothing new. It happened during your father's reign too. People question the status quo when succession of power occurs. There are still some supporters of Joseph Haan around, but it's not anything to worry about. We're monitoring it."

Teo raised his eyebrows. "Joseph Haan is still alive?" He had to be at least a hundred years old.

"No, but he has family in another kingdom. We keep tabs on them, but there's been no suspicious movement."

Teo rubbed his chin. "I want to be kept in the loop. As far as the disgruntled merchants, either they sell to all or they sell to no one. I don't have time to waste on this nonsense."

"I agree, Your Majesty." Alarick shoved his pen in the chest pocket of his jacket. A few advisors frowned but remained silent. It would take time for everyone to get on board with the equality for Foresters that allowed them equal access to the city and all it had to offer. Teo studied the faces of his advisors. Did any of them secretly support Haan? No. They were loyal to him.

A sharp pain stabbed his left eye. If he didn't finish this meeting soon, he'd have a migraine. "This is the last one. It's too nice out to be holed up in this stuffy room."

Teo thought he saw a smile on his uncle's face before Alarick turned to the Wolf Pack, signalling them to bring in the last person. He didn't enjoy these meetings any more than Teo.

An elderly woman with a slight limp moved in front of the king. Her long hair was pulled severely back in a bun, the streaks of grey making a striped pattern across her head. She was tall and lean, but the washed-out blue eyes boring into him raised the hairs on the back of Teo's neck. He forced himself to meet her stare. *Don't show fear.* Where had that thought come from? He wasn't afraid of an old lady.

"How may I help you, Madam?"

"My name is Marta Jergus. I am a Forester." Her chin raised a little at the admission. The Foresters weren't the wallflowers he'd always believed. The woman held out a package, which a Wolf Pack guard relieved her of. "I came to give you this. I found it in the forest, but it's not native to it."

The guard checked the package but, deeming it safe, passed it to Alarick, who peeked into the opening. He frowned. Teo leaned closer, peering into the box. Blue leaves. What were they?

The woman held up her hand. "Don't touch them. I was sweeping under some bushes near my home when I noticed blue beneath a pile of twigs. I grabbed it, thinking it was fabric. I don't know where the plant came from—the best I can figure is it blew into my yard in that windstorm last week. It doesn't seem natural. My hands tingled when I picked it up. Maybe I'm allergic, but you need to be careful."

She locked eyes with Teo. Again, the hairs on his neck rose. His gut told him she was talking about more than the foreign plant.

"Why bring it to me?"

"You're the new king. You said you want things to be different. So do I. I brought it to you because I think it has trouble for the Foresters written all over it. You said you would be a king that represented every-one in Wolf Kingdom, so I'm trusting you'll protect us from whatever might pose a threat."

A challenge, to see if he'd do as he had said he would. He levelled his gaze to hers. "Thank you, Ms. Jergus, for bringing this to my attention. We'll look into it."

"It's trouble." She nodded her head once as if agreeing with herself, then strode from the room, not waiting for an escort.

Teo side-eyed his uncle, who had re-wrapped the package tightly.

"That's all for today. Enjoy the rest of your day." Teo stood, gesturing for his uncle to come near. "That was strange."

"Hmm. I agree."

Teo's eyes narrowed. "Don't touch it with your bare hands. It sounds as though it is toxic. She was challenging me to step up and put my words into action."

"Indeed." Alarick clapped Teo's shoulder. "She has nothing to worry about. I believe you will be a king who does represent everyone in Wolf Kingdom."

Teo blew out a breath. "I hope I don't disappoint her."

"You won't." Alarick lifted the package. "I'll deal with this."

"Let me know what you find out."

His uncle nodded before heading out the door, leaving Teo alone in the large room. He rolled his shoulders, then tilted his head, the sunbeams warming his skin and washing away the doubts and worries of the day.

Playing hooky had been a fantasy today. He sighed, picturing walking the streets of the city, people-watching. That would be the best way for him to take the temperature of the kingdom. And maybe see a certain courier. He smiled as an image of Rider shoved aside the memory of the strange plant and the name Haan for a brief moment. But the stack of files on his desk was a reality check, reminding Teo that he wasn't free to do as he wished.

After all, he had a kingdom to run.

Chapter Two
Rider

"THIS IS THE LAST of the vaccine, Dad." Rider carefully squeezed the box between a jug of milk and a bowl of leftover stew in the refrigerator of her kitchen. Tomorrow she'd deliver it to the medical offices in the city. As of right now, she was done working for the day. Straightening, she glanced over the door of the fridge at her father, who sat at the large wooden table.

"I hope they won't need it, but it's insurance against any rogue cases of the Lupine flu." Her father looked up from reading the newspaper. "Thanks for boxing it up."

Before closing the door, Rider pulled out an apple from the crisper. She wiped it against her shirt, then took a bite, juice squirting out the side of her mouth.

"He's done well, sweetie. The disease is almost eradicated. No new cases in the last week. That's a first. It took a lot of courage to terminate the trade deal with Falls District and ChemTech, especially considering their already strained relations after Teo left Tania at the altar."

She swiped her sleeve across her mouth, shoving away the thought of Teo marrying that girl from the Peacock clan. "I know. But you deserved to be reinstated as the supplier of the vaccine and medications to Wolf Kingdom." Teo's father, King Duko, had replaced Dr. Hood as the main purveyor of medicine with a company from another district that made synthetic drugs. Teo had reversed that decision when he became king after his father's death. She wasn't going to give all the credit to Teo, though. Her father had earned the promotion to Chief Medical Officer the king had bestowed on Dr. Hood the month before.

"Your young man is doing what's best for the kingdom, despite the complications it makes for him. That's the sign of a wise ruler." He stood and came over to slide his arm around her shoulders. "I know you're disappointed you haven't seen him much the last two months, but Teo's hands are full. The kingdom needed stabilizing after the flu outbreak. That was his first priority. He's got a lot of work ahead of him, uniting the whole kingdom. Give him time." He held his finger and thumb slightly apart. "And maybe a little grace."

Rider tossed her core into the compost pot sitting in the kitchen sink. Its *thunk* against the tin echoed the sound her heart made as it dropped to her stomach. The eight weeks since Teo had taken the throne had whizzed by but at the same time crawled. Their contact had been sporadic. He'd written four letters, sneaked out of the palace a couple times late at night, and she had been to the palace on unofficial visits. Mostly, she was smuggled in by Seth or someone in the Wolf Pack. She and Teo hung out in his private quarters, talking, playing cards, and kissing.

Heat crawled up her neck at the thought of those kisses. Teo's days were long and tedious—meetings with advisors, councils, and other kingly duties of which she had little understanding. Rider pinched her lips together before blowing out a breath. "I know." Emotions were confusing. Although she wanted to understand Teo's busyness, it still rankled that he had little time for her. She picked up the half-full compost pot by the handle. "I'll dump this and then I'm going for a ride to take advantage of this mild weather."

"Okay, Jenna-girl. See you in a bit."

Rider kissed her father on the cheek before pushing open the back door and stepping out into the sunshine and fresh air. The sky was blue, not a cloud in sight, and Rider only needed a light jacket. If every winter was like this one, she wouldn't complain. She upended the pot, shaking out the peelings and coffee grounds into the wooden composter. After leaving the pot on the stair to carry inside later, Rider unlocked her bike and then hit the paths.

Pedaling through the forest, she wound her way to the city gates. She braked as she approached the large stone wall, her attention captured by a huge banner hanging from it. *Celebrate our new King at his Coronation*. Rider's heart flip-flopped as she stared at a life-sized Teowulf. The picture was eye-popping because the man was too good-looking in that military uniform. His ice-blue eyes stared back at her, and heat flushed over her body. Good grief. She was a goner if a picture made her react that way. She moved forward with the line.

The Wolf Pack, the kingdom's police, no longer sneered and growled at the Foresters entering the city. That had changed when Teo took the throne after his father died. The Pack weren't smiling, but they weren't rude or intimidating when Foresters showed their papers. All due to the new king.

It was a step in the right direction, although Rider wished they didn't have to show papers at all. She sighed, reminding herself all the changes she dreamed about couldn't happen overnight. Eventually, Teo would implement what needed to be done to unify the kingdom. If anyone could do it, he could.

After gaining access to the city, Rider pedaled hard, enjoying the sensation of flying through the streets. Turning left, she smashed into something hard. The next thing she knew, Rider was on her butt with her bike beside her, wheels spinning wildly. She lay stunned but unhurt. Someone moaned. Gingerly, she pushed herself up to sitting. The person she had hit was still lying on the ground, his back to her. *Oh no.* Rider crawled over to him, cussing herself for not slowing down. "Are you okay?"

The black, hooded sweatshirt covered the person's upper torso so she couldn't see his face. A pair of broken glasses lay next to him. Shaking him gently by the arm, she asked again, "Are you okay?"

He turned away from her touch.

"I'm so sorry; it's all my fault. I was going too fast."

His shoulders shook. Was he having a seizure? Writhing in pain? Rider closed the distance between them, fear gripping her like a vise. How long did a seizure last? When she leaned closer, Rider heard not sobbing but laughter.

Wait. What? She rocked back on her heels. "What's so..."

The guy rolled toward her, his icy blue eyes locking on her green ones. Her breath caught as she stared at Teo, tears streaming down his face from laughing so hard.

"What is it with you and bikes, Jenna Hood?"

Rider's nostrils flared. "If you'd stop, look, and listen before entering traffic, you wouldn't have this trouble." She crossed her arms over her chest.

Teo tilted his head back, roaring with laughter. "Traffic? We're in an alley. There is no traffic. Only pedestrians. And mad bikers." He pointed to her. "And you admitted it was your fault."

"That's because I thought you were hurt." She frowned. "*Are* you hurt?"

Teo sat up, brushing off his hands. "No, other than a couple of scrapes on my hands." He picked up his glasses. "These didn't make it, though."

Rider's eyes narrowed. "What are you doing out here, alone and disguised? Where are your bodyguards?"

Teo stood, tossing the glasses into a nearby trash bin. He held out his hand to help her up. She took it, enjoying the warmth his fingers gave off. Even though she was perfectly fine to stand herself, she'd take any chance to touch the man. He pulled her in and whispered, "I've missed you."

"Me too." She sighed as she rested her head on his chest for a second or two.

"I'm sorry we haven't seen much of each other." He kissed the top of her head, then broke their connection by stepping back and dropping her hand. Rider frowned when he glanced around as if worried someone had spotted them.

Teo shoved the sleeves of his hoodie up his arms. "It's not because I don't want to see you. Every time I might have an opportunity, there's another meeting to go to. I'm so sick of meetings."

"I get it, but it doesn't mean I like it." Her gaze swept the area. "Where are your guards?"

"Somewhere near the Falls District where they think I went on a hike." Teo grinned.

She swatted his arm. "Teo."

He grasped her shoulders lightly and walked her to the shadows of the building. "What? I'm resourceful and a creative thinker. Not bad things." His lips brushed hers, all her nerves tingling at the touch. Then he kissed her as if he hadn't seen her in a year, leaving her breathless.

When he pulled back, his own breaths were coming quickly. "I need to get back."

Gratified that he didn't appear as though he wanted to head to the palace, Rider placed her hands on her hips. "Where were you headed?"

He lifted her chin with a finger. "Where do you think?"

Oh.

Teo glanced over his shoulder. "I'll see you soon. I promise." He headed out the opposite way she'd come. As he vanished into the street, Rider grinned and straddled her bike. He'd been coming to her.

Chapter Three
Rider

A WEEK LATER, THE long lines at the city gates moved rapidly but not fast enough for Rider. Dragging her foot on the ground, Rider skidded to a stop, enjoying the mild breeze and warm sunshine. No one could complain about the weather—it had been more springlike than winter this season, meaning she could still bike into the city rather than ski. Riding was so much faster, which she preferred. She walked her bike toward the line, her gaze drawn like a magnet to a banner of Teo proclaiming his coronation in two weeks. The ceremony was more for appearance's sake, since Teo had been crowned king when his father died. Her stomach flipped as she averted her gaze. The stupid thing was going to drive her to distraction because it was hard seeing it every day but not the real person. She hadn't seen Teo since their run-in a week ago.

"Looks heavy."

Rider turned to the low voice, but all she saw was a grey wool coat covering a broad chest. She raised her gaze. The giant towered over her. A square jaw framed a strong-featured face—high cheekbones, elegant nose, and hazel eyes. Honey coloured locks were pulled back from his face. The bike he rolled beside him looked like a toy in his large hands.

"Pardon me?"

He pointed at her black backpack. "It looks like it weighs a hundred pounds." He moved a step closer.

The hair on her arms rose as she shuffled away from the stranger. Flinging her curls over her shoulder, she stared straight ahead. Maybe if she ignored him, he'd get the hint. He didn't; instead, he walked alongside her.

"Hood Medicine," he read the label on her pack. "As in Dr. Hood?"

Rider halted. "You know him?"

"No, but he's a legend from what I hear. Saved the Wolves from the Lupine Flu." He stuck out his hand. "I'm Matrix."

Rider hesitated, then slid her hand into his, surprised by its soft smoothness. Although this guy dressed as though he did manual work, his hands said otherwise. "Matrix is an unusual name."

"It's common where I come from."

"And where's that?"

"Oh, you know, around." He grinned. "What's your name?"

"Rider."

The guards checked the papers of a family a few people ahead of them.

"Talk about unusual handles. Is that your real name?"

"Real enough." As real as she was going to get with a complete stranger. The guard waved her forward. "See ya, Matrix." She tossed the words over her shoulder as she moved to the guard's side, handing over her papers. Most of the guards knew her by sight. She glanced over to where Matrix stood with another guard. His papers weren't familiar, so he wasn't from the area. Hmmm. He'd dodged her question of where he was from. Why was that? She shoved the thought away because she had other things on her mind. Delivery, then the dedication of the new Medical Centre by the royal family. Teo.

She wanted to see Teo, even if it was from a distance. She picked up her pace.

"Slow down!"

Rider ignored the warning from a man standing on the sidewalk. She wasn't out of control, so she continued as she had been. If she wanted a good spot to watch the ceremony, she needed to be quick with her delivery.

The memory of the tall stranger she'd met at the gates flicked through her mind. If she had his height, she wouldn't have to worry about being able to see over peoples' heads. Where was he from? The question nagged at her like a hangnail. Or maybe it was the fact that he'd avoided answering her that had her hackles raised. It was strange.

Rider hit the brakes in front of Dr. Lupine's office. *Focus.* She needed to step up her pace if she wanted to make the dedication in time to see the new king.

Rider left her bike locked up near the medical office, then hurried toward the beautiful new building that ended the street like a period. Maybe more of an exclamation mark. The five stories of glass, chrome, and concrete were simple yet elegant. Rider studied the building, so different than anything she'd see in the forest. Surprisingly, she liked its clean lines. Normally, she preferred the cozy cabins of the forest to the slick architecture of the city.

The building had been commissioned by the late King Duko, but Teo had dedicated it in the name of his brother Bleddyn, who had died of the Lupine Flu. Senselessly. King Duko's hatred and stubbornness had killed his own son because he wouldn't ask Rider's father, Dr. Hood, for help. The king had held back the medicine once he knew where it had come from. Rider swallowed against the ache in her throat.

The lawn in front was already crowded with people. Rider searched for a spot where she could both see and be seen by those on the platform. Spying an opening, she slid into the space between a group of middle-aged women and an elderly couple. *Perfect.*

Glancing around, Rider studied the crowd. It was mostly made up of Wolves, although she spotted a few fellow couriers and Foresters. *That's new.*

Usually, Foresters didn't bother with Wolf news or royalty. Perhaps more change was happening than she'd thought. *That would be awesome.* Teo had received pushback about new policies such as allowing Foresters to come and go into the city as they pleased with no more needless questions at the gates to hassle them and eventually no documentation at all. Giving the Foresters more privileges and rights was making some Wolves upset, but for the Foresters a sense of hope had budded. Someone jostled her elbow, and Rider stumbled forward a step. A shadow fell across her and she glanced back. And up. "Wh... what... are you *following* me?" she sputtered.

Matrix held his hands up, palms facing out. "No, but it's interesting we keep ending up together. Maybe it's a sign."

"We're not together, and it's not a sign." Rider faced forward, crossing her arms over her chest. She couldn't prevent him from standing behind her, but that didn't mean she had to talk to him. Instead, she searched for Teo. Some of the higher-ranking officials were starting to take their places at the front, suggesting the ceremony would begin soon. Rider adjusted her red hoodie, hoping it would catch the eye of the king. She'd secretly hoped Teo might give her a VIP pass today, but he hadn't. She pressed her lips together. It was an unrealistic dream and nothing to get upset over, right?

A hush fell over the crowd as Teo and the owner of the building walked down the stairs to the platform below, followed by the Queen Mother and Seth, the king's brother. Rider was slightly mollified to see that there were no other VIPs.

Teo wore a dark suit that she knew would make his blue eyes stand out. Rider's heart raced, pumping blood and heating her body. A murmur rippled through the crowd as Teo made his way to the podium. A few teen girls giggled nearby, and one of them started crying. Rider rolled her eyes. Teo was the most eligible bachelor in the kingdom now, and everyone had suddenly become a matchmaker for the new young king. Or hoped to be matched to him. Rider shook her head, hoping to jar the thoughts. The tenuous ties between the Wolves and Foresters had Teo hesitating about making their relationship status public. Rider suspected some of that resistance was coming from his advisors. Maybe his mother? Her chest burned, and Rider rubbed it with her palm. If his mother wasn't in favour, what hope did Rider have?

As the owner of the building addressed the crowd, she only had eyes for Teo. He was handsome for sure, but it wasn't only his looks. An air of authority surrounded him. And something else Rider couldn't put her finger on. Did he look older? Perhaps ruling a kingdom did that to you. Or losing two loved ones. His dad had been a jerk, but Duko was still Teo's father, and that relationship had come with some complicated emotions. Teo had hinted he still struggled with his father's actions, but they hadn't had a real conversation about it. Hopefully he was talking to someone, if not her.

She pulled her hood closer to her ears, warding off the chill that had blown in. A light wind ruffled Teo's hair. The young king had been through a lot, and Rider knew Bleddyn's death and Teo's new role weighed heavily on his shoulders. He took his reign seriously. Maybe it was those cares that Rider saw woven into his facial features.

The building owner stepped away from the podium, gesturing for Teo to take the mic. A few people cheered. His rich, deep voice filled the air, warming Rider from the inside out, a small sigh escaping her lips.

"Swooning like all the other girls here." Matrix's whisper next to her ear sounded like a shot, his words jolting her out of her bubble. Rider shifted to the side, frowning—did the guy have no idea of personal space? He chuckled softly, as if she amused him. Resisting the urge to elbow him in the gut, Rider shoved her hands deep into her hoodie's pocket. She took another side-step away from him, focusing again on the platform.

Teo's icy blue eyes locked with hers across a sea of people, causing a zap of electricity. She shivered but not from the frosty air. The world narrowed to the two of them. What was probably only a few seconds felt longer before Teo peeled his eyes away and glanced at another section of the crowd.

The king wrapped up his speech with a heartfelt dedication to his brother Bleddyn, and then Teo, along with his mother and Seth, cut the ceremonial ribbon. Before the snipped ribbon finished fluttering in the cool breeze, the royals were whisked away into the building, probably for some kind of reception.

Around her, people drifted away, back to their jobs and families, but Rider didn't move. She stood still, staring at the doorway where Teo had disappeared, her heart dropping to her stomach. Someone cleared his throat, and she turned to glare at Matrix. "Why are you still here?"

He held his hands up in surrender. "I'm curious about the new king like everyone else who came out today. Is that a crime?"

Rider curled her lip. "No, but stalking is." He *pffted* as she strode away. *Who does he think he is?* She glanced over her shoulder with what she hoped was a murderous look. Matrix's hazel eyes bored into hers, causing her to look away and quicken her steps. A knot coiled in her stomach. She picked up her pace, focusing on her mission. *Find Teo.*

Chapter Four
Matrix

MATRIX GRINNED. THE SPITFIRE had practically run from him. The girl was all fire and ice and prickly as a porcupine. *Not what I expected.* But the challenge she presented intrigued him. The wind whipped around him as he zipped up his jacket. The crowd had acted as a windbreaker, but now he stood alone as people dispersed to their daily activities. Everyone he'd spoken to in the kingdom had marvelled about the mild weather this winter, but where Matrix came from? This was cold weather. The thought of experiencing a "normal" winter made him shiver.

Matrix turned away from the direction the Hood girl had taken. *Wouldn't want her to think I was following her.* The corners of his lips lifted at the thought of her huffing and puffing. This was going to be more fun than he'd anticipated. He'd balked when he had been assigned to the girl because he wanted a more active role in the mission. But she was definitely a looker and fiery. He cracked his neck, letting the tension of the last hour seep out.

People hurried past as he walked the streets of Wolf City—parents wheeling their babies in strollers, couriers whizzing by on bikes, cars and small trucks snaking through the city. He'd noticed the low speed limits here, which made sense since pedestrian traffic was high. On the surface, it looked like Wolf City had survived the sickness that had plagued them a couple of months ago. Underneath that surface, though, dissension and unrest clearly simmered throughout the kingdom. People's faces wore scowls not smiles, and Matrix had noticed small groups of two or three Wolves talking, gesturing wildly. He'd heard phrases such as, "We don't mix" and "Foresters need to stay in the forest."

Grief was also etched into those faces. Too many had died with the flu. He'd had a conversation with a family who'd lost their father, and now even the children had to find jobs to make ends meet. They wondered if all that could have been done, had been. Matrix had assumed the role of tourist with the family, and they hadn't held back in sharing their woes. Wolf City wasn't as strong as it wanted people to believe. And perhaps the new king wasn't as different from his father as he wanted everyone to think. Soon the people would have another option if Matrix was successful with his mission. He didn't intend to fail.

Matrix paused before the gates to the palace, peering through the rungs of the wrought iron at the imposing building. What other weaknesses lurked behind the gated doors? Perhaps this mission would be easier than he'd expected. He rubbed his hands together, blowing on them to ward off the chill. How did people survive the cold here? He'd been freezing since he'd arrived a few weeks ago to scout out the place.

A guard approached him. "Can I help you?"

Matrix smiled. "No, just taking in the sights. It's such a beautiful building."

"Indeed." The guard nodded before strolling away.

Matrix studied the building, his fingers clutching the cold iron. Soon, if everything went according to plan, it would all be his.

Chapter Five
Teo

TEO PEERED OUT THE window of the limo, searching for a red hood. Nothing. Unclenching his fingers, he inhaled deeply, the smell of the leather interior filling his nostrils. The headrest cushioned his head as his body sank into the buttery seat. He glanced out of the corner of his eye at the street. One minute with Jenna, that was all he'd wanted—why was that such an impossibility now? *I'm the king, and I can't see the one person I want to.* She'd been there in the crowd, her red hood beckoning him. That electric shock when their eyes met—had anyone else felt it? He'd lost his train of thought, almost bumbling his speech. Like some thirteen-year-old boy, all Teo wanted to do was gawk at her.

At the click of the door opening, Teo turned his head toward the other side of the vehicle. His mother and uncle were settling across from him. The Queen Mother neatly tucked her grey-blue coat around her legs before buckling herself in. "A beautiful speech, Teowulf." His mother always called him by his full name when out on official business, even when no one else was around.

His uncle reached over and patted his arm. "That was an inspired speech today. Bleddyn, I'm sure, is smirking somewhere, because he finally got you to confess how truly great you thought he was." Alarick smiled warmly. "You did good, son."

A lump swelled in Teo's throat, cutting off any response. He'd dreamed of hearing those words from his dad for years. Now that would never happen. His father had gone to his grave disappointed in his son and heir. Still, it was something to hear it from his uncle, wasn't it? Maybe, although the knot in his stomach disagreed.

"She was here," Teo whispered, staring out the window.

The leather creaked as his uncle shifted his position. He imagined his mother giving Alarick a "look."

"We saw Jenna, or rather her red hood, in the crowd. It was a nice gesture of support on her part."

Teo stared at his uncle, whose tone was sterile, formal. Where had the guy gone who had holed up with Jenna and her dad while he was exiled? The one who liked the Hoods?

He opened his mouth to say something, but his mother's hand on his knee stopped him. Her hand was pale against his dark suit pants, and he stared at it. "Son, you know the kingdom is in a tenuous place right now. I'm not sure the new king romancing a Forester, even if she is Dr. Hood's daughter, will go over well with your people. They're having a hard enough time with the equality bill you passed, giving Foresters the same rights and privileges as Wolves."

Teo locked gazes with his mother. He knew all this from the town hall meetings. What she didn't understand were his feelings for Jenna. His parents' marriage had been arranged by his grandparents, with no thought to love. Had she ever felt for Duko what he felt for Jenna? Probably not, since Duko had only seemed to care about himself. Had he been different as a younger man? From what his mother had said about their life together, Teo doubted it.

"I'm not saying forever, Teo. Only... wait." She squeezed his knee before removing her hand.

Teo drummed his fingers on the armrest as the car rolled into traffic behind the Wolf Pack guards who surrounded the king's car. He searched the people gathered on the sidewalks until a flash of the unique red rewarded his persistence. *There.* He sat up. Standing on the corner, bike beside her, Jenna waited for the procession to pass. Once again, their eyes met, sending a jolt through Teo's body like an electric shock. Then they were past her.

He resisted the urge to turn and stare out the back window. *That's not behaviour befitting a king.* His mother's voice echoed in his head. Words she'd said repeatedly to him and his brothers when they were growing up.

Although his mother was applying more lipstick, he knew she watched him, so Teo schooled his features into a blank canvas. Closing his eyes, he hoped to doze on the ride back to the palace. At least if he pretended to sleep, his mother wouldn't give any more unwanted advice. As he shut out the rest of the world, his thoughts drifted back to Jenna. *They can't stop me from thinking about her.*

Sleep was elusive, however, so Teo jumped out of the car the minute it pulled into the portico at the palace. He needed a few minutes to himself.

"Teo!"

The tone of his mother's voice halted him in his tracks. He ground his teeth. Who had the authority here? She was treating him like a teenager, not a king. Frowning, he faced her.

"We have a meeting in the south blue room in twenty minutes. Freshen up and then meet me there."

"There's no meeting on the schedule."

"I scheduled it last minute. There was no time to tell you before the dedication. Please." She hurried past him into the darkened passageway, leaving no room for argument.

Teo shot his uncle a glance. "Do you know what this is about?"

Alarick shook his head. "I'm in the dark too."

"You're telling me neither the king nor his advisor have any idea what my mother is up to? Who is in control here?" Teo growled.

"Easy, Teowulf. It might be nothing more than details about your upcoming coronation." His uncle didn't sound as if he believed his own words. "At the very least, everyone is adjusting to the new roles here at the palace. Why not extend a little grace?"

Uncle Alarick was right, but Teo huffed out a breath. The last place he wanted to be was in another meeting. After hurrying to his quarters, he changed clothes and splashed cold water on his face. He'd do as his mother asked, then he'd disappear for a bit, intent on his own agenda for the day, including seeing Jenna. He would make it happen. He was the king, after all.

The blue room was decorated in shades of blue—sky-blue leather sofas, sapphire drapes, and royal-blue carpets so plush Teo was tempted to remove his shoes. As far back as he could remember, this had always been called the blue room because of the décor. After picking up his teacup, which looked ridiculous in his large hand, Teo lifted it to his lips, eyeing the man who was engaged in a lively discussion with his mother. Middle-aged, tall, muscular, and handsome, the years had been kind to the stranger. The man clearly came from a good gene pool.

His mother's laugh tinkled, but it raised Teo's hackles. He didn't find the man humorous at all, especially the way he kept touching Teo's mother's arm. And he was sitting altogether too close to her. Didn't the guy respect personal space? Despite his good looks, he reminded Teo of a slick salesman, making him want to move things along quickly. He slugged back the rest of his drink, then gazed at his uncle, who stared into his tea.

Setting his cup on the coffee table in front of him, Teo cleared his throat. His mother's eyes narrowed, but he held his ground. He didn't want to be in this room all day. "I'm sorry, but I have other obligations to attend to. Would it be possible to get on to business?"

The man—*what was his name again?*—nodded. "Your Majesty, of course. Thank you for making time to see me today."

Sirhaan, that was it. Pronounced Siran. Reminded Teo of a snake. Shoving aside the thought of a forked tongue flicking from the man's mouth, Teo said, "Of course. But first, how is it that you know my mother?" Because that was the main answer Teo wanted.

"Teo, that's irrelevant to our meeting." His mother smoothed the cobalt linen napkin on her lap.

"I don't think it is. Humour me." Teo motioned for the man to proceed.

"He's being a protective son—nothing wrong with that." Sirhaan patted his mother's knee. Teo straightened. He wanted to smack the man's hands away from his mother.

She smiled, resting her hand on Sirhaan's forearm. "We met in the Lake District when I travelled there last month for a couple of weeks." His mother had taken a much-needed vacation to grieve the loss of her son and possibly her husband. Teo knew his mother had loved his father in her own way, but his treatment of their family had been cruel. Probably she mourned what she'd dreamed her life might have been, dreams that had never materialized. That was all guesswork on Teo's part because his mother had never spoken about their relationship in depth, other than the day he was supposed to marry Tania. That day his mom had hinted she had made things work with Duko, but it hadn't been the fairytale ending everyone had hoped for.

"We struck up a friendship and have been in contact ever since. I think you should listen to what he has to say." As though she'd finally gotten the message, his mother hurried the story along. Colour filled her cheeks, the dark smudges under her eyes had faded, and she was more apt to smile these days. Did Sirhaan have something to do with that?

Teo narrowed his eyes. "Go on."

The man leaned forward. "I have in my possession something that should interest you, Your Majesty. I am a descendant of the Wolf clan, although I haven't lived here for years. I was a nomad in my younger life, not calling any place home until I arrived in the Lake District where I reconnected with family. In my travels, I've dallied in trade and inventions, particularly weapons, swords, knives, and small explosives. I'm particularly proud of a body armour that feels like a second skin." Sirhaan ran a hand down his suitcoat, as though he currently wore the armour. "Upon travelling in Wolf Kingdom, I've noticed that your security is lacking. Your weapons are old, making you vulnerable to attack. With the recent succession, I think it's advantageous to stop the gaps I've seen. I can help you in that area."

Teo inhaled sharply, glancing at his mother and then his uncle, who was frowning at the man. What was going on? His reign was going to be a legacy of peace, not war. She knew that was what he desired more than anything, and here she was bringing a war monger to the palace? Teo clenched his jaw as the vein in his neck throbbed.

The Queen Mother smiled at Sirhaan before turning her gaze to her son. "Hear him out, Teo. You too, Alarick. Sirhaan makes a valid point, and his concern is for you, Teo, and all of Wolf Kingdom."

Sure, it was. Teo schooled his features into a blank canvas, but his stomach churned. He'd hear the man out and then Teo would banish him from the city.

Chapter Six
Rider

T HE FLAMES DANCED AND sparks crackled as Rider shoved another log into the woodstove. The day's sunlight had given way to cloud and rain this evening, along with a chill that, like a bad cough, wouldn't go away. Rider pulled the blanket tighter around her shoulders, curling up in the chair beside the heat source. The novel she'd been thinking about reading sat unopened in her lap. Images of Teo from the dedication earlier today were all her mind seemed determined to focus on. The dark suit and white shirt had fit in all the right places. He definitely cleaned up nice. His hair was longer now that he no longer served with the Wolf Pack, and it suited him. He'd left his rebellious youth behind and become a man overnight. Her stomach danced at the memory of his face, the electricity zapping between them as their eyes locked. He'd seen her. Warmth filled her chest.

Sharp raps against the wood of the front door jolted Rider out of her daydreaming. Her eyes focused as Ethan let himself in.

"Hey." Her friend shucked off his wet coat, then hung it on a hook. Running his hand through his wet hair, Ethan sank onto the sofa.

Rider nudged him with her toe. "Hey, stranger. Haven't seen you in a while."

He removed his glasses, cleaning them with the hem of his shirt. "Two courier jobs take up a lot of time. But it's all good, 'cause I'm rolling in the dough *and* I think I'll have enough to travel next year."

She clapped her hands. "That's awesome, Ethan! I'm so happy for you."

"Me too. I can't wait to visit new kingdoms. Not that I won't miss home, my family, and... you." His gaze lingered on her. "Why don't you come with me?"

Rider flipped her book onto the side table as she hopped out of her chair. "Do you want something to drink? I think Dad made some of his berry juice." She hurried to the kitchen and pulled glasses out of the cupboard, avoiding answering his question.

Ethan followed her, settling a hip against the counter but remaining silent. Waiting.

Rider huffed out a breath. "I can't go with you, Ethan. We've already discussed this—I need to help Dad."

"That's an excuse. Your dad can handle his business. You don't want to come."

Rider stared at the ruby-red juice. It wasn't a lie. She didn't want to go. She wanted to stay near Teo.

"So, uh, did you go into the city today?"

"Um, yeah, I had a delivery too."

"Did you see him?"

"Who?"

He rolled his eyes. "Who do you think?"

Rider poured the juice, the red liquid filling the glasses. "I might have been around the new medical centre when the dedication was happening." She handed him his drink.

Ethan sipped it. "You're too good for him, you know. He's not even acting like your boyfriend." He set his glass on the counter firmly, juice sloshing over the edge.

"You have no idea what Teo is up against, or what he's thinking. He's got a lot to do before he can pursue... personal things."

Ethan crossed his arms over his chest. "Really? Because if I were him, you'd be my priority." His Adam's apple bobbed as he stared at her. After dropping his gaze, he shrugged. "I'm just saying."

Rider grabbed a rag, swiped at the spilled juice, wishing she could restart this conversation.

"Thank you for your concern, but I can take care of myself. You don't need to worry about me. Teo isn't going to let me down. I trust him. You should too." She squeezed his shoulder. "You're a good friend."

Ethan winced at that last word, then turned to stare out the window, his back to her. "I think he's yanking your chain." His shoulders tensed. "Never trust a wolf. Remember?"

Heat filled Rider's chest. "Where's this coming from? Teo, his uncle, and brother have more than proven that we can trust them. *Especially Teo.* I thought we were past this prejudice, at least here in this house."

Ethan swung his gaze to meet hers. "I'm not sure I'm buying it. Yes, he's made changes, but would he risk everything to date a Forester?"

"Stop." Rider covered her ears as she glared at her friend. "I don't want to hear it."

He shook his head, long strides taking him back to the front door quickly. He grabbed his jacket but didn't bother putting it on, only tugged the door open, letting in the stormy night. "Eventually you'll have to listen." The door clicked behind him.

Rider drew in a deep breath and let it out again. She'd never fought with Ethan like that. They'd had their disagreements as kids, but he'd never left angry. She gripped the back of the sofa to stop her fingers from trembling. *He's wrong about Teo. Isn't he?*

Chapter Seven
Matrix

MATRIX SAT AT THE back of the pub, the dim lighting shrouding faces in shadows. The perfect place to meet his partner. The smell of greasy fish and chips made his stomach rumble as though he hadn't eaten in weeks. The cold was making him hungry—was that human hibernation? He'd always lived in a warm climate. Drumming his fingers on the table, he squinted at the clock on the wall across the room. *He's always late.* His partner was his father's oldest brother, but Matrix found the guy insufferable. Unfortunately, he played a vital role in the mission. Water trickled down Matrix's glass, wetting his fingers. He sipped the ale, coughing as his taste buds rejected it. It was the worst draught he'd ever drunk.

"What's the matter, too strong for you?"

Matrix cleared his throat and then forced a smile. "Not at all. More like I'm surprised you're only five minutes late rather than your usual twenty."

His uncle slid into the opposite seat, shaking raindrops from his coat. "I'm not late; you're early."

Matrix rolled his eyes. Most people were intimidated by his uncle's large frame, but Matrix, who was as tall if not taller, was not. His uncle ignored him as he tapped the table with his index finger. "You make contact with the girl?"

"Yes. I waited at the gates until she showed, which wasn't long after I got there. The info we received was correct. She delivers meds like clockwork daily, although today she was in a hurry to get to the dedication." Matrix wiped his fingers on a napkin. "Jenna Hood is feistier than I'd anticipated. She didn't seem to take to me."

"Can you blame her?" His uncle chuckled, although the sound was more mocking than amused. "I thought you said everyone loves you."

Matrix scowled. "They do. But she's different. There's a slight problem."

His uncle lifted a dark eyebrow. "Besides not taking to you?"

"She's enamoured with the new king. She barely took her eyes off him at the dedication, except to accuse me of being a stalker."

His uncle smacked the table, rattling the dishes. "You're supposed to be sweeping her off her feet. We need Dr. Hood on our side. They have to like you, not be afraid of you."

"I can handle them, Unc—"

"Sirhaan. Don't call me uncle here."

"Sorry." Matrix spread his hands. "It might take a little longer than we'd hoped, but it'll happen. Don't worry, I've got it under control." Matrix forced a grin, hoping his uncle wouldn't see past the façade. Inside, his stomach coiled tight. Jenna hadn't given him a chance to question her about being a courier for Hood medicine, let alone request a meeting with Dr. Hood.

"There's no room for flexibility in our time frame. Win her over now—do whatever you need to do." Sirhaan stood, the chair scraping the floor in his haste. Matrix winced as his uncle hurried out of the pub. After slugging back the rest of his drink, Matrix hauled his large frame from the cramped seat. His thoughts whirled as he plotted how to catch a girl who was in love with someone else.

Good thing he enjoyed a challenge.

Matrix left the pub soon after Sirhaan. The rain had stopped, but he didn't want to get caught if it started again. He journeyed from the city to the forest, his long legs eating up the distance. Wrapping his scarf tighter around his neck, he congratulated himself on remembering it this morning before heading out to the dedication. He missed the mild temperatures of the Lake District. Shivering, he blew on his hands as he walked the lonely path through the woods. Cold was bad, but damp cold was torture. An owl hooted in a nearby tree, making Matrix jump. He wasn't used to all the nature. A park lay to his right and a solitary figure sat on the swings, his shoulders slumped, his head bowed as if he was studying the ground. Was that who he thought it was?

His curiosity piqued, Matrix wandered over to sit on a slightly damp swing, leaving one in between them. He recognized the kid as Jenna Hood's friend and fellow courier. The reports from Sirhaan's spies had been thorough, except when it came to her crush on the new king. That was a major screw-up on their part. What else had they missed? The creak of the swing brought Matrix back to the task at hand. Maybe Ethan could help him win Jenna over.

"Must be a girl."

Ethan glanced at Matrix as he pushed his dark-framed glasses up the bridge of his nose. "What?"

"A girl." Matrix spoke louder and motioned to the guy. "To have put that look on your face."

Ethan sighed loudly—all the answer Matrix needed. Dude had it bad. His mother had always told him the best way to get people to talk was to shut up and listen.

Ethan lifted a shoulder, let it drop.

Matrix studied him. How to get the guy to open up to a virtual stranger? "I'm new here, so I don't know anyone. You could talk about anyone and I would have no clue."

Ethan kicked at the pea-sized stones that covered the ground below the swings. "I've seen you around. Where did you move from?"

"The Lake District. Name's Matrix." He could be honest with Ethan because he needed Ethan to be honest with him.

"The Lake District? You mean Paradise. At least you don't have to worry about the cold and snow there. Why come here?"

"Family business." Matrix pushed off the ground with both feet, until he swung slowly back and forth. "So, what happened with the girl?"

"I'm in the friend zone forever," Ethan groaned.

"Ouch."

"It doesn't matter." He clamped his mouth shut.

Okay. Matrix lifted his brow. "You're going to give up that easily?"

"She's into someone else. And she's my best friend." Ethan jumped off the swing. Guess the conversation was over. "I gotta go. I'll probably see you around." With that, he took off, his sneakers crunching on the stones, leaving Matrix alone.

She's my best friend. Ethan Moss was in love with Jenna Hood. Matrix smiled. A love triangle. He could use this information to his advantage. Maybe they didn't need Dr. Hood after all. Sure, it would be good to get the old man on their side, but Ethan might prove more valuable to their plan. The knot uncoiled in his stomach as he rocked back and forth on the swing.

Chapter Eight

Teo

PAPERS AND MAPS SPANNED the king's large mahogany desk like an ocean of paper goods. Teo had read every single page twice, studying the maps until his eyes crossed, but the tightness in his chest remained like an unwanted parasite. Sirhaan's reports about weaknesses in security in Wolf City were alarming. Teo hadn't realized there was a significant number of exposed points along the perimeter of the wall. He leaned his head against the back of his leather chair, staring at the white ceiling. What should he do with Sirhaan's suggestions? His mother had insisted he read the findings of Sirhaan's investigation. Unwanted investigation, from Teo's standpoint. But he couldn't argue with the results. He needed to speak with General Scar, whom Teo had promoted from commander to general when he took the throne, and his uncle Alarick.

He collected the papers together, tapping them on the desk and hoping for a diversion that involved a red hood. It had been two days since the dedication, and a certain bike courier had haunted his thoughts the entire forty-eight hours. If he could only see Jenna, things would fall into place. Her presence refreshed him, and her optimism cleared his head. Gave him a new perspective.

A sharp rap on the door jerked him upright as Seth poked his head around it. Teo motioned him in, pointing to the chair across from his desk.

His brother sank onto the cushioned seat with a grunt. His military uniform was rumpled and dust speckled his trousers and boots. Dark smudges under his eyes emphasized his pale face.

Teo frowned. "Did you pull a double shift?"

Seth rubbed his eyes. "Yeah."

"Why?"

Seth unbuttoned his jacket. "Short staffed." He waved at the papers piled on Teo's desk. "What's going on?"

"You first." Teo moved a glass paperweight onto the pile of maps.

"You'll be getting a report. In fact, I thought you'd have it by now. It's not my place." Seth stifled a yawn.

"You're my brother and a member of the Wolf Pack. It *is* your place. Tell me."

Seth raised an eyebrow. "Wow. You sound authoritative. Kingly. That's impressive." He smirked.

"I'll show you how kingly I can be if you don't spill it. Now."

"A couple from the forest found a patch of land that appeared to have been burned. It was in a far lot of land where they rarely go, but they'd had some issues with flooding, given the mild spell. They found what looked like burned, decaying plants. Bright blue like the one the woman dropped off at the last town hall. Some of the officers went to investigate, so I had to pull the double on patrol."

Teo's fingers gripped the arms of his chair. "Why was I not alerted to this? The Wolf Pack should have come to me as soon as they heard."

Seth scrubbed his hands over his face. "I thought they had."

"Where was this found?"

"On the northwestern border of the forest. That's all I know."

"Which is more than me," Teo muttered. Why hadn't he been informed?

Seth held up his hands. "General Scar was going to call in a botanist to see if he could identify it. Maybe they're waiting to hear the results before they report to you. You've got a lot on your plate."

Teo massaged his throbbing temples. "Dr. Hood needs to be brought into this. He knows every plant in the forest."

"We don't know who is growing the plants. It could be a Forester—the burned field is in the forest, and the woman who came to the palace is also a Forester. I think you need to exercise caution when it comes to the Hoods."

Teo shook his head. "If a Forester is growing them, why would the woman and the couple come forward? That doesn't make sense. Besides, Dr. Hood is the most qualified to identify the plant, and he doesn't need to know why we're asking." He rolled his shoulders. "And what are you implying, anyway? You know the Hoods. They're trustworthy."

Seth levelled his gaze at Teo. "People are talking. They think you are getting too chummy with Foresters. They're afraid you'll favour them in your attempt for equality. You're asking our people to change deep, ingrained ideas overnight. It's not that easy for everyone. They're struggling." Seth picked at a loose thread on his jacket. "Is she worth the risk of losing our people's respect? Of causing prickly, unnecessary complications?"

Teo snorted. "Maybe I think they're necessary. Besides, I barely see Jenna."

"You're acting like a lovesick teenager when you have a country to run."

Teo stilled. "Is that everything?"

Seth didn't respond.

"Good. You've made your point." Teo dragged a map in front of him, pretending to study it. He'd tell Seth about Sirhaan later. At the moment, he wanted his little brother out of his sight. As if reading his mind, Seth strode from the room—dismissed.

Teo rubbed his sternum. Seth didn't deserve to be treated like a common soldier. Teo wasn't acting like a lovesick fool, was he? But hadn't he been mooning over Jenna before Seth came in? Teo chucked a pen at the closed door. *I may be king, but this is the loneliest I've ever been.* He propped his elbows on the desk and lowered his head to his hands as memories of Bleddyn flickered through his mind. His brother's stupid jokes that no one laughed at except himself. And then everyone joined in because Bleddyn's chortle made you laugh. And the way his brother always listened to him, even when he didn't agree. Teo had trusted Bleddyn. *I miss you, brother.* Teo sighed. He hadn't extended that same courtesy to Seth today; instead, Teo had been angry and dismissive.

Two hours later, Teo was still chained to his desk. General Scar had dropped off the report, and Teo had given him an earful about keeping him in the dark about the latest developments on the plants. He'd also filled him in on Sirhaan's report, to which General Scar had only scowled and said he'd look into it.

Teo stared at the report of the field of plants the general had dropped off. The small field was located behind brush and near the back of the acreage owned by the Nelsons. The couple rarely went that far back on their property, so whoever had planted there knew their comings and goings. When it had been harvested was a mystery. Whoever had done it didn't want anyone to know about it. The report went on to state that the entire section of field had not been burned, as first thought, only a few plants.

The leaves in the photo were charred, making it hard to distinguish shape, but the deep blue colour with green veins was something Teo wouldn't forget. Pretty. General Scar had taken Dr. Lupine to the area where the bits of plant were and asked the doctor if he'd ever seen anything like it. The doctor confirmed he'd seen a similar coloured plant at a conference in another kingdom, one with a different climate. Apparently, scientists were experimenting with this particular foliage.

Dr. Lupine had been fascinated until he'd learned what the plant was used for—drugs that caused biological changes to the brain. Large amounts could be lethal. At that point, Dr. Lupine walked away, horrified at the prospect that a country could use it for ill gain. Teo scrubbed his face. So pretty but toxic.

If it was the same plant. Could there be similar plants with that colouring? The report stated the patch was about half an acre, which was a lot of leaves. According to Dr. Lupine, he estimated that it only took a small amount to be toxic, although he admitted that was conjecture.

Teo moved the file around, searching for Sirhaan's documents on the security breaches. A deadly plant grown in the forest and weakness in the security of the city—the muscles in Teo's neck and shoulders tightened. He needed a second opinion about the plants. Dr. Hood had a vast knowledge, and regardless of what his family thought about his relationship with Jenna or her father, Teo needed answers.

What if it is Hood growing it? Teo closed his eyes, blocking out the thought. *No.* Why would Dr. Hood work to save the Wolves with the flu and then try to attack them? He trusted Jenna and her father. Duko's warning to stay away from the forest played like a broken record in his mind, as hard as he tried to block it. His father was wrong. And besides, Teo wasn't Duko.

Teo shrugged the black jacket over his sweater, then pulled the beanie low on his head. Flipping up the jacket hood, he strode to the back of his closet, knelt, and pressed his fingers on the wood above the floorboards. The click of a latch signaled his freedom for a few hours. Rising, Teo felt for the uneven seam in the wall. When he found it, he rolled the door across the panels.

After slipping through the opening, he slid the door back into place and then jogged down the dark passageway. He'd found the secret entrance when he moved rooms after becoming king. Refusing his father's chambers, Teo had selected a different suite of rooms, suitable for a king but without all the reminders of his father. Who had previously occupied the room was a mystery, since it had been empty for as long as Teo could remember. It didn't matter, he was grateful that someone's desire to leave unnoticed at some point in the past meant he could do the same now. He'd used it multiple times to escape the guards and wander the city. It was fascinating to watch people when they thought no one was looking. Today it was a means to talk to Dr. Hood and see Jenna. Nothing would stand in the way of seeing her today. He jogged the dark passage, intent on getting to the light and freedom.

Chapter Nine
Rider

IT'D BEEN TWO DAYS since the dedication of the new medical building and the last time Rider had seen Teo. And Ethan. She frowned as she measured dried herbs into a stone bowl. The kitchen was bright with the afternoon sunlight. Snow had fallen the night before, leaving the world white and clean.

The sound of the stone pestle grinding against dry herbs was surprisingly satisfying. She added another teaspoon and worked her wrist until it throbbed from the turning motion. The earthy fragrance from the smashed oregano revived her brain. Rider stretched her wrists, the memory of the hurt in Ethan's eyes at the mention of them being only friends at the forefront of her thoughts. Why did things have to get so complicated?

Rider dumped the herb into a container. Turning on the hot water, she held the pestle under it, watching as the refuse disappeared into the drain. After setting it on a towel, she did the same with the bowl.

Tap, tap, tap.

A shadow moved by the back door. Ethan. Rider flung open the door and her breath caught. It wasn't Ethan.

"Didn't your dad ever tell you not to open the door to strangers?"

Smiling, she pulled Teo into the kitchen. "What are you doing here?" She wrapped her arms around his neck, inhaling the smell of the outdoors along with his sage and citrus cologne. He felt so good. She squeezed him again.

Teo chuckled, the air tickling her ear. "You're going to suffocate me, although I wouldn't mind being hugged to death."

She tilted her head back, unwilling to let go. "How did you get here? Where is the Wolf Pack?"

"I slipped out by myself." He kissed her nose, then her jawbone. Rider clung tighter to his neck as her knees weakened.

"By yourself? How is that even possible?"

Teo rested his forehead against hers. "I have my ways." Pulling her closer, his lips grazed hers. Although they were cold, his kiss sent heat through her veins. She ran her fingers through his hair at the nape of his neck. Sighing, he whispered, "I missed you."

"I missed you too."

"I'm sorry I haven't been able to visit you—I wanted to, but..." Teo let the sentence trail off.

"I get it." She did, although a part of her wondered why he couldn't make time for her more often. Rider shoved the thought away. Right now, she'd enjoy his presence and worry about the rest later.

Teo twined their fingers and led her to the kitchen table. She sank onto a chair, not letting go of his hand.

With his free hand, he pulled off his beanie, then unzipped his jacket. "Wolves are balking at the new policies I've put into place regarding the Foresters. It's going to take time for everyone to get used to them. So, we have to keep us," he pointed between them, "under wraps. I don't want you and your dad to be given any more grief than you've already experienced. We need to be patient."

Rider tugged her hand from his. "Is this you or your advisors speaking?"

"It's the right thing to do at the moment." He balled his beanie in his hands.

She studied the dark smudges under his eyes and his pale complexion. Did worry about his people keep him up at night? She sighed. "Okay, I guess we can keep it between us. For now."

"Thank you." His shoulders relaxed as he glanced around the cozy room. "I can't stay long, but I wanted to come by, see you and your dad. Is he here?"

"He's in his office." Rider stood. "I'll get him."

"Actually, do you mind if I go knock on the door?"

Rider stepped aside and held out her hand. "Go right ahead."

Teo cupped her cheek. "It's pharmaceutical business—super boring."

"You can knock and go in. He's not going to deny the king." She bit her tongue—she'd meant to tease, but it had sounded sarcastic instead.

Red infused Teo's cheeks as his body stiffened. He dropped his hand and strode to her father's office. When Rider heard her dad calling for Teo to enter, she pursed her lips. What did he need to talk to her dad about? She drummed her fingers on the worn surface of the kitchen table. Fifteen minutes later, the door opened and both men emerged.

Her dad grinned. "Not every day we get royalty in our house. Can you stay for tea?"

"I'd love to Dr. Hood, but if I stay any longer, the chances of me slipping back into the city without being discovered by the Wolf Pack will disappear. They think I'm having a royal nap to ward off a migraine at the moment, but that won't hold them off much longer. And I'd like to keep my ability to escape the castle from everyone as long as I can." Teo held his hand out to her father. "Thank you for your help. I'm sorry I didn't come sooner."

"Anytime. I mean that." He shook Teo's hand. "I better get back to work." He let Teo go and headed in the direction of his office.

Teo watched her dad retreat. "He's a good man."

"I know." Rider walked over to him and laid her hand on his forearm. "I'm sorry for my snarky comment earlier."

Teo chuckled. "Jenna, I don't know what I'd do if you weren't you. Snark, spitfire, feistiness. I love it all." He did up his jacket, fiddling with the zipper. "But I really do need to go." He tugged her to him, pressed his lips against her temple, then brushed her lips, lingering there. Rider wished the moment could last, but he pulled away and slipped out the door, shutting it softly behind him.

She touched her mouth, fingering the invisible imprint he'd left. Too jittery from his kiss, Rider shrugged on her coat, then yanked a toque over her curls. Shivers ran over her body as she stepped out into the chilliness. Although the sun shone, winter had returned. Her breath made puffs as she stood in her backyard. What had Teo talked to her father about? And why couldn't he tell her? She walked around to the front of the house and set off on the path away from the city. Was he sick? Or was it because he wasn't sleeping? She rubbed her arms, hoping Teo trusted her enough to share any secrets he might have.

Chapter Ten
Matrix

THE COFFEE WAS STRONG and hot, the nuttiness of the blend teasing Matrix's taste buds as he surveyed the restaurant. Two women chatted at the next table, their hands waving in the air. An older gentleman nursed an espresso while reading the paper, his large hand dwarfing the small cup, and two teenage girls sat slurping some iced concoction that made Matrix want to gag. He opened his sandwich and removed the tomato. The door flew open, and Jenna Hood burst into the place, along with a gust of chilly air. Matrix straightened in his seat. With her wind-blown locks tangled around her toque and her flushed cheeks, she could rival any beauty queen. He understood what the king saw in her. Matrix took a bite of his sandwich, chewed. *You're not here to admire the sights.*

He tracked Jenna's movements until her eyes met his. Smiling at the fortuitous turn of events, he waved her over. Would she come?

She didn't disappoint. "Hey there." The steam from her cup floated in front of her face.

"Hey." He gestured to the chair beside him.

She glanced around the space, looking as if she wanted to be any-where else. "This place is busy. I don't usually come here."

"Join me?" he pressed.

After another brief hesitation, she slid onto the seat, crowding his space at the small table. When a waft of honeysuckle drifted by his nose, he found he didn't mind. "Why don't you come here often? Something wrong with the coffee?"

"Wolf-owned." She didn't offer any other explanation as she sipped from her mug. "It's cold out there. After this mild turn, I'm not used to it."

Matrix bit into his sandwich, chewed, and then swallowed. "Is it always this cold?"

"In the winter, usually. This year is an anomaly. Summer can be hot. Spring and autumn are delightful." Her hands cupped the mug, but her eyes never left his face. "I forgot where you said you were from?"

Persistent. He'd played the mysterious stranger long enough. It wasn't working in his favour. "I'm from the Lake District. It's pretty mild there year-round." He'd lived there the last few years. Close enough.

"I've never been. It's in the west, right?"

"That's right. It's beautiful country. You should go sometime."

"Why did you move here then?"

"Work-related." Matrix licked mustard off his thumb.

"You look too young to work full-time."

"I'll take that as a compliment. It's a family business. I finished school early, so I could help out more."

"I help my dad out too."

"Right, the famed Dr. Hood. What's he like? I've heard a lot about him since I moved here. Saving the Wolves and all that. I'd love to meet him."

Jenna picked up a cane sugar packet, tapping it against the table top. "I'm a little biased." She grinned. She had a great smile when she chose to use it. "He's a genius—knows every plant out there. What it does and how it can or can't heal. And he's kind and generous."

"Sounds like a great guy." Matrix forced his features to relax. The pharmacist knew every plant? He tucked that nugget away to tell Sirhaan. They couldn't have the pharmacist ratting them out if he ever saw the plant. Winning over Dr. Hood seemed more like a long shot every day, especially since Matrix couldn't seem to finagle a meeting with him. Ethan's face popped into Matrix's mind. The lovesick BFF was going to come in handy.

Jenna opened the package of sugar, spilling it on the table. She lifted the tip of her finger to her lips and licked off the excess sugar. "Tell me more about the Lake District."

Interesting change of subject, and she didn't take the bait to introduce him to her father. Matrix told her about the beaches and white sand, how he liked to swim and snorkel. He'd been busy preparing for the mission and dodging the Howells' spies, but he had managed to enjoy the surroundings when he could find the time. Now he was glad he had.

"I'm curious about the new Wolf king. I think we're about the same age. That's pretty young to sit on the throne of a large kingdom."

She cleared her throat. "King Teo is..." She stared off into nothing, a dreamy look softening her face.

Matrix clamped his molars together. *The swooning is annoying.*

Jenna laughed, her cheeks pinking. "He's also kind and generous. Not like his father. He grew up under Duko's hate, but Teo is going to unify the kingdom, especially the Wolves and the Foresters."

Matrix knew all about Duko. "You seem pretty sure about that happy ending."

Rider shrugged. "He's being transparent."

"Is he now?"

Her blue eyes narrowed. "You doubt him?"

"Never trust a Wolf. Isn't that the Foresters' motto?"

Rider choked on the sip she'd taken and set down her cup. "What do you mean?"

"C'mon, you've never heard that before? I've only been here a short while, and I've probably heard it ten times."

"It's not like that anymore. You'd better forget that if you're going to fit in." She stood. "I've gotta go. I've still got work to do. See you around."

Matrix watched her walk away. He'd hit a nerve. Grinning, he took another swig of the strong brew. *Good.* Sowing seeds of disunity was so amusing. People got riled up over nothing.

After finishing his coffee, he stood but quickly sat down again as Ethan sauntered into the place. The way his eyes flicked to Matrix, he remembered him. Matrix lifted his hand in greeting. "Hey, how's it going?"

Ethan walked over. "Okay. Matrix, right?"

"Right. Sorry I didn't catch your name."

"Ethan." He glanced at the menu board. "Just finishing my courier route. Thought I'd warm up with a hot drink."

"Want to join me? I'm dreading going out into the cold, so putting it off a few more minutes is not a hardship."

"Sure." Ethan ordered his drink before taking the chair across from Matrix.

"Did you figure out your girl problems?"

He sighed. "Nope."

"So, still in the friend zone." Could he get Ethan to open up?

"I will never leave that zone."

"That's tough, man."

"The thing is, she's too good for him. He doesn't deserve her."

"They never do. Look, don't feel bad, we've all been there. Dissed by some girl."

"She's not like that." Ethan poured sugar into his tea.

They never are.

"I've known her forever. We were... are just friends. Like I said, she's already involved."

"No chance to win her away from the guy?"

Ethan snorted. "Not likely."

Matrix raised his eyebrows. "Are they married? Engaged?"

"No. It's just... not going to happen."

"Whatever you say, but until a ring is on the finger, she's fair game, in my opinion." He glanced around the cafe. "You need a distraction."

"Like what? I've already got two jobs."

"You said earlier you're a courier?"

Ethan slugged a mouthful of tea. "Yeah, for Caps 'n Stems Truffle and Mushroom Farms and for Dr. Hood."

"Dr. Hood? I've heard great things about the man since I moved here."

"He is a good man, an outstanding pharmacist." Ethan glanced at his watch. "I gotta roll." He pushed back the chair and stood. "See ya around."

"If you want a distraction, let me know. I have something I need help with, and I think you're the person for the job."

Was that interest that flickered across his face? Hope flared in Matrix' chest.

"Maybe."

"What have you got to lose?" Matrix lifted a shoulder, a bored expression on his face. Inside, the blood roared through his veins—he had to get Ethan to bite. "Could be fun."

Ethan eyed him before tossing his cup into the garbage and striding out of the shop, lifting a hand in farewell.

Fun for Matrix, at least.

Chapter Eleven

Teo

"WHICH DO YOU PREFER to wear tonight, the military black or the blue dress uniform? Teo?"

Teo blinked, bringing himself out of his daydream about Jenna. His mother stood at the entrance to his bedroom, holding uniforms in each of her hands and clearly waiting for his reply.

"Sorry, Mom, I zoned out there. What did you ask?" It had been three long days since he'd seen Jenna. Instead of being with her, like he wanted, his time had been filled with mind-numbing, last-minute details about the coronation, suit fittings, and countless meetings.

The Queen Mother shook each hanger slightly. "Which would you prefer to wear tonight to the dinner?"

"I don't care."

"You should."

"I've been to a gazillion suit fittings for the coronation—I'm suited out. I. Don't. Care."

"Your coronation is a week away, and the only thing that isn't ready is the king."

Teo rolled his eyes. "It's a formality, Mother. I was already sworn in after Father died."

"It's not about you. It's for the people of your kingdom. They need to witness you crowned, so there is no dispute about who is in power. All the clans need to remember that we are their reigning sovereignty." His mother's delicate eyebrows furrowed. "There are certain Wolves who need to be reminded of their place."

"I know, Mom. You don't need to worry, though. The Wolf Pack has our back. Has *my* back. I'll be fine." She was concerned, which was why she'd brought in that creep, Sirhaan. Thankfully, he was long gone. One thing Teo hoped to gain from all the fuss was the signal to his people that change was coming. A new day with a new king. Then all the suit fittings, dinner parties, and hand-shaking would be worth it. He studied the suits and pointed. "The black one." *Please be done.*

"I agree. Now," his mother hung the clothing over the back of the closet door and picked up a folder, "we need to..."

Teo groaned and flopped onto the couch as his mother droned on about tonight's state dinner.

Tap, tap, tap. He sat up. *Please, please let this be an escape.*

His mother's secretary peeked around the corner of the door. "Please excuse the interruption, Your Majesty, but Sirhaan is here for the Queen Mother. He said he had an appointment."

Teo stood and clasped his hands behind his back to keep from pumping a fist. Then the woman's words registered. *Sirhaan. Wait. Why is he still in Wolf City?* Teo's chest tightened as he watched his mother, who was busy gathering up her notes from the table in the dressing room.

"I lost track of the time. We'll finish this later." She hurried from Teo's room, leaving him alone. Why was Sirhaan back? Teo's gut churned at the look on his mother's face as she practically ran from the room. What had that been, joy? He cracked a window, suddenly woozy. Whatever new perfume his mother was wearing, Teo didn't like it. He'd noticed it when she'd entered, but then the mention of Sirhaan's name had drowned out everything else. He leaned close to the screen, breathing deeply.

I thought I got rid of that man when I declined his idea to outfit the kingdom with those nasty weapons. Modernization, Sirhaan called it. From what Teo could tell, it was cruel and inhumane. Even for your worst enemy. *So why does mother have an appointment with him? Without me?*

The formal dining room sparkled like a diamond in a gold setting, and Teo blinked. The crystal chandelier as well as the glasses on the table twinkled in the candlelight from the centrepieces. His eyes adjusting to the glitz, he glanced about the room while he remained unnoticed. Friends, other rulers and dignitaries from the clans of the kingdom, had been arriving in Wolf City for the coronation next week. Teo sighed at all the events his calendar was jammed with for the next eight days. In the corner, his mother spoke to the Governor of the Falls District and part of the Peacock clan. Teo made a mental note to avoid them. He cast a furtive glance around for Tania, his ex—if you could call her that—but thankfully he didn't see her. The Peacock clan hadn't been happy when he left her standing at the altar almost three months ago. So far, he hadn't come up with a way to smooth over the ruffled feathers and hurt feelings. He sighed—that was a problem for another day. Scouting the floor, he spotted Seth in the opposite direction of the governor. Teo moved toward him.

"Excuse me, Your Majesty?"

A tall shadow fell across Teo. Sirhaan. What was he doing here? Had he been on the guest list? Had his mother invited him?

Teo cast a longing glance at Seth, but his brother hadn't noticed him. He schooled his features into a polite calm. "What can I do for you?"

"I wanted to thank you. It's a real privilege and pleasure to be included in these festivities tonight."

Teo stepped to the side, forcing a thin-lipped smile. "Please enjoy yourself. If you'll excuse me, I need to speak with my brother." He let out a breath as he strode across the room. Seth broke off his conversation with a courtier, who was a family friend, to meet Teo halfway. "Who's that?"

Grabbing a flute of something as a waiter passed by, Teo motioned Seth to a more secluded spot at the side of the room. "Sirhaan. I can't remember his last name." Teo frowned. Had the man given it? Or was he one of those people who went by only one name? "He wanted to sell us weapons. Some pretty nasty things. I declined. He took it upon himself to study our security and came up with a list of our weak points. The wall has some exposed areas that are concerning. I spoke to General Scar about them and he's checking into it."

"What's wrong with that? Sounds like he's trying to help."

"I guess." Teo chewed his bottom lip. "I thought I'd seen the last of him, but mother had an 'appointment' with him today. She practically ran from my room. I haven't been able to get her to put down her To Do file for the coronation all week. Sirhaan shows up and she's gone like that." He snapped his fingers. "Now he's here." He took a swig from the flute. "I don't like it."

Seth narrowed his eyes. "Because of the weapons or because of his interest in Mother?"

Teo cast a glance over his shoulder, catching his mother and Sirhaan smiling and chatting. His mouth dropped open. *Was his mother blushing?*

"Stop staring and show some manners. You're the king," Seth murmured.

"I wondered if Mother had a bit of a crush but thought—hoped—I was imagining it."

"Weapons weren't his only objective when he came to Wolf City, by the looks of it." Seth sipped his drink. "But it's the happiest I've seen her in a long while." His brother shrugged.

Teo's mouth slackened. "Are you kidding me?" But as the words left his lips, recent images of his mother smiling, laughing, and generally lighter in spirit flicked through his mind. Could Seth be right? He eyed the man sharing a drink with the Queen Mother. Sirhaan's dark suit was well-made, and he looked every inch the gentleman. Still, Teo couldn't shake the bad vibe he got from the man. "I don't like the guy."

Seth clapped a hand on his brother's shoulder. "I don't think the king has any say in this particular matter." He smirked before walking toward a pretty redhead.

Teo swallowed the sour taste in his mouth. *I wish Jenna was here.* An ache throbbed in his chest. His mother could see whom she wanted, but she stopped Teo from inviting Jenna? A portly gentleman maneuvered through the crowd toward him. Pushing away thoughts of his favourite bike rider so he wouldn't run from the room, Teo clasped the man's sweaty hand, greeting the dignitary like an old friend. As the man spoke at length on his thoughts about the forest and his agenda for trade with other kingdoms, Teo feigned interest. Maybe his mother was right to keep Jenna away because Teo wouldn't wish the schmoozing that came with his role and life on her. No, she deserved far better than that.

The soft mattress cushioned Teo's body as he fell on it, facedown. Too tired to even undress, he lay there, eyes closed. In an attempt to stop his swirling thoughts, he squeezed his eyes tighter. Sleep was what he was after, but his mind had other ideas. Teo groaned, rolled onto his back, and stared at the ceiling, a blank canvas for the thoughts parading through his mind. His mother's hand on Sirhaan's arm as she laughed at something he said. The clamouring by neighbouring clans to get the new king's ear. The weapons Sirhaan had claimed he had access too. Teo's stomach burned. The mysterious patches of harvested plants that had appeared within the borders of the forest. Who planted and harvested them? If they were what Dr. Hood thought they were, Teo didn't only have to worry about Sirhaan's weapons. Those plants were dangerous and all fingers pointed to the forest.

That's not going to help unify the kingdom.

It wasn't going to win any points with Jenna either. He rubbed his fingers together, his skin remembering the silkiness of her locks, her soft skin and lips. The memory of her scent wrapped around him. Her eyes that he would willing drown in if he ever got the chance. Instead of sleeping, Teo lay wide awake, his heart racing. He swung his legs to the ground, got up, turned on the shower. As the hot water ran off his body, he let all the worry and the responsibilities of the last few weeks run with the water down the drain. Exhausted, he turned the taps off, dressed in a T-shirt and boxers, and once again flopped on the bed, pulling the covers over him.

All night, he dreamed of a curly-haired courier wearing a red hood.

Chapter Twelve
Rider

RIDER HELD HER BREATH as she ran her trembling fingers over the gold embossed lettering.

You are cordially invited to the coronation
of Teowulf Dolphus Howell
on Saturday, February 4
at 11 o'clock in the morning
at Westmount Cathedral

He hadn't forgotten. A second invite on the kitchen table caught her eye. Warmth spread through her chest as she lifted the one made out to her father—one of the hottest and hardest to get tickets in the kingdom. With only a week to go until the celebration, she had been fighting a niggling worry they would be overlooked. Not that she thought they had a right to be there, but she'd hoped.

Squealing like a little piglet, Rider hopped around the kitchen, the parchment clutched in her fingers. Footsteps echoed in the hall before her dad entered the kitchen. His eyes twinkled as he pointed to the mail. "I see you got the invitations."

Her throaty laugh bubbled up and out like a water geyser. "I can hardly wait." She stood still, her eyes widening. "I've got to find something to wear, like yesterday." Her brows creased. "You'll need new clothes too. I don't think lab coats are an acceptable choice for a crowning for a king," she teased.

He sighed loudly, but the smile didn't leave his eyes. "I guess a shopping day is in order."

"Really?"

"I can't have my girl going to the new king's coronation in a second-hand dress now, can I?'

"Can we afford that?"

Her dad's eyes softened. "You don't need to worry about that Jenna-girl. I've been putting money aside for a rainy day. This is definitely a rainy day. Go buy yourself something pretty."

Rider flung her arms around her dad's neck, kissing his cheek. "Thank you." She danced all the way to her bedroom. *I'm going to the king's coronation.*

That afternoon, Rider stood inside a dress shop in Wolf City, surrounded by beautiful dresses in every colour hanging from racks along the walls. Her fingers glided over an emerald satin ballgown, landing on the price tag. One glance at it and Rider dropped the tag as if it burned her fingertips. She licked her dry lips as she glanced around the shop, hoping she looked like she bought fancy dresses every day while also trying to be invisible.

Who was she fooling? Not the saleswoman who eyed her like a hawk its prey. Rider had never been in a Wolf dress shop because Wolves frowned upon Foresters buying their luxury items. She slouched behind a rack of blouses, hoping to get out of the crosshairs of the woman behind the counter. Maybe she'd forget about Rider if she couldn't see her. Things hadn't changed all that much, after all. Foresters still weren't welcomed everywhere inside the gates. Rider rubbed her stomach, glancing once more at the saleswoman. *You belong here too.* Rider lifted her chin as she searched the racks in earnest for a dress she could afford. She'd been invited by the king; she deserved to shop for a dress here.

Several minutes later, Rider blew a strand of hair out of her face. Even the sales weren't bargains; this shop was way out of her means. The shopkeeper had obviously figured that out already, as she eyed Rider stonily, tapping her long fingernail on the counter. Heat crawled up Rider's neck. If only her dad had been free to come with her, but he'd had a meeting come up unexpectedly. All her bravado gone, Rider shoved through the doors to the fresh air outside.

Compared to the forest, it wasn't all that fresh, but it was better than the pretentious air in the store. Trudging up the street, Rider racked her brain. Where could she buy a dress without being treated like a pariah?

A mother and little girl walked by hand-in-hand, laughing and chatting. They stopped for a minute, the mother adjusting the girl's jacket. She had dark hair tied back in a long braid. Her mother swept wisps of hair off her daughter's face before leaning down to kiss the girl's cheek. They shared a smile. Rider followed their progress up the street, her eyes blurring. *Mom, I wish you were here.* She'd know where to go and what kind of dress to buy.

"Rider."

"Hey, Ethan." She waved, but her gaze fixed on the person behind her friend. "Matrix." She pointed between them. "How do you guys know each other?"

"I could ask you the same question." Ethan cocked an eyebrow, his tone sharper than normal.

Rider made a face. What was Ethan's problem? "We met waiting in line at the gates. For some weird reason we keep bumping into each other." Was that coincidence?

"That's strange that I would befriend each of you separately." Matrix tugged at his gloves.

"Did you meet at the gates too?"

"No, in the forest. Just happened on each other." Ethan seemed in a hurry to drop this line of conversation.

Rider inclined her head at Matrix. "You get around."

"If I want to meet people, I've got to go places. Is that against the law here?"

"Nope—making an observation." Like she was also observing the guy was a bit defensive. Hmmm. Rider swung her keyring around her finger. "What have you been up to, Ethan? I haven't seen you in a while."

"Working." Ethan kicked a pebble off the walkway.

Okaay. Awkwardness filled the silence. Rider glanced over her shoulder. She needed to move on, since this conversation wasn't going anywhere. Ethan was obviously still mad at her for the *friends only* comment she'd made.

Before she could make her getaway, Matrix asked, "What are you doing here in the city?"

"Shopping." She could do one-word answers too.

Matrix leaned against a lamp pole. "What are you looking for? I happen to be a very good shopper."

Ethan's eyebrows hiked up.

Matrix elbowed him. "What? Guys don't shop here?"

"No. I mean, yeah, they do. It's not my idea of a good time, that's all."

Matrix rubbed his hands together and stared at Rider.

Rider shoved her keys into her jeans' front pocket. "Nothing."

Ethan snorted. "You never shop. There's got to be a reason."

Sometimes she hated that Ethan knew her so well. She sighed. "A dress. I'm looking for a dress. I got an invite to the coronation. Did you get one?" She glanced at her friend.

"Yup. Not planning on going." Ethan stared at his sneakers.

"Why not?"

Ethan threw his head back, huffing. What did that mean? Rider thought Ethan liked Teo. Or he had.

Matrix cleared his throat. "For the new king? Wow, that's the event of the season."

"We're *friends* with the king."

Matrix nodded. "I didn't realize you were that good of friends. Must be close if you got an invitation." He pointed to himself. "I don't know much about dresses, but I'd be happy to come along and give a guy's opinion."

Ethan scowled at Matrix.

She didn't want or need Matrix's help. "The city's prices are out of my range. I'm done for today. But thanks for your offer." She waved as she hurried away from the pair, a sigh of relief escaping as she put distance between them. That had been awkward on so many levels.

Her stomach dropped as she remembered Ethan's displeasure. And Matrix? What was up with him?

The city gates rose in front of her and Rider slid her papers from her pocket. Thankfully, the line was short. Once the woman ahead of her was finished, Rider held out her documents to the guard. Before he could take them, a shadow fell between them.

"I'll take this one, Officer West." Seth smiled.

Rider's stomach flip-flopped. Would he take her to see Teo? She inclined her head. "Your Royal Highness. What's going on?"

"My lucky day. I was just about to head out to your house. You got your invitation?"

She nodded, her lips curving up. Goosebumps jumped out on her arms. Even though the dress shopping had been a fiasco, Rider was still excited about the big event.

"Good. I've been sent on a mission on my brother's behalf."

Rider tilted her head. "What do you mean?"

"Come with me."

She followed Teo's brother to a little shop on a cobblestone side street. After knocking once, Seth opened the door and peered around it. "Evange. It's me, Seth. I've brought our honoured guest." He motioned for Rider to go in ahead of him.

No Teo, but Rider knew he was busy. Although a tiny little part of her wanted him to come find her and take her shopping, she forced herself to concentrate on the present moment instead of wishing for something that wasn't going to happen.

Sweet orange and cinnamon teased Rider's nostrils as she entered the elegant front showroom. Several comfortable chairs sat around a three-way mirror with a pedestal in the centre. Soft grey paint covered the walls, interrupted by two large windows, beautifully draped in rose-coloured curtains. A petite, middle-aged woman with spiky white hair stood next to the mirror.

"You must be Jenna. Please come in, dear." The woman smiled as she took Rider's hands in her own. "Thank you, Seth. You can go now."

Rider cast a glance at Seth, who smiled at them. "See you later, Jenna. Enjoy."

The woman squeezed Rider's fingers gently. "I'm sure you're wondering what's going on. The new king requested that I help you find a dress for the coronation. And anything else you may need. He's taken care of everything, so you don't need to worry about cost." She led Rider to a green velveteen chair, then chose a matching one across from her. "I'm Evange Silver. I've been a friend of the king's family for years. I've dressed the Queen Mother numerous times. In case you need a reference." She winked. Where were the scowls and pursed lips Rider had received in the other dress shops?

The woman's words registered with Rider. Did the woman think she had to give her resume to Rider? "Th-thank you. I wasn't expecting this." She ran her sweaty palms over the soft arms of the chair before clasping them in her lap. "I, ah, I was shopping, and it was so overwhelming and..." Heat flamed in her cheeks.

Evange reached over and patted Rider's knee. "I'm sorry if a few of my counterparts weren't very welcoming." She clapped her hands. "Moving onto happier thoughts. I'm glad we caught you before you purchased something. I've taken the liberty of pulling a few dresses for you to consider, so let's start there, shall we?"

Rider let out a little sigh of relief and wiped at the tear that had escaped at the woman's kindness and Teo's thoughtfulness.

Swirls of jade swished about Rider's knees as she twirled in the tea-length dress. She felt like a princess. A giggle escaped as Rider's eyes met Evange's twinkling ones in the mirror. Rider didn't care if she was acting like a little kid; at this moment she felt like a kid in a candy shop. A finger tapping her chin, Evange circled Rider, who stood on the dais. Every now and then, the woman would tug here and straighten a seam there. Finally, she smiled and pronounced, "I believe we've found the one. What do you think?"

"I love it. I feel so pretty." Rider stared at her reflection. The dress fit perfectly and made her look like a grown-up.

"You're a beautiful girl, regardless of what you wear."

Rider sniffed. This woman, a Wolf, wasn't faking kindness. She had gone out of her way to make Rider feel welcome and had made it her mission to make all Rider's wishes come true. Evange was her own personal fairy godmother.

"What about those shoes?"

Rider grimaced. "Ugh, they're a little high. I'm afraid I'll trip and fall."

"Nonsense. You need some lessons in walking and..." Evange pulled Rider's shoulders back, "... better posture. You'll be fine."

Thoughts of tripping and falling in the aisle of the cathedral filled her mind. *Stop.* If Evange had faith in her, maybe Rider would manage to not kill or humiliate herself.

"Now, for the ball gown."

Rider frowned. "I thought it was only the coronation."

"Oh, darling, there's always a ball to celebrate the coronation of the new king. You must have a gown for it. The king said so." She winked. "And what the king wants, the king gets. Now go change out of that dress and wait for me to pick a few from the rack over there." Evange pointed to several gowns hanging in the corner. Tulle skirts, lace, and satin cascaded from the hangers.

Rider carefully stepped from the pedestal. She'd been so focused on the actual coronation that the ball had slipped her mind. Another dance at the palace. At least it wasn't a masquerade. She carefully stepped out of the jade dress.

"How do you feel about the colour peach?" Evange called.

"I love the fruit but not so much the colour."

"Hmm, I agree. That's not your colour." The woman appeared with an armful of dresses. As she hung them on hooks, she gave Rider instructions. "Go through these and try on any that strike your fancy. If you need help, let me know." She disappeared around the partition.

Rider fingered the dresses, feeling the different fabrics. A beautiful champagne dress caught her attention. She pulled it from the rack and held it up against her body, its full skirts draping around her. The bodice was embroidered with red thread and glass beads that sparkled when the light hit them. The memory of last year's ball came back, when Teo was a prince, not the king, and Bleddyn was still alive. *So much has changed.*

Carefully removing the dress from its hanger, Rider stepped into it and pulled it up over her body. It felt like a hug, it fit her so well. She slipped on the heels again, a grin forming as she walked out to Evange, the skirts swishing around her legs.

This was the one.

Chapter Thirteen
Matrix

M ATRIX HAD MESSED UP. Ethan, walking beside him, had gone into silent mode since Jenna left them earlier, confirming Matrix's suspicion she was the girl Ethan was fixated on. "What's wrong?"

"That's my best friend. You know, the one who said I was a great friend but that was it?"

Matrix winced. No guy ever wanted to hear those words. He almost felt sorry for Ethan. "That's rough."

"It didn't help things that you practically begged to shop with her." Ethan glared at him.

"I was offering my expertise. I'm a good judge of style, if I do say so myself." Matrix pretended to dust off an imaginary suit jacket.

Ethan rolled his eyes.

Matrix clenched his fists at his sides—he wanted to shake the kid. No wonder Jenna wasn't interested; the dude had no spine. As they passed a menswear shop, Matrix noted the mannequins in tuxes in the front window. He grabbed Ethan by the shoulder, halting him. "You're going to need something to wear."

"For what?" Ethan shrugged out of Matrix's hold.

"The coronation." Matrix held the door, but Ethan didn't budge from his position on the sidewalk.

"Do you want to win the girl or not?" Matrix huffed.

Ethan turned away. "You don't understand."

"Enlighten me."

Ethan glanced furtively around the street. A few people milled around, but no one near them. He stepped closer to Matrix. "You can't tell *anyone* this," he hissed.

Never one to say no to gossip, Matrix leaned in.

"It's the prince. I mean...the new king."

Matrix raised his eyebrows, feigning surprise. "The other guy is King Teowulf? Why is this a secret? Unless... is that a fanciful wish on Jenna's part? I know she said they were friends."

"No. I wish it was. Look, you can't repeat that, okay? No one, and I mean absolutely no one, knows."

"You do."

"I'm one of a few select people because I helped them with the vaccinations. Plus, I'm Rider's best friend. I haven't even told my parents."

"I don't get what the big deal is." Matrix could do without all the drama.

Ethan shoved his glasses up his nose. "You definitely aren't from around here. He's a Wolf, she's a Forester. Never the two shall meet. Or date." Ethan's tone implied the *duh*.

"That's dumb." Matrix's eyes narrowed. "You agree they shouldn't date. You don't like Wolves and aren't buying into the king's new policies, is that it?"

"No, that's not true. It's mostly the royals I don't like. Teo is full of himself. Rider will never be his first priority. She deserves so much more."

"He is a king." Why was he defending Teo to this kid?

Ethan waved his hand as if batting away the logic of Matrix's comment. "She's too in love to notice she has no place at the palace. The king used her and Dr. Hood to try and save his brother and the kingdom. Since then, he's barely been around, but she's blind to it all. I never thought Rider would be that girl."

"Don't give up yet. Maybe there's hope." Matrix seriously doubted it, but he wasn't about to tell Ethan that. He had to get Rider's best friend to buy into his plan.

Ethan stared at the suits on the mannequins in the shop window. "What do you mean?"

"Why not show Rider the king's true colours?" What looked like interest skittered across Ethan's features, and Matrix pounced. "I mean, if he's being an idiot, let's make her see it. I'll help you."

Ethan's Adam apple bounced in his throat.

C'mon, dude.

"Okay. Sure. Let's do it."

"Atta boy." Matrix grinned like a kid who'd discovered a cache of candy. "You're going to need a new suit."

Chapter Fourteen
Teo

T HE CLICK, CLACK OF heels hitting the marble floors registered too late as Teo sat engrossed in a map of the surrounding forest and counties of Wolf Kingdom. Each county was overseen by a clan, and the Wolf king reigned over it all. He tried not to let the size of it overwhelm him, but some days it did.

"Teo."

Teo hung his head, muttering under his breath. What did she want now? He was so tired of talking about the coronation. Glancing up from the map, he nodded at his mother. She strode in, shaking a sheet of paper.

"What's this?"

Teo held out his hand. "I don't know because I can't see what you're holding."

She thrust it into his hand. Teo scanned the paper, his heart racing at the printed words. He schooled his features into boredom. "It's a bill."

"I know that. It's from Evange's boutique, but I got my dresses from her weeks ago. This isn't my bill. Whose is it?"

Teo dropped the paper onto the map he'd been reading. "It's none of your business. I used my personal money. I don't need to report it to you or anyone."

His mother tapped the bill with a long, manicured nail. "You can't fool me. It's for the Hood girl, isn't it? You invited her."

"It's *my* coronation, I should be able to invite who I want." Teo ground the words out between clenched teeth. "Speaking of which, why is Sirhaan still around? I thought he left."

"He's harmless."

"I don't trust him. He's a weapons dealer," Teo growled.

She strolled to the window and pulled back the curtain. "That doesn't make him a villain." The heavy material dropped from her hand as she faced him. "I enjoy his company, not that it's any of your business."

Teo huffed out a breath at her echo of his own words. "It's not the same thing as me paying for a dress for Jenna out of my *personal* funds. Sirhaan sells weapons and wants to distribute them here. I said no. I'm asking again why he's still here."

"With your father gone, I get lonely. Sirhaan makes me laugh and is a good conversationalist. I enjoy being around him. One day you'll understand."

"Wait. You get to enjoy Sirhaan's company," Teo finger quoted the last two words, "but I can't invite Jenna and Dr. Hood? I might remind you that the Lupine flu is over due to them. Or did you forget?"

"Teo." His mother's tone was firm, unyielding. The kind she used when he had crossed a line when he was thirteen and tested her patience with his mouthiness.

"I'm asking for this one thing."

"You're the king, Teo. You serve the people; it's not about what *you want* anymore."

"Father always did what he wanted." The words spilled out before Teo could rein them in. Ugh. He wished he could take them back. He never wanted to be like his dad.

His mother hiked her well-groomed eyebrows. "You want to rule like your father, is that it?"

Teo ran his hands through his hair. "No. *No.* I... I want to have people there who *I* care about. You, Seth, Uncle Alarick, Jenna, and Dr. Hood. Is that too much to ask?" Teo sank into his chair, shoving a pen out of the way. He wanted to throw more than a pen. "One day. That's all I'm asking for."

Her face softened. "Make sure you take care of the bill discreetly." She exited the room, letting the door click softly behind her.

A warmth spread over Teo as he examined the bill. He'd won this round with his mother. Sirhaan still made him uneasy, but he let it go because he wanted Jenna at the coronation more. The bill of sale didn't give details. What had she chosen to wear? His heart kicked up its tempo as he thought about her in his arms, dancing. Suddenly the coronation didn't seem like such a chore. *I might even enjoy this.*

The week had sped by in a series of meetings with foreign dignitaries visiting for the coronation as well as parties to celebrate the new king. Every night, Teo dropped into bed, asleep before his head hit the silk-covered pillow. By coronation day, all he craved was a little solitude, wishful thinking on his part. Instead, he did the next best thing—he played football with his brother in a rare, unscheduled ten minutes. Lifting his face to the sun, Teo let its rays warm his cheeks.

"Incoming!"

He cut his gaze to the football flying at him, grabbing it out of mid-air before it landed on his nose. "Hey!"

Seth pointed at him. "You need to get your head in the game, or you'll have a black eye for your coronation and I'll be in the dog house with mother."

Teo drilled the ball back at his brother. It fell short, straight into the ground. Seth ran to pick it up.

"Relax. You're way too tense." He threw the ball to the left of Teo, making him jump for it.

"Maybe if you threw more accurately, I might be able to," Teo grunted.

"It's not my skills, bro. You've been wound tighter than a windup toy this past week." He deftly pulled the ball from mid-air. Seth definitely had the superior skills when it came to football. "What's going on? It's a lot of pomp and ceremony—we've done it a million times over the years."

Teo ran backwards, plucking the ball from its flight, bringing it close to his chest. "It's my coronation. It's a little different than cutting ribbons and planting trees. People are waiting for me to mess up. If I make a mistake, it will become the headline of the day." Teo molded his hands around the textured skin of the ball, its roughness grounding him. "What if I fail? What if I'm a lousy king, like Father?"

"You're nothing like Father. The fact that you went to Dr. Hood for help with the Lupine flu screams you're different than dear old Dad. You're human—you'll make mistakes, but if you own them and learn from them, it'll be fine. No one is expecting you to be perfect."

Teo appreciated Seth's words, but he wasn't sure he believed him. He threw the ball in a perfect arc. "It's not just the coronation. Why is Sirhaan still around? I said no to the weapons and thought that was the last of him. But he's still here, hanging around Mother. What does he want?"

"Didn't we already discuss this? I think that's rather obvious." Seth waggled his eyebrows.

Teo drilled the ball at his brother. "Ugh. Don't do that. Father's only just passed. This guy shows up and moves in, like she's his for the taking. It looks bad. Why doesn't she see that? And she's on my back for inviting Jenna to *my* coronation."

Seth let the ball fly past him. "First, stop pummelling me with the ball. I don't feel like being covered in bruises." He stalked over to where the ball had landed and picked it up. Throwing it back and forth between his hands, he walked up to Teo. "Maybe she's flattered by all the attention. Father barely registered her presence the last few years. Sirhaan is probably a distraction from losing Bleddyn and all the other changes. I wouldn't worry too much."

"Maybe." Teo swiped a trickle of sweat from his brow. "I miss Bleddyn. He should be here for this," he rasped. What would Bleddyn make of all the fuss of the crowning of the heir? He'd be having a ball teasing Teo, that was what.

"I miss him too." Seth stared off into the distance. "He would love this."

"Yeah, he'd be rubbing my nose in it all." Teo huffed a laugh, loosening the tightness in his throat. "I should probably go inside and finish one of the several tedious duties that still need to be done before the ceremony."

Seth clapped him on the shoulder. "Yeah, we've got a king to crown today. And some beautiful women to charm."

Teo's shoulders eased as he walked with his brother to the palace entrance. "There's only one girl I want to charm today."

The crowds were at least ten people deep, creating a sea of heads over the sidewalks and streets. Teo stared at the scene outside his car window. He waved at a little boy holding a Wolf Kingdom flag. The boy's eyes went wide, as he pointed at the royal limo.

"I can't believe the number of people who came out for this. It looks like the whole city and half the kingdom is here." Teo leaned forward slightly to get a look around his brother, trying to see out the other side of the car.

"It's a big deal. You represent a new beginning for Wolf Kingdom. People are hoping things are going to change for the better. They're putting their trust in you."

No pressure. "I'm not so sure about that. There's been a lot of pushback from the new policies I've put in place regarding the forest." Teo watched as a guy, hanging from a light pole, waved a sign with Teo's face on it. In bold letters, it read, **Long Live the King**. He lifted his hand in acknowledgement, hoping the dude didn't fall. "I think everyone came for the free food and drink."

"Brilliant strategy, by the way. It's a given they'll party in the streets, but at least this way there are controls in place." Seth fiddled with his military collar. "But I'm sure that's not the only reason they've gathered today."

The car made the final turn into the cathedral's drive. Teo gulped water from a bottle, hoping to ease his dry mouth. Even through the glass, the roar of the crowd shook the vehicle. "I guess it doesn't matter why they came." Had they come for him or for the party and the pomp and circumstance? It wasn't every day a new king was crowned. He didn't have an answer, but part of him desired them to be here because they wanted and supported him as king.

Wolf Pack surged around the vehicle, opening doors for the brothers. The noise swelled until Teo could feel the rumble in his chest. Once on the steps, he turned and waved a final time before being ushered into the foyer of the cathedral. Seth followed on his heels.

The actual coronation ceremony wasn't for another hour, but his mother wanted him there early to go over a few last-minute details. The woman was obsessed with details. Since she'd arrived in her own car, she was already there, waiting inside the doors of the cathedral. The Queen Mother was elegant in her cream dress and matching coat and hat. She held out her hands to him as he walked to her. "Darling, look at those crowds. This is what the city needed—what we needed." She kissed him on the cheek. "You're so handsome. I'm sure all the girls are swooning today."

Teo rolled his eyes, but he couldn't help smiling, since his mother appeared so happy. At least he was the reason today, not Sirhaan.

She brushed the fabric of his jacket. "I'm so proud of you, Teowulf." Wrapping her arms around his waist, she squeezed gently. "You can do this. Now," she stepped back, "enjoy today."

Teo focused on his surroundings and all the players in the ceremony who were present and waiting instead of the weapons dealer as he headed toward the archbishop, who would perform the crowning ceremony. Teo extended his hand, making it clear the bishop didn't need to bow. No need for formalities at this point. The archbishop's firm grip eased Teo's nerves.

"Your Majesty. It's an honour. Are you ready?"

Teo inhaled deeply in an attempt to calm the swirling butterflies in his stomach. "As ready as I'll ever be." He wiped his palms on his pants discreetly. *This is real.*

Chapter Fifteen
Rider

RIDER WALKED ARM IN arm alongside her father to the cathedral. It was a beautiful, sunny, crisp winter morning. Butterflies fluttered wildly in her stomach as they strolled along the cobblestone walk that led to the front doors of the church.

Her jade skirt danced around her knees as she carefully stepped in heels that should be illegal. Thankfully, Evange had been correct when she'd told Rider all she needed to walk gracefully in high heels was good posture and to practice. Who knew? A gust of wind whipped around her face, and she lifted her hand to hold her hat in place. It was small with a little veil covering her forehead. The girl who liked to wear the red hoodie had been transformed, at least for today.

She glanced at her father, dashing in his black morning coat and charcoal trousers. He winked at her. What were two Foresters doing attending the Wolf king's coronation as invited guests?

Two of the Wolf Pack guards were checking invitations and directing folks where to enter. Her dad pulled the invitations out of his breast pocket.

The guard pointed to a side entrance with large wooden doors that stood open with ushers waiting outside. The heavy floral scent of lilies, roses, and carnations teased her nose as Rider and her father followed an usher into the foyer. The floral arrangements were as big as she was. Obviously, they had been brought in from warmer parts of the kingdom.

Seating arrangements had been set ahead of time, although Rider had no idea where their seats were. She followed the guard toward the front. Her eyes widened as he led them by one row after another.

He's made a mistake. Finally, he stopped past the halfway mark and motioned Rider and her dad into the pew.

Rider gaped at the usher. "Are you sure this is correct?"

He rolled his eyes. "It's as close as you can get if you're not a dignitary or courtier."

Heat filled Rider's cheeks. "No, I didn't mean it's not good, only that I thought we'd be farther back." Like in the back row.

"Oh." The young man glanced at the invite. "These are the correct seats. The king himself requested you be as close as possible."

"Th-thanks." Rider sank onto the upholstered seat.

Her dad whistled softly.

She lifted a trembling hand to her chest. "I can't believe this. Am I dreaming? Is someone going to pinch me, and I'll wake up from this fairy tale?"

"It's no dream, Jenna-girl."

The seats quickly filled with people from all over the kingdom. Governors, royalty from other kingdoms, and a few celebrities were spread throughout the room. A famous model, whom Teo was rumoured to date once upon a time, sat three rows over.

Rider flicked her gaze to the front so she wouldn't be caught staring. "I feel like a coronation crasher," she whispered in her dad's ear.

He tapped the invitation against his palm. "You belong here, Rider. Don't doubt that."

At her father's words, the butterflies settled. Teo had requested her presence and seated her as close as he could. She would enjoy those blessings.

Bugles sounded the arrival of the coronation party. A hush fell over the room. At the appearance of the archbishop at the back of the cathedral, everyone rose, like a wave cascading over the sanctuary. Teo, looking solemn, walked behind the bishop, then Seth and the Queen Mother. Others followed, but Rider didn't know who they were and she didn't care. Her eyes remained glued to the handsome king as he strode purposefully up the aisle.

When he neared their row, Teo's eyes connected with hers, the corners of his mouth lifting slightly. For a few seconds, it was just the two of them, the people, the place fading away. The moment was fleeting, but it was all Rider needed. She fanned her flushed cheeks with the ceremony's program.

Teo looked fine. His suit fit him perfectly. Rider smiled—all those fittings he complained about had been worth it. He'd had his hair trimmed since the last time she'd seen him. It still wasn't military short, but it enhanced his beautiful features.

The bishop took his place at the podium. "Welcome family, friends, and special guests, on this special and sacred day. Please be seated." In his long robes and peaked hat, the man added a sense of the holy to the occasion. He turned to Teo, who remained standing, although his brother and mother had taken seats in the front row.

If anyone doubted his ability to rule, his air of confidence, broad shoulders, and straight posture erased all questions. Rider knew it wasn't only his physical looks that would grant him favour, but his kindness of heart, his love for his people, and his desire to see justice and equality in his land. Those qualities would, in the end, win his peoples' hearts and loyalties.

The bishop whispered loudly, "Are you ready?" The ripple of laughter in the room added brevity to the serious moment.

Teo offered a wobbly smile, nodding. The bishop draped the Imperial robe around Teo's shoulders, which, according to legend, weighed ten pounds. Teo had told Rider that the people knew the future king would be able to lead the kingdom if he could hold his head high while carrying the weight of the robe. Rider had rolled her eyes at the time, but now, as she stared at him in the robe, she got the significance of the legend. As the bishop straightened the garment, Teo lifted his chin slightly, and looked right at her, as if to say *See?* She covered her mouth with her hand, holding back a laugh.

The bishop must have caught Teo's look because the older gentleman said, "It's heavy?"

Teo chuckled as he faced his family. Rider could just make out Seth giving his big brother two thumbs up. Laughter rang out throughout the church at the brothers' camaraderie. Thankful they could share a moment on this special day, warmth spread through Rider's chest.

"You wear it well." The man nodded, as if confirming that truth for anyone who might be in doubt. He held up the signet ring. "This ring's seal makes all laws legal and binding. Wear it with authority." He slid it on Teo's little finger. The king made a fist as he stared at the ornate ring. Rider had seen the seal on official statements from the palace, usually orders from King Duko that weren't in the forest's favour. Things would be different now because he was no longer the wearer of the ring.

The last ceremonial item was the sword, resting on its side on the palms of the man of the cloth. The blade gleamed in the light. The hilt was metal and leather. Did it weigh more than the robe? How would Teo stand strong under all that weight? Not just physical weight but the weight of ruling a people? As the new king accepted the weapon by the hilt, his hand appeared to shake. Rider leaned forward. Had she seen it or was it her imagination? Teo had always seemed confident about his role as the heir to the throne. He'd always known he would be king one day. Was he nervous about the ceremony or something more? Did he doubt himself?

Her glance slid back to his hand, the sword firmly in place. Not a tremor or wobble was to be seen. Maybe she had imagined it.

Teo lowered himself to one knee, the hilt of the sword in one hand, the tip resting on the carpet. An attendant carried the ornate velvet cushion that held the crown to the archbishop.

The crown was nothing extravagant—a simple silver band coming together in front to form a pointed tip, a diamond in the centre and rubies on either side. Sunlight caught the gems, flashing red and rainbow streams of light, until the bishop lifted the crown off the cushion and held it over Teo's head.

"I crown you King of Wolf Kingdom." The bishop's voice rang throughout the space as he nestled the band just above Teo's brow.

Emotions bubbled up, culminating in a lump the size of a boulder in Rider's throat. As Teo knelt, head bowed, he looked vulnerable yet strong. What an odd combination. Her heart banged against her ribcage. The thought that she'd follow him anywhere rose with the music of her heart.

The bishop spoke the vows, bringing Rider back to the ceremony. "Do you, Teowulf, solemnly pledge yourself to lead with wisdom of mind, a heart full of love, and courage to defend your people?"

Teo placed his hand over his heart. "I solemnly pledge to lead my people with wisdom of mind, a heart full of love, and courage to defend all my kingdom."

Was that Rider's imagination or did Teo just look at her? At her dad? A tingle jittered down her spine.

"God save the king! Long live the king!" The bishop helped Teo to standing.

Rider rose to her feet and shouted with the other guests, "Long live the king! God save the king!"

Teo contemplated the crowd as his attendants arranged the long robe around him. They then escorted him to the throne, made of mahogany with a wolf print engraved at the top and overlaid in silver.

The guests sat, while the Queen Mother, Seth, Alarick, and Teo's court of advisors, one by one, knelt before Teo, pledging their allegiance to him and the crown.

"I'd love to see a Forester on that court," her father whispered.

She squeezed his hand. "One day, Dad." That was the hope Teo brought to the throne—he wouldn't let them down.

After the lengthy line of advisors and courtiers had passed by Teo, the archbishop stepped to the forefront. "I present to you, the people of Wolf Kingdom, your king. Long live the king. God save the king."

Goosebumps popped on her arms, and Rider rubbed them. "Long live the king. God save the king."

A photographer took pictures as the bells of the cathedral rang out. The crowds outside and inside cheered, but her eyes never strayed from Teo, even as her vision blurred. *I wonder what he's thinking right now?* If it was her, Rider would be fainting under the enormity of it all. He was officially *king*.

Teo glanced in her direction. Nodding, he waved to his people, but he kept his focus on her. She smiled and was rewarded by Teo's lips curling up at the corners. The crowd cheered even louder, clearly unaware he was making eyes at a Forester. Rider hugged that thought to herself.

The archbishop motioned Teo forward, and they led the long procession to the carriage that awaited the new king outside. Seth and the Queen Mother would ride with him. The parade would wend through the city and back to the palace, where Teo would host a luncheon for the leaders of the other realms and various dignitaries. *Glad I'm not going to that.*

Her dad squeezed her arm. "Ready to head home and get ready for the ball?"

"Absolutely." Rider leaned her head on her dad's shoulder, still caught up in the fairy tale of the coronation ceremony and Teo's gaze on her. She couldn't wait for tonight.

Chapter Sixteen
Matrix

FOR THE HUNDREDTH TIME, Matrix wished for ear plugs as the cheers of the people reached maximum decibels. There had been no invite to the coronation of the new Wolf King for Matrix, not that he'd expected one. Instead, he stood on the street in front of the cathedral along with the rest of Wolf City and those from the different kingdom clans. He'd been there since before dawn because he wanted to keep an eye on Jenna, but he was also curious. What if his family had stayed in power? How different would this day be?

A group of men with pink, blue, and green hair, probably from the Peacock clan, stood in front of Matrix. Several people with the ruddy complexions the Bear clan were noted for waited off to his left.

Also mingled in with the masses were several Foresters Matrix recognized from his time living there. An older woman with tiny glasses glared at him. Granny. He'd met her his first week there, a nosy old thing. He'd deflected her questions and tried to avoid her at all costs, likely the reason for the stink eye. He shifted his weight, trying but failing to keep a modest amount of personal space around him. It was claustrophobic.

As the wooden doors of the cathedral opened, silence descended as though a switch had been flipped. King Teowulf appeared, framed by the large arches, setting up a perfect picture. The simple crown glinted in the sunlight. After a brief hesitation, the young man stepped out onto the steps, and the crowd erupted. If Matrix had found it loud before...

The king, for his part, appeared slightly overwhelmed. Matrix balled his hands at his sides. The dude had everything Matrix desired. *But not for long.*

King Teo waved, increasing the noise factor. Girls screamed nearby, nearly blowing out Matrix's ear drums. The new sovereign was the most eligible bachelor in the kingdom. The Queen Mother and the youngest brother took their places beside and slightly behind the king. Teo glanced back at his mother, sharing a smile with her that was photo perfect. Cameras clicked all around him. No doubt that shot would be on the front pages of every newspaper. He, however, saw something other than a perfect photo op. *Still looking to Mom for direction.* Maybe Sirhaan was more correct about the Queen Mother having a lot of sway than Matrix had given him credit for.

What did it matter? That was Sirhaan's department. Matrix's assignment was different. He had to take care of the girl. He shifted his focus to the entrance of the cathedral. Wolf Pack surrounded the royal family as they made their way to the covered carriage. After they were seated, the guards on horses left, followed by the carriage and then other security vehicles.

Hemmed in by thousands of people, Matrix wasn't going anywhere. Once the procession was gone, guests flowed out the doorways of the massive building. Rider and her dad exited out the side along with others who were all gussied up in hats and morning coats. Rider's dress swirled around her knees, and she fussed with her small hat as she and her father hurried away.

Matrix stared after them, ignoring the crush and jabs of people now anxious to get moving. Rider was his assignment and he was failing. She was still all gaga over Teowulf, and he was no closer to meeting Dr. Hood. Matrix's stomach turned over. It was time to change the plan.

When all the coronation guests were gone, the Wolf Pack removed the front barriers, motioning people out from behind in an orderly fashion. Frowning, he moved with the tide of people. According to Sirhaan, the Queen had advised against the Hoods being invited, but the new king had gone ahead and done it anyway. Maybe he wasn't as tied to the apron strings as Matrix first thought. *He's not afraid to be his own person.* Again, that was not Matrix's problem.

Shoving his hands into his jacket pockets, Matrix crossed the street with other pedestrians who were trying to get one last glimpse of the newly crowned sovereign. A sneer crossed his features. The new king was not *his* king, and if Matrix had his way, Teo's reign would be short. He'd figure out a way to get Jenna on his side.

The guy has it bad. From behind the large evergreen, Matrix studied Ethan as he dumped a load of mushrooms into a large wooden crate in the back of a beat-up truck. The rusted front bumper as well as the patch along the bottom of the passenger door spoke of better days. The truffle and mushroom farm wasn't exactly a scurry of activity. Besides Ethan, Matrix could only see two workers through the open doors of a nearby greenhouse. Either the others were off for the coronation or there wasn't much work in the off season. Maybe both.

Ethan's scowl made Matrix smile. *The dude is going to be useful.*

Rider's image from the cathedral this morning filled Matrix's mind. The way a tendril of hair had blown around her graceful neck. Her bright green eyes. He understood Ethan's infatuation. Too bad winning her over wasn't going to pan out. *Don't be an idiot.* Matrix strode over to the lovesick mope, shaking off any further thoughts of the Hood girl.

"I was told I could find you here. You didn't go to the ceremony?"

Ethan tossed an empty bucket onto the ground, ignoring Matrix. This was going to be easier than Matrix had hoped. The guy was in the right frame of mind to seek revenge.

"You missed your chance. I saw her coming out of the cathedral."

For the first time, Ethan glanced at Matrix. "So?"

"If you're not around, how do you plan to win her over?"

Ethan brushed dirt from his gloves. "I couldn't watch her drool all over him. I need to accept we're just friends. That's all we're ever going to be."

Matrix slammed his hands down on either side of the crate. "Really?" He wanted to shake Ethan. "You're wasting good opportunities here. You're still going to the ball, right?"

Ethan eyed Matrix. "Do I have a choice?"

"Nope. What time are you done?"

"In a few minutes."

"Good. We've got work to do."

Ethan dumped another bucket of mushrooms into the crate. "What are you talking about?"

"Why are you letting him win so easily?" Matrix picked up a wayward mushroom from the bed of the truck and tossed it into the crate. "You're gonna give the new king some competition, and I'm going to help you."

"Right. Because I have lots of money and stylists and can give Rider the world."

Matrix held up his hands. "You're going to roll over and play dead? You're not even going to try?"

Ethan slammed the bucket down next to the crate and waved his hands up and down his lanky body. "Look at me. Am I competition for King Teowulf?"

Matrix smirked. "Like I said, we've got work to do." He swung his arm around Ethan and steered him towards his new future.

Standing in his bedroom in the small cabin he'd rented, Matrix surveyed his work. A bit of spit and polish, as his pop used to say, did the job rather well. Gone was the brooding, pathetic person dumping mushrooms into a crate a few hours ago. In his place stood a good-looking young man in a fitted dark suit, clean-shaven with his hair slicked back.

"You clean up nice, Ethan." Matrix pulled a pair of cuff links out of a box he'd retrieved from his dresser.

"I feel naked without my glasses."

"The contacts are better. Less geeky."

"Gee, thanks."

Matrix shrugged. "You want to make an impression or not? You can keep your glasses in your pocket." He motioned for Ethan to hold out his wrists so he could insert the links. Matrix surveyed Ethan before wandering over to his neatly made bed and picking a purple tie from his drawer, laying it on the bed with a white shirt and dark trousers.

"What's that?"

"My outfit. Like it?"

"How did you score an invite?"

Matrix shrugged on the white, collared shirt. "I'm your plus one, buddy. That's what friends are for, right?"

Ethan frowned. "You don't have to do that."

Matrix buttoned the shirt quickly. "Why, are you taking someone else? I'm hurt."

"No, but I don't want any distractions." Ethan swallowed so hard his Adam's Apple bounced.

"I won't distract you. Think of me as your wingman." Matrix slung the tie around his neck, winding it into a knot. "I'll simply be there for moral support."

The party at the palace was in full swing by the time Matrix and Ethan arrived. Matrix's heart raced as they climbed the stairs to the arched entrance where the Wolf Pack was patrolling and event people were checking invitation lists. He inhaled deeply. *Stop acting like an amateur.* He ran his hand lightly over the breast of his jacket, straightening his tie.

Ethan stepped forward and handed his invitation over, cool as a cucumber.

The woman, dressed in black from head to toe, studied the piece of paper. "Who's your guest?" She made a mark on her clipboard.

"Matrix..." Ethan glanced at him out of the corner of his eye.

"Smith," Matrix mouthed.

"Smith. He's a friend."

Matrix dipped his head. The guy was a social moron. The woman didn't care who Matrix was, and he was freely giving out too much information.

Matrix lifted his head to meet the woman's gaze before she waved them through. Swiping the sweat off his brow, he let out the breath he'd been holding. *Step one complete.*

As they entered the ballroom, Matrix's jaw dropped at the splendour. Large windows let in the pinky golden hue from the setting sun. The chandeliers sparkled almost as much as the jewels that bedecked every woman and man. His gaze crisscrossed the room until it locked with Sirhaan's, who stood next to the Queen Mother on the dais at the front of the room. Impressive. Matrix inclined his head toward his uncle and offered a quick salute. Sirhaan's mouth turned up at the corners before he faced the Queen Mother and whispered in her ear. The couple laughed as Matrix returned his attention to the room full of people. He'd noted the new king beside his mother, but the person he was looking for wasn't with him. *Where is she?*

"I don't see Rider." Ethan echoed Matrix's thoughts.

He shrugged. "Probably wants to make a grand entrance."

Ethan gave him a strange look. "Rider? No way. You don't know her like I do. Rider doesn't like being the centre of attention."

His words floated over Matrix, who stood transfixed by the vision in the gold dress in the doorway. Beside him, Ethan sucked in a sharp breath. Matrix was having a difficult time breathing himself as he gaped at Jenna Hood. She, however, only had eyes for the new king, who'd risen upon her entrance and walked toward her, his gloved hand held out.

Ethan faced Matrix, his brows furrowed. "I don't get it. She's not like that."

"Maybe you don't know her all that well either." Recovering from his own stupor, he clapped Ethan on the shoulder. Time to get this show on the road. "Why don't we get a drink? There are some lovely ladies over there, who I'm sure would love to talk to someone as handsome as you. You need to boost your ego before we approach Jenna." He guided Ethan over to the far corner where a waiter was serving punch. "I'll get drinks, you go introduce yourself."

"No, I'll wait."

Matrix gave him a little shove into the group of women, so Ethan had no choice but to talk to them as Matrix hurried over to the punch. After filling a glass, he turned away, dropping what he'd been hiding in his hand into the liquid. He swirled it a little as he approached Ethan and two stunning blondes who were all smiles. Smirking, he handed the glass to Ethan. "Here you go. Drink up."

Chapter Seventeen
Teo

THE COLOURS OF THE rich gowns and the noise of a thousand voices mingling with the strains of the band, and the smell of roasted meat assaulted Teo's senses. He sagged against his chair as he searched the mass of people for the one face he wanted to see. *She's not here yet.*

Jenna had been at the coronation. He'd noticed her as he made his way up the long aisle to the front of the large sanctuary. Her bright green eyes gazing at him were all that had kept him from bolting in the other direction. She had looked almost ethereal in the teal dress and small hat framing her dark locks. *Like a forest fae.*

They'd locked eyes a few times throughout the long ceremony. Not that he didn't take his vows to his country seriously, he did, but he was also making those vows to her and her people, the Foresters. One day he hoped he'd make another kind of vow to her. He tucked that dream away. For now.

Movement at the doors captured his attention. Air whooshed from his lungs as Jenna, stunning in a gold ballgown, stood framed in the large arched entrance, overwhelmed if the wide eyes and tense look on her face were any indication. He smiled. Of course she was uncomfortable—Evange had transformed her into a dream. Long gone was the hoodie-wearing courier. Not that he minded that look, but tonight, Jenna was a goddess. Evange deserved every penny he'd spent and more. He'd have to send her a huge bonus cheque. Teo's eyes drifted to Dr. Hood, who stood slightly behind Jenna, dashing in a charcoal tux, before returning to Jenna.

His gaze locked on hers, and she smiled, the tension easing from her features as her face lit up in an invitation meant only for him. Teo stood, propelled to her as if by a magnet. The crowd parted for him, creating a path directly to her. His smile was so wide it hurt his cheeks, but he didn't care as he held out his gloved hand. Her cheeks reddened, which was adorable. Warmth spread through his chest at the knowledge that he had that kind of effect on her. All he wanted was to take her in his arms. When he stopped in front of her, she dropped a well-formed curtsy. Evange must have helped her with that too.

Her hand set his ablaze as he brought it to his lips, kissing her knuckles softly. He didn't mind; he'd let her touch burn him any time. "I'm so glad you're here," he murmured.

"All possible because of you. I don't even know how to thank you for the dresses."

"You being here is all the thanks I need." Reluctantly, he let her go and held out his hand to her father. "Dr. Hood."

Jenna's dad hesitated before grasping Teo's hand and shaking it. "Your Majesty. Thank you for inviting us. It's an honour." He bowed slightly.

"The privilege is mine. Please enjoy yourself this evening. If you don't mind, sir, I'd like to steal your daughter and escort her into the room."

"Enjoy yourselves." The doctor squeezed Jenna's hand before weaving through the maze of people, heading over to where Dr. Lupine and other medical people were chatting.

As they strolled farther into the room, Teo kept Jenna close to his side, the tantalizing smell of her shampoo and the feel of her touch on his arm making him a little dizzy. Someone cleared a throat behind them. Seth. Teo stopped and raised his eyebrow as they turned to face his brother.

"You look beautiful, Jenna." Seth kissed the back of her hand before facing Teo. "Are you going to go over and greet Mother?" It wasn't a question.

His brother was giving him orders? Why did his family always run interference when it came to the Hoods? "Eventually. We were going to dance first." He kept his tone even, but he stared hard at Seth. *Go away.*

"She's anxious to greet Jenna. In fact, that's why I'm here, to make sure you stop there first." Seth turned to Jenna, "Save me a dance later?"

"I'd love to. Thanks."

Resisting the urge to growl at his brother, Teo changed course and led Jenna to his mother. As they moved to the dais, the silence of the room screamed, and he could feel the watchful eyes of the guests boring into his back. If he was uncomfortable, how did Jenna feel? Her shallow breathing wasn't a good sign. "Breathe," he whispered as he squeezed her hand.

"Easy for you to say," she murmured.

"Be yourself." Teo inhaled deeply, his own stomach fluttering. Since his mother had advised against inviting the Hoods, she wouldn't be happy with his special treatment of the girl—singling her out in front of the kingdom.

As he thought, her eyes flashed as he and Jenna approached, but that was the only sign she wasn't happy. He had to give it to his mother; she had a good poker face. She was striking, her grey hair with its black stripe twisted in an updo and her small tiara studded with diamonds glittering in the light. He stopped at the edge of the dais and bowed slightly "Mother, you remember Jenna Hood."

Jenna curtsied.

"It's a pleasure to see you again, Jenna." The Queen Mother smiled, but it was the one she used for professional events.

"Th-thank you, Your Majesty."

His mother gestured to Sirhaan, who stood a little behind her. "This is Sirhaan, a friend."

Sirhaan extended his hand to Jenna. "No need to curtsy, my dear, I'm not royalty." He chuckled. "It's a pleasure to meet you finally. I've heard much about you."

Teo's eyes narrowed. What had he heard about her? Had his mother spoken about the Hoods? The hairs on the back of Teo's neck raised. He didn't like the way Sirhaan studied Jenna, like a fox hunting prey.

He stepped slightly in front, blocking her from Sirhaan's view. Anxious to leave the man's presence, Teo faced his mother, ready to make an excuse to leave. As if reading his mind, she gestured to the tables laden with food.

"Make sure Jenna tries some of our delicacies. The egg cups are your favourites, and I'm sure she'd like to sample them."

"I will, but first we're going to dance." He nodded at his mother before escorting Jenna onto the dance floor, twirling her away from him and then back, holding her close. Over her shoulder, Teo spotted Ethan following their every move. It had been months since Teo had seen Jenna's best friend. He should talk to him later. A whiff of honeysuckle brought his attention back to the girl in his arms. "Have I told you how beautiful you are?"

She slid her hand down his chest. "You are looking dashing yourself, Your Majesty."

He pulled her closer and whispered in her ear, "I'm still Teo to you."

She stepped back, both of them smiling like goofy kids sharing a joke. The song ended, but Teo held her firmly in place, challenging the other men who circled them to approach. For the next few minutes, Teo wasn't sharing. After two more songs, he let Seth cut in. After that, two other young men took Jenna for a whirl before Teo reclaimed her as his dance partner. As they started to waltz, Ethan approached. Teo groaned softly as he halted their steps.

"Congratulations, Your Majesty." Ethan bowed, wobbling slightly before regaining his balance.

"Ethan, good to see you." Teo studied Jenna's best friend. He seemed off.

"You look so handsome." Jenna left Teo's arms and hugged her friend. A sharp pain stabbed Teo's chest.

"You're the most beautiful-ist girl here." Ethan smiled. Was he drunk?

Jenna laughed. "Dance with me later?"

"Why not now?" He held out his hand.

"Oh. Uh..." Jenna glanced between Teo and Ethan. "I'm going to dance with Teo, but after that, I'd love to."

Ethan's mouth pressed together in a thin line. He looked as if he might object, but then he nodded. "Sure." He slurred the word a little before turning and weaving through the dancers.

Maybe Teo had imagined Ethan's instability, since Jenna didn't seem concerned. He shoved away the nagging thought as he held out his hand to her. "Shall we try again?" As if on cue, the first strains of another waltz filled the room, and Teo's arms encircled Jenna's waist. She was taller than the usual girls he danced with, and he liked being able to look at her face without ducking his head too much. Her eyes reflected the twinkle of the chandeliers as he pulled her closer than was probably appropriate. He didn't care. "You did great with my mom."

She laughed, her breath tickling his neck and igniting goosebumps. "I don't think I'll ever get used to greeting the Queen Mother. I thought I was going to faint."

"Never. You're fearless."

"I'm not fearless. Where did you get that idea?" she scoffed, as she straightened his lapel.

Teo stuttered a step but quickly recovered before he tripped her up. "Are you kidding? My kingdom was saved from the Lupine Flu because you wouldn't give up."

"I believe in my dad. That's why I didn't give up. I'm definitely not fearless. This kind of thing," she tilted her head, "makes me nervous."

"Don't be. Balls come and go. They mean nothing in the end. You're the bravest person I know."

Teo leaned in, his nose brushing her ear. The tiny sigh that escaped her lips sent his blood roaring. If they could stay this way forever, he wouldn't complain.

As the music faded, he led her onto the terrace, hoping to get away from the stares of the other dancers and guests. Small, flickering lanterns lit the outside, casting a romantic hue over the space. The air was chilly, but a small fire pit kept it warm enough to linger for a minute or two. Teo held his hands out to the flames.

"It's lovely out here." Jenna wandered over to the railing and stared at the courtyard below, also lit with small lanterns hanging from the branches of the trees.

Teo opened his mouth to reply, but a blur of black in his peripheral vision grabbed his attention a second before he stumbled sideways, away from the fire. He hit the hard ground with a grunt, blinking. Whatever—whoever—had hit him was hauled off him by the Wolf Pack, who had rushed from the shadows. Teo searched for Jenna, locating her just as his guards surrounded him. They were also encasing her in a human shield, he gratefully noted. One of the guards held out a hand to help Teo up.

"Your Majesty, are you hurt?"

Teo assessed himself. "No, I'm fine. Ms. Hood, is she okay?"

"Yes, sire."

Teo's gut uncoiled. He peered around the guards, searching the area for his assaulter. *What just happened?*

Chapter Eighteen
Rider

R IDER WRAPPED HER ARMS around her stomach, trying to hold in all
the crazy emotions whirling through her. One minute, Teo and
she had been alone, then the Wolf Pack rushed her, appearing out of
nowhere like ninjas. Surrounded by a human wall of large men, Rider
tried to peek over their shoulders to see what was happening. She
caught a glimpse of two guards holding down someone who was lying
face-down on the ground. Hair the colour of straw stuck out between
the limbs, feet, and black suits. Muffled sounds mixed with grunts came
from the melee.

Her heart plummeted. *Ethan?*

As Rider's knees weakened, she grabbed at something solid and
came up with a guard's arm. He turned, stabilizing her. "Are you okay,
miss?"

"Yes, sorry. Teo, uh, the king, is he harmed?"

The guard didn't respond. Panic clawed up her throat, cutting off
her breath. Only when she spotted the top of Teo's head behind a
wall of Wolf Pack guards did she breathe. He moved to his left, letting
Rider catch a glimpse of his pale, drawn features. As Rider moved to
him, the men around her shifted, closing in tighter. Okaay. She wasn't
going anywhere. Where was Ethan? Had that been him or someone
who looked like him? She bit her thumbnail. Had Ethan attacked Teo?
She peeked over the shoulder of the hulk in front of her, grateful for
the added height of her heels. *Thank you, Evange.*

The guards yanked a dishevelled Ethan to his feet, his face a dark
red and his nose bleeding.

She covered her mouth with her hand. Ethan had done the unthinkable—tried to assault the king.

"You don't deserve her. She's—" he shouted, his words slurring.

One of the guards grabbed Ethan by his lapels. "Shut up, scum. One more thing comes out of your mouth, and I'll kill you with my bare hands."

General Scar ran over, Seth and Alarick on the general's heels.

"Is the king secure?" Seth sounded frantic.

"I'm fine." Teo's voice rose from amidst what looked like a hundred guards. "Can I leave this human prison?"

A giant stepped aside, allowing Teo to step out from behind the human shield. He smoothed his jacket as he walked to his brother and uncle.

"I'm not sure that's a good idea, Your Majesty. You need to stay behind the guards." A tall, lean guard Rider recognized from the gate patrol handed something shiny to General Scar.

"What is it?" Seth leaned forward.

"He had a small dagger on him. It fell on the ground when we tackled him."

What? Ethan had a knife on him? That was impossible—he'd hated carrying even a pocket knife on him when he was a kid.

The Queen Mother strode through the terrace doors, her hands clutched to her chest. "Teo, are you okay?"

"Everyone is okay." Seth slid an arm around his mother, who studied the circle of people.

"Who's responsible for this act of terrorism?"

The guards dragged Ethan over to stand in front of her. If looks could kill, Ethan would have been eviscerated by the one she levelled at him. "Remove this assassin to the jails now. Find out how he got an invitation and who his associates are." Her gaze flicked to the men who surrounded Rider. Involuntarily, she stepped behind her own human shield. Rider had no doubt who the Queen Mother was referring to—her. Heat filled Rider's face, but before she could object, Teo held his hand up.

"I sent him the invitation because he helped us defeat the Lupine Flu. I'm sure this is a misunderstanding."

Please let that be all it is.

"A misunderstanding?" The Queen Mother's voice rose. She motioned for the men to take Ethan away.

"No." Rider pushed against the hulk holding her back.

"Let her out." Teo's voice filled the space.

Rider spilled out from behind the guard only to see Ethan hand-cuffed and being led away. "Teo's right. This has to be a misunderstanding."

The Queen Mother swung her cold gaze to her. "You'll address your king with respect. And if you know something the rest of us don't, I suggest you speak up now."

What? Was that an accusation?

"Mother." Teo's low voice held a hint of warning.

"Question everyone out here at the time of the attack. I want a full report." She directed that order to General Scar. "Thankfully, few people realize this happened. Let's keep it that way." She whirled toward Teo. "We need to return to the ballroom."

"I need a minute." Teo straightened the cuffs of his dinner jacket.

After she studied her son a minute more, deep lines of concern grooved in her forehead, his mother nodded before she headed back to the festivities, a man falling in beside her. Sirhaan. Rider glanced at Teo, who was frowning as he watched the two of them. Who was this guy? Did the Queen Mother have a boyfriend?

A few people had gathered by the doors to the terrace, but the Wolf Pack moved them away. "Nothing to see. Only a slight mishap," one of the guards said as he rounded up the gawkers. Among them, a familiar figure stood on the fringe. Matrix. How did he get an invitation?

Before she could question him, Teo grabbed her hand. "I'm sorry, Jenna. Are you okay?"

"Yeah, but Ethan—"

"I'll check on him and find out what's going on."

"I want to come."

"No, you need to stay here. Find your father."

"Ethan is my best friend. I have to talk to him."

"No." Teo had never used that tone with her before.

She stilled, stared at him. *He's the king.*

"Go find your father. I'll let you know if I find out anything." He squeezed her fingers gently before hurrying away, the Wolf Pack guards enfolding him in their midst.

"Perhaps you'd like to dance? Or is that not permitted by the king either?"

Matrix's voice grated on Rider's frayed nerves. She turned, brushing by his outstretched hand. He stepped in her path. "What else are you going to do? You can't follow either of them."

Rider stared past Matrix, her nostrils flaring. Why did he have to be right? She couldn't get down to the cells where they'd probably taken Ethan. Where Teo had gone too.

"I don't want to dance. It will make it look like I don't care what happened to Teo."

"There's nothing you can do at the moment. Enjoy the party."

Dancers glided by the open doors but they blurred before her eyes.

"I can't enjoy myself when my best friend attacked my... the king. They will think I'm horrible."

"Who will?"

The Queen Mother, for starters. Wolves in general. Rider crossed her arms over her stomach. "People."

"The Queen Mother already thinks you're guilty by association."

Her eyes narrowed. "What are you talking about? I had nothing to do with what happened."

"Tell that to everyone who saw you dancing with the king. The Wolves, the Royals, they're already wary of Foresters, are they not?" He held his hand out to her again. "Or you can show them you have nothing to hide."

Rider hesitated, then grabbed his large hand, ignoring his smug look. She did have nothing to hide and few options at the moment. When they reached the dance floor, Matrix pulled her close, too close. She caught a whiff of soap and woods before she stepped back, creating space between them. Matrix was a good dancer, their steps keeping time, but Rider didn't even register the beat.

"From my standpoint, unity between the Foresters and the Wolves seems tenuous at best. You don't think that a Forester attacking the new king isn't going to make headlines, despite what the Queen Mother does to cover it up? People will freak out. You were dancing with the king; who's to say you and Ethan weren't working together? Especially when word gets out you're friends."

Rider tried to pull away, but Matrix tugged her closer.

"That's a lie," she hissed.

"Is it?" His locks tickled her ear as he shook his head. "People believe what they want. Do you think you'll have any chance with Teo now? It's obvious his mother won't allow it," he whispered.

Heat spread across Rider's cheeks. "You don't know anything about us," she hissed.

"Don't be a fool." He abruptly released her, and she stumbled slightly before regaining her balance. She whirled away from him, hurrying to the exit and into the hallway. Seth was there, speaking with two guards.

"Where's Teo?" Her words rushed out.

Seth excused himself from the guards. "He's gone with Ethan."

"I want to see him."

"No one is allowed down there." Seth propped a shoulder against a tapestry on the wall depicting the life-cycle of his clan's namesake. His taught jaw belied his easy stance. If Rider tried to step past him, she knew he'd stop her. "Ethan's in serious trouble. He had a *weapon*. There's a good chance he'll be charged with treason. You should head home. It will get out that he's a friend of yours. You need to go where you'll be safe."

What did that mean? No one would come after her. Rider lifted her chin. "No, I'm not leaving. Ethan is my friend."

Teo appeared around the corner, several guards at his heels. Rider ran to him. "Where's Ethan?"

Before the words were out of her mouth, two of the guards stepped in front of Teo. What? Did they think she posed a threat?

"It's okay. She's not going to hurt me." Teo pushed between the two bulky men.

"Where's Ethan?" Rider repeated her question, ignoring the confusing emotions swirling inside her.

He exchanged a look with Seth. "He's in a holding cell. I'm going back, but I wanted to make sure you had a safe escort home."

"I'm not leaving." Rider stood her ground, feet apart, not that anyone could tell in her ballgown. Instead of inhibiting her, the high heels made her feel fierce.

Teo scrubbed a hand over his eyes. "It's for your own protection. I don't want people making assumptions about you and Ethan."

"This isn't Ethan. He would never hurt a fly. He won't even kill a spider—he takes them outside and lets them go." She wanted to yell and shake him but she resisted, forcing her tone to remain even. One Forester assaulting the king was enough for coronation day. How had it come to this?

"I agree it doesn't make sense, but we need to let the Wolf Pack investigate. He was *armed*." He shoved a hand into his pants pocket, avoiding her gaze. "Jenna, please don't tell me you knew about any of this."

Rider's head jerked. "What? No. How could you even think that? I can't believe you would even ask me that." Her eyes burned, but she blinked the tears away. He might as well have stabbed her himself. "He was jealous of you. I did know that, but it was dumb. I didn't think he'd ever act on it. I knew nothing about what his plans were for tonight. He told me he wasn't coming."

Teo's eyes darkened and he reached for her, but she shook her head as she stepped out of his reach.

"Jenna, I'm sorry." He drove his fingers through his hair. "I didn't mean... I don't understand any of this."

Dr. Hood appeared with a Wolf Pack guard. "What's this about Ethan causing trouble?"

Seth pushed away from the tapestry, leaving it swinging slightly against the wall. "He attacked the king tonight and had a weapon on him."

"What?" Her dad's eyebrows shot up.

"He tackled Teo outside, but the Wolf Pack jumped him. He carried a dagger *but he didn't use it.*" Rider glared at Seth and Teo.

Teo lowered his hand to his side. "Dr. Hood, it's not safe for you to be here. When word gets out about your connection to Ethan... I'm sorry, but you both need to leave. Please be careful." Teo nodded to one of the Wolf Pack. "Kindly escort the Hoods home."

Her father glanced between her and Teo. "Are you okay, Jenna-girl?"

She wasn't harmed physically, but Teo had sliced open her heart with his suspicions and actions. Rider lifted her chin. "I'm fine, Dad."

"Your Majesty? Are you harmed? Can I help you?"

"Thank you, but I'm not hurt. I'll probably just have a few bruises tomorrow." Teo's laugh was strained.

Dr. Hood held out his arm to Rider. "Let's go. There's not much we can do at the moment."

Avoiding Teo's gaze, Rider took her father's arm and followed the guards, ignoring the urge to look over her shoulder at the king. She didn't want to know whether he was looking at her or not. If he was sorry about what he said or not. How could he question her loyalty? She almost wished she did have a physical wound because it would hurt less. Although she leaned against her father's strong body, Rider held her head high, determined not to let anyone see how hurt she was, or accuse her of acting guilty. After all, she had nothing to be guilty about.

As they left the palace, the weight in her stomach grew. Teo's parting words echoed in her head. They'd sounded like more than a dismissal. They had felt like goodbye.

Chapter Nineteen
Matrix

MATRIX BACKED INTO THE shadows of the dark corner in the hall outside the ballroom. A large, thick potted shrub with lights strung through its branches had proven to be a good place to watch the events unfolding in the hallway without being noticed. He'd followed Rider out of the ballroom and then slipped behind the plant. The group had been too caught up in the Ethan saga to notice him.

He smiled. The kid had come through for him. His grin grew wider as Teo ordered Rider, who looked like she might cry, from the castle. A wedge had been inserted between Teo and the Hood girl. Would it be wide enough for Matrix to insert himself between them?

Dr. Hood left with his daughter and a guard. Teo stood staring after them, but Jenna never looked back. A lightness spread through Matrix's chest. Finally, Teo and his brother, accompanied by the remaining guards, strode in the opposite direction, probably to the holding cell. Matrix stepped out from his hiding place. A large, gilded mirror hung on the wall across from the shrub. After taking a moment to adjust his tie, Matrix studied his reflection. It was past time for him and his family to claim what was rightfully theirs. Tonight, they'd taken the first step to getting the crown back.

The ballroom doors opened, music and laughter infiltrating the quiet. The festivities hadn't stopped. Matrix frowned—that part hadn't gone to plan. Ethan was supposed to take Teo down in the ballroom, but the king had gone outside with Jenna. And the Wolf Pack had acted quickly, so few had witnessed the skirmish with Ethan. Most of the crowd was oblivious to the earlier attempt on the king's life. Matrix sighed. He'd known the Forester would never kill the king, but he'd counted on most of the people in the ballroom witnessing the attack. Another detour of the plan. Sirhaan would have his head. Somehow, Matrix needed to fix this.

He scanned the room, his gaze landing on a few settees near the terrace doors. Several women and a couple of men lounged on them while drinking champagne. A few well-placed juicy bits of gossip could go a long way. Matrix plastered on his charming smile as he sauntered up to the group. This could be fun.

Chapter Twenty

Teo

TEO'S MOTHER'S HEELS CLICKED loudly behind him as he stalked to the holding cell in the basement of the palace. A whiff of stale air imbued with a hint of urine activated Teo's gag reflex. *Breathe through your mouth.* He let out a stream of air. Several floors above, partners danced, people ate and drank, but Teo wasn't in the mood. With Jenna gone, there was no reason to return to the ball. More than that, he wanted answers, and the only way to get them was to question Ethan.

"Teo! Stop." The clicking of his mother's heels on the cement floor grew louder. "You need to go back to the ball. It's your duty. We will take care of the terrorist." Her voice pitched higher. If Teo didn't know better, he'd think his mother was on the verge of hysteria. Which was ridiculous because he was fine. Only a little shaken.

Teo ignored her. He needed first dibs on speaking with Jenna's friend. The memory of the look on her face when he'd asked if she knew about Ethan's assault, sliced through his heart. *Idiot.* He knew she was trustworthy, yet he'd allowed his fear to jade him for a moment, cause him to question her loyalty. His thoughts had been irrational, but the words had spouted out before he could rein them in.

After entering the holding area, he let the door slam behind him, effectively cutting off his mother's entreaties. The officer in charge looked up from the desk where he sat reading. Recognizing Teo, the guard hastily shoved the book aside, standing to attention so fast his chair legs scraped against the floor.

"At ease, Pinch. Where's the prisoner?"

"Your Majesty. He's in the end cell. He's out of it, though."

Teo's eye narrowed as he caught sight of Ethan, sprawled on a cot and muttering to himself.

"What's he saying?"

"It's gibberish. We think he's had a breakdown of some kind."

Teo strode to the bars of Ethan's cell, sniffing. "What's that smell?" Like burnt candy, the odor clung to the air.

The guard made a face. "We don't know, Your Majesty. We thought it might be some kind of cologne from the forest."

Teo doubted it. He'd never smelled anything like it on Ethan or Dr. Hood. Something niggled his brain. Or had he? It was vaguely familiar, but Teo couldn't place it. Gripping two of the bars, he called, "Ethan."

Ethan rolled over to face the wall.

"Talk to me now, and this can all be wrapped up by tomorrow."

Ethan muttered words Teo didn't understand. He shoved away from the bars in frustration. "No one is to touch this prisoner until he is lucid. Do you understand?"

"Yes, sir."

The door to the holding cell flew open and his mother rushed in, Sirhaan by her side. Teo fisted his hands. That guy was like a bad rash, never going away.

"Teo." He hadn't heard that much ice in her voice since he and his brothers were wrestling and broke a priceless lamp. "Go back to the ball. Let the Wolf Pack take care of the prisoner."

Teo planted his feet shoulder-width apart and crossed his arms. "No one is to touch him until he's coherent."

"He's a terrorist. That's all we need to know. He had a dagger. He was going to kill you."

"He never pulled the weapon. We don't know anything for sure."

Sirhaan stepped to his mother's side. "Your Majesty, if I may?"

Teo opened his mouth to refuse, but his mother nodded to Sirhaan. "I'd value your wise counsel."

Teo shot his mother a death glare.

"Your Majesty, your mother is right. The prisoner had a dagger—a man with a weapon does not have peace on his mind. It's of utmost importance that you act swiftly to assure your kingdom that you and the Wolf Pack are in control of this situation. Your message to the forest and any other possible enemies must be immediate and forceful. You will not tolerate threats to your reign. Show them your strength and fierceness."

"Sirhaan is right, Teo. Listen to us."

Teo ran his hand over his hair, scrubbing it a little. Were they right? *I can't look weak, or our enemies will move against us. What about the Haans?*

Shoving the doubts aside, Teo said, "I hear you, but I want to give him a couple of hours to see if he becomes more lucid. He's not making sense right now. Besides, he can't hurt me while he's in a cell. Since few people witnessed the attack, we have a bit of time."

His mother let out a breath and nodded. Sirhaan smiled tightly.

After giving instructions to the guard to monitor Ethan and let Teo know if anything changed, he motioned for his mother and Sirhaan to go ahead of him and followed them out. Teo had only been king for a short time, but the strange fields of plants being grown and harvested right under his nose and now this threat were making the first days of his reign trying. Who was trustworthy? A vise clamped around his head, making it throb as they made their way up the stairs.

His mother took hold of his arm as Teo started to pass by the entrance to the ballroom.

"You need to go back in there."

"I've got a headache, Mother. It's been a long night."

She dropped her hand. "Another headache?"

Sirhaan took a bottle out of his pocket. "I have something that could help."

Teo eyed the bottle. "Is that from Dr. Hood?"

Sirhaan shifted his gaze to the bottle. "No, it's from my own pharmacist. But she's as good as Dr. Hood."

No way he was taking medication from a man he didn't know or trust. "I'll be fine. Maybe water will help." His mother wasn't wrong. He did need to return to the ball, show everyone he was perfectly healthy, and everything was under control. Teo extended his arm to his mother. Time to go back to work.

Chapter Twenty-One
Rider

THE MORNING AFTER THE coronation, Rider sat on her bed, her knees pulled up to her chest as she stared at the gown hanging on the closet door. Sighing, she squeezed her eyes shut as images of the night before—being surrounded by the hulking Wolf Pack, Ethan on the ground being held like a criminal, the Queen Mother's accusing glare, Teo questioning her loyalty—flashed through her mind. Her heart squeezed as if a boa constrictor had wound itself around it. Opening her eyes, she gazed at the beautiful beadwork, embroidery, and fabric of the dress. Unfortunately, the gown didn't magically provide answers as to why her fairytale evening had turned into a nightmare. She rested her temple against her knees, her vision blurring.

How did we get here? Where is Ethan right now? And Teo? She swallowed, shoving thoughts of him away. A pounding at the front door roused her, and she leaped off her bed, tearing down the stairs to the front room as her father opened the door. Ethan's parents stood huddled together on the front stoop.

"Come in." Her dad ushered them into the warm house.

Mr. Moss yanked off his toque. "Thank goodness you're home."

"Have a seat."

As they settled on the couch before the fire, Rider studied them. Mrs. Moss's face was pale with red blotches around her eyes and cheeks. Her hair was messy and her clothes dishevelled. Mr. Moss's complexion was grey. Neither looked as though they had slept last night.

Rider sank onto the edge of a chair across from them. "Where's Ethan?" The words were out before she could stop them.

Mrs. Moss brought her hand up to her mouth to choke back sobs. Her husband circled his arm around his wife.

Dr. Hood glanced at Rider. "Sorry," she whispered.

Mr. Moss held up his hand. "No, don't be. I know you're worried about him too."

"Let's give the Mosses a minute, Jenna-girl. Will you please make us some tea?"

Rider headed into the kitchen, keeping one ear open to the conversation in the front room. As she set the kettle to boil, all she heard was Mrs. Moss sobbing. Rider pulled four china cups and a pot of honey from the cupboard before stuffing the lemon wedges left over from breakfast, in a bowl. After pouring the boiled water in the teapot, she set everything on a tray and carried it to the living room. Mrs. Moss was no longer sobbing, and Rider breathed a little easier.

"Thanks, honey." Her dad took the tray from her and poured tea into the cups before leaning back in his chair. "What can you tell us?"

Mr. Moss blew on the steaming liquid. "Not much. Ethan seemed a little down the last couple of weeks. We thought it was girl trouble."

Rider stared into her tea cup, the steam heating her already warm cheeks.

"He's been hanging around with a new boy to the area, Matrix, who seems nice enough. Ethan hadn't planned to go to the coronation ball but changed his mind at the last minute, which we were happy about. He needed to get out and stop moping. The next thing we know, Wolf Pack guards are pounding on our door." Mr. Moss's shoulders slumped.

Ethan's mother hadn't moved to pick up her tea. She glanced at Rider. "Do you know anything? Has Ethan said anything to you about the king or this new friend?"

Rider set her cup on the coffee table. He'd said that Teo didn't deserve her, but did she really want to tell them she'd rejected Ethan's interest? She hadn't expected him to act on his anger. "Not really, no, although I did know he was hanging around Matrix. Last night, Teo and I were out on the terrace getting some air. The next thing I knew, Ethan was lunging at Teo, yelling. It all happened so fast. But earlier he'd seemed off." She chewed her bottom lip. "He was slurring his words and unsteady on his feet. I wondered if he'd had too much to drink or was under the influence." She stopped, not wanting to say more and incriminate her friend further.

Her father furrowed his brows. "Was Ethan taking any kind of drugs?"

Both parents shook their heads vehemently. "Definitely not."

Dr. Hood pursed his lips. "What have you heard from the palace?"

Mr. Moss let out a shaky breath. "He's being held in the prisoner block at the moment, awaiting charges." His cup rattled against the saucer, and he leaned forward to set it on the table. "He could be charged with treason." His voice broke on the last word.

Rider's stomach dropped. "But they haven't charged him yet? That's good, isn't it?"

Mr. Moss sat forward, his forearms on his thighs. "No, he's not been charged. We're hoping that's a positive sign."

"Do you think the new king will be lenient, considering Ethan helped with saving the kingdom from the epidemic?" Hope sparked in Mrs. Moss's eyes.

Rider stared at her hands. After last night, she had no clue how Teo would respond. "I don't know. That's what doesn't make sense. Why help the Wolves and then turn against the king?" A little niggle left her unsettled. *He's jealous of Teo.*

Mrs. Moss covered her face with both hands. "We're as confused as you. This isn't our Ethan."

Rider agreed. Ethan Moss was one of the kindest and gentlest people she knew. Even if she'd turned him down, he'd never go after Teo, no matter how jealous he was.

Mr. Moss stared at the floor. "Rider, you're friends with the new king; is there any way you could talk to him?" He lifted his gaze, meeting Rider's eyes.

"The king sent us home, and I haven't heard from him today. I don't know if I can contact him, but I can try."

"Please, we would be so grateful."

Somehow, someway, she had to see Teo. Ethan's life might just depend on it.

<hr>

Dr. Hood closed the door on the retreating figures of Mr. and Mrs. Moss before returning to the living room and stacking cups and plates on the tray. "You said Ethan seemed unsteady and was slurring his words before he rushed at Teo?"

"Yes. It was weird."

"Something isn't right. Have you ever known him to take drugs or to have a reaction to medication?"

"No. Never."

"Hmm, because it sounds like he was on something. Who was he with again?"

Rider picked up the tray. "He came with Matrix, that guy his parents said he's recently started hanging around with. He's only been in the area a short while."

Her dad followed her into the kitchen, carrying the teapot. "How well do you know him?"

"I don't. I've run into him a couple of times. He gives me weird vibes. I'm not sure I trust him."

Her father set the pot in the sink. "Maybe we need to find out more about this guy."

"I can meet up with him, feel him out."

Her father shook his head. "I don't like that idea. If he is dangerous, I don't want you anywhere near him."

Was Matrix dangerous?

"For now, contact Teo and try to find out what's happening with Ethan. They should have laid charges by now. I'll ask around about this Matrix."

"If Teo's suspicious about anything that happened, he'll make sure they thoroughly investigate before he does anything drastic. He knows

Ethan wouldn't act like that. He's not like Duko. He'll make sure there is proof first."

"That's something to be thankful for. Ethan might not be around if Duko was still king."

Rider swallowed past a lump in her throat. "I know." *What were you thinking, Ethan?*

Rider stared at the closed city gates. A couple of people she recognized from the other side of the forest headed her way, so she flagged them down. "Why is the gate closed?" They hadn't been closed since the Lupine Flu.

Mrs. Calley, whose husband was a carpenter, lifted her hands. "The notice only says they are closed until further notice because the Foresters are a threat to the new king."

"What?" Rider's eyes widened.

"It's a conspiracy. The Wolves don't want us to have equal rights with them." Another man, a blacksmith Rider knew, chimed in. "They're setting this kid up so they can renege on their promises."

Rider doubted the conspiracy, but she knew a lot of Wolves took issue with the new equal rights policy Teo had implemented. But the king wouldn't go back on his promises, would he?

Rider excused herself and raced to the gates, skidding to a stop before the sign that hung from the wrought iron bars. Wolf Pack watched from the top of the wall, but none stood on the ground out front. Their gazes bore into Rider, raising the hairs on her neck. She ran her finger over the black letters.

Due to the attempt on King Teowulf's life, these gates will remain closed until the investigation is completed.

So much for keeping things under wraps. Ethan's arrest, combined with the notice informing everyone of the assassination attempt, spelled trouble for the forest. Had Teo ordered this? No, he couldn't have because this kind of self-preservation went against all he stood for. Surely he didn't believe Ethan meant him harm? Rider pedalled furiously all the way home. She had to find another way to contact Teo. And she had to do it soon.

Rider shivered as the bitter north wind whirled around her. Her foot slipped off the pedal at the sight of someone blocking her path. Matrix.

"You're in my way." Rider tried to veer around him, but he grabbed her handlebars. She planted a foot on the ground. "Wh-what are you doing? Let go."

Matrix released the bike but didn't step aside. "I guess you saw that the gates are closed." It was a statement, not a question. "Maybe the new king isn't all he's pretending to be. Perhaps he's as paranoid as they say his father was."

Rider's eyes narrowed. "That's not true. Teo is not Duko. He'll figure it out. He knows Ethan."

"Does he? You're assuming a lot. One, that Ethan is innocent. Two, that King Teowulf will give your friend the benefit of the doubt." He counted off on his fingers.

"I know both of them. Ethan wouldn't harm a flea. And Teo is not his father. He'll investigate until he finds the truth, that Ethan is innocent."

"I didn't take you for naïve. Ethan had a dagger on him. He clearly planned to kill the king. That's treason."

Rider jumped off her bike, her nostrils flaring, and let it fall to the ground with a crash. "I know Ethan. There's no way he meant to harm Teo." She planted both hands on her hips. "Wait a minute— you were with him. I should be asking what you know."

Matrix held his palms up. "Don't look at me. He was fine, then all of sudden he lost it. The next thing I knew, he disappeared and I heard a ruckus on the balcony. It was like he had some kind of breakdown."

"A breakdown?"

"Yeah. He was depressed about you and Teo."

"That's ridiculous. He wouldn't risk his life over a broken heart."

Matrix lifted a shoulder. "People have killed and overthrown kingdoms for much less."

Rider ignored his comment. "Have the Wolf Pack questioned you?"

"Why would they? Nobody knew I was with him, and I plan on keeping it that way. I didn't know anything about what he had planned."

"Ethan's parents know you went with Ethan. I know." Something flickered across Matrix's face but was gone before Rider could decipher it. "The Wolves are blaming us. This will hurt the unity of the kingdom and drive a deeper wedge between the Foresters and the Wolves You have to tell the palace what you know."

"No. I. Don't." Matrix leaned into her space

"It could help Ethan." Rider contemplated the small stones scattered across the pathway, tempted to pick them up and toss them in the guy's face. "I thought you were his friend."

"Hey, obviously my judgment was off. I'm staying out of it. Like I said, I don't know anything."

Rider glared at him as she climbed back on her bike. "You're a jerk. I need to go." She swerved away from him, wanting to put as much distance as she could between them. If she thought it might help Ethan, she wouldn't hesitate to tell Teo that Matrix had been there with her friend.

Chapter
Twenty-Two
Matrix

ALTHOUGH HE'D WRAPPED HIS coat tightly around him, Matrix still shivered as the wind bit at his exposed face and neck. The shadows of the tall pine trees blocked the sun, erasing any of its warmth. Jiggling his foot, he glanced at his watch. The man was never on time. He shoved away the memory of his encounter with Jenna. No one could prove he'd drugged Ethan. All Matrix needed to do was play dumb if he was questioned, but he wasn't about to volunteer to talk to anyone.

A bird call filled the air. His shoulders eased as he whistled back. Sirhaan appeared at the wall like a magician conjuring himself for his audience. It wasn't magic that made him appear, though. Rather, it was a hole in the wall that had so far gone unnoticed by the Wolf Pack. *They think they are so clever, sealing up that hidden doorway but forgetting to check the rest of the wall for weaknesses.* This particular access was near the forest and thus covered by bracken and ivy. Tall pines hid the wall on both sides, so it was given little attention by the Wolf Pack.

Sirhaan hadn't been wrong about the weak defences of the Wolves. Matrix had leaped on that ineptness, and now he and his uncle had as much access to each other as they wanted. They were still careful, however, sounding the whistle before approaching. If no call came back, it meant it was not safe to meet.

Matrix stepped out of the shadows, tilting his head toward a small alcove of trees. At least they would block the wind and provide privacy. *Can't be too careful.*

When they reached it, Matrix stopped and eyed his uncle. "Is the gate closure your doing?"

Sirhaan's smug smile irritated Matrix. "Of course. The queen is easy prey. The poor woman has been neglected for years. All I do is pay her attention and she falls all over herself to please me. I didn't have to use any of the drug to influence her." He rubbed his knuckles against his chest. Matrix snorted. His uncle thought he was some kind of god with women.

"Add a little insecurity about the safety of her son, as well as a pinch of mistrust about the forest—framing the boy was a good idea—and *voila*, the gates are locked shut." He chuckled quietly. "It's too easy."

Matrix shifted his weight from one foot to the other. "Don't get cocky. Teowulf is not a fool. None of the Howells are."

Sirhaan's icy glare cut into him as strongly as the north wind had, but Matrix didn't back down.

Sirhaan's thumb rubbed the smooth metal of the belt buckle of his coat. "I have everything under control. The new king will be taken care of. If you've done your part, that is."

Matrix decided not to mention that he'd been noticed as Ethan's plus one. Instead, he pulled a brown glass bottle from his jacket pocket. "It's right here. That should be all you need. If not, you know how to reach me."

Sirhaan reached for the bottle, but Matrix shifted it out of his reach. "I'm not kidding when I say don't get cocky."

"*I'm* not kidding when I say I know what I'm doing. You take care of the red hood and her dear old dad, and I'll take care of the royals." Sirhaan grabbed the bottle out of Matrix's hand and slid it into his breast pocket. "If we do our jobs, the Foresters and Wolves will soon be at each other's throats, and we will be in a position to strike. Finally, we'll have what rightfully belongs to us."

Matrix nodded, turned on his heel, and strode away.

Chapter Twenty-Three

Teo

HAD HIS CORONATION HAPPENED only twenty-four hours ago? Teo threw the soft wool blanket off him, suddenly hot. He'd hoped to grab a quick nap after a sleepless night, but his mind wouldn't cooperate with his body.

He wanted—no needed—answers to why Ethan had attacked him, but answers were as fleeting as sleep. How could an entire military and intel network come up blank? Ethan was a bike courier and a Forester, but he'd managed to bring a weapon into the ball without anyone knowing. That was the part that confused Teo. Ethan was a simple guy who didn't strike him as the violent, jealous type. His actions were completely at odds with his character, at least what Teo knew of it. Had he been wrong about Jenna's friend all this time?

Teo swung his legs over the side of his bed at the same time his brother burst into his bedroom.

"Ever heard of knocking?" Irritation laced Teo's words.

Seth ignored the dig. "Mother is on the war path, and she's headed this way. She wants action regarding the traitor."

"He's not a traitor."

"No? And how do you know that?"

"Because I know *him*. Something isn't right." If only he could put his finger on it.

"You know Mother only wants to keep you safe, right?"

"I understand her concerns, but I can take care of myself. I'm not helpless. Besides, I have personal guards on me twenty-four seven." Teo glanced over his brother's shoulder. "How far behind is Mother?"

"She was right behind me but got stopped by her secretary. Why?"

Teo grabbed his suit jacket from the end of the bed, where he'd flung it earlier. "I have someone to visit before I see her."

"If you mean the prisoner, that's a terrible idea. Mother isn't wrong to want to keep you away from him for your protection. I'm in total agreement. Since I know you won't listen, though, I'm coming with you."

Teo flicked the lights off as he exited the room. "Suit yourself."

Muttering, Seth followed Teo to the stairs. Thankfully, their mother was nowhere to be seen.

The prisoner holding area was crowded for housing only one inmate. Two guards stood at the doorway, another sat at the desk, and two more stood by Ethan's cell. The young man lay curled in a ball, his back to everyone. Although Teo thought it was a bit of overkill to have that many guards, he nodded his appreciation to them before stopping at the bars. He studied Ethan.

"Open it, Turner" Teo ordered the guard nearest the locked door.

Seth shifted beside him. "Not a good idea."

"Sir, with all due respect, the Queen has ordered no one is to enter." Turner's face was as red as his hair.

"I believe I outrank her, Turner."

Seth laid his arm across the bars of the door as if he could physically keep Teo out. "Are you crazy?" he whispered.

After dragging his brother's arm away from the bars, Teo motioned the guard to open the door. Ethan hadn't moved.

Turner turned the key in the lock. Teo clapped him on the back. "I'll take the flack from the Queen if she finds out." He spoke loudly enough for everyone to hear. *No one wants to get on the wrong side of Mother.* He didn't blame them. "All but Turner please leave the room." Without a word, the men and women moved outside. How gratifying to have orders obeyed without a fight.

Seth threw up his hands in frustration, turning his back on Teo for a minute before he appeared to think better of it and faced the cell.

Turner held open the door. "I'm right here, Your Majesty."

"Thank you." But Teo wasn't worried. A sickly sweet odour assaulted his nostrils. "What's that smell?"

Turner made a face. "Don't know. We thought someone spilled something on him."

Teo swallowed against his gag reflex. "Ethan."

Still no movement. Turner barked, "Your king speaks. Get to your feet."

Ethan slowly rolled over and off the cot, his feet hitting the floor as though they were made of stone. He lifted his head as he shoved himself to standing. Despite the defiance in his eyes, he swayed on his feet.

"Ethan, it's me, Teo. Talk to me."

"I have nothing to say to you."

"Don't be stupid. You know you're to be charged with treason, right? That carries a sentence of death if you're found guilty."

Ethan's face paled, and he grabbed the chain nailed to the wall to hold up the cot.

Teo took a step closer. "What's going on?"

Ethan swayed again. Seth shoved past Teo, grabbing Ethan's arm. "Your king asked you a question."

Ethan's greasy hair stuck up in clumps, and dark smudges highlighted his pale face. Jenna would freak out if she saw him.

Ethan coughed, and Seth dropped his arm. They were all a little on edge still when it came to sickness. Not that Teo thought Ethan was sick. At least not the kind you could catch. Even so, he lowered himself to the cot and stuck the pillow, if you could call it such, behind his back. Teo let the breach in protocol go, as the guy looked as if he might fall over.

Ethan scrubbed his face with both hands before lowering them to his lap. "I don't know what happened. Matrix and I went to the ball. After I approached you and Rider and she wouldn't dance with me, I was in a rage like I've never been before. It was like I was having an out-of-body experience."

"What do you mean?"

"My body took over as if it had a mind of its own. The next thing I knew, I followed you outside and tackled you."

Teo leaned his shoulder against the bars of the cell. "Where did the dagger come from?"

Ethan blinked. "What dagger?"

"You didn't bring a concealed dagger to the ball?"

"Of course not! Why would I do that?"

The horror on his face would be hard to fake. Teo glanced at Seth, who raised his brows.

"To be clear, you know nothing about a dagger?" Teo pressed.

"No!"

"Why were you in a rage that I was with Jenna?"

Ethan gripped the edge of his cot with both hands. "Because."

"Because...?" Like a piece of a puzzle, the answer slid into place. "You're in love with her."

His silence was all the answer Teo needed.

"I can understand why."

"You understand nothing. Do you think it's going to work between you and her? You're the Wolf King and she is a Forester. In your dreams will your mother allow you to date her. She's so hung up on you that she can't see it," he spat.

His mother had no say in his love life. But was what Ethan spewing at least partly true?

"So, you brought a dagger to kill the king because of a girl." Seth traced a crack in the cell wall with one finger and then, as though thinking better of it, wiped the finger on his pants.

"No. I told you I don't know anything about a dagger."

"Yet it was on your person." Seth stepped closer.

"Seth." Teo warned. His brother stopped but didn't move back. Teo pushed away from the bars. "How did you get it past security?"

Ethan tilted his head to lean it against the cinder block wall. "I told you, I don't remember having a weapon." He squeezed his eyes shut.

"Ethan, you didn't take any drugs, did you?"

"Of course not." Ethan scoffed, his eyes still closed. "I barely take anything for a headache."

They were going in circles. Motioning for Seth to follow, Teo left the cell. Turner locked the door then followed them to the guard's desk.

"I want the prisoner to be tested for drugs ASAP. Call Dr. Lupine to do the tests."

Turner picked up the phone and made the call.

"Do you think it's too late for a tox report?" Seth washed his hands in a sink attached to the wall. A coffee pot sat on the counter next to it, but the liquid in the pot looked like tar.

Teo shrugged. "It's worth a shot. Call the other guards in."

Seth went to the door and ordered the other guards back to their posts.

"Dr. Lupine will come right away," Turner reported.

Seth whispered in Teo's ear, "You believe him?"

"I do. The guy's scared of his own shadow, so why would he try to jump me? I've got at least twenty pounds on him."

"Love makes us do crazy things," Seth deadpanned.

Teo tapped two fingers on the desk, ignoring Seth's verbal jab. "Thank you, Turner. I'll be back later." As he led Seth out of the cell area, he asked, "Did you smell that sweet odour?"

Seth pinched the bridge of his nose. "No, my sinuses are acting up."

"I think it was coming off Ethan. I can't place it, but I know I've smelled it before." Teo strode along the corridor, his boots echoing off the stone walls. "I also want to speak with this Matrix. If he was with Ethan, he may know something. Why wasn't he held for questioning?"

"No one knew he'd come with a friend until the Mosses mentioned it. The guest lists went missing in all the confusion. We've been trying to locate this Matrix, but he's a ghost."

Teo took the stairs leading to the living quarters of the castle two at a time. "Of course he is."

"Don't be discouraged. We'll figure it out." Seth stopped, groaning. "We have a perfectly good elevator, you know."

"You're Wolf Pack, what's a few stairs to you?" Teo grinned as he continued to climb, his footsteps muted on the ornate carpet. His amusement grew as Seth muttered under his breath behind him. He enjoyed their friendly spats, but it was his brother's 'We'll figure it out' that warmed Teo's insides. He wasn't alone in all this mess.

Teo drummed his fingers on the arms of his black leather desk chair. After glancing at the clock again, he stood, straightening his clothes before pacing the room. It was after noon, two hours since he'd sent for Dr. Lupine to test Ethan's blood. After another minute, Teo threw open the door and addressed the guard on duty outside.

"I need to know Dr. Lupine's findings. He should be done by now. Find out."

The guard rushed away as Teo shut the door. He picked up his empty paper coffee cup, crumpled it, then tossed it into the garbage. Seth had interviewed several Wolf Pack guards who'd been on duty last night but had turned up nothing. Not one of them had talked to, let alone remembered, Matrix. And the guest list? Gone without a trace. Teo doubted it had simply gotten lost—that was too convenient.

A knock rattled the door. "Come in."

The guard entered and saluted. "Your Majesty."

"Report."

"Dr. Lupine arrived to do the tests, but the Queen Mother stopped him."

A rushing sound filled Teo's ears. "What? I gave a direct order. Who agreed to overturn it?" He was the ruling sovereign, not his mother.

The guard swallowed. "I'm not sure, Your Majesty."

Teo pointed at the guard. "The Wolf Pack obey my orders. Go and escort Dr. Lupine to the prisoner's cell. Stay there until the tests are completed. You will not return here until you have the results in hand. Do you understand?"

"Yes, Your Majesty." The young man hurried away.

Teo strode to his mother's office, which was around a corner and down the hallway. He yanked open the door, ignoring his mother's secretary as he headed into his mother's personal office space. He didn't care about privacy or respect, since she'd shown him little of either since he took the throne. She'd kept Sirhaan around, even though Teo had made it clear he wanted him out. Because of her disapproval of Jenna, Teo had resorted to sneaking around and keeping her a secret. He stopped short when he spotted his mother sitting beside Sirhaan on the small loveseat. If he'd been a bull, that man was the red cape.

His mother leapt to her feet. "Teo, you can't just barge in here—"

"Get out," he growled, pointing at Sirhaan.

His mother's face paled. "Teo."

"Get out now."

Sirhaan rose, a placid smile on his face. "It's fine, Ruby. I'll leave you two alone."

Was that a smirk? Teo bared his teeth as the man passed his way.

"What is the meaning of this?" His mother's sharp tone drew his attention back to her. "This is my private office and you were rude to my guest."

Teo clenched his fists and pulled himself to his full height. He couldn't lose his temper in front of his mother. He had to act like an adult. "Did you call off Dr. Lupine from testing Ethan?"

"Yes, I did. It wasn't necessary. He wasn't drugged." She walked to a tall bookcase and straightened a few books.

"We don't know that."

"Sirhaan is an expert in behaviour, and he said the prisoner gave no indication he was on drugs. He studied him after the Wolf Pack arrested him and before he was taken to the holding cell. He said this boy displayed a classic case of a psychotic breakdown. He's dangerous. Besides, it would be seen as a weakness to let him off because of a toxicology report."

"He saw him for all of five minutes and you believe him?"

She picked up a framed picture of Teo and his brothers, caressing it with her finger. "He is wise—"

Teo grabbed the photo out of her hand. "You barely know him. And I am king. You, Sirhaan, and everyone else, are to obey *my* orders. If I want to explore a theory of drugs, I will, and it's not up to you to decide if it's okay."

His mother tugged the photo out of Teo's hands and set it back on the shelf. She pointed to his ten-year old image. "Calm down—you're acting like a child."

Her words hit Teo as if she'd slapped him across his face.

"Who is in control here? That's what I'm asking."

"You are, dear, but accepting help is not a weakness." She turned to face him, her hands on her hips. "You sound like your father."

"I am nothing like Duko," Teo rasped. He felt sick to his stomach.

"Listen to me. Sirhaan has been trained as a behaviour expert so he doesn't sell weapons to people who shouldn't have them. He's able to recognize drug abuse and mental crisis. What he saw with that Forester was not drug abuse."

It made sense that the guy would be trained to spot erratic behaviour and addiction, but Teo still didn't trust the man. "Mother, I'll ask advice from... people I've known for more than two seconds, like Alarick and Dr Lupine." Dr. Hood, even.

"Don't be a fool. They aren't objective like Sirhaan. He brings fresh eyes and a perspective your uncle and Dr. Lupine don't have. Besides, you're wasting time. We need to deal with the terrorist so others won't try to attack you, too. My first priority is your safety."

"I'm not going to rule in fear. Nor am I sending a possibly innocent man to his death until I know for sure he's guilty. I'd rather fight off assassins than have to live with that." He cast a glance at the photo of him, Bleddyn, and Seth grinning at the camera, their hair mussed from wrestling in the back courtyard. Suddenly his limbs weighed a hundred pounds. "Let me rule the way I see fit, or dethrone me." He locked eyes with his mother before he turned and let himself out, the door clicking firmly shut behind him.

Chapter Twenty-Four
Rider

R IDER CHEWED HER THUMBNAIL as she paced the front room of her cottage—the threatening grey skies mirroring her inner turmoil. She needed to contact Teo, but now that the gates were closed and the Foresters' loyalties suspect, she didn't know how. Rider winced as she tore new skin away from her thumb. Brushing the stinging area against her thigh, she sat on the sofa, pulled a pillow close to her chest, and rested her chin on it.

Think. How did one send a message to a king who had locked himself away in a city? Walk up to the gates, rattling the bars and screaming until someone let her in? Or arrested her? Scale the wall?

Her father walked in through the front door. "Good, you're here."

The ache in her thumb pulsed. "What is it?'

He waved a sheet of paper. "It's good news. Dr. Lupine needs our help."

She tossed the pillow to the side. "How did you...? With what?"

"A Wolf Pack guard intercepted me as I walked home from Granny's. Her sore throat is coming along, by the way. Anyway, the guard approached and handed me this paper from Dr. Lupine. Your man is suspicious; he's requested the doctor do tests on Ethan. The Queen Mother interfered the first time, but Dr. Lupine was summoned back to the palace, escorted by one of the king's personal guards. Once Dr. Lupine gets blood from Ethan, he's coming here to do the testing, so the palace can't interfere with the results. The king approved it."

If Dr. Lupine came to her house... "I can send a message to Teo through Dr. Lupine."

"Sounds like a plan."

Rider followed her father into the kitchen. He pulled a loaf of bread out of the breadbox.

"Do you think Teo really believes Ethan was drugged?" Rider passed the butter dish to her dad.

"I think he's questioning the validity of Ethan's actions."

"But the Queen Mother?"

"Is not the reigning sovereign. He overrules her. And obviously, he did." He slathered the butter on the bread, set it on a plate, and handed it to her.

Rider took it. "I'll get that message ready now." Leaving the plate on the table, she dashed up to her room.

Dear Teo,

I'm so sorry Ethan ruined the coronation ball. I wish we'd had more time together. I tried to see you, but the gates are closed to the Foresters, which makes me sick. Foresters are uneasy, and shutting us out sends the message we don't belong and aren't wanted. You know Ethan would never harm you. Do you think someone set him up? That's the only thing that makes sense to me. He doesn't even like knives, so why would he carry one? I'm begging you, please don't do anything rash until you find out the truth. Please open the gates. I miss you and wish I could see you again.

Jenna

Rider reread the note before folding it and inserting it in an envelope. The front door opened and then closed. She raced down the stairs to find Dr. Lupine standing in the front room, speaking with her father. The doctor smiled. "Rider, good to see you."

"Dr. Lupine. How did you get out of the city?" Had they opened the gates?

Dr. Lupine glanced at his bag, shifting it to his other hand. "Wolves can go as they please. And I'm doing the king's bidding."

"Teo himself asked for my dad's help?" That was better than Rider had hoped.

"Not exactly, although he did approve the suggestion when I mentioned it to him. When it comes to natural drugs, your father is the best toxicologist."

Dr. Hood motioned for the Wolf to sit. "You think if Ethan was drugged, it came from a plant?"

Dr. Lupine sat, letting out a small sigh as he set his bag on his lap. "Yes." He ran his hand over the worn leather medicine bag. "I saw the sign on the gates, and already I'm hearing rumours about a forest conspiracy to take over the city. I know Ethan a little bit, and I can't imagine him attacking the king. If he was drugged, why wouldn't the person responsible want to lay blame on the forest? They'd choose a natural drug so it would look even more suspicious for the Foresters."

Someone was framing the forest people? Rider's jaw gaped.

"Let's get started then." Her father stood and motioned for Dr. Lupine to follow him to his office.

"Wait. Dr. Lupine, would you be able to get this letter to the king?" Rider held out the envelope.

"I'll try, but I can't promise anything. Security is tight around the king."

It was something. "Thank you." Would her words have any sway over Teo? Would Ethan be released? *Please, Teo, say yes.*

Chapter
Twenty-Five

Teo

T HE PAPER CRINKLED IN Teo's hands as he read it for the hundredth time. He'd didn't really have to, since he'd memorized every word, but he needed the visual of her handwriting, to touch the paper that she'd held in her hand that very day. As he sank into his desk chair, Teo set it on top of the piles of paper waiting for him. He massaged his temples.

"Headache, Your Majesty?"

Teo jerked and then, catching sight of Sirhaan in the open doorway, grimaced. Why had he left his door open? He slid a file over the letter. "A minor ache. Nothing to concern yourself over."

"If I may, I have a pain reliever that works wonders for headaches."

I wouldn't trust you with my enemy. "I'm fine. No need to worry yourself." Teo picked up a pen, then slid over a stack of files, hoping the man would take the hint and disappear.

"You seem to suffer a lot with headaches, if you don't mind me saying."

Actually, I do mind. "As I said, I'm fine. Thank you." His tone was curt.

Sirhaan bowed slightly, then hurried away. After closing the door, Teo stared at his messy desk. His stomach rolled. Was he hungry or just tired? Maybe he needed refreshment to give him energy and rid himself of the ache in his head. After ringing for tea, Teo sifted through the reports.

Sirhaan was annoying, but he hadn't pursued the weapons deal so he was the least of Teo's problems. Dr. Lupine's toxicology report, which had come back within two hours of Teo ordering it the second time, was inconclusive. He could not confirm any drug in Ethan's system. Dead end. *How can I listen to Jenna with no evidence her friend was under the influence?*

The door opened. "Your Majesty."

Teo slammed the pen down. How many times did he have to tell the man no?

Sirhaan walked in carrying a tray. "I was on my way to my room when I saw your butler. I thought I'd save him the trip."

"Er, thanks. But that's his job."

Sirhaan set the tray on the side table, the china rattling.

Wait, why do you have a room here? "I was unaware you were staying." Teo let the unsaid question linger between them.

"Your mother invited me. She's a generous host."

"She is." Perhaps if he kept his words few, the man would leave.

As if he could read Teo's mind, Sirhaan said, "I'll let you get back to work, Your Majesty." For the second time, Teo watched the man exit his office.

He squeezed a wedge of lemon, watching the juice trickle over his fingers into his tea. His mother was free to invite whomever she wanted, but Sirhaan staying in the palace unsettled Teo. A spicy aroma wafted by as he lifted his cup, and he sniffed. The tea had a sweet scent, although it was faint. He sipped it, but the tea didn't taste sweet. Must be his imagination. Hopefully the caffeine would take care of the pain in his temple.

Taking another sip, Teo burned his tongue. Hurriedly, he put the cup back on the tray, deciding to let it cool while he had a chat with his mother. He was going to get to the bottom of what was going on between her and Sirhaan. *Then I'm kicking him out.*

After being directed to the courtyard greenhouse by his mother's assistant, Teo entered the steamy building. His mother strolled through her rose garden, snipping flowers with a lethal-looking pair of gardening shears. She placed the perfect flower in a basket she had hung over the crook of her elbow.

"Hello, Teo. What can I do for you?" She studied a bud, then moved on to another fully formed rose.

"Why does Sirhaan have rooms here, and why wasn't I told about it before this?"

Snip. The flower came off the bush and into the basket. His mother worked rhythmically—studying, cutting, moving to the next rose.

Teo tapped his foot, half hypnotized by his mother's hands.

"He's travelled a long way. I thought being hospitable in light of your rude response to his request to help us protect ourselves was the right thing to do."

"I wasn't rude. I simply told him no."

She placed the shears in the basket. "You've been nothing but rude to my friend. You need a few lessons in diplomacy, my son. Sirhaan was quite offended by your very curt no. You didn't even let him finish his presentation."

"We don't need his war weapons. All the clans live peacefully with each other."

"What about that terrorist from the forest?"

"Mother." Teo wasn't getting into it with her again. "Why didn't you tell me you asked him to stay?" Deflection was good.

"Because hospitality is my job until you find a suitable wife."

Teo snorted. "Isn't that a little stereotypical?"

"Would you like to discuss a marriage?"

Not the change in subject he wanted. Teo stepped back. "No, thank you." His mother's face blurred.

Her fingers wound around his forearm, grounding him. Gradually, her face came back into focus.

"Teo, are you okay? You're white as a snow wolf." She lifted the back of her free hand to his forehead.

Teo moved back, out of her reach. "I'm fine. Just a bit dizzy for a second. Must be all the fragrance from the flowers." He pinched between his eyes. "Next time I want to know when we have guests."

The Queen Mother frowned but didn't reply. Teo hurried out of the humidity of the building, inhaling the crisp air of the courtyard before she could ask any more questions about how he felt. The last thing he needed was for her to worry about his health on top of Ethan. *Maybe my blood sugar is low.* He'd been too keyed up to eat breakfast this morning and lunch had passed hours ago. Rerouting, Teo wandered to the castle kitchen in search of something more nutritious than tea and pastries. If he couldn't best this bout of headaches and dizziness, he wouldn't be able to think clearly enough to resolve the situation with Ethan, hopefully in a way that wouldn't drive a wedge between him and Jenna.

Garlic, salt, and other spices satisfied Teo's taste buds. As he bit into the last half of his sandwich, juice dribbled down his chin. Swiping it with a napkin while he chewed, Teo savoured the taste of the beef along with the tang of the mustard. He was hungrier than he'd realized.

"There you are." Seth slid next to him on the bench at the large table.

"Here I am."

"For being the ruling sovereign, you're hard to find."

Teo took another bite, mumbling through a mouthful, "I was hungry."

"I met Mother in the courtyard. She wasn't happy. What did you do now?"

"Have you noticed that nothing ever is done to her liking these days? She's almost as controlling as Father."

"She's not anything like Father."

Teo wiped his fingers on a napkin, shoving down the niggle of guilt. He was letting his frustration with her colour his perspective. "You're right, she's not like Duko. However, she isn't letting certain things go easily. And Sirhaan isn't helping matters."

Seth picked a carrot stick off Teo's plate, bit it. "He's okay. A little pushy sometimes." He crunched the veggie, the sound grating on Teo's nerves.

"A little? He's inserted himself into the palace like a nasty case of fleas."

"You're overreacting because you don't like the guy..."

"I don't trust him. There's a difference. Something's off with him."

"You're stressed with the coronation, Ethan, the mysterious plants. There's a lot going on. I think your tolerance is low."

Was it simply that too much was happening right now? "It's more than that." *I think.* "I'm going to have Uncle Alarick investigate Sirhaan's business in the Lake District and surrounding area. I want to know everything I can about him—especially if he has designs on Mother." The sandwich he'd eaten turned to lead in his stomach. Time to change the subject. "The toxicology reports came back negative. A drug was the only thing that would explain Ethan's actions."

"Or he wanted to kill you." Seth levelled his gaze at Teo. "You can't rule that out."

Teo tossed his napkin on the plate. He didn't want to think of the repercussions of Ethan planning his assassination. "Maybe, but I don't believe it."

"You don't have to believe it for it to be true."

"You really think he planned to kill me?" Teo shoved his plate away.

Seth shrugged. "I don't know, but you have to consider the possibility."

"Did you notice the smell on him?"

"That gross, cheap, sweet cologne?" Seth faked a gag.

Teo grimaced. Someone needed to teach the kid the value of less is more when it came to scents. "Yeah, that one."

"Do you think that had something to do with what happened?"

Teo frowned. "How could it?"

"I have no idea." Seth traced a circle on the table with his finger. "I know you don't want to hear this, but Mother's pushing for a quick trial... and execution."

"She's not in charge. I'm king. I make the final ruling."

"Then pardon him."

Teo raised his eyebrows. "Pardon a possible assassin? That will cause a riot in the city. What if he did mean to hurt me?" He shuddered. "We can't send the message that we'll go easy on people who want me dead. I certainly don't want my enemies thinking that. Father would roll over in his grave."

"Definitely right on that count." Seth poured himself a glass of water. "What are you going to do?"

"That, brother, is the million-dollar question."

Chapter
Twenty-Six
Rider

WARMTH CRESTED OVER RIDER as she approached the city, and it wasn't because she was hiking that fast. It was what she saw ahead of her. The gates were wide open. Teo had seen reason—he must have.

Did that mean Ethan had been released? It had been thirty-six hours since he'd attacked Teo; was that long enough for them to figure out her friend was innocent? Her heart raced.

Rider jogged the rest of the way to the wall, merging into the long line. "What's the hold up?"

Mr. Potts, an older gentleman from the forest who ran a local museum about the habitats of forest creatures, glanced at her. "Back to the old ways. Checking papers, detaining anyone suspicious or because they feel like it. The new king is as paranoid as his father."

Rider winced at the bitter undertones in her neighbour's voice. Tempted to argue, she bit her tongue. The man wouldn't listen—he'd never been a supporter of Teo and his policies. Teo complained that too many Wolves hadn't accepted the new ways, but Mr. Potts and a few other Foresters were also set in their beliefs. *Never trust a Wolf* was written in a more than a few Foresters' DNA.

As the line inched along, a few people were escorted away by guards, probably to be questioned or detained. This giant step backwards wasn't helping matters for either side. Rider gripped her backpack straps until they cut into her palms. Why had Teo gone back on his word? He didn't believe the Foresters would rebel, did he? Because the notion was laughable.

White fire surged through her veins as a burly guard approached her, holding out his hand.

"Papers."

Rider shoved the papers at him. Too forcefully. He narrowed his eyes as he stared at her. "What's your name?"

"Jenna Hood," she said evenly, no tremor in her voice. *You'd be dead without my father's help.*

"Come with me." He grabbed her by the arm.

"Let go." She pulled, but his grip was a vice. Another guard came up and grabbed her other arm, and they walked her to the guard offices.

"Stop fighting me," the first guard hissed. Rider didn't recognize him. Muscular and bald, he must be one of the new hires after the flu took out several officers. His scowl looked as if it was a permanent feature. "Take her to the Commanding Officer. His orders." He let go of her arm.

The second guard led her down a hall. Rider's mind whirled. Commanding Officer? Who was that? She tried to go through the guards she knew or had become acquainted with through Teo and Seth.

"In here." He opened a door to the left of the entrance to the offices. After hesitating a moment, Rider entered, taking a seat on one of two wooden chairs. A large pine table took up the rest of the space. Another door on the far wall was partially closed. The guard strode over to it, knocked twice, then leaned into the room, muttering something Rider couldn't make out. Popping back out, he gestured for her to come over. "You can go in."

Rider's heart beat an erratic rhythm, but she schooled her features into a bored expression, as though she did this every day, until she saw Seth standing there. Air whooshed out of her. "Your Highness. Is Teo all—

"He's fine. Come in." He beckoned her forward. "And you're not in trouble." He grinned, and Rider's shoulders dropped an inch or two.

"Why would I think that?" Rider sank onto a chair beside the desk, her legs suddenly weak. She couldn't let Seth see her sweat.

The prince rolled his eyes. "Because you attract it like it's your job." He leaned a hip against the desk. "I need your help. Teo needs a distrac— to see you. I thought it might clear his head if you visited. And you know Ethan better than either of us. Maybe you could shed some light on this whole disaster."

"Ethan's innocent."

Seth pursed his lips. "That remains to be seen. But any evidence you can provide would be appreciated. In the meantime, I'll take you to Teo."

"Wait, how did you know I was coming? Does he know I'm here?"

"No. I've been waiting for you since we opened the gates this morning, hoping you'd show, and I got lucky. Teo is at a museum opening right now, but his afternoon is free. At least for a couple of hours." He glanced at his watch. "He should be finishing up. Let's go catch up with him."

"You couldn't have just come and knocked on my door?"

"I didn't want anyone to know." He tilted his head. "Do you want to see him or not?"

Rider stood up quickly, before Seth could change his mind about taking her to his brother. "No. I mean, yes. I do." Of course, she wanted to see Teo. She'd missed him, but she also wanted to give him a piece of her mind about Ethan, about closing the gates, and the treatment of the Foresters. She had a lot to say to him.

Rider hurried to keep up with Seth and two guards. One of the guards jumped into a small car, his long limbs banging against the dashboard. Rider smiled as she slid in the backseat with Seth. The other guard squeezed himself into the passenger seat, and they sped to the palace. Before today, she'd never driven anywhere in the city; she'd always ridden her bike or walked. She gripped the back of the driver's seat as they whizzed around a biker and another small vehicle.

Pedestrians walked along the cobblestones, shopping and going about normal life, but on every corner a couple of Wolf Pack stood, watching, their mouths in grim lines, hands resting on their weapons.

Those guns would keep Teo safe, she told herself, but they left a sour taste in her mouth.

"Did Teo order this?" She gestured to the Wolf Pack on the street.

"He agreed to it after Mother insisted. It was this or the gates remain closed. General Scar refused to open them unless the military had control of the city."

"Who ordered new weapons?" she whispered, not wanting the guards upfront to overhear.

"They are trials. It was part of the deal to open the gates." Seth kept his own voice low as he shot a look toward the front. "Stop asking questions, Rider. You'll get yourself into trouble. I'm not supposed to be talking to you about this."

Rider clamped her lips shut, although she had more questions. The vehicle approached the palace and, as if by magic, the wrought-iron gates opened to allow them through. Wolf Pack crawled over the grounds.

They stopped near a side entrance Rider hadn't seen before. When she followed Seth inside, jackets, boots, and umbrellas crowded the entrance hall. The Howell family entrance. A small bench, upholstered in bright red fabric, invited one to sit down and remove their shoes. Teo's boots lay tangled with his running shoes. A nearby military jacket hung on a hook, BLEDDYN written across the front pocket. Rider swallowed against the lump in her throat. Seth followed her line of sight, then motioned her forward.

"Teo's this way."

Rider shook her hands out at her sides, hoping Seth didn't notice. Desire to see Teo and the urge to smack him warred within her.

Seth rapped lightly on a large wooden door before poking his head into the room. "Package delivery." He stepped back with a smirk—the first glimpse of the joking brother she'd seen all day—motioning Rider into the room ahead of him.

Teo sat on a leather couch in jeans and a T-shirt. He was throwing a small ball back and forth between his hands—until he laid eyes on her. Then the ball dropped, bouncing across the floor. "Jenna. What... what are you doing here?"

Before she could respond, Teo closed the distance between them, engulfing her in his strong arms. Her body melted into the heat of his as they held each other. Maybe she'd hug first, throttle later. Much later.

The snick of the door closing behind them signalled they were alone. Teo kissed the top of her head, then he cupped her cheek, bringing her face up. "How are you here?" He caressed her jawline, his light touch igniting flames on her skin. Her stomach flipped-flopped like it had when she'd done somersaults as a kid.

"I... they stopped me at the gates. The next thing I knew, Seth was escorting me here, along with some well-armed Wolf Pack."

His gaze dropped to her lips before he leaned in and brushed them with his soft ones. As he deepened the kiss, she wrapped her arms around his neck, her fingers sliding through his silky locks. The longer hair was a definite bonus. His scent wrapped around her, and she lost herself in his closeness.

Too soon, he pulled back. "You are here, right? I'm not imagining it?"

"I'm here." Delicious shivers sparked along her arms as he ran his hands up and down them. He leaned his forehead against hers. She allowed herself a moment to just be with him, and then she opened her mouth "Is Ethan okay?"

Teo raised his head and dropped his hands to his sides, all the shivery sparks vanishing between them. "For now." His jaw hardened.

"Can you tell me anything else?"

Teo paced a few steps before returning to her. "There's nothing to tell. You know what the tox report said, right?"

"No. My dad wouldn't tell me something that confidential." It hurt to think Teo would think so little of her father.

"It doesn't matter. The less you know, the better."

"Why are you shutting me out? I know Ethan best. I can help you."

"It's for your own protection. If the Wolves find out you're best friends with Ethan, things could implode, even more than they have."

"My protection? This sounds more like your own self-preservation. My best friend would never hurt me. Or you." She poked her finger in his chest.

Teo grabbed her finger. "He had a dagger and he assaulted me—because of you."

"Me?" She yanked her hand away.

"Right before he attacked me, he yelled that I wasn't good enough for you. Didn't you hear him? What did he mean by those words?"

Rider sank onto the sofa. "A while ago, he admitted he had a crush on me. I said we were good friends, but that was all it would ever be."

"Might have been nice to know that."

"You think that's why he went after you? That's ridiculous."

Teo squatted in front of Rider. "I have no idea why he did what he did. That's what I'm trying to find out."

"It was hurtful that you sent me away when I'm your best bet to help you both. And then you ghosted me."

He tugged on her wrists until she met his gaze. "Jenna, my first priority is to keep you safe."

"From whom? You already have Ethan in custody."

"We're not sure he isn't working with someone else."

She narrowed her eyes. "What? Have you spoken to him?"

"Of course I have. He's fine and being treated well. I made sure." He studied her. "He's hazy on the details of that night, which is why we believe it's possible he was drugged. If he was, then another person or party must be involved whether Ethan knew or not."

"If that's the case, Ethan didn't know." Rider chewed her bottom lip. "He's been set up. Someone doped him up, then set him loose. I wouldn't believe it if I hadn't witnessed him tackle you."

"The tox report came back inconclusive. We don't know for sure whether he was drugged or not." Teo moved to sit beside her, tugging her into his side. "We're turning up every rock and searching all crevices for answers, but Ethan's in serious trouble. My mother wants him tried for treason and then given the death penalty."

Rider covered her mouth with her hand. "I can't believe this is happening."

Teo squeezed her tighter. "That makes two of us. Besides admitting to crushing on you, has Ethan been acting weird lately?"

"No." She grimaced. "Except he's been hanging out with this new guy, Matrix."

"I've heard. Do you know him?"

"We've run into each other a few times."

He stiffened. "You haven't mentioned him either."

"It's been a little hard to get in touch with you." Rider didn't like Teo's tone. What was he implying?

Teo flinched. "I'm sorry. I'm trying, but it's complicated. I can barely walk out of my bedroom without being bombarded with reports, warnings, or my mother."

His mother? Realization dawned. "Because I'm a Forester."

"No. It's about easing the wolves into equality—being with you in public makes everything trickier. Especially now."

"Right." Rider sucked in her cheeks. "Is that how you feel too?"

A slight hesitation. "My feelings for you haven't changed. We need to be patient, though, and take it slow. Ethan's actions have put everyone on edge."

Rider rubbed her chest. His words were a sucker punch to her heart. Swallowing past the lump in her throat, she forced her attention back to her friend. "Where did Ethan get the dagger?"

"What?" Teo furrowed his brow.

"Where did Ethan get the dagger?"

"He says he didn't know he had one."

"He was armed without knowing it?" Rider's voice rose.

"That's what he claims."

Ethan wouldn't lie about that. Or would he? Rider bit her thumb nail. The Ethan Rider knew wouldn't have attacked Teo in the first place, let alone carried a weapon to a coronation ball. "Do you think it was planted on him?"

"If he was drugged, then it's a definite possibility. It adds to the motive and makes it look like treason rather than assault."

"We need to get to the truth. Please don't do anything until then."

"Jenna, I can't make any promises. The Wolf Pack will investigate and present their findings. I'll go on their recommendations."

Rider jumped up. "What? Even though you know he's innocent?"

Teo heaved himself off the couch. "I don't know he is. He attacked me. He possessed a weapon. It's advantageous to show our enemies we won't put up with any kind of aggressive behaviour, especially in these first few months of my reign. Besides, I'm not going to pull a Duko, doing whatever I want or think is right, undermining the authority of the Wolf Pack."

"What you think is right? Ethan is innocent. You need to execute justice. For him." She stared at Teo, her eyes wide. "I don't even know who you are right now."

"I am the king. I have responsibilities—"

"You have the responsibility to do the honourable thing, which is to let an innocent man go."

Teo's nostrils flared. "I know you're friends, but why are you advocating so hard? There is a chance he's guilty. Is something going on between you two?"

Jenna stepped back. "You're being ridiculous. There is nothing going on between Ethan and me. He is my friend. End of story. But I believe in him like a true friend does."

"What I'm hearing is that you believe in Ethan more than you believe in me. You don't trust me."

"You're putting words in my mouth." Rider huffed.

"Am I? You're telling me I'm ridiculous, making assumptions, and not doing enough to help a possible assassin."

Rider leaned in so close, she could feel his breath on her face. "What I'm telling you is you're a jerk."

He hissed as if she'd hit him. "If that's how you feel."

Remorse struck her immediately. He looked so hurt... "Teo." She reached for him, but he walked away, toward the door.

"I'm sorry, Jenna. It makes me crazy that you would side with Ethan over me."

"I'm not. I'm asking for your help."

"I'm not sure there's much more I can do to help him." Teo's tone was cold.

Rider stared. "You're the king. Your word is law. Let him go. That's not repeating your father's mistakes. You know he's innocent. Let him go and start looking for the real threat."

Teo stared at her a moment before stalking from the room and closing the door behind him, leaving her alone in the personal quarters of the king.

Chapter Twenty-Seven
Matrix

MATRIX SHOVED HIS HANDS deep into his pants pockets, trying vainly to get them warm. Blue skies in the Lake District meant warmth, but here in Wolf Kingdom, the sun lied. It shone brightly, but it was anything but warm. He glanced sideways at his uncle, who appeared impervious to the cold in a light jacket. His smug expression irked Matrix. It had been three days since the coronation, and Ethan was still sitting in a cell. The plan was working, thanks to Matrix. Trouble was brewing in the palace and, more significantly, between the king and his little girlfriend, according to one of Sirhaan's spies in the palace—a maid who served in the dining room and cleaned their apartments. The royal family spoke candidly at their meals, apparently forgetting the servants had ears.

He ran his tongue over his incisor tooth. It was still a little ragged from when he'd had it ground down before arriving in Wolf Kingdom—a minor sacrifice to get the throne back.

Matrix glanced sideways at his uncle as they walked the city streets. "You've done good," he ground out. Even though it was Matrix who set up Ethan, Sirhaan was taking all the credit. If it kept the peace between them, Matrix would keep up that façade.

Sirhaan tossed his empty coffee cup in a nearby garbage. "It was easy. All I had to do was listen to the queen and play the sympathetic confidante. Once I was given a room, I started making myself indispensable. The poor butler is run off his feet, so I made myself available to deliver food and drinks to the king. The maid keeps me informed of interesting conversations and tidbits. It's amazing how invisible she is to the royals."

"From what she overheard between Jenna and the king, things are rocky in that corner. And it sounds as if the drug is doing its work." Stoking the man's ego was smarter than the alternative.

"The drug is brilliant. King Teowulf is becoming moderately paranoid, chased by flashes of anger." Sirhaan studied his fingernails. "Your man in prison is a nice distraction, which plays upon the Queen Mother's fears. She can barely stand to have Teo out of my sight since she hired me to protect her son and Wolf Kingdom, although the king has no idea she did that. He doesn't like me hanging around." Sirhaan chuckled.

Matrix clenched his fists in his pockets. "Speaking of Teo, what are the next steps?"

"I've given him two doses already, with more coming. He'll be putty in my hands in no time."

"How long before he goes over the edge?"

Sirhaan blew out a breath. "We can't hurry things, but I'd say in a couple of weeks our new beloved king will be as jaded as his father and ready to fight any threat to his kingdom, using our weapons, of course, which the Queen Mother persuaded General Scar to test out."

Matrix nodded. "Excellent."

"I'm glad you approve, since you seem to be failing with the Hood girl."

Matrix didn't miss the sarcasm in Sirhaan's voice. "It's not failure. Our intel was wrong, and it's requiring more of a detour than we originally thought to get to her father."

Sirhaan halted, his eyes cold and hard. "She's supposed to be distracted with her deteriorating relationship with the king. We need to keep her and her father busy protecting the forest's interests—namely fighting the Wolves to clear their names, a lost cause because the Wolves will never trust the Foresters now that the assassin is from there. You need to make your move, since she is no longer sure where she stands with the king."

Matrix checked to make sure no one was close by who could over-hear. He leaned closer to his uncle and lowered his voice. "As I've said, it's going to be more difficult than we'd originally thought. She doesn't like me much. And I don't think I'll make any inroads with Dr. Hood either. From what I've learned about him, he'll never agree to produce a bioweapon."

"I think you're right about Dr. Hood. Let's keep him occupied with clearing the forest's name. I've learned that Wolf City owes Falls District from a previous failed trade deal. Our new king left Governor Adams' daughter high and dry at the altar and he's chomping at the bit for payback, which could work in our favour. I think he'll be more than willing to produce our weapon."

Some good news at last. Matrix's body felt lighter, the stress of having to sway Dr. Hood removed.

Sirhaan stepped past Matrix. "I'm heading back to the palace. Keep me informed of the Hoods' actions. Maybe try and get the girl to like you. Be the shoulder for her to cry on if necessary." His uncle's tone grated on Matrix. He'd been the one to set up Ethan, which opened the door to disunity and weapons. Yet the man couldn't even acknowledge Matrix's part in the success. He watched his uncle disappear into the crowd of pedestrians.

Matrix sighed. He could be the friend in times of disappoint-ment—hadn't he just been the crying shoulder for Ethan? Gaining the throne was worth anything, including putting up with his uncle's ego and the humiliation of his own failed attempts to get the Hood girl to give him a second glance.

Chapter
Twenty-Eight
Teo

*W*HOA. TEO STUTTERED TO a halt as he stared at Ethan's pale face, dark smudges circling his eyes and greasy hair limp. Jenna's friend sat slumped against the wall, his legs drawn to his chest, forehead resting on his knees. He didn't bother to lift his head.

"I want a lawyer. I've been here three days. Either charge me or let me go."

"That's quite a bit of bravado for someone who is being charged with treason."

"What have I got to lose?" His voice was muted.

Ethan wasn't wrong. The guy wasn't going anywhere. Not if Teo's mother had anything to do with it. The Wolf Pack had uncovered nothing—no second person or party, no motive other than unrequited love. Teo grabbed hold of a bar and leaned his weight on his arm. Kingdoms had been overthrown for less. Which was why King Teowulf had to send a strong message that he wasn't a push-over. And his throne wasn't up for grabs. If Ethan walked free, would there be more attempts because Wolf Kingdom's enemies saw him as easy prey?

Memories of his father pacing his study, heated conversations behind closed doors, and the endless renewing of papers for those in the forest and elsewhere flicked across Teo's mind. Bile rose in his throat. Was he turning into his father after all? He closed his eyes, inhaled, then let all the air out through his teeth.

Ethan lifted his head. "Are you okay?"

Teo straightened. *Pull it together, man.* "The tests came back negative. No drugs in your system. Charges will be laid later today."

"Will someone notify my parents?" Ethan's voice shook on the last word.

Teo steeled his emotions—he couldn't go soft now. "Wolf Pack will pay them a visit after you are formally charged."

Ethan lunged across the cell, his fingers gripping the bars. Teo stepped back.

"You can't do this to me. I'm innocent. I helped you save the Wolves from the Lupine Flu. Why would I turn on you? Have you spoken with Rider?"

The words sliced through Teo's heart, reminding him of their last conversation. Jenna didn't understand his duties to the kingdom. She'd shown where her loyalties lay.

"Teo."

"That's *King Teo*. You'd be wise to remember that."

Ethan's eyes widened.

"Jenna had nothing to add or detract from the evidence we've gathered." Teo dropped his gaze to the floor, rubbing his jaw. "Your lawyer's been called. He'll be here shortly." He turned and strode out of the holding area. The last thing he heard as he rounded the corner was Ethan yelling, "No! I'm innocent."

Ugh. Teo moaned as he stumbled into his room. His head throbbed as though he'd banged it against a stone wall. After popping his neck, Teo found no relief from the relentless pain. He flung himself on his bed and pulled a pillow over his head. Maybe sleep would help.

What felt like seconds later, he jolted upright, dazed, his head still pounding. Another rap on the door made him groan. Darkness permeated the room, and he fumbled for the light on the bedside table, wincing at its brightness. Shading his eyes, he stumbled across the room, cracking open the door.

Seth shoved into his room. "Wake up."

Teo ran his hand gingerly over his still-banging head. Why was his little brother in his room?

"Why are you sleeping when they've laid charges against Ethan and in about fifteen minutes the State dinner is set to begin? You've already missed cocktails with the VIP's. Mother is covering for you, but she's not happy."

"My head. I laid down and passed out." The room tilted, and he grabbed the back of a chair. "I know they laid charges."

"And you thought it would be a good idea to take a nap?" Seth's long legs took him to Teo's closet, where his dress uniform was hanging. Grabbing it, he thrust it at Teo. "You look horrible."

Teo grimaced. "Thanks, bro. You're so encouraging." Even saying the words hurt his head.

"Get yourself together. Splash cold water on your face, get dressed, and get downstairs. I'll go make peace with mother."

"Tell them I'm sick. My head is killing me." The thought of all the lights and scents soured Teo's stomach. What would happen if he vomited in front of everyone? He shoved the thought away, not wanting to jinx it.

Seth held out a small brown bottle. "Mother sent this. It's from Dr. Hood. A pain reliever."

"How did she know I was under the weather?"

"Your dizzy spell in the greenhouse tipped her off. And I might have encouraged that thought. It was the only reason I could think of that you'd miss something this important. Am I right?"

Teo studied his brother. "Yes."

Seth shook the bottle. "Well, take some of this and get better. You're the king, after all. You have responsibilities."

"I'm well aware." Teo took the bottle and tipped it back to gulp a swig, grimacing at the bitter taste. "I'll be there in ten minutes."

Seth tapped his watch. "Clock's ticking." He rushed out the door.

Teo headed to the bathroom. After turning on the faucet, he let the water run cold before splashing his face. He rubbed a hand over his stubbled jaw, then grabbed his shaving kit from the drawer. Quickly ridding himself of his five o'clock shadow, he dressed and, with one final longing glance at his bed, hurried downstairs to show the world he was not easy prey.

Chapter
Twenty-Nine
Rider

R IDER STARED AT THE king of Wolf Kingdom standing at the podium on the palace steps, handsome in his suit and tie. It had been five long, short days since the coronation—how could time become so twisted? A woman moving closer to the front of the barrier jostled Rider. A baby cried nearby, but Rider focused only on the king and the words coming out of his mouth. *I can't believe this.*

"Ethan Moss will be tried in court, and we trust that our justice system will do its job to determine guilt or innocence. Thank you." His gaze flicked in her direction but quickly moved on.

Rider ground her teeth. A palace PR woman stepped to the mic as Teo moved aside.

"His Royal Highness will not be answering any questions at this time. Thank you for coming out today. Further details will be released as we get them." The woman ushered Teo into the palace.

Rider's legs wouldn't move as she continued to stare at the now empty palace steps.

What had just happened? She shook her head.

"Looks like our friend is in a bit of trouble."

Ugh. Matrix. Rider whirled on him. "Friend? What kind of friend lets him rush the new king with a weapon?"

Matrix held his hands palms up. "Whoa. I didn't know he was going to do that. What kind of jerk do you think I am?"

Rider put her hands on her hips. "That's what I'm trying to figure out."

"You've got the wrong guy."

She rolled her eyes. Yeah, right. "You were at the ball with him, so that makes you a prime suspect in my books."

The wind had picked up, and Matrix pulled his beanie over his ears. "Yeah, I was his wing-man. Sue me."

Why had Ethan trusted this guy? "You failed at your job. Isn't the wing-man supposed to have his back and keep him *out of trouble?*"

A faint redness crept up Matrix's neck. "It's a little hard to have someone's back when they don't fill you in on their plans."

"That's a lame excuse. You must know something that can help him. Who else was near him?"

"Only the hundreds of people at the ball," he scoffed. "What are you implying?"

Rider bit her bottom lip. "Nothing. I just wondered if he'd spoken to anyone else about his plans." She quickly covered up her slip—probably not a good idea to let Matrix know about the suspicions of a second party.

"I went to the ball with him. He seemed fine, then suddenly he's ranting about you and Teowulf. He disappeared, and the next time I see him is on the terrace, covered by Wolf Pack." Matrix shrugged. "That's all I know, and that's what I told the investigators."

"You spoke to the investigators?" Teo hadn't mentioned that.

He shrugged. "They'd heard I was with Ethan at the ball. I spoke to them yesterday."

Rider pinched her lips together. "I need to go speak to the Mosses. See if I can do anything."

"Why don't you speak to the king?"

She eyed Matrix. "I've already spoken to him. He couldn't do anything more."

Matrix raised an eyebrow. "I find that hard to believe. If I were king, I'd be trying everything I could think of to get Ethan off."

Rider agreed, but guilt niggled her stomach. "I have to go."

He stepped in front of her. "Let me help you."

"Like you helped Ethan? You want to be my wing-man?"

"You can't save Ethan by yourself." He gestured with his thumb behind him. "I don't think Teowulf is going to be much help."

Rider winced. She shoved against his chest but didn't get far. The guy was made of pure muscle. "Get out of my way." She didn't trust him.

"I can help."

She stared up at his face, his jaw set stubbornly. Maybe it would be better to keep him close, so she'd know what he was up to. "Suit yourself." She side-stepped around him. "Keep up."

"No bike?"

"It's icy on the paths."

He fell in step with her. "Was that so hard, asking for help?"

"I didn't ask... but maybe two heads are better than one. For Ethan's sake, I'll try anything." She only hoped she didn't live to regret the decision.

Chapter Thirty
Matrix

MATRIX PICKED UP HIS pace, his long legs having no trouble keeping up with Jenna. *She's a handful.* But he could handle her. Her dark locks bounced against her back as she hoofed it through the streets of the city. Her steely determination and feistiness would make her an excellent asset to their side. If only he could figure out how to get in her good graces. Matrix frowned. He hated failure. But wait, he was going to the Mosses with her, wasn't he? He hadn't failed. Maybe this was the opening he needed.

The gates out of the city loomed ahead. Jenna reached for her papers. Her smug face amused Matrix.

"If that was your version of speed-walking, it was a stroll for these long legs." He wasn't about to let her think she'd tired him out. Maybe he was out of shape, but he'd never admit it.

Her gaze roved over him, and he shifted his weight from one foot to the other. The line inched forward, and she turned to face the front. Matrix eyed the guard patrol, his stomach knotting. "They certainly are a lot more uptight about papers and such now."

Rider sighed. "Yeah, they've reverted back to what it was like when King Duko ruled. We'd made progress too with Teo on the throne. But now..."

"We'd?"

Rider folded and unfolded her documents. "Yeah... okay, *he'd* made progress with unifying the Foresters and the Wolves. But it was our dream—we both desired to see it happen. Wolves and Foresters are stronger together, if only people would open their minds."

She was talking about more than Wolves and Foresters. Ethan had been right on that count; she was blinded by love.

He cleared his throat. "You realize he's the Wolf King, and you are a commoner, not to mention a Forester. You can't believe after today that anything will ever happen between you two." He couldn't resist throwing a dose of reality on her fantasy.

To his satisfaction, her cheeks turned a delicate pink, enhancing her green eyes. Matrix understood why Teo had a thing for her. *Focus. If you can get her to doubt the guy, you'll be in.*

She lifted her chin. "I don't think it's any of your business."

"Hey, I'm only trying to help. If you continue to live in LaLa land, you're no use to Ethan. The king's made his position clear. He's going to execute your friend for treason. Get real, Jenna."

"Shush." She nodded towards the guards who were only a couple of metres away now.

Matrix stilled his trembling fingers as he handed over his papers. The guard eyed him, but Matrix levelled his own gaze at the surly man. He wasn't about to be intimidated by a Wolf, especially in front of the girl. Stuffing the papers back into his bag, he crossed over the threshold to the forest and waited for Jenna.

She breezed by him. "Like I said, keep up." Tossing her head, she hustled down the path.

Matrix stared at her for a few seconds before breaking into a jog, not in the least afraid of losing her. Exactly how much trouble was she going to be, anyway?

Chapter
Thirty-One
Teo

TEO ROLLED HIS HEAD from side to side. The pain in his temples had receded to a dull ache, but the dinner the evening before had been agony. His mother's heated glare hadn't helped. Nor had the endless bragging of the pompous VIPs. Some didn't even pretend humility; they spouted off all their successes and accomplishments like a resume, hoping to impress Teo. By the end of the evening, Teo couldn't wait to go to bed and put an end to the day.

He didn't think anything could hurt worse than his head until he faced Jenna's disappointed frown and puppy-dog eyes at the press conference this morning. The last thing he desired was to hurt her, but from her expression, he'd done that and more. Teo closed his eyes and lowered his head to his hands. Every time he made a decision, he either ticked someone off or hurt a person he cared for. He was always the bad guy. *I have no clue what I'm doing, or what I should be doing.* He wasn't fit to be king. For the first time, he wished he could talk to his father—at least Duko would understand the pressure Teo was under.

He lifted his head. Wow. Where had that thought come from? His stomach turned sour.

Grabbing a fistful of hair, he pulled and then released it. After a minute, he opened his eyes and straightened in his desk chair. The room swayed. He rubbed his eyes and tried again. No more tilting. Gingerly, he clambered to his feet. Definitely needed to go for a walk and get out of this prison.

The smell of butter and garlic enticed him into the large, bright palace kitchen. His stomach growled. When had he last eaten?

"Your Majesty."

Teo smiled at the head chef whom he'd known all his life. "It's good to see you, Chef LaFleur."

"It's my privilege to serve you. What can I make for you?"

"I'd like some tea and maybe a beef sandwich? I can make it myself."

"No, it's my kitchen, my rules." He smiled. "I can send it up to you if you'd like."

Already, the tension had eased from Teo's shoulders and his head felt clearer. "I'd rather stay. If you don't mind."

"Absolutely. Have a seat and I'll get your food ready."

"Let me at least make the tea. I feel helpless sitting here watching you."

Chef LaFleur gestured to the tea kettle. "If you insist."

"I know how to boil water, if you're worried." Teo chuckled as he filled the large kettle with water and set it on the stove, then stared at the set of dials. "Um." He leaned closer, checking the dials. Maybe he *didn't* know how to boil water.

The chef nudged him aside, turned the gas on, and lit the burner.

"Thanks. I guess I'm useless at even making tea."

"You can easily learn, but that's not your job at the moment." The chef swiped his knife against a sharpening stone several times before carving the beef into thin slices.

Teo took a seat at the large wooden harvest table that looked as if it could sit at least fourteen people comfortably. He and his brothers used to come here and sit, eating tins of cookies and drinking gallons of milk. *Bleddyn. I miss you.* Teo drew circles on the wood, trying to keep the lump in his throat manageable. The kettle whistled, calling him back to the present, and he stood and grabbed the kettle off the element. After checking to make sure it was the correct one, he turned the dial to shut off the gas.

The chef smiled. "See? Learned something already."

Teo chuckled as warmth spread through his chest. It was stupid to feel such satisfaction at learning how to operate the stove, but he'd failed at so much lately, he'd take the win.

"Sit." Chef LaFleur slid a plate with a sandwich loaded with beef, horseradish, and tangy mustard on the table as Teo filled the mug with hot water. When he finished, he sat and stared at the food, his mouth watering. "Thank you. This looks amazing."

"It's my pleasure, Your Majesty." Chef LaFleur stepped away.

"Wait. Do you have time to join me?"

Surprise etched across the chef's face, but he nodded and lowered himself onto a chair across from Teo.

"My brothers and me, we used to make midnight raids on the kitchen."

LaFleur laughed. "I know. I was a sous chef then, and part of my job was to take inventory of the larder. Some mornings there were sizeable holes."

Teo choked on his tea. "How come you never ratted us out?"

"You were hungry, growing boys. I wasn't about to let you starve."

Teo took a bite of his sandwich and chewed. "This is great," he said around the mouthful. "I didn't realize I was so hungry."

"If you don't mind my saying, you look like you could use some extra meat on those bones."

Teo mopped up a little horseradish with the bread. "I never understood the huge pressures my father faced as king." He stilled, not having meant to say that aloud.

If LaFleur was surprised, he didn't let on. "How could you? You were a kid. It's like parenting; you don't know how hard it is until you're in the mess of it."

"You're right. But now I wish I had cut him a little slack."

LaFleur clasped his hands in front of him. "Hindsight is twenty-twenty. Learn from past mistakes and forge a new future."

Teo swiped his fingers on a napkin. "Yeah. I suppose you're right." He grabbed his plate and mug and stood. "Thanks, Chef."

LaFleur took the dishes from Teo. "Anytime. And our conversation won't leave this kitchen."

The warmth in Teo's chest deepened. "I appreciate it."

"You're always welcome here, Your Majesty."

Teo nodded and then left the room, whistling as he walked back to his office. Opening his door, he startled. Seth sat in the leather chair on the far side of the desk. Teo closed the door. "You scared the daylights out of me. What are you doing sitting here?"

Seth snickered. "You should have seen your face."

"Not funny." Teo cleared his throat. "What do you want?"

"Relax, Teo. You're way too serious. What happened to my devil-may-care brother? I miss him."

"Whatever. I have work to do—I don't have time for childish games."

Seth scowled. "Fine. I'm here at Mother's request." He set a small brown bottle on the desk. "More medicine from Dr. Hood. To help with your headaches."

Teo eyed the bottle. The stuff he'd taken the other night seemed to have worked. "She went to Dr. Hood?"

"He's our main supplier for medicine. Where else would she go?"

"No, I mean... never mind."

Seth swung the chair around and picked up a framed photo of the three brothers from Teo's bookshelf, running his finger over it. "I miss him," he whispered.

Teo stilled. "Me too."

Seth set the photo on the desk. "How are the headaches? You seem to be suffering with them more than usual."

"I'm fine. It's the stress with Ethan and the mysterious gardens, not to mention the tension between the Foresters and the Wolves." He ticked the problems off on his fingers. "Need I go on?"

"No. Your plate is full." Seth rounded the desk, and clapped a hand on Teo's shoulder. "I'm here for you, Teo. Whatever you need."

Teo sighed. "Thank you."

Seth nodded and left.

Teo took the chair his brother had vacated, propped his elbows on his desk, and rested his forehead on his clasped hands. Closing his eyes, he rubbed his temples. A moment later, he straightened and reached for the brown bottle. After unscrewing the top, he sprinkled two drops into his water and chugged it back. He'd lied to Seth because he wasn't fine. His head felt as though it was going to blow off most days. How had his father handled all the stress? Maybe that's why he'd been a little crazy, paranoid. Teo leaned back in the chair and closed his eyes.

No. No matter what, I will never be like him.

Chapter
Thirty-Two
Rider

T HE DRAWN CURTAINS BLOCKED out the sunlight, making the living room feel stuffy. Rider rubbed her palms over her thighs as she stared at Ethan's parents, sitting next to each other on a small love seat. Their grey faces and the dark smudges under their eyes mimicked how Rider felt.

She leaned forward on a rocking chair. "There's nothing you can add to Ethan's alibi? He wasn't acting strange before the ball? Did he seem fearful?" Surely there had to be some clue. Rider wasn't giving up until she found it.

Mr. Moss pushed his glasses up his nose for the hundredth time, mimicking Ethan's habit. Rider rubbed her chest, pushing the painful reminder away. "He was a bit depressed, but he said he'd had a miscommunication with a friend. It didn't seem like anything more than that, so we let it go. He was working a lot with the two jobs, but he seemed to be handling it fine."

Mrs. Moss tugged on her long braid, the same straw colour as Ethan's hair. "He's not an assassin."

"I agree. Something's not adding up. I'm not giving up until I figure out what." But they were running out of time.

"We're going to visit him this afternoon. Our lawyer arranged it."

"I'm so glad. Ask Ethan again to tell you what happened. We're missing something." Rider stood, hugged the Mosses, then let herself out, Matrix trailing behind. Rider ignored him as they walked. *I wish you'd go away.*

"That was a waste of time."

"No, it wasn't. They were happy to see us, to know someone cares."

Matrix blew on his hands. "I meant in terms of helping Ethan."

Rider stopped, her shoulders slumping. "I'm not sure anyone can help him."

"Didn't I hear you tell the Mosses you were going to figure it out? You're giving up that easily?"

Rider scrubbed her face. "I know, but I'm at a loss as to what to do now. Ethan doesn't remember anything. You don't either, and you were with him. His parents have no clue. I don't know who else to talk to... I'm drawing a blank."

"And the king won't listen to you."

Rider bit her cheek.

"The truth hurts, doesn't it?"

She didn't respond.

"You have to face the truth. Teo's not going to help Ethan. Even your king has his limits, and right now he's got someone behind bars who looks like he wanted to kill him. If Teo did want to, and that's a big if, he has to think about his reign, the message he wants to send the kingdom and its enemies. If he looks weak, it could get him killed."

Rider's stomach dropped. She didn't want anything bad to happen to either Teo or Ethan. "Ethan is innocent."

"Then you're going to have to prove it."

"What is it you want, Matrix?"

Matrix held his hand up as if surrendering. Why did she get the idea that he never gave up? "Hey, I'm trying to help. I'd like to think we're friends. Plus, I like this place, and I'd hate to see it turn into a war zone between the city and the forest."

A chill shivered down Rider's spine at his words. "It's not going to come to a war between us. We're peaceful. We won't fight the Wolves. We never have."

"That explains a lot."

She frowned. "What do you mean?"

"Now I understand why the Wolves dominate Foresters, and why the Wolves are weaponizing themselves and the forest isn't."

The chill on her skin froze as she gaped at Matrix. "What are you talking about?"

"I saw an armoured vehicle arrive at a warehouse on the far side of the city. Huge crates with the word *GUNS* painted on them."

Rider inhaled, but it felt as if there was no oxygen to breathe. "What? No. Teo wouldn't do that."

"Sure about that?"

No, she wasn't, but she had no intention of letting Matrix know that. "Y-yes, I'm sure."

"Maybe you're right. It could be the Queen Mother. She seems to be more in control than Teo."

Rider scrunched her face. "That's not true. This conversation is over." She strode away, her arms pumping. Surprised he didn't follow, she breathed deeply of the pine-scented air, hoping to clear the fear and confusion from her mind. What did Matrix know? The city wasn't arming itself. Teo would never allow it. Although, she hadn't believed he would press charges against Ethan, either. The memory of the guard's new firearm on his belt blipped into her mind. Maybe Matrix *was* right about Teo's mom. *I wouldn't put it pass the Queen Mother to armour up.* Because the Teo Rider knew wouldn't ever do that. She pushed on, her legs burning as she increased her pace.

Even if it was true that the Queen Mother had ordered the weapons, Rider felt sick at what that implied about Teo. It did him no favours to be seen tied to his mother's apron strings.

Chapter Thirty-Three
Matrix

*S*IRHAAN WASN'T GOING TO *be happy.* Matrix clenched his jaw as he strode through the forest, ignoring the cardinal's song in a nearby tree. He had messed up. Why had he told Jenna about the weapons shipment? And then pointing the finger at the Queen Mother? *Stupid.* He'd had to place the blame somewhere. His chest tightened as he remembered seeing the armoured truck delivering crates of guns to the warehouse. A fact Sirhaan had forgotten to mention to him. Matrix didn't care about the weapons, but Sirhaan acting on his own without informing his partner? Matrix rubbed the ache in his stomach that had been there since he'd seen those crates unloaded. *Why is he keeping me in the dark?*

Matrix jogged the rest of the way to his cabin, anticipating a warm fire to ward off the chill in his bones. He pulled the key from his pocket and inserted it into the lock, but the door pushed open easily. He stiffened as Sirhaan appeared in front of him.

"How did you get in?" His tone was harsher than he'd meant it.

Sirhaan scowled. "I'm in charge of this mission; you don't think I don't have a key? I didn't take you for naive, Matrix."

"You almost gave me a heart attack." Matrix threw his keys on a side table. They skidded across the surface before clattering to the floor. Both men ignored them. "What do you want?"

"I want a report on how it's going with the girl." Sirhaan leaned his weight against the back of a leather chair.

"I want to know why you had weapons delivered here but neglected to tell me."

His uncle shrugged. "It didn't concern you."

"How does it not concern me when it's part of the mission? I need to know what's going on in all areas."

"How did you find out?" Sirhaan studied his fingers.

"I saw them being delivered to the warehouse when I was over there buying supplies."

"Well, now you know. Tell me about the girl."

Matrix clearly wasn't getting any more information from Sirhaan. He blew out a breath. "Everything is going as planned." *Except my big mouth telling Jenna about the weapons.* "You're keeping the king distracted, and she's doubting their relationship as well as his promise to unify the kingdom. The rift between them is growing and, as that happens, so will the rift between Wolf City and the forest."

Sirhaan rubbed his hands together. He reminded Matrix of a snake, ready to strike. "Excellent. Only a few more days until the drug takes over and our young king won't know up from down. I'll make sure of that. The headaches are getting bad, and he's more irritated by the day." He chuckled softly. "This is the best entertainment I've had in years."

"What about Ethan?"

"Collateral damage. He'll be tried and found guilty of treason, then executed, which will destroy any goodwill the Foresters have for the Wolves. The girl will hate the king, which will appear to push him over the edge. He'll declare war on the forest, and all those lovely weapons will be pulled out, ready to be used against those granola-loving people. Then, in the chaos, we'll take over from those incompetent Wolves and rule the kingdom. I've arranged a meeting with Governor Adams regarding the bioweapon."

"It sounds so neat and tidy. Too bad that's not reality." Matrix grabbed a few pieces of tinder from the metal box.

"Such a doubter, Matrix. What's gotten into you?" Sirhaan narrowed his eyes. "Did you mess up with the girl?"

No. Yes. Matrix forced himself to meet the older man's piercing gaze. "Everything is fine. I'm saying things never go as planned. Don't get cocky. We're dealing with people who have feelings and can act irrationally." He knelt by the stone hearth, creating a teepee with the wood.

"We've accounted for their idiotic feelings. Hate is as powerful as any gun or bomb. We wield it correctly, and we rule the world."

Matrix struck a match against the stone hearth, then touched the flame to the paper. It flared bright orange and yellow, and a small breath of heat hit his hands. He blew on the flame before turning to face his uncle. Maybe it was time to put Sirhaan in the hot seat. "I want to know why you kept me in the dark about the shipment of weapons."

Sirhaan's lips thinned. "Back to this?"

"We're partners. I need to know what's going on with your part of the mission."

"I had a window to bring a shipment in, so I did. That's it. I need to go." Swinging open the door, Sirhaan hesitated, letting the chilly air into the house. His uncle's stare bore into Matrix. "Don't be a fool and fall for the girl." The door clicked sharply behind him.

Matrix frowned at the closed door. There was no way he could know Matrix had told Jenna about the weapons. So why would he warn Matrix about falling for her?

Sirhaan had it wrong. Matrix had control over his feelings. He scrubbed a hand over his face. Then why did he pin it on the Queen Mother when Jenna seemed upset Teo might have done such a thing? *I'm supposed to be making her hate him.* The hurt on Rider's face had done weird things to his chest, so he'd lied. Neither the Queen Mother nor Teo knew about the weapons. Sirhaan had arranged it all behind their backs. Did it matter who she blamed—Teo or his mother? As long as the wedge between her and the royals deepened, the hostility would spread like poison throughout the kingdom. That was what mattered. Sirhaan didn't need to worry; Matrix was sticking to the plan. He wasn't falling for the girl.

Chapter
Thirty-Four

Teo

T EO DRUMMED HIS FINGERS on the long table in the meeting room, studying General Scar as he gave his daily brief to the king, his advisors, and the military strategists. Six days had passed since his coronation. Time had crawled since that fateful evening, yet his Wolf Pack still had no definitive answers.

"In conclusion, it's my opinion that Ethan Moss is not guilty of anything more than carrying a concealed weapon and a broken heart." General Scar gathered his papers together.

Teo's pulse quickened. He didn't like the broken heart comment, but he shoved the thought away. Why did his insides squeeze like a vise when he thought of Ethan crushing on Jenna? "General, I don't need more opinions. The people of this city don't care what we think—they want facts. We need to take action one way or another. It's been a week since Ethan attempted to attack me."

"Yes, your Majesty. I'm sorry."

"If we're finished here, I have somewhere else I need to be. Thank you all for coming." Teo stalked out of the room, ignoring the stares and slack jaws. His shoulders dropped an inch as the door snicked closed behind him, shutting him off from everyone's opinions, disapproving glares, and attitudes. A persistent ringing in his ears had him on edge, and heat spread from his insides outward. He flung open the doors to his favourite courtyard. For him at least, this little act of rebellion was his only freedom. Crisp air cooled his warm cheeks and feverish brow.

Footsteps rang across the yard, as his brother and mother advanced toward him. Teo glanced at the sky then back to his family, his mother shoving past Seth.

"What do you think you're doing? You don't walk out on a strategic meeting with the Wolf Pack and our defence generals. What is wrong with you?"

He glared at her. "Nothing is wrong with me, Mother. They were blathering on about opinions when we require action. I need evidence if I'm going to hold Ethan; otherwise, I let him go. We can't hold a prisoner indefinitely. We have no evidence, so I'm dropping the charges and releasing him."

Seth stood beside his mother, shaking his head. "That's crazy. It's like a proclamation to come try and assassinate you."

"It's not. There is no evidence that Ethan meant to do anything but separate me and Jenna. Maybe punch me like any other guy who's with the girl you want." He got that.

"Your father will be rolling over in his grave."

Teo snarled. "I am not my father. Ethan's not an assassin, and if I want to date a girl from the forest I will."

His mother laughed. "Being king means you don't get to do what you want. Your life belongs to the kingdom now. This is the way it is." Her hard tone softened. "You need to accept that and get on with the business of the kingdom."

He turned, his back to his brother and mother, staring at the courtyard. She was right, but his heart wouldn't fall in line with the rules of the crown. "I will. I am," he lied before pivoting and brushing past them. He stumbled to his quarters, feeling as though he had the weight of the world on his back but no way to hold it up.

Teo pushed open the door to the holding centre and motioned to the guard at the desk. He must be new, as Teo didn't recognize him. "Draw up the paperwork for the prisoner's release. Charges are dropped. He's free to go."

The guard hesitated.

"Do it now." Teo bit out the words. Why did everyone doubt him?

The man pulled a paper from a file. Teo pointed to Ethan, who stood at the bars of his cell.

"You're free to go as soon as the paperwork is done. There's no evidence to hold you, so I'm dropping the charges. Maybe I'm nuts, but I don't believe you meant to kill me. Maybe knock my lights out." One corner of his lips lifted. He could respect that. "But if you ever try something like this again, Moss, I will eat you alive."

Ethan's Adam's apple bobbed in this throat.

"There's one thing I need from you as a show of goodwill. If you hear about anything strange in the forest, come to me. Don't go to anyone else."

He nodded, his eyes never leaving Teo.

Teo turned and left the holding centre, the knot in his stomach loosening. He rolled his shoulders as he strolled to his office. Seth sat on the bench in the hallway outside it.

Teo jabbed his key in the lock. "What are you doing here?"

"I wanted to check on you. You seem out of sorts."

"I'm fine." Now that he'd made a decision about the prisoner.

"What do you mean?"

"I freed Ethan."

Seth jumped up. "You did what?"

"I let him go. We had nothing on him other than a concealed weapon." Teo shoved open his office door.

Seth blew out a breath. "You're digging your own grave."

"No, I'm not. He's not an assassin. He'd shoot himself in his foot before he'd hit a target." Teo rolled his eyes. "Besides, he helped us with the Lupine flu—why would he come after me now?"

"I don't know. Because of Jenna?"

Teo shook his head. "He risks execution for unrequited love? No way."

"Mother is going to freak."

He slapped Seth on the shoulder. "I'll handle Mother. Besides, *I'm* the king. Everyone seems to forget that."

His brother eyed him warily. "Then maybe you should start acting like it."

A roar rushed through his ears, and he grabbed Seth by the lapels of his jacket and shoved him hard against the wall. He growled, "Maybe you better start remembering it." After pushing him into the wall once more, Teo snarled, then let go. Seth stumbled before regaining his footing, his eyes wide. Teo's stomach churned. He'd never turned on his brother before. He brushed past Seth, into his office, slamming the door behind him.

Teo leaned against the door, clenching his trembling fists. *Get control of yourself.* The room shifted, and Teo staggered to the desk, slumping in his chair. He rubbed his temples as pain shot through his eyes. Nausea rolled through him, and he clamped his mouth shut, dragging breath in through his nostrils.

The door to his office swung open. He lifted his head, expecting Seth, but his mother stood before him. She opened her mouth but then shut it, her features smoothing out, softening. "Are you sick?"

Clearing his throat, he shook his head. "I'm fine. I assume you're here about Ethan. I need you to leave it alone."

"You need to increase the Wolf Pack who guard you."

He nodded. "Fine." *I don't have the strength to argue with you.*

Concern flitted across her face. "Do you have a headache again?"

"I just need some rest."

"Teo." She reached out a hand, as though she might feel his forehead again. Before she could touch him, though, she pulled it back and nodded. "I'll speak to General Scar about increasing your personal guard."

Before he could respond, she turned and left. The room swirled and his stomach heaved. He grabbed a glass filled with water and took a sip before making his way to the couch and flopping down on it, fatigue washing over him. Images of Jenna floated through his mind, and he dreamed about dancing with her in a red dress with a hood.

Chapter
Thirty-Five
Rider

"**Y**OU'RE HERE! I CAN'T believe you're free."

Rider embraced Ethan, not wanting to let him go. After a minute or two, she pulled back, smiling at her best friend. His hair was mussed and he was thin, but she didn't think he'd ever looked better. He held up his arm and pinched it as if to make sure he wasn't dreaming. She laughed as she slung her arm around Ethan's shoulders. A cool north wind blew, swaying the bare tree branches above them. Rider pulled her hood up over her hair as they sat on the wooden porch steps of his home. When she'd received word of Ethan's release, she'd run to his place. "So Teo walked in and ordered your release?"

Ethan nudged her in the side with his elbow. "I suppose I have you to thank for that."

Rider's eyes widened. "I tried, but nothing I said seemed to change his mind." She grimaced.

Ethan raised his eyebrows. "Something did, and you're the one with the most influence over him." He stared at his shoes. "I'm sorry. For all of it. I have no idea what came over me, but I never wanted to harm you. Or Teo."

"I know and so does Teo, which is why you're free" She clung to his arm. "He's a good guy."

Ethan studied her. Rider could see the wheels churning inside his head. She waited.

"It was interesting sitting in that cell—you're invisible to people unless they're addressing you. The guards never shut up when no one is around. They have some pretty strong opinions about matters in the kingdom."

"What do you mean?" She loosened her grip.

"Some agree with Teo and want things to change, but others are opposed. They want us to stay put in the forest. I also overheard them talk about the Howells. The Queen Mother isn't as supportive of Teo as we'd hoped." Ethan stretched out his long legs and crossed one ankle over the other. "Teo came down a couple of times... he didn't look too good."

Rider huddled deeper into her jacket. "I know he's stressed. Seth brought me to the palace once while you were being held. I think he hoped to cheer up Teo, but we ended up fighting."

"About what?"

Rider stared out at the frozen front lawn.

"You fought about me?"

"I told him he was the king and his word was law. He seemed to be confused as to whether you were guilty or not, which made me angry. How could he doubt your loyalty? He accused me of taking your side."

Ethan blew out a breath, creating a puff of vapour. "Thanks for coming to my defence. He obviously listened because, from what I could tell, he went against everyone's advice by releasing me."

That wasn't going to endear him to his people. Rider nibbled her lip.

"My release—is it going to cause him problems with the Wolves?"

"I think so, but Teo's not naïve."

"He had a strange request when he told me I could go."

"Oh?"

"He asked me to report back to only him if I heard anything strange here in the forest."

Rider furrowed her brow. "What did he mean by strange?"

"Out of the ordinary, I guess. Rebellion maybe?" Ethan shrugged.

She frowned. Why was he worrying about that? She shoved the troublesome thought aside for later. She had someone else on her mind. "Speaking of trouble. How well do you know Matrix?"

"We've hung out some. He's a nice guy."

"Yet he always seems to be around when trouble happens. Have you noticed that?"

"Can't say that I have. I know he was with me the night of the ball, but we separated after having a drink. I was too interested in finding you to be good company."

"Why did you bring him?"

Ethan groaned. "He was supposed to be my wing-man."

Rider snorted. "I thought part of a wing-man's job was to keep you *out* of trouble."

"Yeah, but..."

"Be careful around him, okay? I don't trust him."

"At this point, I don't feel like leaving this property. I'm afraid if I slip up at all, I'll be back in jail."

"Laying low is a good plan. But I think I need to check on Teo. He has to know we aren't going to rebel."

"No. Laying low is a good idea for you too. How do you plan to check on him when you can't get to him?"

Rider grinned as she shoved off the stoop. "I'll figure out a way."

"I was afraid you'd say that." Ethan stood too. "Let me help you. You can't do it alone."

"Laying low, remember? You have to stay out of sight for a while. It's not safe."

"And you need to be careful." Ethan grabbed her hand and gently squeezed it. "Thanks for stopping by. You're a good friend, Rider."

"I'll see you soon." Rider headed home, her thoughts filled with ideas on how to see the new king.

You could always make an appointment. The Queen Mother's face floated before Rider. Then Seth's. Nope.

Alarick? But she hadn't seen him for a long time. Which was weird. In the past, he'd hardly left Teo's side. Was that why Teo was stressed and looking ill?

Rider bit her thumb nail, then pulled it away, shaking her hands out. She rolled off her bed, pacing her room.

A soft knock interrupted her thoughts. Her dad peeked around the edge of the door. "How's Ethan doing?"

"He's good, considering he's been in jail for a week. At least he wasn't treated badly. Teo wouldn't allow it."

"I believe you're right." He stepped into the room. "What's up?"

Rider sank onto the edge of her bed. "Have you seen Alarick lately?"

Her dad scrunched his brow. "No, now that you mention it, I haven't. I heard he'd gone away on official palace business. One of the guys who delivers to the palace mentioned it while I was at the coffee shop."

Rider pursed her lips.

"Why?"

"Ethan said that Teo appeared ill and stressed the couple of times he came to Ethan's cell to talk to him. Alarick looks out for Teo, and I realized I haven't seen him since the coronation. Do you think something's wrong with Teo?"

"Probably stress. I can't imagine running a kingdom with so many opposing and varying opinions. He probably needs time to acclimatize to his new responsibilities." He patted the door frame. "I'll let you get back to what you were doing."

Rider sprawled on her stomach on her bed. Usually, her dad could reassure her, but today the pit in her stomach was still heavy after talking to him. She had to see Teo and make sure for herself that he was okay.

Rider leaned her bike against the brick building across from the guard house and city gates. It had been an icy, slippery ride but worth the risk. She scanned the guards' faces. *He's got to be here somewhere. He's my only way in.*

Fifteen minutes later, the shift changed and Seth walked out of the office. A slow smile danced on Rider's lips, and her shoulders lightened as if a heavy pack of meds had been lifted off them. She stepped into the street and strode towards Seth. He turned to say something to another guard but stopped when his eyes met hers. He held up a finger, spoke to the guard, then motioned for Rider to follow him. She hurried to catch up to his long strides as he rounded the corner of the guard building.

When she came around the corner, he'd stopped and folded his arms across his chest, and she skidded to a stop to avoid banging into him. "What's up, Rider? Ethan made it home okay?"

"Yes, he did. Thank you." Rider licked her dry lips. "I need to see Teo. Can you arrange it?" Her words tumbled out.

Seth stared over the top of her head. "You realize he's a little busy right now?"

Heat flooded Rider's cheeks, but she couldn't let Seth talk down to her. She straightened her spine. "Of course I do."

"I can take him a message, but I can't guarantee a meeting."

She rubbed her hands together to warm them. "Is he okay?"

Seth's brow puckered. "What do you mean?"

"Ethan thought your brother looked ill. I want to make sure he's not sick."

A shadow crossed Seth's face but faded quickly, a smile replacing it that looked a little forced. "He's fine. Ethan saw him for maybe five minutes the whole time he was imprisoned. What does he know?"

Rider shoved her gloves into her jacket pocket. "Can you arrange a meeting or not?" she pushed.

"I can try, but I'm not promising anything."

"A few days ago, you pulled me in to take me to him, and now you're stonewalling me. What's going on?"

Seth stepped away from her, spreading his hands in front of him. "I'll try, Jenna, that's all I can do. I'll send word if I'm able to arrange something." He strode toward the gates. Rider stared after his retreating back. Did Teo not want to see her? Rider kicked a loose stone several yards. She didn't know what to do or think. And worse, she was at the mercy of a Wolf.

Chapter Thirty-Six

Teo

T HE FRESH AIR WHIPPED around Teo's face, soothing his aching head as he walked away from the tunnel. He pulled his hoodie low over his brow, slumping his shoulders as he headed to the café near the palace and hoping he'd blend in and look like any other young adult male. He and Seth had pulled a switch to evade his guards. At the moment, Seth was hanging out in Teo's apartment, pretending to sleep, while Teo had slipped out the hidden door in his closet.

He quickened his pace along the cobblestoned walkway, anticipating his meeting with Jenna—a surprise for her. She was anticipating a guard with a meet-up plan, but yesterday, when Seth gave Teo her message, he'd decided to go in person. No need for another middle man.

A wooden sign painted bright blue with gold lettering and hanging over the door of the bakery came into view. His breath caught as he spotted her sitting out front at a table, nursing a hot drink, steam rising from the mug. Teo crept up to the table and dropped onto the seat beside her.

Rider glanced up from her drink. "I'm sorry. I'm waiting for someone. That seat's taken."

"Jenna."

Her full lips opened, her green eyes widening.

He subtly shook his head. "Follow me." He took her gloved hand, which fit perfectly in his, then pulled her to her feet. He didn't let go as they hurried along the street.

"Where are we going?"

"You'll see." Teo smiled as he pulled her down an alley to a door. After pulling a key from his pocket, he unlocked it and tugged her inside. "This is Uncle Alarick's apartment—he's away on business."

That explained his absence. "He has a home away from the palace?"

"Yes, a retreat, so to speak. Why?"

"He needs a retreat from being waited on, from luxury?" She rolled her eyes.

"Freedom from being under the microscope." He took off the dark-framed glasses he used for a disguise.

Rider inclined her head. "I can't believe how much glasses changes your appearance. It always fools me." She eyed him up and down. "You look skinny. I'm not sure I would have recognized you if I was passing you in the street."

Teo frowned. How could his girlfriend not know him? He met her gaze, the concern in her eyes soothing his irritation. Shrugging, he said, "You didn't recognize me when I sat next to you."

"True."

He sighed. "It's hard to have an appetite when your girlfriend's friend is locked up because he's accused of attempting to assassinate you." He tossed the glasses on a nearby table. "As for those, they worked before, didn't they?"

She grinned at his reference to their first meeting. Warmth spread through his chest. At least it was still a good memory for her—she couldn't be that upset with him. He pulled her to him, catching a whiff of her honeysuckle shampoo. He wanted to breathe that smell in and memorize it to pull out when he needed a break from all the troubles that weighed on him. "I've missed you," he whispered into her hair.

She wrapped her arms around his waist and hugged him tight. "Me too."

They stayed locked together until she pushed away and cupped his jaw. Her eyes swept over his face. "I wanted to make sure you were okay."

"Seth mentioned that. Why wouldn't I be?" It was better Jenna didn't know more than she already did.

"Ethan thought you looked sick." Her hand dropped to his chest, over his heart. A jolt of electricity ran over him, increasing his heart beat. How did she wield so much power he could feel her electricity even through his clothing?

"Thank you for releasing him."

He contemplated her. Did she not know he'd do anything for her?

"There wasn't enough evidence to hold him for treason, and I wasn't about to press charges for assault." He pulled her gently back to him. "I'm fine. The whole affair with Ethan was stressful." His eyes dropped to her full lips, begging to be kissed. Teo leaned in and captured them with his own, heat rushing through his veins. This moment, this girl, was what he desired more than any kingdom. "I don't want to talk about Ethan." He whispered the words against her lips. Running his hands up her back, he pulled her in even closer. Her sigh reverberated through him, settling in his chest.

"Are you okay?"

"I'm good." He could hear her smile in her words.

He leaned his chin on her head. "I'm glad."

At last, she loosened her grip, her green eyes holding his. "Isn't there some way we can stay in touch? Why are we still hiding our relationship?"

Blinking, he tried to process the change in subject. He didn't want to talk about that. In fact, talking was the last thing on his mind. "I don't want to, but there's a lot of mistrust between the Wolves and the Foresters. Ethan's stunt didn't help that."

She opened her mouth but he shook his head to cut her off. "Relations have deteriorated. We'd made significant progress, but now we're back to square one. I can't jeopardize any future progress."

"It doesn't have to be like that. Maybe if people see us together it will help. They might follow your example and give the Foresters a chance because you are."

Pain jabbed at his temple, and he rubbed the spot. *Not now.* "Teo?"

Teo rolled his head to ease the tension. "Maybe."

Rider covered his cheeks with her cool hands. "What is it?"

"Nothing. A bit of a headache. Don't worry about it." He caught her fingers and brought them close to his chest. "Look, I don't want to waste our time talking about headaches or business." He pulled her close again. "Dance with me."

"There's no music," she objected.

"We don't need music. We'll make our own." He swayed her to the song playing in his head, relishing the feel of her in his arms. They fit together perfectly. A sharp rap at the door, followed by two quick ones, interrupted them. Sighing, he glanced over Jenna's head. What would happen if he ignored it?

"Aren't you going to answer it?"

"It's Seth. It's our code, and he's the only one who knows I'm here." Reluctantly, Teo let her go and strode to the door, opening it a crack. His brother, pale and drawn, leaned against the doorframe.

"You need to come now. It's an emergency," he huffed.

"What is it?" Teo opened the door to let his brother in.

Seth didn't move, only peered over Teo's shoulder at Jenna before giving Teo a single shake of his head. Teo's stomach bottomed out.

His brother leaned in, whispering, "Jenna needs to get back to the forest *now*."

Teo glanced back at Jenna. He pulled Seth inside, closed the door, then walked over to her. "I have to go. I need you to return to the forest now."

She glanced between them. "No, I want to stay here with you. Why do you always send me away?"

Teo tried to take hold of her hands, but she stepped back, out of his grasp.

"Jenna, listen to me. Go home. I'll be in touch. I promise."

She jammed her hands into her armpits, staring at Seth. "Why do you look like you've seen a ghost? What's going on?"

Seth cleared his throat. "It's official palace business. I'm sorry, but Teo's right— you need to go home now."

Rider scowled. "I don't take orders from Wolves."

Teo's head throbbed. "Jenna, I don't know what—"

"Ethan's dead," Seth blurted. His eyes widened as he clamped his jaw shut. Too late.

The room tilted, Teo's stomach going with it, and he clutched the back of a nearby chair. His gaze flicked to Jenna, who stood still as stone.

"What?" she rasped. She sounded dazed, as though she couldn't comprehend the words Seth had uttered.

"I'm sorry, Jenna. I shouldn't have... You must get back to the forest." His brother turned to Teo. "And you need to get to the palace."

Teo, ignoring Seth, pulled Jenna close, but she stood ramrod straight in his arms, shaking her head.

"No. I just talked to him."

Teo rubbed her back. "I'm so sorry, Jenna." His eyes bore into his brother. "You make sure she gets home safely." Seth nodded. He looked like he wanted to cry.

Teo swallowed over the lump growing in his own throat. "I have to go." It was the last thing he wanted to do. He didn't want to leave her side. What if...? He removed the terrible what ifs from his mind. "Please be safe." He kissed her forehead and strode to the door, flinging it open. After pulling it closed behind him, he pulled his hoodie low and sprinted towards the palace.

Teo swallowed against the threatening bile in his throat as he studied the pictures of Ethan's body lying in a dark puddle.

General Scar's voice was low. "Your Majesty, as you can see, he was found along a path in the forest, barely breathing. By the time emergency personnel got there, he was dead. Bled out from a knife wound."

"Who found him?"

"A couple of kids playing nearby."

Teo winced. They'd need to talk to someone after seeing such a horrific sight. He covered his eyes with his palm. "Do we know who did this?"

"No. There was no evidence left behind except the note."

The note. Teo fingered the bag holding it. *Dear Foresters. This is how we treat traitors. The Wolves.* He'd memorized the words that were now etched forever in blood on his hands. How could he have been stupid enough to let Ethan go without any kind of protection?

"It was pinned to his jacket."

"This is bad." Whoever did this wasn't trying to hide their motive or the fact they were Wolves.

The General's silence was all the confirmation Teo needed. He turned and stared out the window. This would undo the last of the goodwill the two clans had established. Everything Teo had hoped to do to unite the kingdom was being dismantled by some unknown hand.

The older gentleman cleared his throat. "We need to close the gates. To protect the Foresters, as well as to protect ourselves."

Was Jenna home safe? "Give an hour warning, so all Foresters can leave. Don't tell them we're closing the gates. Issue a curfew stating that they must be out of the city and home in an hour. Then close the gates until further notice."

"Yes, Your Majesty. We'll be increasing our security coverage for you and your mother and brother, too." General Scar stared at him, his lips forming a thin line. "No more clandestine meetings." He saluted before spinning around and marching from Teo's office.

Heat rushed up Teo's neck. *Guess that's why he's the general.* Nothing got by him. His gaze dropped to the photos, and Teo's stomach turned over. Scooping them up, he slid them into the folder, wishing it would all go away. He sank onto his chair, his head in his hands.

"Son, you look terrible." His mother's voice cut through the fog, and he glanced up. She leaned against the door frame. "I wanted to check on how you were doing."

How he was doing? How did she think he was doing? He'd let Ethan go, and now the guy was dead.

Sirhaan appeared behind her, and Teo muttered a word he rarely said under his breath.

"Sire, you must be relieved that your enemy is dead."

Was this guy for real? Teo stared at him coldly. "He was my friend. He helped stop the Lupine Flu. You don't know what you're talking about."

"With all due respect, he was a suspected assassin. He's no longer a threat to you or your family. You released him, but he got what he deserved in the end."

Chills skittered up Teo's spine. "I did not mean for this to happen. I never believed Ethan meant to harm me." He clasped his trembling hands together, hoping Sirhaan wouldn't notice.

"I'm sorry, I didn't mean to offend."

His mother tucked a stray lock of hair into her chignon. "Perhaps we need to let Teo have some time. It's a shock."

Sirhaan nodded. "Of course."

"If you need anything, Teo, I'll be in my suites." She stepped closer, rubbing his shoulder. "I'll talk to you later." The pair departed, leaving Teo alone. Was he responsible for Ethan's death? *If I hadn't released him, he'd be alive right now.* Teo's mind wouldn't let it go. Jenna's stricken face flashed before his eyes. She would never forgive him for this.

Chapter
Thirty-Seven
Rider

RIDER STUMBLED ALONG THE road to the city gates. Only Seth's firm grip on her elbow kept her from sprawling headfirst onto the path. He didn't utter a word, for which Rider was grateful—her mind couldn't form a coherent thought. As added security, a Wolf Pack guard brought up the rear.

People milled around the entrance to the city, some she recognized as neighbours and friends. Did they know about Ethan? Rider ducked her head so she didn't have to look anyone in the eye and breathed through her nostrils, hoping to keep the sobs locked inside. Seth waved a guard over, whispering in her ear. The woman followed as Seth navigated Rider away from the crowds and into the offices. The trio moved quickly through the building and then out through an exit Rider didn't know existed.

"For VIPs."

Under other circumstances, Rider might have laughed. She was no VIP.

The door clicked behind the other guard. Seth set a quick pace, his hand never leaving Rider's elbow. She pushed her hood back, the crisp air reviving her. As they approached the treeline of the forest, Rider tugged her arm free of his grasp.

"I can make it home from here." She didn't want Seth or the other guard, who trailed along behind them, to witness her losing it. And if the lump in her throat was any indication, Rider didn't have much time before she began bawling her eyes out.

"I'm sorry, but Teo ordered me to make sure you got there safely."

No point in arguing with the king's orders. She coughed, hoping to dislodge the now boulder in her throat. After a few more minutes of trudging along the path, her cabin came into view. A soft cry escaped when she caught a glimpse of her dad standing at the edge of the yard, waiting. He jogged to meet the sad group, wrapping his strong arms around her.

"Jenna-girl, I was so worried." He stroked her hair, the tender touch releasing the floodgates. She sobbed into his chest.

"Thank you, Seth, for bringing her home safely."

She heard her dad's words and Seth's and the guard's retreating footsteps, but she didn't lift her head. They stayed in the front yard until her sobs receded. After Rider stepped back and swiped the tears off her cheeks with her fingers, he rested a hand on her back and led her inside.

"Ethan..." she croaked out.

"I know, honey. I'm so sorry." Her father's voice shook.

"How do you know?" Rider wiped her eyes on her sleeve. It hadn't been more than a half hour since she left Teo's uncle's apartment. How could her world change that much in such a short time?

"I was part of the medical personnel called when they found his body." Her dad drew in a shaky breath.

"I was with Teo when he got the news. Ethan was st-stabbed?"

"Yes. Dr. Lupine is taking care of... his body. The Wolves need to do an autopsy."

Bile rose in her throat, and Rider held her hand over her mouth, afraid she'd vomit. Her dad rubbed her back.

"There was a note. It was written in bold lettering so it was hard not to see it." His eyes were glassy.

"What did it say?"

"Dear Foresters, this is how we treat traitors. The Wolves."

Rider's stomach revolted and she ran to the bathroom, gagging. Clutching the porcelain bowl, she heaved everything she'd eaten. When there was nothing left, she wiped her mouth, standing on shaky legs. Her dad handed her a damp cloth. "Wipe your face, then come drink some ginger tea."

The warm cloth soothed her. After rinsing her mouth, she walked back to the couch, sinking into its soft cushions. Her dad handed her a mug of ginger tea, the spicy, scented steam already calming her stomach.

"I don't understand. Teo released Ethan because he was innocent. Why would the Wolves believe otherwise?"

"He was released but not declared innocent. Insufficient evidence. I guess many Wolves still thought he was guilty, despite the king's orders."

Tears trickled down her cheeks, dropping onto her hoodie. After setting her tea on the coffee table, she faced her dad. "This is bad, isn't it? I mean not only Ethan... but for the forest."

His eyes locked with hers. A quaver went through her at the fear she saw in their depths. He took a sip of his own tea before answering. "Yeah, Jenna-girl, it is. But we'll figure it out. Teo's smart and he's on our side. We'll do whatever we can to help him."

Rider picked her mug up and wrapped her hands around its warmth. Staring at the amber liquid, she hoped her dad was right. Teo might be on their side, but could he fix the implications Ethan's death had for the Foresters? Even if he could, no one would be able to bring Ethan back.

Chapter
Thirty-Eight
Matrix

"WHAT WERE YOU THINKING?" Matrix spread his hands out in front of him before yanking Sirhaan into his house. After checking to make sure no one was watching, Matrix slammed the door.

Sirhaan pushed Matrix against the door, holding him there with one hand firmly pressed to his chest. "You dare to question me?"

Matrix shoved his uncle off him. "There was no need to kill him. You said you had the king in hand."

Sirhaan ran his palms down his jacket, straightening the material where Matrix had grabbed it. "This destroys the little unity that was forming between the Foresters and Wolves. They'll kill each other now. You're welcome."

Was the man insane? Matrix hadn't counted on Sirhaan killing the guy. His uncle had veered so far south of their plan. "Are you still giving the king the meds?"

Sirhaan scoffed. "Of course. I need him on the edge of rage and insanity so he'll fight the forest. And anyone else who thinks they deserve our crown. King Teo needs to be rabid."

His uncle's smile sent a chill down Matrix's spine.

Matrix strode to the kitchen sink and turned on the faucet. After filling a glass, he drank it down, stalling for time. He needed to gather his wits about him. "What's the next move, since you've taken out my guy?"

Sirhaan put his hands together as if he was praying, then tipped them to point his fingertips at Matrix. "You need to keep the girl away from the king. He's useless to me when he's near her."

A silent groan welled up inside Matrix. He hadn't made any inroads with Jenna. She still didn't trust him or even like him.

"Nephew?"

Matrix glanced at his uncle.

"Is that going to be a problem?"

"No, no problem." He would have to come up with a different plan. He'd given up trying to charm her or be her shoulder to cry on. Maybe she needed a little more force. *There's a thought.*

Sirhaan strode to the door, grabbing its handle. "Soon we'll have control like we were always meant to. We're smarter, more lethal, and deserve to rule. We are the Howells' worst enemy, and they don't even know we're right in their backyard."

"Don't get cocky," Matrix warned. He wouldn't let Sirhaan ruin everything. The Wolves didn't know they were being stalked, and it needed to stay that way.

Chapter Thirty-Nine

Teo

T EO POUNDED ON THE door to Seth's apartment, then jiggled the doorknob.

"Okay, okay," Seth yelled from the other side.

Before he opened it all the way, Teo shoved past. "Was she okay?" The words raced to get out of his mouth.

Seth shut the door before facing Teo. "What do you think? Her best friend is dead."

Teo hung his head. He didn't need to think; Jenna was heartbroken.

"Dr. Hood was waiting outside when we got there. He knew about Ethan."

Teo ran a hand over his head. "I know. He was called in when they found the body out of courtesy because the forest is his jurisdiction. But General Scar and Dr. Lupine took over since the circumstances have to do with me." The tension in Teo's shoulders eased slightly, knowing that Dr. Hood had been there for Jenna. What would it have been like to have a father like him? Too late to worry about that now. The past was the past, and Duko had been his father. No sense wishing for a do-over. Teo sank into a leather chair, his limbs heavy. "I can't believe Ethan's dead."

Seth sat down, resting his head against the back of the other wing-back chair. "What do you make of it?"

Teo gripped the arm rests as though they were a life preserver and he was drowning in the ocean. "I can barely wrap my mind around it. Did I make a mistake releasing him? He'd still be alive if he was in jail."

"Don't go there, Teo. You had no way of knowing. It's not your fault."

"I feel like I signed his death warrant by releasing him."

"Now you can predict the future?"

No, but looking back, it seemed obvious that Ethan would be in danger, given that not everyone agreed with the decision to free him. "I... Sirhaan implied that by letting him out, I knowingly put him in danger—like I planned for this to happen. What if the Foresters think the same?" Teo scrubbed a hand over his face.

Seth leaned forward. "When did you start listening to Sirhaan?"

"I try not to, but those words coming out of his mouth were like a sucker punch to my gut. If that slime bucket is thinking it, maybe everyone is. Even Jenna."

"She doesn't. If there's one thing you can count on, it's Jenna not hiding her feelings or thoughts."

But she hadn't shared that Ethan had feelings for her. "Maybe. Did I act like father? He'd have had no qualms about letting Ethan go, even knowing he'd sentenced him to death."

"Teo. Look at me."

Teo locked eyes with Seth.

"You are nothing like our father. You had no idea what would happen. One of the best things about you, brother, is that you believe in people. You expect the best from them. Father never did. Jenna knows that." Seth stood, walking to the window. He wiped away condensation with his sleeve. "I don't trust Sirhaan. Your instincts are right."

"We both need to keep our eyes and ears open, especially around him." Teo came up beside his brother. The bare trees stood like sentries around the square yard. Black bark and white wisps of snow created a beauty different from the greens of summer. The green house stood on the other side of the quad, its windows steamy.

"Agreed." Seth ran his hands over his stomach. "I need to burn off some energy. Mom asked me to chop wood."

That sounded good. Teo grabbed a jacket out of Seth's closet and followed his brother. His mother had always given her sons chores to do, insisting they learn the merits of hard work. All three boys had enjoyed the physicality of chopping wood, so for their private use, Seth still took care of it. Teo did when he could get away with it. The Wolf Pack got nervous when the king carried an axe.

The chopping yard was near the family entrance to the castle. Guards stood around the perimeter every hundred metres or so. Seth glanced at Teo, who raised his eyebrows. General Scar was not taking any risks with Teo's safety.

After shedding his coat, Seth grabbed a chunk of wood and set it on the block. Teo stood off to the side, far enough away to not be in the line of any projectile. His mind ran in circles, going over every possible scenario where he could have done something differently with Ethan. *I am not Duko.* He repeated the words over and over, but his heart didn't believe it. Had he harboured any ill will towards the young man? Had he secretly hoped something would happen? *You're being paranoid.*

Seth finished with the piece of wood. Teo picked up a pair of work gloves left behind on a log. After tugging them on, he grabbed the kindling and threw it on the pile outside a small shed.

After enough wood was cut to last the rest of the winter and most of the next, Teo and Seth sank onto a couple of stumps. Seth's butler had delivered a thermos of tea earlier, and Seth unscrewed the lid and poured two tin cups full. He handed one to Teo.

Teo sipped it, the liquid soothing the cold and the dryness of his throat. Seth offered him a scone, but Teo declined. His stomach was still roiling and his head ached. He removed the small bottle of meds from his pocket and sprinkled a few drops into his tea. A faint, sweet scent wafted by his nose.

"What's that?" Seth mumbled around a bit of the buttery pastry, distracting Teo from the smell.

"The medicine from Dr. Hood."

Seth swallowed. "Another headache? How many do you get a week?"

"I don't know." The brain fog was getting bad. He was forgetting details. Teo shook his head, hoping to loosen the memory.

"Why don't you go see a doctor?"

"The elixir is working. Besides, Dr. Lupine would only tell me it's stress."

After draining his drink, Seth rolled the mug back and forth between his hands. "I can't lose you too. Why don't you get checked out?"

Teo slugged back his tea, suddenly thirsty. "If they don't stop, I'll go see a doctor, okay? Right now, they're under control, and I don't have time. Nor do I want rumours getting out that I'm sick. That's all I need."

Seth gathered up the thermos and tin of scones. "If you're still getting them in a couple of weeks, make an appointment with Dr. Lupine. Deal?"

Teo rolled his eyes. "Deal. *Mom.*"

The next morning, General Scar stood at the podium in front of the palace, answering questions about Ethan's murder and the gates closing. Teo watched on the monitor in the security room, glad he wasn't the one doing the press conference. Five screens provided surveillance of the crowd listening to the general. Teo, futilely, studied each one, hoping to catch a glimpse of a hood and curls. Of course Jenna wasn't here; he'd ordered the gates temporarily shut. Did she understand he'd had no choice?

His gaze roved over the screens. Faces full of anger, fear, and mistrust stared back at him. Long gone were the joyous expressions of love and cheer from his coronation day. He pinched the bridge of his nose. How had he lost control so quickly? They'd made great strides towards unity and equality with the forest, yet here they were, worse off than when his father ruled.

Maybe he was right all along, and I don't have what it takes to be king. Teo squashed the thought like a bug on a wall. Compassion and firmness didn't have to be mutually exclusive. Could he pull off a reign that combined the two? Doubt crept in, stealing his confidence. Added to that, his foggy head and leaden limbs made him feel as if he was underwater. *I wish Uncle Alarick was here.* But his uncle was following orders and investigating Sirhaan in the Lake District and other places the man had done business. Was Teo overreacting because he didn't like the guy making moves on his mother? He rubbed a smudge on the screen, wishing he could wipe away the loneliness that threatened to engulf him. Although he'd been schooled his whole life for this job, he wasn't prepared for how alone he felt. The desire to call his uncle home so he could help Teo navigate the mess he'd created swamped him.

Shoving back from the table, Teo stood, but the floor moved under him. Or was he moving? Disorientated, he grabbed the counter edge to regain his equilibrium. He felt like he had when, as a kid, he'd sailed on the royal yacht with his dad for the first time. A storm had sprung up, pitching the vessel from side to side. Teo's stomach had revolted at the motion, just like it didn't appreciate the rolling of the room right now. He clamped his teeth shut, glancing around. Had anyone seen? The security guards stared glassy-eyed at monitors nearby, not watching Teo. His personal detail waited in the hall, ordered to escort Teo at all times. He exhaled, his breath shaky, then inhaled. His stomach gradually settled.

Once the room stood still, he trudged back to his office, his security trailing behind him. The office was quiet and cool from the window he'd left open, and he sank onto the wingback chair in front of his desk. His hands trembled in his lap. Perhaps a trip to Dr. Lupine's was warranted.

More than a doctor's visit, he needed answers. Who murdered Ethan? What were the plants secretly growing in the forest and who had planted them? Why was Sirhaan still here? Teo believed he was up to no good, but the guy was like a parasite that wouldn't budge.

Teo straightened. This was a problem he could solve immediately. A jolt of adrenaline shot through his veins as he hurried to his mother's suites. Opening the door, he nodded as he passed her administrative assistant, heading straight to his mother's private office.

"I want Sirhaan out today." He'd barely passed the threshold to her office before the words were out.

His mother glanced up from her calendar, slowly inserted a book-mark between the pages, then closed the book. "Sorry, dear, not going to happen. I am allowed to have personal guests here at the palace. He's staying."

His hands on her desk, Teo leaned close. "I don't trust him. Since he's shown up, we've had nothing but trouble."

His mother scooted her chair back. "He's trying to help us, but you're too pigheaded to see it. If you'd listen, he has some very good ideas for security for the city and our family. For you."

"He wants war so he can sell us more weapons. Have you researched what he's trying to get us to purchase?"

"He's shown me brochures."

"I think we should take a tour of his weapons factories. In fact, I won't even consider it without seeing them."

His mother returned to her pages. "Fine. I'll arrange it if it will finally end your crusade against him. All I'm concerned about is your safety, and it feels as though Sirhaan is the only one who can ensure that."

Teo opened his mouth, then closed it. That was easy. Turning on his heel, he hurried to his office. *Now I'll be able to see what you're up to, Sirhaan.*

Chapter Forty
Rider

B*ANG. BANG. BANG.* RIDER'S eyes protested against opening. *Bang. Bang. Bang.* Rolling over, she pulled the pillow over her head, but it didn't drown out the swell of voices coming from downstairs. Rubbing her eyes, she sat up, then checked the clock beside her bed. Judging by the dimming light, it had to be late. *I must have fallen asleep.* Hopping out of bed, she followed the sound of the voices, hurrying as the volume rose. At the landing, Rider saw a crowd of people in her front room. Her dad's voice boomed over the chatter.

"Please quiet down. I can't hear when everyone's talking at once."

Rider took the steps two at a time, then sidled up to her dad's side. He slipped his arm around her, acknowledging her, his warmth reassuring her. Most of the people in the room she recognized.

Mr. Farley spoke up. "We've got to do something. Those Wolves think we're all out to get them. Now they've shut us out. Again."

A woman with dark red hair, a child on her hip, chimed in. "We've known all our lives we can't trust Wolves, yet we still fell for the new king's lies."

As if her father could sense Rider's hackles rising, he tucked her closer to him. She slid an arm around his waist and squeezed. Her friends and neighbours needed a safe place to voice their concern and grief. Her father, with his calm and wisdom, provided that space.

The owner of the mushroom and truffle farm where Ethan had worked, stepped forward, his hat trembling in his hands. "They killed one of our own. They need to pay. Ethan didn't deserve that." The farmer, with his unkempt hair and haggard features, looked as though he'd aged years.

Rider's breath hitched. Poor Ethan. Her throat closed around the lump forming as she remembered her last conversation with him.

More people voiced similar concerns. After everyone had a chance to air their complaints and concerns, her father raised his hands. "This is hard for everyone. Certainly, Ethan didn't deserve to die. Nor does it make sense that we were given privileges only to have them revoked. However, we need to exercise caution and not make any rash decisions or take actions that will make things worse. King Teo is young, but he's intelligent, and from what I've witnessed, he cares about his whole kingdom, including us. Let's wait and see what happens in the next couple of days. Give him a chance to lead."

Mr. Farley slapped his cap against his thigh. "Lead? He seems as sure of himself as a toddler. He had all these grandiose ideas, but they aren't working. He can't make people change. The Wolves don't like us, and I don't trust them."

Several people shouted, "Aye, aye."

"If we act on our feelings and not our wise judgment, we'll regret it. I don't want to be a part of that. In the end, it will be detrimental to our relationship with the Wolves." Her father's face had reddened. Rider rarely saw her father get riled up.

Voices rose again, some agreeing, others not. Then everything got quiet as Mr. Moss came forward, his shoulders slumped, his eyes sad. He glanced around the room. "Please listen to Dr. Hood. Don't use Ethan as a scapegoat for your vengeance. He believed in unity and equality with the Wolves, and I know he respected King Teo."

Several people raised their eyebrows.

Mr. Moss acknowledged the doubters. "It looks bad, I know, but looks can be deceiving. Ethan told me he never wanted to hurt the king. We don't know for sure what happened at the ball, but I don't believe we have all the facts. Again, circumstances aren't how they look. Ethan would never hurt another human being, and he wouldn't want us too, either. Especially not in his memory." He swiped at his eyes as Rider's own eyes blurred.

"They took him and murdered him. How can you defend them?" Mr. Farley questioned Ethan's dad.

"You're right, he was taken from our yard while his mother and I were out. The men who took him are murderers, but that doesn't mean their actions represent every Wolf. In fact, I believe they represent only a select few. Please don't use Ethan as an excuse to retaliate." He glared at the farmer.

Her father stepped between them, extending his hand to Mr. Moss. "Thank you, Tom." He let Ethan's dad go and turned to face the rest of the group. "Go home. Think carefully about your next actions. Please."

People shuffled out the door, some grumbling but most silent, lost in their own thoughts. Rider locked the door after the last one left. "What are we going to do? People won't sit back and let the Wolves take away our rights. Rights Teo expanded with the assurance that we'd soon have more. Now he's shut the gates in our faces."

Dr. Hood gathered Rider in his arms and held her tight. "I don't know, sweetie.

But we'll figure out something. Teo has a good heart. We need to trust him."

Rider leaned into her father, hoping some of his courage and trust would be passed to her since she had a feeling she would need both going into the future.

Chapter Forty-One
Rider

FOUR DAYS LATER, THE shock of Ethan's murder was still palpable. People lined the walls of the small forest chapel, squeezed together like sardines in the hard pews. Rider crossed her arms so her elbow didn't dig into her dad's side. The woman next to her was almost on Rider's lap. It would be funny if this wasn't her best friend's funeral. If Ethan had been here, he'd be snorting he'd be laughing so hard. At the thought, Rider's glance flicked to the front of the sanctuary where a picture of her best friend sat on an easel. His glasses were a little crooked, his hair messy with that wide grin. Typical Ethan. She smiled back at him. *You'd be so impressed with all the people who turned out for you.*

The woman beside Rider stood, then moved out into the aisle. Strange, but Rider was glad for the room on the bench. She started to shift over, but a guy dressed in a beanie, sunglasses, jeans, and a heavy jacket and scarf, slipped into the vacant spot. Rider sighed, sneaking a glance his way. He hadn't removed his sunglasses, and his collar was raised, obscuring the bottom half of his face. As if he could feel her staring, he turned slightly towards her, dipping his head. Blue eyes met hers. Heat rushed her face as his fingers entwined her own. He was here.

The solemn-faced pallbearers carried the casket past Rider's pew. Her gaze followed it out the sanctuary. The urge to yell 'Stop' rose in her throat, even though she knew Ethan wasn't in there. The casket bore his body but not his soul. She sniffed. Her dad turned, stilling at the sight of her hand in Teo's. Correction. To her father, Teo appeared a stranger.

"It's okay, Dad. He's a *friend*."

Teo nodded, extending his arm. Recognition dawned on Dr. Hood's face as they shook hands.

"I'll meet up with you later, Dad."

"Sure thing. I'm going to speak with the Mosses. I'll see you at home. Be careful." He glanced at Teo, then filed out into the aisle.

Teo tilted his head toward the front of the church. "Come."

They headed away from the back of the church, exiting out the door the pastor had come through earlier into a room that held several chairs and a small table. Perhaps a meeting room. Teo shut the door and pulled off his sunglasses.

"What are you doing here? It's dangerous," she whispered.

"I wasn't going to stay away. I wanted to be here for you, like you were there for me with Bleddyn. Besides, it's important for me to pay my respects. I didn't want Ethan to die. I was trying to avoid that." His voice cracked.

Rider sat on a padded chair, her knees weak. Teo knelt in front of her.

"Are you okay?" He pushed a curl behind her ear.

"Yeah. I'm just glad you're here." Her vision blurred.

"I'm so sorry about Ethan."

A sob escaped her lips, and she covered her mouth with her hand.

Teo pulled her to standing, wrapped his arms around her. "It's okay; you're allowed to cry."

Rider hiccupped as tears slid down her cheeks. Her body shook in Teo's arms. After what seemed like hours, she dried her eyes on her scarf as she pulled away. She eyed his jacket that now had tear stains on it.

He touched his forehead to hers. "I don't mind being your tissue."

She chuckled at his attempt at humour. "Thank you for coming today."

"I wouldn't have missed it. You're not alone." The tenderness in his voice threatened to dissolve her in tears again.

"How'd you get away this time?"

He shrugged. "I know a few tunnels and people who let me slip by them."

"Aren't they worried someone will attack you?" Rider frowned, concerned for his safety.

"Security has never been so tight. But growing up in the palace, we got to know every nook, cranny, and secret passage." He sighed. "Of course, if I'm ever caught, my mother will make sure she locks me in a cell herself."

"Your mom's concern is valid. It's dangerous to be out by yourself." Ethan's murder was all the evidence she needed of that.

"I'm not alone. Seth's outside, also incognito. He's got my back. Other than you, he's the only one I really trust." Teo kissed her temple. "Which is my cue to leave." He grabbed her hand, lifting it and kissing the inside of her wrist. Shivers cascaded down her arm.

"Be safe." He walked away, holding her hand until he had no choice but to let it go.

"You too." Rider whispered as their fingers slid apart. Then he was gone, his absence filling the room. A moment later, she forced herself to go back through the door they'd entered, where she found herself in an empty sanctuary.

Walking over to the easel holding Ethan's picture, she ran a finger over his likeness. *I miss you so much.*

The sound of footfalls on the carpet echoed in the empty room. Had Teo come back? Her hopes fizzled as Matrix came up beside her. She scowled.

"That's the kind of reaction every guy wants." He glanced around the sanctuary. "Expecting someone else?"

Ducking her chin into her scarf, she said, "No."

"You're a very bad liar."

Rider ignored his bait.

Matrix glanced towards Ethan's picture. "Nice funeral. My condolences. I know he was a good friend. This has to be hard for you."

She nodded, not trusting her voice. The guy confused her—one minute he seemed annoying, the next he was nice.

"Where did you go after the service? I tried to get to you, but there were so many people and then you disappeared." The nosy, annoying guy was back.

"I wanted to get away from the crowds." *That much is true.* "Ethan would have loved it that all these people came today." Rider straightened the flowers in the vase by the easel. Matrix's gaze bore into her. Had he seen and recognized Teo?

"Who was the guy who sat beside you?"

So, he had seen him. Was he fishing for information? Rider decided to play it cool, since Matrix couldn't have figured out it was Teo. "Some guy. Why?"

"The lady sitting beside you gave up her seat for him. I figured you knew him."

"She gave up her seat?"

"Yeah, it was like she was saving it for him."

"Weird," she whispered.

"Did you know her?"

"No." Rider planted her hands on her hips. "Why are you interrogating me?"

"I'm not. Just curious, is all. I was sitting at the back and watched the whole thing. I swear she was saving the seat, so I figured you must know him."

"Jenna-girl." Saved by her dad, who stood in the doorway of the sanctuary. "I'm heading out. Walk with me." Her father wasn't asking, and Rider turned away from Ethan's picture.

"I gotta go." She attempted a smile that felt more like a grimace before hurrying up the aisle to her father. When she reached him, she took his hand, practically pulling him outside. Matrix made her uncomfortable at the best of times, but he was way too curious about the stranger for Rider's comfort. All she wanted to do was put as much distance between herself and Matrix as possible.

Chapter Forty-Two
Matrix

MATRIX NARROWED HIS EYES as Rider hustled out of the church. His gut told him she was lying about not knowing the guy who sat beside her. As he squinted at nothing, his mind ticked through the morning as if he was flicking through photos. Rider and her dad had been sitting in the pew when the lady came and sat next to them. A few minutes before the service started, the stranger came up the aisle and the woman stood and left. He took her spot. It was like a choreographed dance, natural but, thinking back now, too precise. The woman had been waiting for him.

Matrix ran his hand over his mouth. The guy had worn sunglasses the whole service. Sunshine had streamed in the windows but still... who did that? His beanie covered his hair so Matrix couldn't tell what colour it was. The coat collar was up, blocking his profile. There was nothing else extraordinary about the guy. He looked like any other young man at the funeral—except for the confidence he'd exuded, as though he belonged. Was he a relative of the Mosses? Did he want a seat near the front or was it Rider he wanted to be close to? Where did she go after the service?

Matrix tapped his chin. Wait, where did the guy go? It'd been so congested that Matrix had lost sight of them as soon as everyone stood up. By the time the place cleared, both were gone, but they hadn't exited through the doors after the casket. *They were together.* His heartrate ramped up as he slammed his fist into his palm. *Teo.*

He'd snuck in, wanting to be near Rider. Probably played the comforting boyfriend. The part Matrix was supposed to play. He tightened his fist until his nails dug into his palm. How had he been so stupid?

Not only had he missed his own chance at comforting Rider, but more significant to their plan, Matrix had failed at driving a deeper wedge between the couple. Sirhaan couldn't find out that Teo had been here and Matrix had messed up again, or he was in jeopardy of losing his place not only in the mission, but in the royal Haan family.

Chapter Forty-Three

Teo

T HE TUNNELS THAT WOVE underground through the city were black as midnight without a moon or stars, and today, they stank like rotten eggs. Teo positioned his scarf farther over his nose, breathing through his mouth.

Seth coughed. "Is this smell worth sneaking out?"

These tunnels were his ticket to freedom, so Teo wasn't complaining. "Breathe through your mouth. It helps."

"Ugh. That sounds gross. I don't want to taste the stink."

Teo flipped the switch of his flashlight and shone the beam on his brother. "Don't be a wuss."

Seth made a retching sound. Teo rolled his eyes. His brother had a sensitive nose. Tonight, it irritated Teo more than usual. He rolled his shoulders, hoping the agitation would ease away, too.

The wooden door that led from the tunnel to the palace came into view. Teo sighed. Seth grabbed the handle, but Teo pulled him back.

"What?" Seth cupped his hand over his nose. "I need to get away from this stench."

"Shush. We don't want anyone to hear us. You go first, then I'll come five minutes later. It will look suspicious if we're coming from the basement, especially if we're together."

"No, you go first. I can't leave the Wolf King here by himself."

"I thought you needed to get fresh air?"

"Not at the cost of your safety."

Seth opened the door and shoved Teo through it. "I'll see you in about fifteen minutes." The door clicked shut in Teo's face.

Teo muttered under his breath as he shrugged out of his coat and pulled off his beanie. Stuffing the sunglasses into his coat pocket, he hurried through the dark basement to the stairs that would take him to his suites. After entering the safety of his rooms, Teo shed his clothes and stepped into the shower. The hot water washed away the grit, grief, and worry. Afterward, he pulled on joggers and a Henley.

Tap. Tap. Tap. Seth must have run here after his own shower. Teo yanked open the door but stopped short when he found Sirhaan.

"These are my private quarters. Why are you here?" he growled.

Sirhaan bowed slightly. "Your Majesty, I need a word."

Teo attempted to shut the door, but the man shoved his foot in the way.

"You'll have to make an appointment with my secretary. Like everyone else. If you'll excuse me." He glared at the man's foot. Sirhaan removed it and held up his hands. Teo shut the door in the guy's face with a satisfying click. *How did Sirhaan get up here?* The royal family suites were not accessible without special permission. And a code to the doors. Only family was allowed up here. And guests that Teo approved. Like Jenna. Sirhaan wasn't on the list. Where was palace security? He'd ditched his personal detail earlier, but the palace security should still be in place.

At another knock, Teo whirled toward the door, but Seth peeked in. "Good, you made it back."

Teo leaned into the opening to scan the hallway. "Did you see him?"

Seth followed his gaze. "Who?"

"Sirhaan. He was just here. Said he wanted a word with me. Palace security was nowhere to be found. I want to know how he got access to this floor."

His brother's brow furrowed. "That's not good."

Teo shuddered. "What does Mother see in him?"

"He pays attention to her. Something dear old Dad never did."

"I want to wipe that smug look off his face."

Seth made an abrupt slashing motion across his throat.

"What—"

Seth pointed to his ear and then circled his finger around the room. Teo's eyes widened. They searched the room, running their fingers under lamp shades and table tops. Seth felt around lighting fixtures and along the tops of cabinets as Teo checked his bedroom and bathrooms. There were no listening devices.

His brother shrugged. "Sorry. Guess I got paranoid for a second."

Teo flipped on a lamp. "You were right to be concerned. It bugs me that he somehow managed to get up here. Do you think Mother gave him the code to my wing?"

"Possibly. But she knows how you feel about him, so I doubt it." Seth glanced at his watch. "I've got a shift at the gates."

"All right. I'll see you later. Thanks for having my back today. I know you thought it was a bad idea to sneak out and go to the funeral."

"Let's hope no one recognized you."

Teo didn't want to think about the consequences to that scenario. It made his head hurt.

"That's what we have publicists for, right?" He yawned. "I need a nap."

Seth had barely closed the door before Teo sprawled onto the bed and pulled a blanket over himself. He'd been so tired lately, likely the stress of having Sirhaan around and everything that had happened with Ethan.

Some solid rest and then hopefully Teo would feel like himself again.

After a good night's sleep, Teo did feel more himself than he had in a long time. He smiled at the woman, Madame Blanc, who'd just handed him an orchid. They stood in a greenhouse in the centre of the city where the Orchid Society staff grew flowers and experimented with different breeds of orchids. Several workers and garden enthusiasts stood around them. The Orchid Society sold hundreds if not thousands of plants each year. They also generously donated plants to hospitals and other charities annually. That was why Teo was here—the society was in the process of presenting a plant to each family who had lost a loved one to the Lupine Flu.

The greenhouse was humid, making Teo uncomfortable in his suit. As soon as he was in the car, he would remove the stupid tie.

"It would be our honour if you'd accept this gift as a token of our appreciation for your support as our patron." Madame Blanc smiled broadly. She reminded Teo of a poodle with her frizzy white hair and pointy nose. He grabbed the pot with both hands. The orchid had white petals, their edges a dusky rose. It was heavier than he expected. Thanking the woman, Teo smiled for the photographers who were crowded to the left. Always the photo op.

The crowd applauded as the final picture was snapped, then Madame Blanc opened the floor. "We will now answer any questions about the science of breeding orchids."

"Your Majesty, do you have any more information on the murder of that assassin?"

Heads swivelled toward the voice as Madame Blanc shook her head. "No, the king is not answering those questions today."

Teo stepped forward, signalling it was okay. If he hid, it would make it worse. He eyed the woman who'd asked the question—an ambassador's wife standing in the front row. She focused on him, eyes narrowed beneath her stylish pink hat, reminding Teo of a cat stalking its prey. Beside her stood another, older woman in a floral dress and cardigan, whose pursed lips and crossed arms made Teo feel as though he was in the principal's office. He shifted the large potted plant to his hip so he could see the ambassador's wife better. "Mrs. Williams, the young man was let go due to lack of evidence. I don't believe Ethan Moss could hurt a flea."

"But he rushed at you with a weapon." The woman didn't back down.

"He didn't have it in his hand. And there were extenuating circumstances." Sweat trickled between his shoulder blades.

"No one has ever explained those."

"They were personal."

A photographer lifted his camera to snap another photo, but this one wasn't posed to look pretty. Thank goodness the only press allowed into today's event was the paparazzi and not reporters. His press secretary had wanted a pleasant surrounding for a good photo op but no press drilling him with questions. So much for that idea. The citizens of Wolf Kingdom had decided to hold their own press conference. Teo wasn't getting out of this unscathed.

"Personal grudge against our king? I'd say that needs to be explained."

Several people nodded in agreement with Mrs. Williams.

"Personal to Mr. Moss." Teo's fingers tightened around the pot. Where was his secretary? Did he look as idiotic as he felt?

Governor Adams from the Falls District stepped forward. What was he doing here? "I think it's a good decision to arm Wolf Kingdom, based on what's happened."

All eyes lasered in on Teo. What was the governor talking about? He searched for his publicist, but the man seemed to have disappeared. Teo cleared his throat, stalling, but before he could speak, Sirhaan moved to the front of the small crowd. Where had he come from? Teo hadn't seen either him or the governor earlier while he gave his speech. Was this an ambush? Had he failed to notice anyone else? Teo's heart galloped in his chest, panic clawing its way up his throat.

"Your Majesty, if I may?" Sirhaan bowed slightly.

So Teo's choices were to appear ignorant of the happenings in his kingdom or shut the guy up and look as though he was hiding something. "Why don't you enlighten our guests, Sirhaan?" And myself.

The smug look on the man irritated Teo. He itched to pitch the plant at his face.

"My pleasure, your Majesty. The weapons Wolf City has decided to arm itself with are necessary for any large city to keep its citizens safe. The Wolf Pack will be fitted with body armour. The gates to the city will be fortified with armour too. Patrols will still be done, but at much less risk to the Pack. Presently, they're sitting ducks up on that wall." He nodded at Teo. "No offence, your Majesty."

Heat climbed up Teo's neck, but he kept his features neutral. "None taken. It sounds like you've been busy."

"All in a day's work."

Teo's publicist pushed forward—finally!—and removed the plant from his hands. "The king is done answering questions." He waited for Teo to stride ahead before following him through the doors to the waiting car. The grim look on the man's face mirrored how Teo felt. Someone had some explaining to do.

Teo stormed into his suites, his mother and Seth close on his heels. The first thing he'd done upon returning to the castle was summon them to his office. After yanking off his tie, he flung it on the floor. Through clenched teeth, he growled, "Tell me what is going on. How do I go to a horticultural event and get ambushed by questions regarding weapons I know nothing about? How are Sirhaan and Governor Adams attending said event, equipped with all the details, while I stand holding a large potted plant and looking like a fool?"

His mother sat on the edge of Teo's desk. Her calm features annoyed Teo. "Sirhaan was going to tell you yesterday. You were too busy... elsewhere." She glared at him. "You trust the Foresters too much. This boy Ethan is a perfect example of your naive faith. He meant to kill you, and then you released him with barely a slap on the wrist. And it's not only the forest. Others will try and take our kingdom from you, Teo, because you're young and naive. Your Father and I had already discussed the possibility of arming the city before he died."

Teo glanced at Seth. "Why is this news to me?" Had his father not trusted him enough to let the heir know about his plans? As the Crown Prince, Teo should have been in on that conversation.

"He wasn't expecting to die. We thought it would be years before you'd take the throne. Duko gave me Sirhaan's name when he fell ill and realized he might not live. He was trying to protect you. It was a fortuitous turn of events to meet Sirhaan on my holiday." She adjusted the sleeve of her filmy blouse. "I'm not going to apologize for looking out for my son and the heir."

"That's not the point. I appreciate that you care, but you should have told me. Instead, I find out about it at a charity function. The news isn't what was going on with the society but rather that the king was ignorant of what was happening in his own city." Teo grabbed a fistful of hair and tugged. The pain to his scalp momentarily relieved the throb that had taken up residence there.

"Governor Adams jumped the gun. He wanted payback for the embarrassment you've caused his family. I'm sorry it came out the way it did." She pushed away from the desk.

The collar of his shirt strangled him. "What are the Foresters supposed to think?" Teo unbuttoned the top button of his shirt.

"That they better watch their step."

Teo's head jerked up at the sharpness in her tone. "When did you start to hate the forest so much? Do you want to make things worse between us? Because Ethan's murder, combined with the note and the fact that the Wolves are arming themselves, is going to cause this situation to explode." Teo rubbed his arms, a chill running over his body.

Seth stepped forward. "Besides the people at the event today, who else knows about the purchase of the weapons?"

His mother shrugged. "No one other than General Scar, Sirhaan, Governor Adams, and myself."

Teo paced back and forth a couple of steps. "What did Alarick say about this?"

The Queen Mother straightened a pile of folders on his desk.

"He doesn't know."

"He's not here." She tapped them together against the top of the desk.

Teo closed his eyes. How could he have been stupid enough to send his uncle out of the city? "Please leave."

"What?" She dropped the folders onto his desk.

"Now."

His mother flinched before her features hardened. "Don't you dare speak to me this way."

Teo shook his head. He'd had enough manipulation by his mother. He'd thought she was on his side. "Do I have to call security?"

Her eyes widened before she straightened her shoulders and strode away. Teo wished he could retract his words. Teo picked up a small glass jug from a table and threw it at the door she'd just exited through.

"Whoa, Teo. Easy." Seth lifted a hand.

Teo whirled on his brother. "Mother and Sirhaan are treating me like a child. I'm the king." He jabbed his chest with his thumb. "Do you understand how stupid I felt today? Suddenly, Governor Adams and then Sirhaan appear out of nowhere, and I had no idea what either of them was talking about. I swear they planned it that way to make me look incompetent in front of my people. I'm supposed to be the one making these decisions, not becoming some pawn in a game I know nothing about."

Seth shoved his hands into his pants pockets, silent.

"How am I supposed to explain this to Jenna and Dr. Hood? They saved us from the flu. They didn't once hesitate to help us, and then we do this?" He strode over to the window, his heavy breathing fogging the glass. Small twinkle lights lit up the area, making it appear magical and romantic. Like a fairytale dream. He, however, was living a nightmare.

Seth murmured, "Maybe she'll understand."

"Do you believe that?"

His brother shook his head before heading to the door. "I'm sorry things went down this way. Are you going to be okay?"

"Yeah." No. He wasn't. In fact, there was a very good possibility he was about to lose everything he'd ever dreamed of having.

Chapter
Forty-Four
Rider

W*OLF CITY IS ARMING* **itself.** She mouthed the words her father had just spoken, hoping they would start to make sense. They didn't. Rider pulled back the curtains, staring at nothing. The light in the front room was dimming in the late afternoon hours. "How can this be?" She spluttered, but a memory of Matrix speaking about a truck delivering weapons niggled her. It *was* true. She hadn't wanted to believe him. She turned away from the window, biting her cheek.

Her dad patted the couch cushion beside him, inviting her to sit. She sank beside him, leaning her head on his shoulder.

Her father still clutched the message a courier had dropped off to him an hour earlier. "Dr. Lupine told me that Wolf City is buying weapons against a possible attack from the forest or any other enemies that might decide to challenge Teo's reign." The oven dinged, signalling the strudel was finished cooking. Her father dropped the paper on the coffee table before heading into the kitchen, Rider at his heels. He tugged on oven mitts before pulling the steaming apple strudel from the oven. The smells of spicy cinnamon and apples wafted in the air, but the homey aroma provided no comfort for Rider.

Chucking the mitts onto the counter, he continued his story. "Apparently, the news came out during an event this morning at the Orchid Society. Governor Adams mentioned it publicly and then that man who has been seen with the queen mother often lately, some kind of weapons expert, apparently, gave more info. Dr. Lupine did say that Teo didn't look too happy."

Rider's chin trembled. "He said nothing at the funeral yesterday, and he had plenty of opportunity to tell me. T-this is a betrayal of all he promised." She swallowed down the bitter disappointment that threatened to spill out in a sob.

"Maybe he couldn't say anything. He is the leader of Wolf Kingdom—there will be things he can't talk to you about." Her father wrapped his arm around her shoulders.

"But this? Unity in the kingdom wasn't just *his* dream. He should have trusted me. Maybe we could have figured something out that didn't involve weapons. Why didn't he come to us and talk it over?"

"In an ideal world, yes, that would have been nice. But even as king, he still has to listen to his advisors. That's the reality of his job, Jenna-girl. He came to the funeral. That's something."

Pain shot through Rider's chest. She rubbed at the tender spot.

"Do you trust him?"

"I'm not sure anymore," she whispered. She pulled a bowl from the cupboard, then measured confectioner's sugar into it. Making a glaze for the strudel was the distraction Rider needed. She stirred in two tablespoons of milk.

After the mixture was combined, she set the bowl aside. Her father swiped his finger along the side of the bowl of the sweet icing. She swatted his hand away. "Dad."

He winked, then licked his finger as he walked to the sink to wash his hands. "That's understandable, but don't lose faith yet. I'm not saying it makes sense, or it's not concerning, but we don't have the information from Teo, and until we do, we can't make assumptions."

He's the king. He's the one who makes those decisions, isn't he?

Rider stood, grabbed her coat, and headed for the door. "I need some air."

"Stay close. It's not safe to wander off on your own."

He didn't need to tell her twice. Rider slipped out the front door into the crisp air. Settling on the porch steps, she stared at the trees across the way. Teo had stood out here one night, a long time ago. It seemed an eternity. She bit her cheek. A shadow fell over her, and she moaned. *Go away.*

Matrix stopped in front of her. "Hey, Jenna."

Rider tilted her head back, glancing at the darkening sky and hoping he'd get the message she wanted to be alone. It didn't work. Matrix sat beside her on the stair.

Would he take the hint if she stayed mute?

Leaning against the top step, he stretched his legs out in front of him, appearing to get comfortable. Maybe he would understand rudeness.

"What do you want?" Her tone was cold.

Matrix tsked. "Is that any way to greet a friend?"

"Who says we're friends?"

He pressed a hand to his chest. "You wound me." He nudged her in the arm, and she edged away from him.

"Obviously, from your mood, you've heard the news."

"Say 'I told you so' and leave."

"That's not why I'm here. I thought you might need a friendly ear."

Rider squinted at him. She couldn't ever get a handle on this guy. Did he want to be friends? Could he be trusted? Maybe she needed to take a leap of faith, since she was short on friends. And he *had* told her the truth about the weapons. "I can't believe they've bought weapons and armour. We've never been a threat. Why would Teo do that?"

"They believe Ethan was part of a bigger plot. Or one of several."

Rider glanced sharply at Matrix. "A plot by whom? A bunch of peace-loving people who live in a forest and have rakes, hoes, and perhaps a bow and arrow? Wow—so threatening."

Matrix's eyebrows rose. "The forest has no weapons?"

"No. Why would we? We don't want to fight anyone, even Wolves. We want to live our lives peacefully. Would we like equality? You bet, but we aren't willing to take lives to get it. We've lived decades oppressed but peaceful." And what good had that done them? Maybe they should have come out with knives unsheathed.

Matrix leaned forward, his elbows on his knees. "Are you sure Foresters wouldn't fight? I've overheard some pretty heated conversations around here."

He had a point. People *were* upset. Would they act crazy?

Matrix contemplated her. "You didn't answer my question."

"No, they wouldn't." She forced the words out.

"Okay. If you say so." His words were laced with doubt, echoing Rider's own fear.

"You are the most annoying person ever."

Matrix laughed.

"Do you purposely spin stuff to make me doubt? Because whatever I say, you argue against it."

"I'm trying to get you to open your mind. You're stubborn."

Rider huffed out a breath. "No, I'm loyal."

Matrix stood. "Whatever you say. Believe the fairy tale of happily ever after if you want, but you're going to regret it. Don't come running to me to save you." He stalked off.

So much for friendship. Rider chewed a fingernail. He'd hit on an already tender spot. Was it all a fairytale? The dreams of equality? Of her and Teo? No one was actually going to attack anyone. *Teo wouldn't do that and neither would any of her neighbours or friends. Right?*

Chapter Forty-Five
Teo

FINGERS OF PAIN GRIPPED Teo's head like a vise as he struggled to stay upright. His mother, sitting across from him, narrowed her eyes as she waited for his response. The rest of the men and women at the long table sat in silence. Teo panted slightly, trying but failing to gather his thoughts. What had she asked him again?

His mother leaned over the table, her fingers splayed out in front of her. "King Teo, what is your response to this?" Her voice was firm, as though willing him to give an answer, although her eyes held a concern she clearly couldn't express in front of the council, not without making him appear weak.

His stomach churned as he tried to think. Bile rose in his throat and he swallowed, hard. Gripping the edges of the table, he hauled himself up. "Ex-excuse me." He shoved his chair out of the way and staggered from the room. In the hallway, he lost his balance and slammed into the wall opposite the door. His fingers grasped empty air as he tried to find something to grab hold of.

Seth appeared at his side, steadying him with his arms. The hallway tilted, then spun. Teo sagged against his brother, clutching Seth's shoulders.

"My head. It's going to explode off me."

"Let's get you to your rooms. Can you walk if you lean against me?"

Teo swallowed again and nodded. He suspected at least some of his advisors had followed him and were watching from the doorway, but he didn't look back. Honestly? He wasn't even sure he cared. The pair made their way to the stairs and up to Teo's suite. Seth helped him to his bed, and Teo sprawled across it. He could hear Seth moving around and then a quilt covered him.

Seth nudged his side. "Take this."

Teo opened one eye and shook his head. "No. My headaches aren't getting any better. They're getting worse."

"I thought you said it was helping." Seth sniffed the bottle, making a face. "It's from Dr. Hood, isn't it?"

"Yeah, but he's off his game here. Must be a bad batch."

"Dr. Hood is never off his game." Seth held the bottle closer.

Teo shoved it away. "No, get me something else."

Seth set the bottle on the table next to the bed and disappeared into the bathroom. When he came back, his hands were empty. "There isn't any other medicine in there."

Teo rolled over, covering his eyes with his forearm. "There should be other old meds." Had he thrown them out? "I kept some from before the flu."

"The shelves are empty."

He waved his arm weakly through the air. "Never mind. Just let me sleep." He was too tired to form words or figure out what had happened to the medicine. Seth handed him a glass of water and he drank, the wet helping his parched throat. Then he sank back against the pillows and let the darkness overtake him.

The room was dark when Teo opened his eyes. He gingerly glanced around, relieved when the movement didn't make his eyes feel as if knives were shredding them. He exhaled as he sat up. The clock told him it was midnight. His growling stomach told him he'd missed at least two meals. He swung his legs over the edge of the bed, then turned on a lamp. The brown bottle of medicine sat next to it, and he picked it up and examined it, turning it around in his hands. Tugging off the lid, he sniffed the opening. A faint, sweet odour filled his nostrils. It was familiar, but he couldn't place it. After returning the bottle to the nightstand, he stood, his stomach grumbling again. Food.

After slipping on a pair of shoes, Teo turned to leave, but at the last minute grabbed the brown bottle and stuffed it in his pants pocket. Then he headed for the kitchen with an appetite he hadn't had in a week.

Teo licked the juice from the beef off his fingers. He hadn't realized how hungry he was. After pouring himself a glass of water, he gulped it down, ignoring his mother as she slid onto the bench opposite him.

"You wonder why you're treated like a child? Scenes like today, when you run off during an important strategy meeting, would be the reason. It was humiliating for me, and you lost respect from people who are under your command, which is an excellent way to encourage a coup."

Teo buttered a piece of bread. Took a bite, chewed, swallowed. He met his mother's eyes, which were anything but motherly. "I was ill. What would you have me do?"

She tapped his plate. "So ill that I find you stuffing your face in the kitchen? Maybe you were sick enough that you had to see that Hood girl?"

Teo tore off another chunk of bread with his teeth. Did she think he'd shirk his duties for a girl? He wanted to see Jenna, but he wasn't so immature as to leave a serious meeting to play hooky. He threw the leftover bread onto his plate, his appetite gone. "I don't know what you want me to say. I was sick, I left, now I feel better."

She sighed. "As you are constantly reminding me, you are an adult, not a child, so I won't coddle you. If you're sick, then say so, instead of running away. Behave like a king and I will treat you as one." His mother stood, opened her mouth, then clamped it shut. She dusted off her hands before striding from the room. Teo shoved the plate away, no longer hungry. Wiping his mouth, he carried his plate to the sink. Thankfully, no one was working this late, so he'd been alone in his humiliation. Did everyone think he was some lovesick teenager who didn't know up from down? Did they think he was playing at being king? He hurried to Seth's suite.

The door was slightly ajar, so Teo entered. Seth sat reading in one of the large leather chairs. He glanced up from his novel, probably another mystery. His brother was addicted to them. "You look better."

"Sleep and some food will do wonders."

Seth set the book aside.

Teo sat on the sofa, the leather cold against his thin shirt. "My mind hasn't felt this clear in a long time, and I have zero head pain. I was better off not taking that medicine," he mused.

"Do you think Dr. Hood could have given you the wrong meds?" Seth paused. "You don't think he would have—"

Teo flung up a hand. "Don't even go there. Why would he save us from the Lupine Flu only to poison me now?"

Seth held up his hands in surrender. "I'm trying to figure things out, that's all. But it seems a little too coincidental with all the other crazy stuff going on."

"I refuse to believe that Dr. Hood is out to get me or any other Wolf. It isn't logical."

"Then what's going on?"

"I don't know. If I did, I think we'd have answers to numerous puzzling questions. How did Mother get the meds? Did Dr. Hood drop them off, or did Dr. Lupine give them to her?"

"I would think she'd get them through Dr. Lupine. I don't think Mother has personally ever spoken to Dr. Hood, other than on official occasions."

"I want to get the meds tested. I'm going to make an appointment with Dr. Lupine and ask him a few questions too."

"Sounds like a good place to start." Seth's features relaxed. "What happens if you start getting the headaches again?"

"Then we'll know it wasn't the meds."

Seth frowned as if he didn't like that response. Teo got up and left his brother. He wanted answers, and the only way to get them was to make an appointment with Dr. Lupine as soon as he could.

Being king had a few perks, home visits by the doctor being one of them. It wasn't even 8 am and Dr. Lupine was already at the palace. Teo watched the man turn the brown bottle in his hands. He unscrewed the lid, sniffed it, and grimaced. "Where did you say you got this again?"

"Mother. She said she got it from Dr. Hood. I thought maybe you gave it to her from your stash."

Dr. Lupine pursed his lips. "It didn't come from my office. Dr. Hood sends me meds, but I never gave your mother any kind of medicine for you. I would have required that I see you in person." Dr. Lupine held the bottle up to the light. It was three-quarters gone.

"Of course. Would Dr. Hood somehow have given my mother medicine?"

"No, he wouldn't. I'm sure I would have heard from him if your mother went to him to get meds for you, since it would have been highly irregular. When we're done here, talk to your mother. I'm going to test this and find out what's in it. It stinks like burnt sugar."

The doctor's words niggled. Teo had smelled that somewhere else.

"But, since you're here, I want to know about the headaches. I'll check you out."

"I've always had migraines, as you know. But lately they've gotten worse and more frequent. I think it's stress. Mother gave me the meds to help, but the headaches only got worse. My brain is foggy, and I'm irritable all the time too."

"Stress can cause headaches. You've certainly had a lot to handle in the last months. I'll check you out, Your Majesty, and then maybe we'll get some answers."

"It's Teo, Dr. Lupine. You've known me since I was born."

Dr. Lupine chuckled. "True, but you deserve the honour and respect of the office, so I'll stick to protocol."

Teo started to protest but then closed his mouth. At some point, he'd have to get used to it. Dr. Lupine thoroughly examined him, took blood samples, and then left, taking the bottle of meds with him. He'd told Teo he would be in touch after testing both it and his blood. When he was gone, the grey walls of his suite closed in on Teo. He wished someone would write the answers to all his questions on those blank walls. He straightened on his chair. Wait. His mother had answers—what better time than the present to get them? He hit a button on his phone. "Can you send Mother to my suite?" Her secretary told him his mother would be right over.

Within minutes, she knocked on the door. Teo opened it.

"What can I do for you, Teo?" Lines ringed her eyes, and she seemed to have aged lately. Her tone was still icy.

Teo led her to the sofa, and they sat. "I'm sorry I embarrassed you at the meeting, but I thought I was going to be sick."

"Perhaps you should have led with that. Cancelled the meeting instead of bolting from the room."

"Where did you get the bottle of medicine you gave me?"

"I told you, Dr. Hood."

"Did he personally give it to you?"

She tugged a throw pillow from behind her setting it aside. "No, he dropped it off here."

"When and why?"

"Sirhaan told me Dr. Hood stopped by and left it after hearing you were suffering from headaches."

Teo jerked forward. "So, Sirhaan gave it to you?"

His mother crossed her arms over her chest. "Yes, he physically handed me the bottle, but it came from Dr. Hood."

"Says Sirhaan."

She winced. "I know you don't like him, but he's not the bad guy you make him out to be. He wants to help us."

Teo pushed to his feet and paced behind the couch. "You didn't speak directly with Dr. Hood." It wasn't a question—Teo already knew the answer, and he didn't like it.

"No, I didn't, and no, I didn't see the red hood either, if that's what you're trying to find out."

"Mother, I'm old enough to see her on my own without trying to manipulate you."

"Why don't you find a nice girl in the kingdom, Teo? It would make life so much simpler."

Teo stopped in his tracks. No way he was having that conversation with her again. "Thanks for the information, Mother. Now, if you'll excuse me." He strode over and pulled open the door of his suite, ending the conversation. His love life wasn't his mother's concern. Teo had other things on his mind—like where Sirhaan had gotten that medicine, because it definitely hadn't come from Dr. Hood.

Chapter Forty-Six
Rider

THE HAIRS ON THE back of Rider's neck stood straight as the Wolf Pack guard's eyes bore into her. She swallowed, annoyed that he intimidated her yet also hopeful because he was asking for her dad. This was a good sign, wasn't it?

"Ah, I'll go find him."

Rider shut the front door of their house, then bolted for her dad's office, throwing open the door.

"Jenna-girl." Her dad glanced up from his medical journal.

"Wolf Pack are at the front door, waiting to escort us to the palace, at the king's request."

Her dad shoved away from his desk. "Any hint as to why he's requested we come?"

She shrugged.

Dr. Hood grabbed his coat off the peg on the wall. As he settled his toque on his head, he nodded toward the front door. "Let's go."

Rider pulled on her red hoodie. Teo had summoned them. Was it good news or bad? She hurried after her father, crossing her fingers that Teo had changed his mind about the weapons and wanted to talk peace.

Upon arriving in Wolf City, Rider and her father were whisked to the palace and shown to a small room that had a long granite counter with a sink along one wall. Tall stools stood next to the counter. Her father raised his eyebrows at her. "By the looks of this lab, I don't think this is a pleasure visit."

Rider's nostrils tingled at the strong smell of bleach. She rubbed her nose as the door swung open, admitting Teo and Seth. Rider's breath caught in her throat as the king's ice-blue eyes locked with hers. He looked good in his dark jeans and blue sweater. His smile warmed her from her head to the tips of her toes. He embraced her, holding her a little longer than necessary.

"I'm so glad to see you," he whispered so only she could hear.

His breath tickled her ear, sending electric zings over her scalp. After releasing her, Teo shook her father's hand. "Thank you, sir, for coming on such short notice."

"I serve at your pleasure, Your Majesty. What is it you need me to do?"

"I have questions I hope you can answer. Dr. Lupine will join us shortly. No one is in trouble. I want an expert opinion." He sat on one stool and motioned for the others to take a seat too.

Rider sat beside her dad on the other tall stools. Seth leaned against the far wall, observing. Teo tugged a small brown bottle from his jeans pocket. "Do you recognize this bottle, Dr. Hood?"

Her father took it from him and examined it. "I use brown bottles like this all the time for elixirs and medicine. If it's one of mine, I can't be sure. I always put a label on any of my medicine bottles, but it could have been removed."

Teo pursed his lips. "Did you give my mother any medicine recently, or drop off medicine here at the palace for me? I've had some bad headaches. Perhaps you heard and wanted to help?"

Dr. Hood used his thumb to rub the smooth glass where a label should have been. "No. I have never interacted with your mother about your health. I had heard you seemed ill from idle gossip in the forest, but I did not bring medicine here. I would never do that unless I had personally examined you and you requested something. My usual course is to give the medicine to the doctors who pass it on to their patients. So, if you received my medicine, it would have been through Dr. Lupine, most likely."

A whole conversation passed with a look between Teo and Seth.

"That's what I thought." Teo faced Rider. "You didn't leave any meds here for me, did you?"

"No, I only deliver what I'm told. I wouldn't give out medicine unless Dad gave the okay."

Dr. Hood opened it and sniffed. "What is this?"

Rider caught a sweet scent that quickly faded when her dad recapped the bottle.

"My mother gave me this bottle of elixir when I complained of headaches. She said it came from you."

Rider picked up the bottle. "Why would she think it came from us?"

A knock sounded on the door, interrupting their conversation. Dr. Lupine entered the small room. "Your Majesty." He nodded at Teo and then smiled at Rider before shaking her father's hand.

After Dr. Lupine settled himself on the last empty stool, Teo addressed Rider's question. "The person who gave it to her said it came from Dr. Hood. My mother didn't question it."

"But you did?" Dr. Hood clasped his hands together.

"Yes, once I realized it was making me sick, I spoke to my mother." Teo gestured to the doctor. "Dr. Lupine is going to tell you about his findings."

The man cleared his throat. "Upon the king's request, I tested this medicine. What I found is concerning. This bottle does contain a mild pain killer, but it's laced with something I've only seen once before. I need another opinion."

Dr. Hood glanced at the file Dr. Lupine passed him. Rider peeked over her dad's shoulder. Photos of a field of harvested plants, a few leaves, and a slide from under a microscope picture were all in the file.

Her dad lifted the file in Teo's direction. "These are what you showed me a few weeks ago, the plants that were found growing in the forest?"

Teo nodded.

Rider reached for one of the photos of the plants.

Her father thumbed through the papers, scanning the lab results. "This is the same plant found in the elixir you were taking?"

Dr. Lupine answered, "Yes."

Rider set the photo back in the file. "I'm confused. Can someone please tell me what's going on?"

Seth pushed away from the wall and wandered over. "Several fields have been secretly planted on the edges of the forest in two or three areas. The plants were harvested before we ever found them and the fields wiped clean, with the exception of a few leaves."

Her stomach squeezed. "In the forest? Who planted them?"

Seth shook his head. "We don't know."

Rider lifted the photo again. "What is it?"

Dr. Hood held up the image of a leaf, one half torn off it. "It's a highly toxic plant. Taken in the right amounts, it can make you sick. Or kill you."

Dr. Lupine tapped the top of the brown bottle. "There were small amounts in this elixir, only enough to cause illness or headaches. I took bloodwork from Teo and found trace amounts of it in his blood. Both tests also revealed traces of synthetic drugs."

Dr. Hood glanced up sharply. "What kind of synthetic drugs?" Her dad wasn't a fan of synthetic drugs unless they were absolutely necessary. He believed in the natural healing powers of plants.

Dr. Lupine tapped a finger on a list of ingredients in the file. "A mood changer, for one."

That didn't sound good. "There's a drug that can change your mood?" How dangerous was that?

Her dad frowned as he stared at the list. "It's highly illegal. It's considered a bioweapon in Wolf Kingdom."

All the air seemed to be sucked out of the room. Teo had been given both the plant and the mood changer?

Dr. Hood stood. "This is serious. What are your theories?"

"There wasn't enough of the toxic plant to kill the king, only make him sick with headaches. Because he's prone to them anyway, I think the plant enhanced that weakness. The question is, if whoever gave this to him didn't want to kill him, then what did they want to accomplish? And why include a mood changer?"

Seth strode over to the counter and picked up the bottle. "We believe someone is setting up the forest. With the mystery fields planted there, Ethan, and now the poisoning of Teo, the source of which supposedly came from you, I'd say someone wants to make the Wolves suspicious of the Foresters. Perhaps strip away any chance for the equality and unity Teo was trying to bring in. But that's only a guess based on circumstantial evidence."

Dr. Hood whistled. "It sounds like a pretty good one."

Rider leaned forward, her hands gripping the edge of the counter. "Why would anyone do this? Foresters aren't bad. We're different than Wolves, but that doesn't make us wrong. We still breathe the same air, eat, and have feelings."

Her dad rested a hand on the file. "Someone is feeding on the inequality between the Foresters and Wolves. My guess is it comes down to greed and power. They are using these prejudices to gain for themselves."

Teo clasped his hands behind his head. "I think you're right. We don't know for sure if it's a Wolf or a Forester. It could be either. Or the other option is an outside source who stood to gain if I was engaged in a conflict between Wolves and Foresters. I spoke to my mother, and the bottle came from a man who's been visiting Wolf City for a while. He gave it to her, explaining that Dr. Hood dropped it off. My mother didn't question him." Teo's jaw hardened. "She appears to like and trust him."

Seth took up the story. "His name is Sirhaan, and he is a weapons dealer. He came here to help us weaponize the city at our mother's request. She and our father had discussed the idea before his death. Another of his paranoid schemes."

Teo scrubbed his face. "You met Sirhaan briefly at the ball, Jenna. Remember?"

"I do, yes." The man had given her bad vibes at the time. Now she knew why.

Teo exhaled. "When Sirhaan came to present his ideas, I told him no, we didn't have a need for those kinds of weapons. If anything happened, Wolf Pack would be able to deal with it. However, I recently learned that my mother went behind my back and ordered armour and weapons for Wolf City. She's been fearful of an attempted coup or assassination, which Ethan's attack didn't help."

Rider shifted on the stool as Matrix's words echoed through her head. He'd been telling the truth about seeing a delivery of weapons.

"We have no proof that this is Sirhaan's doing." Seth pressed both palms to the top of the counter. "In fact, we have no solid evidence for any of the three options. But we agree that creating distrust between us has caused a distraction, which can only bring trouble."

Teo stared at a white board on the wall as though hoping writing would appear. "The question is, what kind of trouble, and who is doing it? What's their endgame? Is Sirhaan a part of it?" His eyes met Rider's. "Personally, I don't believe it's a Forester or a Wolf."

Seth straightened. "As of right now, only the five of us know anything about Teo's poisoning. We need to keep it that way because we don't know for sure who to trust anymore."

Her father's grave expression didn't help Rider's queasy stomach. He rubbed his chin. "That's understandable. You can't be too careful. We are behind you one hundred percent."

Dr. Lupine reached for the file. "Dr. Hood, if you wouldn't mind, I'd like to go over some of my findings. Do you have time?"

"Of course." The two men stood and made their way to a couple of hard plastic chairs in the corner of the room.

"I'm on duty shortly, so I need to go get ready." Seth waved to Rider and Teo before exiting the room.

Teo shifted over to the stool Rider's father had vacated. "Do you have a minute?"

She smiled. "Maybe." She glanced over at her dad. "He might be a while."

Teo grinned. "That's what I was hoping." He took her hand and led her out of the room and down a corridor. Pulling open a large mahogany door, he gestured for her to go ahead. Rider had never been in this room before. It was stylishly decorated with creamy walls and dark leather couches. Game tables and large leather chairs that looked like good places to curl up with a book were scattered around the room. The scent of leather hung in the room. Rider stopped a few feet from the doorway and turned to face him, meeting Teo's gaze steadily.

He drove his fingers through his long hair. "I need to apologize. I think the meds messed up my brain. I know I haven't been the nicest person to be around."

"Thank you for that, but clearly it wasn't your fault."

He took a step closer to her. "I'm glad you came today. I needed to see you, and since your dad was coming…" His cheeks pinked. Was the king blushing?

"You thought you'd waste my time?" Rider teased. "You're so bad."

"I thought you liked the bad boys."

Rider's eyebrows shot up. "What? Who gave you that idea?"

Teo reached for her hand. His thumb rubbed between her thumb and forefinger, making it hard for Rider to focus on anything else. The low tone of Teo's voice brought her back to reality. "You certainly seem to spend a lot of time with that guy, Matrix."

Rider tilted her head. "Are you jealous? I barely know him, other than we keep running into each other. He befriended Ethan, so I wanted to find out what he knew."

"He didn't know anything. We questioned him. And what do you mean you keep running into him?"

"He seems to show up wherever I am—the building dedication, coffee shops, a few other places." Probably not a good idea to mention he'd come to her home.

Teo narrowed his eyes. "Is he some kind of stalker?"

"No. Wolf City isn't that large, so of course I run into him. I don't think he stays at home much."

"Does he have a family?"

"Not that I know of. Maybe an uncle? I can't remember."

Teo raised her hand to his lips, kissing her knuckles. "You need to be careful, Jenna. I can't lose you too."

She tugged her hand free. "I am. Let's forget Matrix, shall we?" She circled her arms around his neck. "I miss you." They were so close she could smell his minty breath and would have been able to count his long eyelashes if they weren't so thick. Every girl she knew would kill to have them.

Teo brushed his lips against hers lightly. The butterflies in her stomach danced in ecstatic joy. He kissed behind her ear, whispering, "I miss you like crazy." Wrapping his arms around her, he pulled her closer. "I wish we could figure us out."

She let her hands fall to his chest, then pushed away. "What's there to figure out?"

The king stared over her shoulder, avoiding looking her in the eyes. "It's complicated. My mother does not approve. She wants me to find a nice Wolf to marry."

"Marry? You're only twenty, Teo."

"The kingdom expects it, and she wants an heir."

"What?" Rider's voice rose an octave as she took a step back. Marriage was one thing, but a family? So soon?

"I'm not saying I want that right now. But she can be manipulative."

The butterflies dropped. The dance ended. "But you're the king. Shouldn't you have a say in your life? You're not under your father's rule anymore."

Teo shoved his hands into the front pockets of his jeans and stared at the floor. His handsome face was definitely thinner, with dark smudges under his eyes. "Jenna, I'm not going to do anything I don't want to do, but please be patient. There is so much going on, and at any time it can all blow up in my face."

She got that he was under a lot of pressure, but one question burned in her mind. "Are you embarrassed by me? Because I'm from the forest?"

Teo's eyes darkened. "Are you kidding? No, I'm not embarrassed by you. Ever. I don't care that you're a Forester. For me, that's a bonus." He closed the space between them, but he didn't touch her. "I want to protect you from things that are beyond your control. The kingdom and Wolf City are not stable. If the wrong people find out about us, I'm afraid they'll use you to get to me. I need you to be safe."

Like his father had done—kidnapping her to manipulate Teo to marry the daughter of the Governor from Falls District. Rider still couldn't be in an enclosed space since her stint being buried alive. She shivered.

"The more discreet we are the better. It's safer for you. And it's not forever." Teo rubbed her arms. "For now, be careful, okay? Especially around this Matrix dude. Don't take any unnecessary risks."

Rider rested her head against his chest. His arms closed around her as he leaned his chin on the top of her head.

"I keep Matrix at a distance. He's sort of annoying."

"Annoying is good." He squeezed her, then let her go when a knock sounded at the door. Teo strode over and opened it.

Dr. Hood stood in the corridor. "Jenna-girl, are you ready to go?"

"Sure, Dad, I'll be right there."

Teo stuck his hand out and shook her dad's. "Thank you, Dr. Hood, for your help today."

"It's my privilege to serve you, Teo."

Rider squeezed Teo's hand, then walked out with her dad.

Teo led them through the hallways to a back family entrance. He nodded to them as they left. "Take care. I'll be in touch."

Rider smiled at him before following her dad out into the frigid air. Dark clouds threatened snow. She pulled her scarf over her mouth and fell into step with her father, hoping the storm would soon blow over.

Chapter
Forty-Seven
Matrix

INSIDE THE SMALL SHED behind his cabin, Matrix bundled up the last of the dried leaves and boxed them in the courier box that would take them to Falls District. The place was warm, and he wiped the sweat from his brow with his shirtsleeve. Carrying the box to the wall beside the door, he dropped it beside the ten other boxes waiting to be shipped to the factory that would make the bioweapons. Matrix yanked off his rubber gloves and pulled the mask from his face, glad to be free of the hot protective gear. *Not sorry to see the last of this plant.*

He chucked both the gloves and the mask into the garbage. The plant was so potent that protection was necessary. Enough of it could kill you or make you extremely sick—like Teo with his migraines. Mixed with the mood changer, the drug was scary. Matrix had no desire to mess with it. *I wonder if Sirhaan has dabbled in it?* The more Matrix got to know his uncle, the sicker he thought the guy was. His unpredictability was making Matrix hypervigilant. Sirhaan had killed Ethan without a second thought. He reminded Matrix of King Duko. *Ironic.*

Matrix had decided there was no way his uncle was taking the throne once they controlled the kingdom. He walked over to the small window and attempted to wipe away the smudges covering it, but it was useless. Staring through the cloudy glass, he followed the movements of a blue jay as it darted from tree to tree. Entertained by the little bird, Matrix leaned closer to the glass. His smile slipped as a familiar form walked toward the shed. *Speak of the devil.* Dark clouds rolled in behind his uncle. Matrix blew out a breath before grabbing the doorknob.

"Matrix, you must have been reading my thoughts."

"Great minds think alike."

Sirhaan ignored the comment. Even though they shared the same DNA, his uncle never thought of Matrix as an equal. That would change soon enough.

"To what do I owe the pleasure?"

Sirhaan glanced around the room. "I see the last of the leaves are ready to go?"

Matrix nodded. "Waiting for the courier."

"Excellent." Sirhaan moved into the centre of the room. "We need to accelerate the plan."

Matrix blinked. "I'm sorry?"

"The king and his brother discovered the meds."

He inhaled sharply. "How? Do they know about us?"

"A fluke. They've been suspicious of me from the beginning, which is why we need to speed things up."

So much for Sirhaan breezing through his mission. "Why didn't you tell me they were suspicious? That would have been good to know." *Since you gave me such a hard time about Jenna.* "What are you going to do?"

Sirhaan smiled. "I'm going to drive the king crazy."

"I want specific details." Because he needed to keep his uncle on plan.

"I'm going to give him a concentrated dose that makes him so angry he won't be able to think straight. Then I'm going to give him a dose of another of our bioweapons that will make him putty in my hands." Sirhaan clapped his hands together, clearly giddy.

Matrix stared. The man was off his rocker. "How are you going to get the king to take the meds since he's already suspicious?"

Sirhaan shook his head. "Matrix, I didn't take you for a doubter."

Careful. He licked his lips. "I'm not. Just being a good partner by making sure we cover every base."

"It's brilliant, if I do say so myself. I'll be called in for questioning, I have no doubt. When I am, I'll inject the king with the meds."

"And the brother?"

"I'll take care of him. You don't need to worry your pretty little head about it. What I need you to do is distract the girl and her father. And if that doesn't work, then you need to deal with them."

"Deal with them?" This was going someplace Matrix didn't want to go. People got killed in war, but he didn't like unnecessary casualties.

"Am I not making myself clear?"

"I'll distract her. You can count on me."

Sirhaan pressed his hands together in a praying position. "Don't let me down, Matrix. Or you'll be sorry."

Seriously? You're threatening me?

Sirhaan cackled. "The look on your face. Priceless. I know you'll come through because we both want revenge for our family. Don't forget that."

Matrix wouldn't forget it or the fact that Sirhaan wasn't fit to lead. No, Matrix would take the crown when the time came and wouldn't give it to anyone else.

Chapter
Forty-Eight
Teo

THE NEXT MORNING, TEO strode down the hall, his Wolf Pack guard right on his heels. He glanced at his watch, picking up his pace. He needed to speak to Seth, but his mother had requested his presence. What did she want? He and Seth were supposed to be questioning Sirhaan today about the bottle of meds, but he couldn't blow off his mother. He didn't need her to come looking for him and stop the interrogation. Halting in front of her office door, he sighed. *Let's get this over with.*

Teo knocked. When there was no answer, he pushed the door open. Strange. Since she wasn't there, he walked in, took a seat, glanced at his watch again. He'd wait five minutes and then he was gone. She'd have to meet with him later. He drummed his fingers on the chair arm. "Mother?" he called.

No answer. Five minutes later, he stood. *Time's up.* He shoved his irritation away so he could focus on the coming confrontation with Sirhaan. Teo needed answers, and he was beginning to suspect only one man could give them to him. At the sound of a soft click behind him, he started to turn. Before he could, a hand came over his mouth and something sharp pinched his neck. A wave of dizziness crashed over him. His knees buckled, but the person who held him from behind shoved him onto a chair. Darkness crept into the periphery of his vision.

A person, man or woman, Teo couldn't tell, stood in front of him, body moving in waves, as though Teo was looking into some distorted mirror. He closed his eyes, trying to calm his pitching stomach. Once the sensation of being on a wild ride eased, Teo pried one eye open. A pair of legs came into view. At least they weren't waving like a flag, so Teo forced his eyelids higher. He opened his mouth, but for some reason his lips felt as if they had weights on them. When he tried lifting a hand, he ended up dropping it like a dead weight.

A chuckle from his captor grated against Teo's nerves. "Shut up." His words were hoarse.

His irritation apparently delighted whoever it was. His cackle grew louder as he slapped his leg, like this was all some joke. "Your Majesty, so irritable."

The voice connected to a face as Teo's heart rate skyrocketed. What had Sirhaan given him? He couldn't move.

"You've had a little cocktail of drugs. A temporary paralysis will occur. Don't worry, though; it will go away soon."

Panic crawled up Teo's chest, squeezing his lungs. His heart whomped against his chest as blackness closed in around his eyes. He was in his mother's office. A vague memory of coming here earlier drifted back to him.

"Your mother has gone to a spa and shopping. I suggested she take a day off. No need to worry about her interrupting us." Sirhaan stood in front of him, holding a small black box that looked like a remote.

"What is that?" Teo mumbled.

Sirhaan dangled it in front of him. "Oh this? Let me give you a demonstration, Your Majesty." He hit a button on the device.

A blinding pain erupted in Teo's temple, and he curled into a ball, his hands covering his head.

"See? Already the paralysis is passing." Sirhaan's voice was filled with delight.

Suddenly Teo's head jerked back as Sirhaan grabbed his hair and leaned in close to Teo's face. "It's linked to something I injected you with. It gives me control over you until I don't need you anymore. You're going to do what I tell you to do or I will hit this button right here." The man let his finger hover over a red button, then pressed it.

Teo gritted his teeth against the pain searing his brain, paralyzing his body.

Sirhaan lifted his finger, shoving Teo's head away. Teo gasped as the abrupt halt of pain left him whiplashed. Sirhaan tapped the remote against his chin as he stared out the windows. "It's too bad, Your Majesty, that your headaches have progressed so violently. I've heard they're debilitating."

"No one will believe that," Teo croaked.

Sirhaan hit the button again, and this time the pain throbbed through his eye. Teo bent over, sure he would vomit all over his mother's expensive rug.

"Tell me why you look sick, Your Majesty."

"I get bad migraines." The words popped out of Teo's mouth. His eyes widened in surprise.

"That's more like it." Sirhaan shoved a glass of water towards him. "Drink up."

Teo jerked back as though Sirhaan was handing him a snake. Sirhaan hit the button again. Pain coursed through his body until Teo cried out.

"Ready to drink it now?"

His hands shaking, Teo reached for the cup. Drops dribbled down his chin, but by some miracle he managed to get most of it in his mouth. The wet felt good against his dry throat, although the sickly sweet odour coming from the glass turned his stomach.

"Drink up or my finger is going to find itself glued to that button."

Teo gagged the rest of the water down. He couldn't resist Sirhaan's commands. What had the guy given him? Sweat beaded his brow. He couldn't think straight and his vision was as foggy as his mind. He swiped at his forehead as the room came back into focus. Where was he? Sirhaan stood in front of him. "What are you doing here?"

"Your Majesty, we have work to do." He raised the remote, which made Teo flinch. Teo didn't know how or why he was in his mother's office, but he did know he didn't like that red button.

"So glad you remembered. Let's try this again. We have work to do."

The words tumbled out of his mouth. "We have work to do." He didn't know what work, only that he needed to get it done. He glanced at Sirhaan. Perhaps that man could help him.

Teo sagged on his bed, barely able to stay in a seated position as Sirhaan pulled out clothing from his closet. He didn't remember how they got back to his rooms. Teo wanted to tear his skin off. Annoyance coiled around him, and he clenched his hands into fists. "You're making a mess. Stop it."

Sirhaan glanced back at him, dropping a shirt onto the floor. "Does it bother you?"

Teo balled the sheets in his hands. "Stop it."

Sirhaan turned back to his rifling, finally pulling out Teo's formal dress uniform for the Wolf Pack. "You need to look like a military leader." The man shoved the hanger at Teo, who fumbled with it, his fingers clumsy.

"Get dressed. Now."

Sirhaan left Teo in his bedroom. He unbuttoned his shirt, focusing on the need to change his clothes. *This is what a leader would wear, like my father did.* Teo frowned. He wasn't like his father, was he? But the idea of looking like a powerful leader appealed to him. He clumsily clothed himself in the military uniform before walking out into the living area. Sirhaan had been glancing through some papers on Teo's coffee table, but he looked up when Teo came in and studied him. "Good. Now we need to discuss strategy."

Teo nodded. Sirhaan seemed to know what he was doing, which was good because Teo couldn't seem to get his brain to work right.

"Sit down." Teo sat. Sirhaan raised an eyebrow. "Maybe I gave you too much serum. You were supposed to be angry, not docile." He waved a hand as if dismissing the thought. "The arming of the wall happens today. The guns are ready to be installed, so order it done. You'll also order Wolf Pack patrols of the forest."

Teo frowned. Patrols of the forest? That didn't sound right. The fog in his brain lifted a little. "Wolves have never patrolled the forest. There's no need to do that. They aren't our enemy."

Sirhaan picked up the remote. "You're wrong about that. They are your enemy. Remember, they tried to kill you."

Pain jabbed Teo's temple, and he doubled over. Just as abruptly, it stopped, its sudden departure leaving Teo on his knees, gasping. Sirhaan knelt in front of him, holding the remote in Teo's face. The ringing in his head jumbled his thoughts. *Was* the forest his enemy? The forest boy had tried to kill him. He'd had something sharp. Foresters were his enemy. Why hadn't he listened to Sirhaan earlier? "We need to arm ourselves against the Foresters; they are our enemies."

Sirhaan smirked. "Glad you're coming around, Your Majesty."

Teo grabbed the edge of the coffee table to steady himself as he stood. "I'm going to set up a meeting with General Scar. We need to get started like yesterday." He took a step, swayed. Taking a deep breath, Teo waited until the room stopped spinning. "Sirhaan, let my mother know."

"With pleasure."

Teo left his suites and headed down the hall. Twenty steps away, the hall tilted, and he flung out his arm to grab at it. He rested his head on his arm and waited for the spinning to stop.

"Your Majesty, are you alright?"

Teo slowly turned his head in the direction of the voice. A maid stood staring at him, wide-eyed.

"I'm fine. Now, get about your business," Teo snarled. The woman paled, then scurried away. Teo squeezed his eyes shut. Why was he out in the hallway? He couldn't remember how he'd gotten here. Suddenly, pain exploded over his right eye, and he hugged the wall until the throbbing receded. Gasping, he looked up. Sirhaan stood outside Teo's mother's office, holding something. "The meeting with General Scar, Your Majesty. You need to schedule it right now."

Yes, the meeting. It was urgent he get that done. Teo lurched away from the wall, stumbling in the direction of his office. As he walked, he slowly regained his balance.

When he reached his office, he unlocked his door and went inside. Going straight to his desk, he picked up the phone to call the General, who answered on the first ring.

"Your Majesty, how can I serve you?"

"I want to set up a meeting to arrange security for the city."

"Your Majesty, I'm confused. I thought we'd done this."

"I want some added measures. Please come to my office at once."

Teo hung up the phone. Sunshine filled the room, which made his head ache and his eyes scream. He shut the blinds. *Better.*

A file lay on his desk and he picked it up. Sinking onto his desk chair, he read the pages while he waited for the general to arrive. He smiled as he closed the file. *Wolf City and Kingdom are in good hands, thanks to Sirhaan and his weapons company. The forest can't hurt us, and we'll be invincible to everyone in the kingdom. I will be the leader my father never was.*

Chapter
Forty-Nine
Rider

A SMILE PLAYED ON Rider's lips as she walked the forest paths in the direction of the city, thoughts of Teo keeping her warm as snow fell gently from the sky. It had turned colder since their meeting at the palace two days ago. She had a couple of errands to run in the city this wintry morning. Hope surged within her heart—Teo was still the same guy. Everything was going to be okay. They only had to find out who was trying to frame the Foresters. Maybe she'd catch a glimpse of him today, or could she possibly surprise him? Would they let her into the palace? Maybe Seth was working at the gates again and he'd escort her to Teo. Her heart beat double-time in anticipation.

Her steps faltered as she came out of the treeline of the forest, the gates looming in the distance. The smile died on her lips, and her heart turned leaden. *What's going on?*

Guns perched along the top of the wall pointed at the forest. Her chest tightened as she stood staring at the long lines of people waiting to enter the city. Guards examined every person's papers, questioning their owners. Most people were turned away, and the few who were allowed entry were escorted in by a guard. No, this wasn't right. Rider ran toward the gates but halted abruptly at the sudden clicking of guns.

"Stop right there." A guard pointed his handgun at her.

Rider raised her hands to shoulder level. "Don't shoot."

"State your business." The guard waved his gun, gesturing her to speak.

"I, uh, I was going to the city." She was still fifty metres from the gates. Why were guards this close to the forest? Two more guards passed her as they headed deeper into the woods. Were they searching for more of the strange plants? Her gut told her no. She glanced at the guy holding the gun on her.

He glared back. "Show me your papers."

Rider stared at him. She recognized him from the gates—he knew who she was. She bit back a retort as she slowly removed her identification from her jacket pocket and held it out to him.

As he perused the documents, Rider studied the guns and Wolf Pack patrols on top of the wall. She had to find Teo. Had someone gotten to him? Was he safe? Because there was no way he'd okayed this.

"Miss, curfew begins tonight at twenty-one hundred hours. No one is to be outside after that time, effective immediately. King's orders."

Rider's mouth slackened. King's orders? Her world tilted, then stabilized. Everything had changed. Why? Rider knew she wouldn't get any answers from the guard so, after grabbing her papers, she ran home. The errands could wait. She needed to inform her father of what was happening.

Throwing open the front door, she yelled, "Dad!"

No answer. Rider jogged from room to room, but her home was empty. Spying the back door to the garden open, she hurried outside. There he was, shovelling the walkway.

He straightened at the sight of her. "Jenna-girl, I thought you'd be longer in the city."

"Something terrible..." Rider couldn't get the words out past the lump forming in her throat.

After setting the shovel against the house, he moved to her, frowning. "What's the matter?"

"There are guns on the walls, and the Wolf Pack are patrolling the forest. There's also a curfew."

Her dad's head jerked. "What?"

"The guns are on top of the wall, pointed at us. You can't miss them. A Wolf Pack guard held a gun on me because I was running to the gates."

Her dad growled. "Are you okay?"

She bit her cheek but her eyes still watered. "Shook me up a bit, that's all. He let me go, but I noticed guards in the forest. Do you think they're searching for more plants?"

What looked like doubt crossed her father's face, and Rider's heart sank. "Let's go see if any of the neighbours have heard anything." As they rounded the corner of the house, a pair of guards, a woman and a man, strode up the front walk. The male officer shoved a paper at Dr. Hood.

"Notice of Curfew. King's Orders. Curfew begins tonight at twenty-one hundred hours."

Rider peered over her dad's shoulder at the piece of paper, which bore the king's seal. Her body quivered. She wanted to tell Teo a thing or two. He'd lied to them.

The paper shook a little in her father's hands. "May I ask why a curfew has been ordered?"

The woman, who had a pronounced overbite, said, "In response to recent security threats, King Teowulf has decided these restrictions are best for everyone. That's all you need to know. Anyone outside their homes after curfew will be arrested. The Wolf Pack is patrolling the forest and surrounding areas to make sure the peace is kept."

"When has the peace never not been kept?" Rider had never heard her father so exasperated.

When the male guard's jaw tightened, Rider grasped her father's arm. "Come on, Dad." She tugged him to the house. *Now is not the time to get into a fight with the Wolf Pack. Although decking Teo felt like a good thing.*

Once inside, they watched from behind the curtains as the guards stood at the end of their walkway, talking. A minute more and they moved on, but the male guard glanced back at their house.

"Dad."

Her father rested a reassuring hand on her shoulder. "The last time I looked, it wasn't against the law to ask a question."

Rider sank onto the couch, pulling her legs under her. "Teo lied to us." She couldn't believe it. She'd trusted him, but he had turned against them. "Do you think they found more evidence against us?"

"I have no idea, Jenna-girl." Her father's tone was grave.

"Do you think something else happened to Teo? I mean, we already know someone tried to poison him. What if they've tried to get to him some other way?" The thought turned her stomach. Why did she always assume the worst of him? She was blaming him when maybe he was in danger.

"I don't know. We need to talk to someone at the palace."

"No one is being allowed in the city. Most Foresters, from what I saw, were turned away or had an escort in." Rider picked at the stitch in the knitted blanket she'd pulled around her. "Do you think the Queen Mother had anything to do with this? Or is this for our protection? Teo might have put a curfew in place if there's a threat to the forest." She knew she was grasping at straws, but couldn't seem to stop.

Her father paced, rubbing his jaw. "It's obvious the Wolves think there's danger, but I'm not sure it's to us. This looks like an obvious attempt to keep us in our place."

"Would another Forester threaten Teo or the palace?" She hated saying the words out loud. "A few were upset here the other night. Even Matrix noticed the tension in the forest."

"I doubt it. All they want is to have a voice—to air their anger and grief. I don't think anyone would act on it. At least no one I know." He sat beside her, pulling her close.

If no one from the forest threatened the Wolves, why did Teo do a one-eighty?

Silence filled the space as they sat with their own thoughts and worries. Finally, Rider straightened. "What should we do?"

"I want to talk to Alarick if he's back. And Dr. Lupine. Did you see anyone you knew at the gates? I'd like to know why they were being turned away."

She remembered seeing a beef farmer there before she turned back. "Mr. Watts was waiting in line at the gates. I was in such a panic to return home, I didn't stick around long enough to see whether he gained entry or not."

Her father glanced at the clock. "It's a place to start. It's just past noon, so we've got a few hours before curfew. They can't arrest us for speaking to one another."

Rider bit her cheek. Under Duko, the Wolf Pack could be real unreasonable brutes.

Had they gone back to that? Because if they had, they would and could find a reason to arrest them. Despite her leaden limbs, Rider stood and held out her hand to her dad. "Let's go see if Mr. Watts has any beef—I feel like stew tonight."

Her dad smiled. "You know, I have a mighty craving for stew too."

Rider was halfway to the door. She shoved worry about Teo aside. They needed information, so that was what she would focus on. As her dad locked their door, she glanced around the area.

"Let's go before they come back. I feel like they're looking for trouble."

Rider grabbed her dad's hand, and they hurried in the direction of the Watts' beef farm, which sat on the edge of the forest in the other direction from the gates, about a fifteen-minute walk from their house. They took lesser-known paths, and soon the red farmhouse came into view. Mr. Watts answered her father's knock.

"Dr. Hood, Rider, what a nice surprise. What can I do for you?"

Her father shook the other man's hand. "Hello, Brian. We wanted to make beef stew for dinner, but we need some beef."

"Come on in."

They followed Mr. Watts into the butcher shop attached to the side of the house. Bile rose in Rider's throat at the smell of raw meat. She breathed through her mouth and wandered around the shop as her father put in his order and paid.

"Anything else?" Mr. Watts smiled.

Her dad held up a finger. "We have a couple of questions."

Mr. Watts pressed his hands to the glass counter of the display case. "Shoot." Rider strode over to where the two men stood. "I saw you in line today at the city gates. They seemed to be turning people away, and I wondered if you got in. Or if you knew why they were refusing people entry."

Mr. Watts blew out a breath. "They let me in because I was delivering meat to the palace. From what I could tell, only specific deliveries were allowed entrance. We all had a Wolf Pack escort too."

"What deliveries?"

Mr. Watts shook his head. "Anything going to the palace was allowed, but security was extremely thick. I didn't even go inside the castle—they sent someone out to get the meat and take it in. That's never happened before." He crossed his arms. "Given the curfew and patrols, it doesn't look like the Wolves trust us anymore. I'm uneasy."

Dr. Hood frowned. "I hope you're wrong about that, but I admit I'm uneasy too." He held up the package of beef. "Thank you for your help. And the beef."

Mr. Watts nodded. "Anytime. You take care now."

He and her father exchanged a look before Rider followed her dad out of the shop, her mind spinning. "I can probably get into the city with a delivery." They hurried along the forest path, headed home. A brisk north wind blew but the snow had stopped.

Her dad shook his head. "I don't like that idea."

"Why not?"

"I don't want you going in by yourself. I'll go."

She jammed her hands into her coat pockets. "Why don't we both go?"

"Too conspicuous."

That might be true. Better if she went alone. "I make deliveries every day, Dad, and they won't stop a package of medicine from entering the city. Not after the Lupine flu. I can get a message to Dr. Lupine."

Her father rubbed his eyes. "I don't know."

"Dad, I can do this. I'll be careful. Teo and Seth will keep me safe." *I hope.* Unless Teo really had turned on them. She pushed the unwanted thought aside. He wouldn't.

Her father exhaled. "Would you go straight to Dr. Lupine and then back home?"

"No, I have to go to the palace. Teo will explain everything. He's the one with the answers."

"If I agree, and that's not for certain, Mr. Watts said the security at the castle was tight, so how would you get inside?"

"Tomorrow the palace will be open for public tours on the main floor. I can deliver the package and then, on my way home, detour back to the palace. I'll pretend I'm on tour. Since I know my way around, I can sneak away from the group and find Teo."

Her dad pursed his lips. "What if they aren't giving tours because of the threat?"

Rider couldn't even think about that. She *had* to get inside, and this was the best way. "They never close the palace—Teo once told me it's bad PR. It's so heavily guarded and the tours never go near the resident suites, so I don't think they'll stop letting groups go through."

"What if you're recognized? And how will you get away from your escort?"

"I'll wear a disguise—Teo gets away with it all the time. I'll figure out the escort later."

Her dad sighed. "I don't like that plan. Far too much could go wrong."

She couldn't argue with that, so Rider didn't try, only leaned her head on her dad's shoulder. "I think it's worth a try. We need answers. Now."

"Okay, but if you can't find Teo, you get out. Okay?"

"I will. I promise." Rider lifted her head. This had to work. Nothing could stop her from talking to Teo. Only he had the answers she and all the Foresters needed and deserved to get.

Chapter Fifty
Matrix

MATRIX PULLED HIS HOOD low as he trailed after Jenna, who was carrying her courier pack and headed in the direction of the city. The forest paths were deserted since everyone was too afraid to run into the Wolf Pack patrols weaving through the forest on a regular basis, so Matrix had to keep more space between him and the girl than he wanted.

Where was Jenna headed? It looked as if the package contained medicine, but why did he get the feeling that wasn't all she was up to? Guess he was going to find out. Fast. There was no way he wasn't going to be spotted—she was too smart to let herself be tailed.

"Jenna, wait up." He jogged to catch up to her.

"What do you want? I don't have time to chat." She picked up her pace.

"I think you may want to hear what I have to say."

She snorted, keeping her pace. "I doubt it."

"I know a way into the city without going through the gates, so you can avoid an escort." It was a risky guess, but Matrix was betting on the fact that her business involved more than delivering medicine.

Jenna glanced at him sharply. "They closed all the openings."

"They missed one. I've used it."

Finally, she stopped. "How did you, who are not from here, find it?"

"I, uh, a family friend once told me about it, and one day I was exploring the city and checked it out. It's still open." No need to go into details like the fact his ancestors used to explore the city and knew it like the backs of their hands. Or that they had drawn maps of any secret tunnels and entrances. *Please buy my story*. Heart hammering, Matrix held his breath.

"Where is it?"

"I'll show you." No way was he going to tell her. This was his ticket into whatever she was scheming.

"Tell me."

"Come." He veered to the left and off the path. She stood still. He glanced over his shoulder. "Are you coming?"

She huffed but followed him. They jumped fallen dead logs and branches until they came out of the forest at a point beyond the sight of the gates. He quickly led Jenna to a place where the bricks were chipped and pressed a hand against one that was almost gone. His finger felt the catch and he released it. The door popped out slightly. He glanced at this feisty girl, her eyebrows almost to her hairline. A warmth spread through his chest.

"How did your friend find this? I know these woods and wall like the back of my hand, and I wasn't aware of it."

Matrix shrugged. "He was raised nearby, and they used it to avoid the Wolf Pack at the gates. Guess you don't know everything." He tugged the door open enough that they could slip through, then pulled it shut. Jenna was already striding in the direction of the palace. Matrix ran to catch up. No way she was going anywhere without him.

Chapter Fifty-One
Teo

"YOUR MAJESTY, YOU LOOK every inch the king."

Teo turned to his side, admiring himself in the mirror. He did look good. The sleek charcoal armour fit his body like a glove. It wasn't bulky or awkward to move in. Kudos to Sirhaan; his company did know how to make body armour.

"Sire, you look imposing and authoritative. You will command respect." Sirhaan smiled.

Exactly what Teo wanted to hear. He was king, and he deserved his people's respect. Would his mother treat him like a king instead of a child if he dressed the part? Maybe this would finally show her that he was capable of leading his country. He ran his hands over his chest, liking the feel of the smooth material. "Well done. It looks great, feels like a second skin."

The man pressed his palms together, bowing. "Thank you. I'm happy you like it." His gazed bore into Teo, piercing his new armour, and he shifted his weight.

A knock on the door stopped further conversation. "Your Majesty, I'm sorry to interrupt." Teo's butler sounded grim. "But Sirhaan is wanted downstairs."

Sirhaan offered another slight bow. "If you'll excuse me, Your Majesty?"

Teo waved the man out, then paced to the window and stared out at the activity on the driveway below. Maids and kitchen hands unloaded carts of vegetables while burly guards carried crates of meat into the kitchen. He turned, facing the mirror once again and admiring his reflection. A king, a warrior. A Wolf. All those who had doubted his leadership could shut up.

His butler entered, handing him a note. Teo glanced at the folded paper, recognizing Seth's handwriting. When was the last time he'd seen his brother? Yesterday? The day before? Time ran together. He shook his head, trying to unscramble his brains before flipping the paper open and scanning it. His brother had left to find Alarick the day before. Teo's nostrils flared. Seth had no business going after Alarick, wherever his uncle had gone. He rubbed his throbbing temples. Why couldn't he remember where Alarick was and what he was doing? And why did Seth think he needed to retrieve the man and bring him back?

I am king. I make the decisions.

Teo quickly penned a reply, ordering Seth back to his post at the Wolf Pack. He sealed it with his stamp and handed it to his butler. As the man walked away, his mother peeked into his room.

"Don't you look magnificent!" She clapped her hands together, her smile wide.

"It's good armour."

"You need to listen to your mother more."

Teo snorted. "I bet you couldn't wait to say that."

She grinned. "How are the plans going?"

"Everything's in place. Sirhaan is good with details and his company moves quickly. We are safe from any possible attacks."

"Excellent. I knew you'd see his value eventually." His mother headed for the door but stopped, glancing over her shoulder. "Don't forget about dinner tonight with the dignitaries from the neighbouring clans."

Teo rolled his eyes.

"Teo—"

He held up a hand. "I'll be there."

She eyed him a moment longer, than left, shutting the door behind her.

Teo, restless with an energy he hadn't had in days, strolled to the main floor of the palace. He had a meeting with the General and Sirhaan in a few minutes. Searching his memory, Teo tried to pinpoint what the meeting was about, but his mind couldn't pluck it out of the fog that had taken residence there. He clenched his fists as he walked, taking the long way to the meeting room, past the general public entrance where there seemed to be some sort of commotion. Why they let guests roam the palace on these tours was beyond him. Perhaps he needed to put a stop to that as well. It couldn't be safe.

"King Teo!"

He halted, turning toward the entrance. Dark curls flew as the guards manhandled the young woman who had called out to him. Familiarity poked at his brain. Did he know her? He searched his memory but once again it was out of reach.

"Teo, it's me." She removed large, dark-framed glasses.

His eyes locked with two emerald ones. He stepped closer, hoping for a better look at the girl.

"Your Majesty." Sirhaan appeared beside him. "Is there a problem?"

Teo studied the girl struggling between two Wolf Pack guards. Her face was pale and her eyes as round as balloons. He took a step toward her, but before he could close the distance, a sharp pain lanced his head and he reared back.

"Not a good idea, Your Majesty. It's only a Forester causing trouble. Let the Wolf Pack escort her back to the tree huggers. She should never have gotten onto the grounds. Your guards will deal with it. It's not your problem."

"Not my problem," Teo intoned.

"Exactly." Sirhaan motioned for Teo to follow him. Flinging a final glance over his shoulder at the girl, he trudged in the opposite direction, after Sirhaan.

When he turned a corner, Sirhaan had stopped to wait for him. He inclined his head toward the entrance as Teo reached him. "Foresters shouldn't be allowed in the city considering the threat they pose. You need to make that decree."

"She didn't look like she could hurt anyone."

Sirhaan wagged his finger. "That's why they are so dangerous. They look innocent and pure, but they are evil, manipulating Wolves to get what they want."

Again, a memory niggled his brain—Teo was forgetting something.

"Remember the assassin Ethan, Your Majesty. Don't forget he tried to kill you."

Teo's face heated and his heart raced. *How dare the Foresters try to remove me from my throne.* "I think we need to make them suffer a bit, don't you?" he spat out.

Sirhaan licked his lips. "I absolutely agree, Your Majesty. What did you have in mind?"

"A complete ban from the city could work."

Sirhaan tapped his chin. "Hm, yes, in the short term, perhaps. But I think you want something with more punch."

"What are you thinking?"

"Perhaps hit them in their pocket books. Why not raise their taxes to, say, ten percent?"

"Their taxes are only five percent at the moment. That's doubling it."

"You want the lesson to count, right?"

"I see your point. After the meeting, we'll arrange it with the treasurer. He's been wanting this for months." Teo shared a smile with Sirhaan, but he tugged on the sleeve of his armour, a pair of green eyes following him in his mind's eye.

Chapter Fifty-Two
Rider

⸻ ◈ ⸻

*H*E'S GONNA LEAVE BRUISES.

The guard's crushing grip around her upper arm made it hard to focus on where Rider was putting her feet as he dragged her along beside him. After struggling with the man most of the way from the palace to the guard house at the gates, exhaustion threatened to weaken Rider's resolve. She'd managed to get inside the palace with the help of Matrix and had stuck close to his side until they were on the tour. Thankfully, two newbie Wolf Pack guards who didn't appear to be older than twelve were tasked with giving the tours. Rider didn't know them, and they didn't know who she was. At least that was what she'd thought until another set of guards approached and apprehended her. Apparently, glasses didn't work as well for her as a disguise as they did for Teo.

At the thought of him, Rider's chest hitched. *Don't go there.* She had to focus on freeing herself because Matrix was a vapour in the wind, having disappeared into the crowd when the guards grabbed her. Yeah, he was no friend of hers. Then she'd spotted Teo and stupidly called to him. He had stood and stared as if she were some kind of freak. As if he had no idea who she was. Heat crawled up her neck at the memory.

The pressure of the guard's fingers digging in brought Rider back to the present. The gates loomed ahead. *If I'm thrown out of the city, how will I get back in?* Panic clawed at her throat, cutting off her airflow. Could she find the door in the wall Matrix had shown her? What if she couldn't locate it? She yanked her arm, but the man tightened the vise as he pulled her up short beside him in front of the officer's house. Her captor spoke to an older gentleman who looked to be a senior officer.

Rider strained to hear what they were saying. If she was expelled from the city, she didn't know what she would do. How had this plan gone sideways so fast? She clicked through the events at the palace. The second set of guards had approached her as if they'd been tipped off, but who knew she was there? She'd told no one.

As soon as the senior guard stalked away, Steel Fingers dragged her into the building, marching her into an empty room at the end of the hall. As a last insult, he shoved her onto a wooden chair so hard, Rider almost toppled over. At least he'd let her arm go. She rubbed at the tender spot as he took up a post by the closed door. She glared at him. She'd done nothing wrong. Why were they holding her? Before she could even venture a guess, the door flew open and Seth and Alarick strode in. Rider's eyes widened.

The guard stood at attention, saluting Seth.

Teo's brother's face was bright red, his mouth taut. "What is going on here?"

The guard's cheeks pinked up as he stammered, "She... uh, she caused a ruckus at the palace. We'd been warned to watch for someone matching her description attempting to breach security, so when she tried to break in, we were told to escort her from the city."

"Who gave these orders?"

"They came from the king's office, sir."

Rider slammed her palm on the table. "No!"

Seth spared her a brief glance before returning his attention to the guard. "Let me get this straight, the king ordered a no admittance to Jenna Hood?"

"Yes, sir."

"Then thank you for doing your duty. I will take it from here. You're excused." The guard glanced between Rider and Seth, then saluted once more before leaving the room. All eyes turned to Rider. Seth blew out a breath. "What is going on?"

A fiery pain stung her bicep, and she rubbed it. "That's what we would like to know. All of a sudden, there's a curfew, Wolf Pack is patrolling the forest, and the wall is armed with guns." She listed the concerns off on her fingers. "This isn't what Teo talked about."

"Why were you escorted from the palace?"

Rider scowled. "It's a public tour, anyone can go. And I thought I might be able to see Teo." She sighed. Maybe it hadn't been a stellar idea after all. "It was the only way I could think of to contact him, but the guards stopped me shortly after the tour began." Rider licked her lips and shut her eyes. "Teo was there, he saw me. I called to him, but he just stared at me like he didn't know me. Then he left with the man who was with your mother at the coronation ball."

"Sirhaan." Seth cupped his neck, a line forming between his eyebrows. "Which makes me concerned."

That guy again. Clearly, he was bad news. Had he done something to Teo? Rider clenched her fists. "Why would Teo be with him? I thought he didn't like the guy."

Rider didn't like the look Seth shared with his uncle.

"He doesn't." The prince's tone was ominous.

Alarick spoke for the first time. "Seth, we need to get to the palace and find out what's going on."

"I agree. But if I let Jenna return to the forest, there's a good chance she won't be able to get back into the city."

Rider's lungs constricted. "That can't happen. Teo's in trouble."

Seth touched his uncle's arm. "Can she stay in your apartment in the city?"

Alarick nodded. "I think that's a good idea." He tugged a set of keys from his pocket, removed one from the ring, and held it out to her. "However, you'll need to keep a low profile until we figure out what's going on. Okay?"

Relief surged through Rider. "Where have you been?"

The older gentleman rolled his eyes. "I was on a merry goose chase. I went to find out more about Sirhaan's company and check out his competitors, so we'd have a better understanding of why he was recommending such extreme security measures for the city."

"And?"

"There are no competitors. At least, there are, but in name only. I've been chasing these illusions for the last few days until Seth found me today. I believe Sirhaan set it up that way so anyone who bothered looking would waste a lot of time."

Seth tugged open the door and peered out. "We need to get to the palace and find out what's happening with Teo. We'll drop you off at Uncle's apartment, Jenna. It's on the way."

Alarick offered his arm. "Promise me you will stay put until you hear from us. We don't know if you're in danger or not."

"Teo wouldn't hurt me."

"From the sounds of things, Teo isn't himself. I don't want to take any chances. Don't leave or do anything to draw attention to yourself."

Rider slid her arm through his. She trusted him but still felt like a school kid scolded by the teacher. "Okay."

Seth grabbed a dark jacket off a hook. "Put this over you. We don't want any questions about where we're taking you, especially since the king supposedly ordered you banned." He jammed a hat over her curls and nodded to a back exit. "We'll go out that way."

Rider slipped the jacket on, wondering idly who was going to miss it. It didn't matter if it got her to the apartment without drawing attention. She shoved her curls under the cap, leaving her neck exposed. A chill shivered down her spine as they left the warmth of the building. Although it was the rear exit, Rider felt as if a hundred eyes watched her. She glanced up to see the guns pointing at the forest. The sound of boots hitting cement from above echoed. A signal, perhaps, that trouble was on its way.

Chapter
Fifty-Three
Matrix

MATRIX PACED THE TEN steps across the alley and back, again and again. His gaze darted around the courtyard surrounding the city gates as he searched for Jenna. Where had she gone? He cursed himself for not stepping in at the palace, but he hadn't wanted to call attention to himself or get caught. Instead, he'd slunk into the shadows and then followed her and the guards back here. What he hadn't expected was the appearance of the king's brother and an older gentleman, Teo's uncle, presumably. Neither was supposed to be in the city, according to Sirhaan. Although the king had sent his advisor away, it had worked in their favour. Of course, Sirhaan was taking all the credit. Thirty minutes later, Jenna and the two men were still in the building.

Matrix ran his fingers through his hair, pulling at it. He'd lost her, given her over to Seth like a wrapped present tied with a bow. Matrix had to get her back. If she returned to the palace, Sirhaan would kill her. He had no doubt. She posed a risk to the plan, as she would overturn all their hard work if she could get through to Teo. Did love actually win the day? Matrix didn't believe it, but if Jenna got too close, she knew enough about plants and drugs to figure out what was going on. And she'd no doubt be able to help Teo get out of the drug's stupor. Sirhaan would never take that chance.

Matrix checked his watch, unable to stand still. He stepped out of the shadows of the alleyway and scouted the area. A path emerged from behind the buildings on the far side of the guard house, and he banged a fist into his palm. Jogging down the road, he peered behind the buildings. No one was there. He glanced up the road in the opposite direction he'd come, squinting to see better. In the distance, he could barely make out three figures walking away from him. Matrix debated whether to follow or wait to see if Jenna would come out of the building. After a moment, he set out after the three, hoping he'd made the right choice.

Chapter Fifty-Four

Teo

TEO BARELY ACKNOWLEDGED THE staff, who curtsied or bowed as he and Sirhaan strode through the hall. The red carpet beneath their feet cushioned their steps. Chandeliers and wallpaper, champagne in colour, created a golden glow Teo had never liked. The designers had told him people expected opulence in a palace, and since this particular space was part of the public tour, it had been left to its gaudiness. Today, Teo wasn't sure what it was he'd disliked. The richness of the furnishings displayed money, which equalled power. Perhaps his offices and suites needed a makeover too. His thoughts drifted to the commotion from before as they passed where the girl had been apprehended. The Wolf Pack had shut down the tours for the day after that.

"Who was that girl?"

Sirhaan waved his hand in a dismissive gesture. "Some lovesick fangirl. Don't give her another thought."

Was she just a fangirl? Her face had sparked a feeling of déjà vu. Teo's steps slowed as he racked his brain for a memory.

"Are you okay, Your Majesty?"

Teo huffed out a breath. "I'm fine—continue with your report." Thinking too hard gave him a headache, anyway.

As Sirhaan boasted about the distribution of the weapons throughout the kingdom, the memory of those eyes the colour of moss in the spring drowned out the words. Teo glanced behind him to the spot where she'd stood. Suddenly, a sharp pain ripped through his head, causing his knees to buckle. Sirhaan's large hand grabbed Teo's elbow to steady him before Teo collapsed to the floor. The man nodded to the guards who were following them. "His Majesty tripped. He's still getting used to the new boots." He chuckled softly, the pretense of joviality belying the fact that he still gripped Teo's arm like a clamp.

Sirhaan leaned in close to Teo's ear. "Your Majesty, the girl is a nobody. Forget her. Now let's move along."

Teo pawed at Sirhaan's fingers, trying to remove them. The pain in his head intensified, and black spots appeared in his vision. He sucked in air as voices increased around him. He stumbled.

A guard reached for him. "Your Majesty, are you... hospital..."

Teo couldn't pay attention to those around him as his eyes went in and out of focus.

"No... perhaps it's a migraine. I'll get him to his room." Teo heard Sirhaan speak but couldn't bring himself to respond.

Teo's stomach lurched as Sirhaan practically dragged him to his rooms, where the man shoved him onto his bed.

"Get some rest, Your Majesty. I'll take over for now." Sirhaan's voice sounded as if he was speaking under water. Then it faded altogether.

Teo was out cold before the door shut.

Moaning, Teo rolled onto his back. The armour he wore was stiff, and a corner of it dug into his neck. He opened one eye, only to shut it as the light from the window pierced his brain like a lightning bolt.

"Teo, wake up!" Someone clapped their hands near his ear.

Jolting, Teo swung an arm at the voice. "Go away."

Cold water dribbled down his face. Teo crawled to the far side of the bed, sputtering. "What do you think you're doing?" His brother's face came into focus. Teo was going to kill him.

Seth flicked more water into his face. "We need you conscious."

Teo threw a pillow at Seth before swiping at the water on his cheeks. Miraculously, his head wasn't pounding. "What do you want?" Gingerly, Teo swung his legs over the edge of the bed. Still no steel band feeling around his skull. His spirits lifted.

"Why are you sleeping in the middle of the day? You didn't take more of that medicine, did you?" Seth's voice was incredulous. *Medicine?* "Of course not." Teo rubbed his hand over his damp hair. "Pain in my head. I couldn't even stand up. Where were you again?"

"You don't remember? I went to find Alarick."

Only a blank void filled his mind. Teo wanted to crawl back under the covers. Nothing made sense.

Seth muttered under his breath, which did nothing to make Teo feel more at ease. That and the fact that not only didn't he remember where Seth had gone, but who was Alarick? He kept that question to himself.

"Teo, you should see a doctor. You don't look good." An older gentleman Teo hadn't noticed earlier stepped closer to the bed.

Should Teo know him? By the looks on his brother's and the man's faces, he should. Teo's heart crashed against his chest. What was going on? "I'll be fine. I don't need a doctor. It's a migraine. That's all." He had to get these people out of his room. He needed time to think and figure out what was happening to him. What if his brother and mother took his crown away because they thought him unfit and mentally unstable?

"Uncle Alarick, speak some sense into him." So, Alarick was his uncle. How did Teo not recognize him? Panic roared through his chest, threatening to let loose in a meltdown. He dug his fingers into the sides of the mattress.

"Teo, a doctor's visit would be wise." The man studied Teo, his gaze boring into him until Teo felt as though he could see into his soul. "You might still have poison in your system that's affecting your head."

Teo blinked. *Poison?* "I'm fine. Like I said, I don't need a doctor." All he needed was to be alone, to figure out if he was going crazy.

"Where is Mother?" Seth grabbed the bedpost.

Teo swallowed. Was he supposed to know? "I-I don't know."

Seth leaned closer to Teo, studying his features. "What's the last thing you do remember? And what are you wearing?"

Teo stood up and ran a hand over the smooth body armour covering his chest. "Armour by Sirhaan's company. It's comfortable—fits like a skin." Until one slept in it. Now it was decidedly uncomfortable. Teo avoided answering the question about what he did remember because it wasn't much.

"Why are you wearing his armour? Jenna said there are forest patrols and curfews in place. All your orders. What are you doing? This isn't what we talked about." Seth's nostrils flared.

Teo furrowed his brow. *Jenna.* Did he know a Jenna? Was she Seth's girlfriend? Maybe. Because surely he'd remember her if she was important? Right?

"Sirhaan felt it was a good idea, considering Ethan, and..." What else? Why had it seemed like a good idea?

A pulse beat in Seth's neck. "Since when are we listening to Sirhaan?"

Teo stood, pressing the backs of his knees into the mattress so he didn't lose his balance. It was important to show strength, not weakness. The floor heaved under him before righting itself. What were they talking about again?

As if reading his mind, Seth repeated his question.

Show strength. No one questioned the king. "Since I said so. I'm the king. I make the rules. This conversation is over." He strode to the bathroom and closed the door behind him, thankful he hadn't tripped. After splashing cold water on his face, he stared at his image in the mirror. His hair stood on end, and his skin was pale as a winter rabbit.

Jenna. Who was she? His mind was hazy; he could see shadows, but when he reached for them, they vanished. His thumped his fist against the sink. *Why can't I remember?*

Chapter Fifty-Five
Rider

T HE STREET WAS EMPTY—IF she'd been on her bike, she could have done wheelies. But she wasn't on her bike. Rider exhaled against the large front window of Alarick's apartment, fogging it. She drew a happy face, then crossed it out. There was nothing happy about what was happening in this city or the forest. Seth and Alarick should have been back by now. The road outside remained empty, even though she willed the men to appear. A sharp pain tore through her thumb as she bit too far on the nail, and she rubbed it against her shirt.

Finally, two figures appeared on the street, and she flung open the door to the apartment. The men hurried up the steps into the foyer.

"Well?" The word was out before they'd even closed the door. "Did you see Teo?"

Seth turned the deadbolt. "You shouldn't be opening the door."

Rider suppressed the desire to scream. Seth and his uncle strode into the front room, Rider practically tripping on their heels. They didn't take off their coats. What did that mean?

"Would either of you please tell me what happened?"

Seth unwound the scarf from his neck. "Teo is definitely not himself."

Rider waited for him to say more but he didn't.

"What do you mean?" she prodded.

"He was confused. Forgetful. He didn't remember that I went to find Uncle Alarick." Seth stared at his boots, which had made a wet mess on the floor.

"What aren't you telling me?" Rider bounced her foot.

"He didn't know who you were."

Rider gaped at him. "What?"

Seth tossed the scarf on the small couch. "He was in bed with a migraine when we arrived. He looked haggard, like he did before, when he was taking the medicine Sirhaan gave him."

"You think Sirhaan is poisoning him again?"

Seth pursed his lips. "Yes. No. I don't know. We've been watchful, so I'm not sure how he slipped it by us if he is poisoning Teo."

Alarick frowned. "It looked to be more than poison. To erase someone's memories requires high-tech meds. Perhaps a bioweapon of some sort."

Rider's heart beat wildly like an animal caged against its will.

Seth picked up Rider's coat that she'd tossed on a chair when she'd arrived earlier. He handed it to her. "Will you come to the palace? I want to study Teo's reaction to you. Maybe it was only the aftereffects of the migraine that made him fuzzy."

Rider snatched the jacket and jammed her arm through an arm hole, but it was the wrong one. She yanked her arm out and then tried again. After managing to pull it on, she zipped it up. "Let's go." She had to see Teo. He'd know her when he laid eyes on her. Of course he would.

Alarick held up his hand. "Whoa. Let's back up a bit. We can't go charging in there without some kind of plan, especially since you were banned from entering." He lifted an eyebrow, his glance directed at her. "If Sirhaan is involved, we need to be careful. He's a liar and a manipulator, and he excels at both."

Seth faced his uncle. "What's the plan then?"

"Can we sneak Jenna in? We don't want Teo seeing her when Sirhaan is around because Teo might act differently if Sirhaan is controlling him. Someone knew Jenna was there this afternoon because they tipped off the Wolf Pack. We don't want a repeat of that."

Seth tapped his chin. "I'll get my butler. He's trustworthy. If Teo doesn't recognize her, we'll pretend she's my girlfriend, and I'll hand her off to James, who'll make sure she gets back here."

"That might work. Go now so you have time to get James on board before Jenna and I arrive. I'll escort Jenna to the palace through the tunnels. Bring Teo to your quarters."

Was that surprise that crossed Seth's face?

"You think you and your brothers were the only ones who knew about the tunnels?" His uncle shook his head in what looked like disbelief.

Rider didn't bother to question what they were talking about because what if Teo didn't recognize her? She twisted her hair into a knot, then let it fall loose again.

Seth laid a hand on her shoulder. "Give me a half hour head start, then come with Uncle Alarick." He hesitated as if weighing his words. "Don't take it personally if Teo doesn't know you. You'll see he's not himself."

She nodded but couldn't respond. The seriousness of Seth's face twisted her stomach.

Seth let himself out.

Uncle Alarick went into the kitchen, calling over his shoulder, "Would you like some tea? I'm in need of a cup myself."

What? No, she did not want tea right now. She wanted to run to the palace and grab Teo, make sure he was okay. Rider trailed after Alarick. "Uh…"

The man filled the kettle before turning on the gas and setting the kettle over the burner. "It will calm you."

"I guess I could use a cup." Rider was not calm. She pulled off her coat and hung it on the back of her chair. "What are your thoughts?" Teo's uncle was one of the wisest people she knew, outside of her dad.

He pulled two mugs from the cupboard. "I'm not positive, but I think Sirhaan is using the bioweapon on Teo."

All the air left the room. "What makes you think that?"

"Do you remember talking about poison when we met with Teo? We mentioned the bioweapons, and one had the ability to change moods?"

Yes, she remembered that scary information. Rider nodded.

"There's also one that can erase memories. I think Teo's being subjected to a number of these drugs."

"I thought they were weapons, not drugs."

"They are weapons in drug form."

An icy chill ran down Rider's spine. "That's scary. How do you know this?"

The kettle hissed and Alarick shut it off. Once he'd poured the hot water in the cups, he handed one to Rider and said, "I learned about these weapons when I researched and visited Sirhaan's factories. I'm sure what I saw in a file was there by mistake, since it contained trial data on prisoners. What I'm seeing with Teo is eerily echoing what I read. Once I saw the file, I got curious and sneaked around." He pulled his tea bag out, placing it on a plate.

"You investigated them."

"A little. That was my job, after all, to know what we were getting into."

"But you said it was a wild goose chase."

"In respect to finding anything about Sirhaan, it was, but not when it came to discovering information on these bioweapons."

Rider blew on her hot drink. "So, you didn't get what you went for, but you ended up getting information that we need now."

"I think so."

They sat in silence, finishing their tea. Finally, Alarick placed his cup in the sink. "We should get going. Seth will be at the palace by now and has hopefully briefed his butler, James." He took Rider's cup and set it in the sink as well.

Rider slipped on the bulky coat and hat and then followed Alarick out the door. They set off for the palace and hopefully some answers.

It always amazed Rider that the family entrance to the palace was easily missed because it was so ordinary. As she followed Teo's uncle, she wondered how many people passed that door every day with no knowledge of where it led. Wolf Pack guarded it like they did any other door. As she was with Alarick, she slipped inside unimpeded.

He hustled along the halls until he reached the double doors that led to Seth's suites. After unlocking the door, Alarick ushered Rider into the living area. She'd never been in Seth's rooms before, but she was surprised by Seth's obvious good taste in furniture and décor. Large comfortable couches and chairs filled the room, along with mahogany side tables. Prints of every season hung on the walls, along with a gorgeous tapestry depicting what looked like the Howell family tree.

Rider slipped off her coat, and before she could do anything with it, a butler appeared and took it from her. James? He smiled warmly. Nodding her thanks, Rider sat and then immediately jumped to her feet. She couldn't sit still. Shaking her hands, she paced in front of the leather couch. Alarick sat calmly on one of the wingback chairs, his arm draped along the padded arm. How could he be so cool and collected?

The door opened and Seth walked in, followed by another man. Rider did a double take when she realized it was Teo. Had she been on the street, Rider wouldn't have recognized him with his pale complexion and the dark rings around his eyes, which were almost solid black orbs. *Is that armour he's wearing?* Her mouth dropped open a little before she clamped it shut. This was worse than she'd imagined.

Teo scowled at his brother. "Why am I here?"

Seth gestured to Rider. "Do you know her?"

Teo flicked a glance over her before facing his brother. "Should I? Another of your girlfriends?"

"You don't know her?"

Teo blew out a huff. "No, I don't. Why would you think I do?"

Eyes burning, Rider clenched her jaw to keep from crying. He wasn't himself—but his dismissal and rejection still hurt.

Alarick stood. "Let me introduce you then. King Teo, this is Jenna."

Teo's eyes locked with hers. Something flickered across his face but was quickly replaced by narrowed eyes.

Rider curtsied. "Your Majesty," she croaked.

Teo nodded curtly at her and then faced his brother, ignoring Rider. "Is that all? I have *important* business to attend to." He turned on his heel before Seth could respond, shutting the door with a sharp click. Rider flinched.

She wouldn't have believed it if she hadn't witnessed it. He had no clue who she was, and he didn't care. Only three days ago, he'd kissed her and held her close. How could he not remember that? She blew out a shaky breath.

"I'm sorry, Jenna. I was hoping that would go differently." Seth rested his hand on her forearm, giving it a gentle squeeze.

Alarick sat back in his chair. "I guess we have our answer. Although there was an instant there where I thought he was trying to place you."

Rider had too, but that was probably their imaginations. They saw what they wanted to.

Seth poured himself a glass of water from a pitcher on a side table and took a couple of swigs. "I saw that too. He's a victim of these bioweapons, I'm positive. Deep down, though, I think there's a trace of him trying to get out. It gives me hope."

Rider didn't feel as optimistic. "How much do you know about these bioweapons? Is the damage permanent to Teo's memory?" *No. No. No.*

Alarick propped his elbows on his thighs. "I don't know. I never got close enough to anyone they've been used on to find out, and the reports I saw didn't say. When they realized I'd come across confidential information, they shut me out, and I was no longer welcome. Seth arrived just in time because my investigation was over and I suspect I was in danger."

Seth poured more water before taking the chair next to his uncle. "I'm going to kill Sirhaan."

Alarick shook his head. "Not before we find out how to reverse the effects of the bioweapon."

"What exactly *is* the weapon?" Rider sat in one of the large chairs, curling her legs under her.

"Good question. In my research, I found several different forms. Like the serum given earlier to Teo or in pill form." Teo's uncle hesitated, "I found evidence of a serum carrying something that is injected into the body so that the markers injected can be controlled and manipulated by a remote. A way to control a person's actions." Alarick grimaced.

Rider wiped her sweaty palms on her jeans. "Do you think that's what happening to Teo?"

Alarick cradled his head in his palms before looking up. "I hope not, but it might explain some of his radical behaviour, like the curfew and arming the wall."

Seth stared at the ceiling as if answers might be written there. "How can we use your knowledge, knowledge we're not supposed to have, to our advantage? Do you think the people in Sirhaan's factories reported you to him?"

"I have no doubt they did, but they didn't know the extent of what I'd found. Just that I know they have bioweapons."

"We can use this info against Sirhaan." Her blood pounded through her veins. "We need a plan."

Seth and his uncle spoke at the same time. "Exactly."

Alarick nodded. "What we really need is your father."

Chapter Fifty-Six
Matrix

⬦

THE NAILS OF MATRIX'S fingers dug into his palms as he squeezed them tighter. Scouring the palace grounds, his jaw tensed, even as he detected nothing. Cursing under his breath, he scanned the ground again. Why had he deserted Jenna when the guards approached her? Idiot. Now he was out in the cold. Literally and metaphorically. He'd lost Jenna's trail when she left the guard house with Seth and the older man. Not wanting to follow too closely, Matrix had left too much space between himself and the trio, losing them on the busy city streets.

I'm going to kill Sirhaan. The man was nowhere to be found, and Matrix needed a way back into the palace. The tours had been cancelled for the day, probably due to Jenna's presence earlier.

Matrix kicked a stone, watching as it bounced into the street. How stupid he'd been. Sirhaan's actions over the last few weeks—ordering and having the weapons delivered, killing Ethan—had all been done without Matrix's knowledge. *He's shutting me out.* A roar built in his ears as he stood, doing nothing. He flexed his hands. Was his uncle going to steal the throne from even his own family?

Two Wolf Pack marched nearby, so Matrix hid behind a tourist map he'd picked up at the castle. Stay or go? The afternoon was waning, but his gut told him to stick around. Then a miracle happened. A vehicle glided out the palace gates, and Matrix caught a glimpse of Jenna and the king's uncle inside it before they turned onto the street. Ducking behind a group of tourists, he watched as the car drove toward the city gates. He'd bet they were going to the forest. However, Matrix needed to deal with his uncle first. No way was Matrix going to be shut out of his own mission. His hand fisted again as he thought about how badly he'd like to correct Sirhaan's assumptions that he could continue to keep Matrix in the dark.

Chapter Fifty-Seven

Teo

THE WORDS ON THE page in front of Teo blurred as though someone had spilled water on them. He blinked once, twice, but they still swam in front of him. He ran a finger between the collar of his armour and his throat. Why was his office so warm? He cleared his throat, stalling. He couldn't read the words, but he didn't want Sirhaan to know that. Show no weakness. Slapping the paper with his palm, he asked Sirhaan, "Where did you get this?" Deflect. Yes, that was good.

Sirhaan spread his hands on Teo's desk, leaning in. "I can't reveal the source, Your Majesty, as I'm sure you understand—they fear for their lives. I assure you they are trustworthy and it's a valid claim."

Teo jabbed his finger at the page. "Explain it to me."

Sirhaan eyed him. "Certainly. The Foresters have been growing illegal plants, probably to poison their enemy—you, the Wolves—or make bioweapons to use against us."

Teo frowned. What was wrong with that statement? It seemed off, but the Foresters *were* their enemies. Weren't they? "How did your *source* come up with this explanation?"

"He overheard a conversation between a farmer and the pharmacist, Dr. Hood."

Teo rubbed his eyes, which felt like sandpaper. Was the man telling him the truth? Didn't the Hood guy work for the Crown? He had a vague recollection of that name... Teo leaned closer and squinted at the paper, but to no use. He growled before a blinding pain ripped through his temples and he jerked back with a gasp.

"This is the truth. We need to act on it now. Arrest Dr. Hood and whoever else might be growing those plants. The Wolf Pack need to seize control of the forest. It's only a matter of time before we are under attack."

As the pain receded, Teo's mind cleared. He breathed deeply. Sirhaan was right. Wolf Kingdom couldn't trust the Foresters, who were neither their friends nor their allies. How could he have been such a fool to believe the lie that they were? His father had warned him to beware of the Foresters. They didn't mix with Wolves. Ever.

Teo rubbed his temples in the tender area. "I'm ordering an arrest warrant for Hood and the farmers suspected of growing these plants. We'll send in the Wolf Pack to search and occupy the forest."

"I've already had the warrants made up. Just need your seal." Sirhaan placed the order in front of Teo. He handed the stamp to Teo and pointed to where he needed to put the king's seal. "You're very wise, Your Majesty." Teo puffed his chest out at the praise. He stamped the papers, then Sirhaan snatched them up. "I'll take these to General Scar. You look exhausted. Why don't you rest a bit?"

Rest, yes, that was what Teo needed. He watched the man leave, a shiver shimmying down his spine. Teo was forgetting something, he felt sure of it. Hood. The arrest. *Who was Dr. Hood again?* The answer lay beyond his grasp, and trying to grab hold of the elusive memory exhausted Teo. He closed his eyes and, within minutes, blackness overtook him.

Teo jerked upright, wincing as his muscles protested sleeping in a chair. Massaging his neck, Teo eyed Seth, who stood on the other side of the desk, frowning. "Have a nice nap?" his brother snapped.

"I don't like your tone. What are you doing here?"

"You need to come with me." Seth stalked out of Teo's office.

Teo frowned. He didn't have to do anything his brother said. Teo was king and it was best Seth remember that.

His brother grasped the front of his shirt with both hands and hauled him up from the chair.

"What are you doing?" Teo kicked at his brother, but the headaches and pain had weakened him.

"You're coming with me." Seth held Teo's arm in an iron grip as he dragged him down the hallway. Teo resisted, but again Seth overpowered him, yanking Teo into his own quarters where their mother sat on a navy leather sofa that seemed to swallow her petite frame.

Seth grabbed a piece of paper off the table in the centre of the room and shoved it into Teo's chest. Teo caught a glimpse of the king's official seal just before Seth began yelling. "What are you doing? Now we're going to occupy the forest and you're arresting Dr. Hood? Have you gone mad?"

Teo's nostrils flared as he pushed the paper and Seth's hand away. "How dare you speak to me that way? The forest is making bioweapons to use against us, and Dr. Hood is leading the charge."

"Lies. Who is telling you these lies?" Spittle flew out of Seth's mouth. Teo had never seen him this angry.

His mother sighed and pinched the bridge of her nose. "They aren't lies, Seth. Sirhaan is being proactive. We need to keep an eye on the forest." She smoothed her hands over her black skirt before clasping them in her lap. "But attacking the forest does seem a bit extreme at the moment."

Seth crumpled the arrest warrant and tossed it onto the floor before picking up an empty glass from Teo's desk and throwing it against the wall, shattering it. "When did Sirhaan become the king's adviser? Isn't that what Uncle Alarick is for? Or General Scar? Or me?" His voice shook on the last word.

Whoa. "They are planning to attack Wolf City. Sirhaan sees this. Are you blind?" Teo grabbed the back of a tall chair. "Sirhaan is knowledgeable about weapons, and he supports my decisions—unlike my own family." The room was swaying, causing his stomach to pitch. He wiped the sweat from his upper lip.

His mother studied him. "We do support you, Teo. I'm on your side, and your brother is as worried as I am." She tilted her head. "Are you okay?"

"I'm fine, Mother."

She glanced at Seth, then returned her attention to Teo. "Although I agree Sirhaan is knowledgeable, Seth has a point too. Using force against the forest is an impulsive and aggressive move. Sirhaan's weapons are meant to keep us safe, not attack parts of our own kingdom, especially when we have no evidence of treason, only conjecture and theories. We don't want to start a war. The patrols are enough, and if we arrest Hood, it sends a strong enough message."

"We have no evidence other than Sirhaan's word." Seth picked up the crumpled paper from the floor and shook it in Teo's direction. "What proof do you have against Dr. Hood?"

Teo shifted his weight so he could lean against the chair without looking as if he needed help standing. "We have proof. Ethan, for one. He tried to assassinate me. He's good friends with Dr. Hood. It doesn't take too much to put two and two together." He rubbed his forehead with the side of his hand. At least, that's what Sirhaan had told him.

"Do you hear yourself? You didn't believe Ethan was an assassin before—that's why you let him go. You're grasping at the wind, buying these crazy conspiracy theories."

Seth's earnest tone stopped Teo. *Had* he believed in Ethan's innocence? He dug his thumb into his temple, hoping the pressure would help him remember, but his mind was as blank as a piece of white canvas. Admitting he had no memory of what had happened with Ethan was not an option. "Sirhaan has another source of intel."

Seth closed the gap between himself and Teo and shoved a finger into Teo's chest. "A second-hand rumour? That's your proof?"

His mother stood, stepping between her two sons. "Boys, take a breath." She gently pushed Seth away. Turning to Teo, she pointed to the chair. "Sit." He sank onto the cushion, grateful to be off his feet although he'd never admit it.

The Queen Mother straightened a blanket that lay across the back of a nearby chair. "Now, tell us what intel you have."

"A report; it's back in my office." Teo weakly waved his arm in the direction of the door. The thought of walking to his office exhausted him.

Seth stared at him. "Let's go get it."

Teo motioned for them to go ahead, but Seth grabbed him by the wrists, yanking him to his feet. Suddenly energized, Teo shoved Seth away.

"Boys." His mother's sharp tone stopped them in their tracks.

Teo stalked out the door. As they entered his office, the man they were arguing about jumped away from Teo's desk.

Sirhaan bowed. "Your Majesty…" he stopped, apparently noticing his mother and brother who had followed him into the room.

Seth lunged toward Sirhaan, but his mother grabbed his arm. Although he shook her off, he stayed where he was, glaring at Sirhaan. "You can't simply waltz into the king's office."

"The door was wide open. I left some sensitive papers here and I was checking—"

"I gave him access." Teo scowled at his brother.

Their mother's furrowed brow smoothed out, replaced by a sweet smile. Was she trying to defuse the tense situation? If so, it would take more than that. When she spoke, her voice was calm, soothing. "Sirhaan, just the person we need to speak to. Perhaps you can clear up a disagreement."

"How can I help?"

Seth jabbed his pointer finger against the top of the desk. "Dr. Hood is not, has never been, and will never be, a threat to the Wolves." He glanced sideways at his brother. "Or any Foresters. I can't believe I'm the one defending the Hoods and the forest."

Teo resisted the urge to slug his brother. "We are taking care of our people."

"The Hoods *are* your people," Seth scoffed. "The forest are your people, too. How have you forgotten?"

The words made Teo's brain hurt— he couldn't process them. The Foresters were the enemy.

Sirhaan rescued Teo. "He hasn't forgotten anything significant. Instead, he's remembered exactly whose son he is."

Seth's face paled as he whirled on Teo. "You never wanted to be our father," he whispered.

Teo's heart raced as he wiped away sweat from his brow. Seth was wrong; his father had been a great king, hadn't he? Sirhaan had told him story after story of his father's feats. He looked to his mother for confirmation. The shocked expression on her face confused him.

"All I'm asking is for you to stop and think about this. Don't rush into anything you'll regret later," his brother pleaded. "Wait twenty-four hours before you take any kind of aggressive action. Please."

Sirhaan shook his head. "Absolutely not. We need to—"

"I think that's a wise plan." His mother's voice carried over Sirhaan. "We don't want any unnecessary bloodshed."

The man's eyes narrowed, but he lifted his hands, palms up. "As you wish, Your Royal Highness, but I'm only concerned for you and your family. Failing to act could have dire consequences."

A shadow flickered across his mother's face. "You've put security in place at the gates and here?"

"Of course."

"Then a twenty-four-hour stay should be fine." She strode to the door and tugged it open. "Now, if you'll excuse us, Sirhaan, I need to speak with my sons about a family matter."

"Of course." Scowling, he strode out of the room.

Teo felt as though an elephant sat on his body. All he wanted to do was lie down. *Get it over with.* "What is your business, Mother?"

She poured three glasses of water from a side table, handed one to Teo. "You need to drink water. You look as though you need to hydrate."

Heat filled his cheeks. He ignored the glass. "I'm not five anymore, Mother. I am the king—"

"Then start acting like it." She placed the glass firmly on the desk, water sloshing over its edge.

Rounding the corner, Teo dropped onto the leather chair, leaving the water where it was. He shoved a file out of his way, sending it to the floor. His mother's tone meant business. At least that was one thing he knew without a doubt.

"Explain to me what's going on between you two. Is this a fight over the Hood girl?" Her eyes flashed.

Teo ran a hand over his forehead. "Who is the Hood girl?"

His mother's jaw dropped. "You don't know who Jenna Hood is?"

Teo spread his hands. "It's a big kingdom; why would I know her?"

Seth tapped the armrest of his chair. "See, Mother? Do you believe me now?"

Teo sighed. Who was this Jenna Hood, and why did she matter? Why were they wasting his time? Protecting his kingdom was what mattered. Wasn't Hood the enemy? So why would he know a Jenna Hood?

Seth spoke to his shoes. "He doesn't remember them. It's like they've been wiped from his mind."

The Queen Mother braced her hip against the side of the desk, facing Seth, her back to Teo. "Explain."

"Alarick thinks that Teo has been poisoned again but with a bioweapon this time."

"That's ridiculous." Teo straightened in his chair. He would have jumped out of it if his legs hadn't felt like they were the weight of a punching bag.

"Let your brother talk." His mother shot Teo a heated look over her shoulder.

Seth jumped to his feet. "Alarick found out that Sirhaan's company makes bioweapons, but they keep it hush hush. They make it with a foreign plant that's extremely toxic. We've found evidence of it growing in the forest."

His mother shifted her weight off the desk, straightened. She raised her eyebrows. "And we're trusting Dr. Hood?"

"Yes. Why would he save us only to then kill us?" Seth wandered to a small bookshelf on the far wall, absently picked up the football that sat on top. He studied it for a minute then rolled it between his hands. "This bioweapon has a mood enhancer as well as a memory blocker." He inclined his head toward Teo. "Which would explain why he doesn't remember the Hoods."

His mother's fingers flew to her throat. "You have proof this isn't a Forester?"

"Alarick can tell you exactly what he witnessed at Sirhaan's factories."

Teo frowned. What was the big deal that he didn't recognize this girl? And how far-fetched was that tale about bioweapons?

His mother grabbed a tissue off Teo's desk and mopped up the spilled water. "Teo, surely you remember the Hoods?" Her voice rose an octave.

"No, I don't. Why do you keep asking me about our enemies?"

She tossed the tissue in the garbage. "Where's Alarick?"

Seth returned the football to its place on the shelf before sliding a sideways glance at Teo. "He went to the forest. Along with General Scar."

Teo smacked his palms against the leather of the arm rests. "This is treason!"

Seth stepped to the desk, leaned so close to Teo he could feel his brother's breath. "If helping you is treason, then so be it. You can't even get out of your chair, you're so weak."

His mother contemplated Teo as though assessing the truth of Seth's words. "You do look sick. Can you get up?"

"Of course." Teo would not show weakness.

"Get up then." His mother waited.

Teo stood. The room pitched, and Teo lurched forward. His mother gasped. She made a grab for him, but Seth was faster and caught him before he hit the ground.

"Alarick went to get Dr. Hood." His mother wasn't asking a question.

"Yes. He's the best pharmacist, and he knows about many plants. We want him to do tests on Teo."

His mother inhaled, nodded, her pinched features making her look haggard. "I agree. We need answers. We'll wait in my quarters."

"I'm not being tested." Teo yanked free of his brother, but when the floor threatened to come up to meet him, Seth pushed him back into his chair. Teo swallowed against the bile pushing up his throat. He'd rest a little bit and then he'd go search out Sirhaan. His eyes drooped. A little rest was all he needed so he could figure this all out. The blackness closed in once again.

Chapter
Fifty-Eight
Rider

FORESTERS GATHERED IN SMALL groups in the front room of Rider's home, whispering and furtively casting glances at the king's uncle and the general of the Wolf Pack, who sat side by side on a small loveseat near the fireplace. They dwarfed the small couch, which any other time would have been comical. A fire burned brightly in the hearth, and with so many people inside, Rider found the temperature uncomfortable.

She glanced around the room, recognizing most of the men and women. Several neighbours had witnessed Rider's arrival with Alarick about twenty minutes ago, followed shortly after by the entrance of General Scar. Alarick had wanted the general's presence for security as well as to update the military leader on what they suspected about Teo.

The neighbours told others, and suddenly there was an impromptu meeting at the Hood home, as her father had graciously ushered everyone in out of the cold. More than a few Foresters were demanding information from him, namely why Wolves from the royal family and military were here in his house. However, Rider had lost track of where her father had disappeared to, and he hadn't yet answered any questions.

Rider shrugged out of her sweater as she weaved among the groups of people. Granny waved from a chair in the corner, near the window. Rider hadn't seen the woman in weeks, so she changed direction and knelt in front of the woman, kissing her cheek. The elderly woman clasped Rider's fingers. "It's so good to see you, sweetie. Don't you worry, it will all work out."

Rider forced a smile. Granny had always hoped the forest and city people would unite and work together. She'd inspired Rider to dream about it too. Now they were facing a possible war. How could the older woman say it would all work out? "I hope so."

The dark looks Rider's neighbours were giving Alarick and General Scar suggested working it out was not their top priority. General Scar sipped tea on the far side of the room. His gaze met Rider's and he lifted his cup to her.

Rider scanned the room. "Where's Dad?" She directed her gaze back to Granny.

"Went to his office to retrieve something."

How long did it take to find whatever it was he was looking for? The people crowded into the house were fidgeting and restless. Before Rider could search for her father, Dr. Hood strode into the room, carrying a canvas bag that he used on house calls. Rider exhaled. Hopefully that meant he was ready to go to the palace.

"I want to assure everyone that General Scar and Alarick are trustworthy. Again, let's not act hastily. We don't want to cause any harm."

"Harm?" One of the farmers who lived across the other end of the forest jabbed his thumb at the guests from the palace. "We're not the ones causing harm. They're threatening to attack us."

General Scar placed his teacup on a side table, then stood. "Folks, we are not attacking you. Yes, we've put in security measures, but those are for everyone's safety."

A few men laughed, although it didn't sound as if they found the general's words humorous. General Scar held up his hands. "We're here to ask Dr. Hood to come to the palace to help us. Why would we do that if we were going to attack?"

"How do we know this isn't a trap for Dr. Hood?" One of the couriers who had worked with Ethan at the truffle farm stepped forward, clutching his hat to his chest.

Alarick stood too and stepped forward. "You'll have to trust us."

At those words, everyone started talking. Dr. Hood waved his hands. "Please. Everyone."

The voices faded as the Foresters focused on her father.

"I trust Alarick and General Scar, so I will go with them and help them as best I can.

Please, I urge you all to keep your heads about you. Obey the curfew and don't antagonize the guards. Give us a chance to figure this out in a peaceful way. We have a reputation as law-abiding citizens; let's not ruin it."

Granny patted Rider's hair. Rider glanced up at the older woman, then scooted aside as Granny slowly stood. "I agree. Let these men figure it out. We are Foresters and we are a proud people, but we are also a peaceful people. Appearances are deceiving, and I don't believe everything is as it should be at the palace. We need to wait and let Dr. Hood and these men," she gestured to the Wolves, "handle it for now."

The neighbours and friends around Rider remained silent for a moment before nodding in agreement. Granny didn't say much, but when she did, people listened.

"Thank you, Granny." Rider slid her arm around the woman's waist, hugging her from the side.

"Your father is going to figure it out. And Teo is a good man." The older woman smiled.

Rider hoped Granny was right on all counts, but she had to admit she wasn't sure about anything anymore.

The small vehicle carrying Rider, her father, Alarick, and the general wasn't going fast enough for Rider's liking. Her stomach rolled whenever she thought of the unknowns that waited for them at the palace. Was this a trap like the courier had suggested? She glanced at the general. No, she didn't believe that. Her father had stated publicly that he trusted them, and he wouldn't have let her come if he thought her safety was in doubt.

And Teo? What would he be like? Worse than before? Her heart squeezed. Her father would help him. Surely, if anyone could figure it out, her dad could.

She glanced around at the small group. General Scar was driving, and Rider sat behind him. She'd noticed earlier that he didn't carry a gun, only a dagger. Did he not want the new weapons?

Alarick was calm. Perhaps handling Duko for decades had made him more resilient in a crisis. *I wouldn't have wanted that kind of training in a million years.*

Her father's fingers closed around her own, sending a warmth through Rider. Her heart slowed to a canter from the gallop it had been beating since leaving the forest. If she was with her father, she was safe. Casting another glance at the leaders around her, Rider decided to trust them. They had only acted in ways that were best for the kingdom, as far as she could tell. The old Teo trusted them, and he'd proven to be a good judge of character.

The wrought iron fence surrounding the palace came into view. General Scar stopped the car, and the four of them got out. Once again, Rider found herself at the Howell family entrance to the palace. Guards approached but General Scar stopped them. "They're cleared to enter on my orders."

The two guards at the door saluted, then stepped aside, although their gazes bored into Rider's back. The four of them hurried up the stairs to the family suites, and General Scar rapped firmly against the wooden door.

"Come in." The Queen Mother's voice was firm.

When they entered, she sat on a love seat, her hands clasped in her lap. Her pale pink blouse and black skirt emphasized the gray streak in her hair. She looked older than the last time Rider had seen her, and her expression was wary.

Seth stood behind her, fingers pressing into the cushioned back of the seat. His face was pale, his lips set in a grim line. *He's already lost one brother.* Rider blinked the thought away, only to spot the subject of it.

Teo slumped in a chair to the right of his family, glowering at the carpeted floor. Despite the black look, his shoulders sagged, and he looked as if he hadn't slept for months. How could a person's features change that fast? The tension in the room was palpable. When Teo lifted his head, his gaze collided with hers, sending a jolt through her. A small gasp left her mouth when he sneered at her, erasing any hope that he was okay.

Had he ever looked at her with such disgust or contempt? Not even in the Forest Business Centre office the day they met. Heat crawled up her neck, but she shook it off, lifting her chin slightly. He wasn't going to treat her as though she was nothing, even if he had lost his memory.

Before she could drop in a curtsy, the Queen Mother said, "Please have a seat. Forget the formalities. I think we're beyond that." She waited until they were settled before nodding at Teo. "King Teo, you remember Dr. Hood and his daughter, Jenna." Before Teo could answer, the Queen Mother continued, "So good to see you both again. Thank you for coming. Would you care for tea?"

"No thank you, Your Majesty," Rider's father replied as he took a seat.

Rider, tongue-tied, shook her head. After Teo's reaction to her, Rider kept her focus on the Queen Mother. How strange that Teo and his mother had switched roles. Just weeks ago, Teo wanted Rider here but his mother did not.

"Alarick, please tell us why you are here with your friends."

Teo snorted at the word *friends*. Rider clasped her hands tightly together to keep from swatting him in the head. At the same time, her eyes burned. *He's sick, remember that.*

Alarick shifted in his chair. "Your Highness, we feel that your life, as well as those of your subjects, has been threatened. We believe that a bioweapon, much like ones I stumbled upon while doing research on Sirhaan's company, is being used against you. Against us all."

For the first time since they'd arrived, Teo spoke. "Do you hear yourselves? You all sound crazy, yet you have the audacity to imply I'm the one who's ill." He swiped at his upper lip, then rubbed his hand on his thigh.

Rider glanced at her dad, who studied the king closely.

Teo's mother sipped her tea, ignoring her son's comments. She placed the cup on the table before addressing the group. "These are serious accusations against Sirhaan. From my perspective, he's only trying to protect us and the throne. Yes, he deals in weapons, but he's never mentioned bioweapons. Now Seth tells me that you found evidence of them at his factories and foreign plants used in the making of the bioweapons have also been found in the forest. Is that correct, Alarick?"

Alarick nodded. "His companies deal in the bioweapons, but it's all behind scenes or the black market. I saw it with my own eyes, although I wasn't supposed to."

The queen glanced between her brother-in-law and Dr. Hood. "I met Sirhaan months ago and invited him to stay here at the palace. He didn't coerce me at all. If you have any evidence that he might be doing something to harm Teo or anyone in the kingdom, I will personally banish him and make sure he never returns, but how do we know the Foresters aren't growing these plants and creating bioweapons?"

Rider hadn't expected Teo's mother to be so open to hearing evidence against Sirhaan. Respect for the woman rose.

Dr. Hood pulled a file out of his bag and handed it to Alarick, who opened it and passed the queen mother a photo. "Foresters are the ones who reported finding the plants. It would take sophisticated technology like that used by Sirhaan's companies to actually make the weapon. We've brought Dr. Hood here today to do some tests. The plant would leave traces in the blood if it's ingested. We'd also ask that Dr. Lupine be allowed to join us."

Teo heaved himself up. "No. There will be no tests." He swayed slightly.

Alarick jumped up, grabbed Teo's arm. "If we're wrong, then you can gloat and tell us you told us so."

Teo sagged against him, and his uncle helped him back into the chair. "I'll be doing more than that." His voice was hoarse, diminishing the threat. The king didn't look as though he could blow a candle out, let alone carry out a violent threat.

Rider stared at him. Who *was* this stranger? Her father spoke up. "We need to take a sample of the king's blood."

"I'm not giving you an ounce of my blood," Teo snarled, baring his teeth.

Alarick lifted the file his sister-in-law had placed on the table and studied the contents. "Here's how I see it. If you give us a sample and it's negative, Sirhaan's in the clear."

Rider bit her lip. If the test was negative, what did that mean for Teo? For the Foresters? Sirhaan had to be guilty. Right?

Teo drummed his thumb on his thigh. "Here's how *I* see it. Dr. Hood is a member of the terrorists who want to take over the city, and giving him my blood will empower him to tell more lies." His tone was harsh.

The Queen Mother winced. "You want to take a blood sample from my son to prove your theory that Sirhaan is behind the unrest and is using Teo as a pawn?" The wariness Rider had seen in her eyes filtered into her words.

"Mother." Seth moved to sit beside her. "We need proof either way."

She glanced at the picture she still held. "How toxic is this plant?"

"Worst case scenario—it can kill." Her father's voice was calm, but Rider's stomach clenched like a boa constrictor suffocating its prey.

The Queen Mother sucked in a breath before glancing at her oldest son. "Is it only blood tests you want to do?"

"For now. It's a place to start. We may need to do other tests, but I assure you they are non-invasive. Only a little time-consuming."

Teo opened his mouth, but his mother shot him a look. "We have nothing to lose, Teo, by agreeing to this. If it's true, it could save your life. If it's all lies, then we proceed with our plans. It's a simple drawing of blood. A few minutes of your time."

Teo pressed his palms to his temples as if his head hurt.

"This may help your headaches. Maybe Dr. Hood can test for that too?" The Queen Mother glanced at Rider's dad, her eyes wide.

"Yes, we can look into that too."

Teo lifted his head, squinting. "Whatever."

The Queen Mother clapped her hands, and Teo flinched. "Let's get going then. We have no time to waste."

A lightness filled Rider's chest. Teo was going to get help.

Her father pulled his bag off the floor next to his chair, where he'd set it when he came in. "Your Highness, I'm going to take a blood sample. We can do it right here if that's okay with you?"

Teo slumped in his seat but nodded, looking sick and dejected.

Her father pulled out a syringe and two vials. "Jenna-girl, can you help me out here?"

Rider took the vials from her dad, avoiding eye contact with Teo. When she did sneak a glance, his dilated pupils met hers. She smiled tentatively, but the only reaction was stony silence.

Her chest tightened. Would her dad be able to help Teo recover his memory, or would she forever be a stranger to him now?

Chapter Fifty-Nine
Matrix

T HE POUNDING WAS LOUD and persistent. Matrix cracked open one eye, wincing at the bright light streaming in the window. *What time is it?* He'd waited at the palace a while, but neither Jenna nor her dad had come out. Matrix had no choice but to return to the forest. He'd decided to rest and figure out his next move. He rolled over and threw the blanket over his head, but the pounding continued and he gave up and crawled out of bed. Rubbing his face, he walked over to the door and pulled it open. Sirhaan stood outside his face red. He shoved Matrix aside and strode into the cabin.

"Make yourself at home." Matrix closed the door.

"I don't care for your sarcasm."

"I don't care for you barging in here, nor do I care to be ignored. I was at the palace earlier and you completely shut me out. I decided to get some sleep, which was quite enjoyable until I was rudely awakened."

Sirhaan picked up the glass of water Matrix had left on the counter. He slugged it back, wincing. "Don't you have anything stronger?" He coughed.

"I didn't invite you here."

"We've got trouble. Dr. Hood, his daughter, and the king's uncle showed up."

Matrix jutted out his chin. "I thought you had the queen mother in your back pocket." Oh, that felt good to throw out there.

Sirhaan clenched his fist. "I think she's more afraid of the headaches and memory loss than her son being assassinated."

Matrix scowled. "I tried to tell you trouble was headed your way, but did you listen?" He glared at the older man. "I think it's time someone else took charge. You can't seem to do your job."

Sirhaan scoffed. "As if you can talk. This is merely a setback."

"Losing control of the king and the queen mother is a setback?"

Sirhaan's features hardened.

"I'm taking over."

His uncle sneered. "You?"

Matrix smiled as he pulled out a needle. "Yes, me. We're doing things my way now. If you're not willing to go along, how 'bout we see how you like your own bioweapon." He waved the needle as he tugged a remote from his jacket pocket.

His uncle stepped back. "You wouldn't."

"If you don't do what I want, then yes, I would. I'm in control now."

Matrix leaned against the doorframe of his small cabin, staring out into the dark night. He wrapped his hands around a cup of coffee, relishing the warmth. Raising the mug to his lips, he sipped. Sirhaan had slunk back to the city only an hour ago. Matrix smiled to himself. It felt good to gain control. His uncle was an incompetent idiot. If only Matrix had realized that sooner.

He turned his thoughts away from his uncle—Matrix had solved that problem. At the sight of the needle and remote, his uncle had been putty in Matrix's hand. Now, if only he could find a solution to his other problem. The starless night did nothing to calm his churning stomach. *Why don't you admit the truth?*

He threw the rest of his coffee onto the snow, staining the pristine white covering. He hadn't expected Jenna Hood to be anything more than a patsy, a pawn to use to get what he wanted, which was control of Wolf Kingdom. Instead, he'd developed a crush. A little crush. Stupid. He could not afford to let a girl derail him from claiming what was rightfully his—the crown. Still... did he dare think it? If he could convince her to come with him and be his partner, they'd make a great team. *She loves Teo.*

Shoving the thought aside, he shut the door to the cold. He'd convince her that the Teo she knew was gone—the bioweapon was no joke. Sirhaan had administered a huge amount to the king over the last few weeks, and there was a good chance the effects were irreversible.

Matrix spat. It didn't matter whether Teo got better or not, the man was weak, a trait Matrix hated. He would make him pay for his weakness and in the process, ensure that there was no way Teo would get the girl.

Chapter Sixty

Teo

THE THROBBING IN TEO's temples did nothing to ease his irritation at everyone in the room. His glance jumped from person to person, landing on his mother and uncle huddled together making plans. Plans he should be included in—if only he could lift himself out of this chair. He tried lifting his leg but barely raised it an inch. His jaw muscles tensed, increasing the throbbing. He tore his gaze from his traitorous mother and let it fall on his brother, who was busy staring at the ceiling. Teo smirked. Everyone was avoiding him as they waited for the results of the blood tests.

All except her. Emerald eyes met his as he shifted his attention to the Hood girl, who sat across the room. A roar started in his head as the blood whooshed through his veins. Was this what it felt like to anticipate an enemy's pounce? Was she his enemy? He didn't know, but he was sure he wouldn't forget someone who looked like her. His family was lying to him. How long had they been betraying him?

Dr. Hood walked into the room, his features mild. He had a very gentle bedside manner and didn't look as though he could hurt a flea. How could the two of them be his enemies? Confusion flooded his mind. None of it made sense.

"Your Majesties, the blood tests have confirmed that the king has indeed been poisoned by a bioweapon that is known to be produced by Sirhaan's company. The bioweapon is largely composed of an extremely toxic, highly controversial plant. You need a permit to grow it in Wolf Kingdom, which to my knowledge no one has been given in the more than seventy years records have been kept." He handed the report to the Queen Mother. "The good news is, the effects can be treated, and it should be possible to fully remove the toxins and other synthetic drugs from the king's system."

His mother's shoulders sagged. Was she relieved or disappointed by the results?

Teo blinked. Poisoned? They'd told him the truth? No, it was another lie. "It's the headaches. I suffer from migraines. There's no poison. He's lying to gain control." Because Sirhaan was helping him against the Foresters, wasn't he?

The pharmacist strode over, lowering himself to sit on the low, square table in front of Teo. He leaned forward to peer into Teo's eyes. "I'm not lying. I don't want control of Wolf Kingdom, but someone does. Sirhaan has been your constant companion for days, I'm told. He has access to the weapon. Think it through."

Teo stared at the man but couldn't process his words. His temples throbbed.

The pharmacist twisted the watch on his wrist. "Your Majesty, I'll have to give you several injections over the next few hours and then daily for about a week. You should start to feel better quickly, including the headaches going away. Let me help you."

Teo lifted his gaze to meet the doctor's. He expected to see hate and hardness but found kindness and concern instead. Could this man really provide relief from the awful, unrelenting headaches and foggy brain? He opened his mouth but couldn't push out words. His hand wouldn't obey his brain's commands when he attempted to move it. Concern passed over Dr. Hood's face.

"What's happening?" Teo's mother sounded frightened.

Dr. Hood's soothing voice floated by. "The bioweapon's wearing off. Sirhaan hasn't been close enough to give him another dose. We need to keep him away from Teo. The weapon is so powerful that once it's on the decline, the body is rendered useless for a while. From what I've read, Teo's aware of his surroundings, but the drug is blocking his brain from sending signals so he can't talk or move." The doctor gripped Teo's forearms. "Your Majesty, is that true? Blink once for yes and twice for no."

Teo blinked once. His mother covered her mouth with her hand. Teo's eyes shifted to the side as Dr. Hood rolled up his sleeve and jabbed a needle into his upper arm. Cold travelled through his veins, chilling him.

Shivers racked Teo's body. Dr. Hood lifted a blanket from the sofa and laid it across Teo. "This is supposed to happen. The meds are targeting the weapons markers or synthetic drugs in your blood. It should stop in a minute or two, as soon as your body adjusts."

Teo sank lower into the chair. Like the girl, this man seemed familiar, but his mind formed only shadows. It made his head hurt trying to understand everything that had happened, so he closed his eyes. He'd figure it out later when he had more energy.

Moonlight streamed through the window, the only source of light in the dark room. Teo yawned, stretching as he sat up. Why was he lying on the couch? *Where am I?* Memories flooded back. A throbbing in his left shoulder reminded him of the injection. He rubbed it as he glanced around recognizing his own suite. Had his brother brought him here? Everyone was gone. He stood up, found his legs were solid, and had started towards the bathroom when he heard a noise from the darkest corner of the room. He slowly turned in that direction. "Who's there?"

"I-I'm sorry. I didn't mean to startle you." The Hood girl's voice was soft, like a caress against his cheek.

Teo shuffled toward the sound of her voice. "What are you doing here?"

In the dull light, she stood, rubbing her hands along her thighs.

"I..." She cleared her throat. "I wanted to make sure you were okay. Dad was going to stay, but I told him I'd take the first watch."

Jenna. The rest was a blank. His family seemed so concerned that he didn't know her. Why was that? Her curly hair was slightly messy. Had she been asleep? He stared for a moment before pointing to the bathroom. "I need some water."

He didn't wait for her reply, just crossed the room and closed the door behind him. Flicking on the light, he grabbed the sides of the sink and leaned forward, staring at his reflection in the mirror. Dark smudges under his eyes, along with his pale skin, made him look like a zombie. His hair was long and mussed up. The mirror wasn't doing him any favours. When was the last time he'd eaten? Teo had no idea, only that he was gaunt.

After turning the faucet on, he splashed cold water on his face and then cupped his hands to catch the liquid and slurp it up like a man who had been trapped in a desert for days. His thirst quenched, Teo dried his face and turned back to the closed door. Maybe she'd left. When he opened the door, though, he spied her sitting on the couch, bent over, her forehead resting on her hands. She'd turned on a dim light so the room had a warm glow to it. Thankfully, it didn't bother his eyes or head.

"I'm fine, you can go."

She straightened. "Uh, my father wants someone here for the night. He's coming in an hour to give you another shot and take watch." She glanced sideways at the door to the suite.

"Let me guess, there's also a guard out there."

She fidgeted with her hands before slipping them under her thighs and shrugging. "We need to protect you from Sirhaan, who has vanished."

"Who's guarding the door?"

"Seth." She spoke the word so softly, Teo had to lean forward to hear it.

Of course his brother was.

"How are you feeling?"

"Like a boulder hit me." He sat in the chair beside the couch, where he now remembered passing out. He was tired and sore, but his headache was a memory, a nightmare. For the first time in a long time, sleep had refreshed him. "But better than I did. Everything is still foggy." He tapped his temple.

"Each shot should make you feel stronger and clear your mind."

"They said I know you."

She stared at the ground. "Yes, we were... friends."

"But you're a Forester. How did we meet?"

A brief lifting of her lips. "In the city. We ran into each other a few times." A small laugh tinkled through the room. He liked the sound and the way it made him feel warm.

"Was it funny?"

"Um... Not exactly. We first met when I had to get new papers and you were working at the FBC. Then later, you stepped into the path of my bike."

That didn't sound like a funny story. "*I* stepped into the path of your bike. *You* ran me over?"

"No, *you* stepped out into the road without even looking and I had nowhere to go to get out of your way."

He pointed to himself. "So, it was *my* fault."

She grinned at him. "Totally."

Sassy. Teo smiled. "I wish I could remember because I get the feeling you're seeing this through a biased lens."

"I wouldn't trust your brain right now. It's not working quite right." Her words stole the joy from the air, and her smile slipped from her lips. "I'm sorry, I didn't mean..."

He ran his hand through his hair, which needed a wash. "No need to apologize."

"My father's medicine will work, and you'll be as good as new." She sounded so sure of herself, of her father.

"Will I get my memories back?"

She lifted a shoulder, let it drop. That wasn't reassuring.

"Some memories are gone, but others are there. People and places have been removed. Is that what the weapon does, selectively remove things from your mind?"

"I think it's part of it, yes."

"Obviously I don't remember you, your father, or much about the forest. Only that Wolves don't trust you."

She snorted, then coughed into her hand as if to cover it up. "It's a mutual feeling. At least, it was. It's not your fault you can't remember."

Teo blew out a breath. He'd failed his people. "I feel like it is. I should have been on my guard. I should have seen it coming."

"How could you? Sirhaan was sly, and he manipulated and fooled everyone, including your mother."

Teo rested his hands on his thighs. "I'm the leader in this kingdom. I should have been more careful." He couldn't remember how Sirhaan had poisoned him, only the pain the man seemed to be able to inflict. In fact, Teo didn't have a lot of memories of the last week or so.

"Being a king doesn't make you invincible. You're as human as the rest of us, even if you come from the Wolf clan."

He wanted to believe her. *I should have seen what Sirhaan was up to. I should have been able to resist the weapon.*

As if she could read his mind, she whispered, "It's a weapon, a powerful one. No one could resist it, at least not on their own. Stop blaming yourself."

"If it's that powerful, then we're all in danger. Every one of us."

A soft knock sounded on the door before Dr. Hood slipped into the room. "Ah, Your Majesty, it's good to see you up and looking more rested. How are you feeling? No nausea or dizziness?"

"No."

Dr. Hood nodded. "Good. Then I'll give you another dose."

The girl stood. "I should be going."

The man pulled a syringe out of his bag. "Make sure Seth escorts you to your room."

"Dad." Her voice raised up a bit.

"He's finished his shift, so I asked him to go with you."

She threw up her hands and stalked to the door.

Teo watched the father-daughter dynamics, mildly amused. *She's a bit of a handful.* As she opened the door, Teo caught a glimpse of his brother, leaning against the wall, waiting for the girl. The door shut behind her, blocking the scene from Teo.

"Is your daughter seeing my brother?"

Dr. Hood paused, the needle in the air. "No. Why do you ask?"

Teo shrugged. "I don't know. Just thought there was a little tension there."

Dr. Hood rolled up Teo's sleeve. "You're reading it wrong. She's interested in someone else."

Teo winced at the prick on his skin. Why was he so sensitive to everything? The pharmacist placed a cotton ball over the injection site. Cold spread through his arm again as the chills overtook him. Teo slumped back on the couch, pulling the blanket up around his shoulders. "W-why is it s-s-o cold?"

"Part of the side-effects."

"I failed chemistry."

Dr. Hood laughed. "That's okay. I didn't, so if you'll trust me, you will be fine."

"I trusted Sirhaan."

The laughter died on Dr. Hood's lips. "As the medicine works and your body rids itself of the weapon, it's my hope you'll regain all your memories. You'll know you can trust me, Jenna, your brother, and uncle. In the meantime, I hope you can use those keen senses and believe that I'm sincere in my quest to help you get better. Get you back to your old self."

Teo studied the man. He wanted all of that too. In the meantime, all he could do was hope the doctor was telling Teo the truth.

Chapter Sixty-One
Rider

L EAVING TEO WITH HER father, Rider walked beside Seth to a suite they'd reserved for her family. For the first time in days, Rider's body felt light, her thoughts hopeful. Her father's medicine was going to work on Teo. It had too. She didn't want to contemplate what would happen if it didn't. If Teo didn't get his memories back. If she became nothing more than another of his subjects. Her father was an excellent pharmacist. She had to trust he would find a solution if this didn't work.

"How is he?" Seth's deep voice brought her back to the present.

"He seems better. Clearer. Still not much memory though."

Seth opened the door to the hallway that housed the guest suites.

"He wasn't irritated or as confused. He willingly spoke to me, and he seemed to remember that he knew me at one time, although he couldn't place when or how." She chewed her thumb nail, then dropped her hand. "Do you think we'll get him back? I mean, this can't be permanent, can it?"

"He'll get there. Give it time." Seth stopped at a large oak door. "This is yours." When he pushed the door open, Rider glimpsed a spacious room, lit by the golden glow of a lamp, welcoming her. Her mouth formed an O. At least two of her bedrooms back home would fit in here.

"I hope everything is to your liking. If you need anything, hit this button." He pointed to a black button on the wall beside the door.

"Thank you. It's beautiful. I can't possibly think I'll need anything else."

"If you do, don't hesitate to ask. My family is indebted to you and your father. My mother is especially grateful and wanted me to convey her appreciation. She will no doubt thank you profusely in person when she can." Seth smiled.

Rider waved off the comment. "Anyone would have done what they could to help."

"Maybe." Seth shrugged. "After the way my father treated you, and now Teo, I'm not so sure you're right." He drove the toe of his boot through the plush, cream-coloured carpet. "I wasn't sure about you and your father at first, but you've proven you are loyal subjects and good people."

"You've proven that too, Seth."

He rubbed his stubbly chin, the dim light enhancing the dark circles under his eyes. "He'll be okay. We have to have faith. Get some rest."

After he'd closed the door behind him, Jenna flopped face down on the soft covers of the bed, praying Teo would be back to his old self by the morning's light.

⚓ ♨ ⚓

The sunlight streaming in the windows woke Rider. She rolled over in her bed, glancing at the clock on the bedside table. Her half-closed eyes flew open. How was it ten in the morning? Throwing off the covers, Rider bolted for the bathroom where she splashed warm water onto her face. Feeling around for the towel she'd seen last night, her fingers closed around the soft fabric, and she lifted it to her face and wiped off the water. After hanging the towel on the gold-coloured rack on the wall, she studied her reflection, finger combing her hair in an unsuccessful attempt to tame the dark curls. Giving up, she pulled a toothbrush out of her bag, brushed her teeth, then ran for the door. *You need an escort.* Rider ignored her father's voice in her head. *It's not far to Teo's room,* she argued with the imaginary voice.

Shutting the door behind her, she scanned one end of the hallway and then the other. Empty. Her father was being overprotective; she'd run to Teo's room and be back in the family suites within minutes. What could possibly happen?

Not giving herself time to answer that, Rider started along the hallway. After turning a corner, she passed by a tall plant in an alcove. A shadow moved behind it, and she whirled toward it, her heart pounding. "Who's there?"

Matrix stepped into view. Clutching her chest, Rider laughed in relief. "Matrix! You scared the living daylights out of me." Her laughter faded when he didn't return the chuckle. "What are you doing here? How did you get inside the palace?" She rubbed her sweaty palms against her pants as red flags waved wildly in her mind. No one was around. Where were all the palace workers? And security?

He leaned in close. "I have friends here too."

What was that supposed to mean? Her heart thudded against her rib cage as she tried to side-step around him. Matrix moved with her, blocking her path. When he reached out, she jerked back. "I-I need to go. Stop fooling around. It's not funny."

He shot out an arm like a snake striking, latching onto her wrist. She tugged but his grip was as tight as a handcuff. "I'm not fooling around, Jenna. You need to come with me."

She struggled to un-attach herself, but Matrix's grip only tightened. Rider scowled at him. "You're hurting me. Let go."

The steel grip loosened, although he didn't let go. "Teo is in trouble, and I can help. My friends can help."

"What do you mean? He's getting help. My father is helping him."

A dark shadow crossed Matrix' face but quickly disappeared. "That's great. Why don't we go see how the king is doing together?"

Rider stared at him. If he was inside the palace, then he had been vetted. Perhaps if she went with him, she could lose him or send him away. "Okay." Instead of heading towards Teo's suites, though, Matrix tugged her the opposite direction.

"This is the wrong way," she protested, blood rushing through her veins.

"They've moved Teo to another room. The head maid is a friend." Matrix's grip on her wrist tightened. The hair on Rider's neck bristled. She dragged her feet, but he yanked her forward.

The area they were in was not familiar to Rider. No maids or butlers or any of the royal family appeared to be around. When she opened her mouth to question him again, Matrix clamped his hand over her lips and then shoved her against the wall. She planted her free hand on his chest and pushed, but it was like trying to move a cement block.

"Listen to me. The king is a lost cause. He is never going to allow equality between the Wolves and the Foresters. You can't trust Teo, but you can trust me." Matrix's eyes darkened. "The Howells stole Wolf Kingdom from my family. We're taking it back. And when we do, we'll make sure the Foresters are treated with respect and dignity."

Rider dragged a breath in through her nose, wishing he'd remove his hand from her mouth.

"This can go smoothly. If you fight me, though, I'll have to take matters into my own hands. In my pocket is a syringe full of the bioweapon, which I'll jab you with if you make any sound or motion that draws attention to us. I don't want to have to do that."

Rider forced her body to relax. Maybe if she appeared to go along with him, an opportunity to escape might present itself.

"That's so much better, little red hood." He lifted his hand from her mouth an inch and waited. She stayed mute.

He smirked. "Good girl."

"You set up Ethan," she hissed.

Matrix tilted his head, his eyes roving over her face. "I knew you were smart. I didn't have him killed, though. I wanted no part of that."

Did he think that absolved him?

"Who are your friends here at the palace? Sirhaan?"

Although he'd removed his hand, Matrix still held her against the wall with his body. "A guard or two who are sick of the Howells. A king who is a tyrant followed by a weak patsy of the forest isn't endearing to most Wolves. We have more friends than you know."

Matrix stepped back, releasing her from the wall, although he regained his grip on her wrist. "They stole my inheritance, and I want it back. I'm sure you can understand that. If they stole the forest from you, you'd want it back too."

"That's absurd. The Wolves aren't going to kick us out of the forest." They would never do that. "You're insane. It's not your inheritance. Teo will never give up Wolf Kingdom."

"I suppose not... which is why I'm going to kill him."

Rider lunged forward, but he pulled her up short by the wrist. Her feet were almost off the floor, her arm stretched overhead as if she were an elastic band.

"Jenna, I don't want to hurt you. We'd make a great team. I can help you protect the forest and make sure you get all the respect you deserve."

She tried kicking him but couldn't get enough leverage since her feet barely touched the floor.

He was so tall and strong.

"Or I can shoot you full of the bioweapon. There's lots where this dose came from. Enough to make *you* willing to be the one to kill him." Matrix twirled a curl between his thumb and forefinger. "Like I said, though, I'd hate to do that to you." He let the curl bounce out of his grasp.

He'd make her kill Teo?

He lowered his arm, and her feet hit the floor. "That's what I thought. Now follow me." Still gripping her wrist, he yanked her along behind him until he came to a door that blended in with the wall. He knocked three times before opening it and shoving her ahead of him into a room the size of a closet. A few boxes lined one wall with a familiar looking man leaning against them. He did not look happy.

"I believe you know Sirhaan."

Rider had forgotten how nice looking Sirhaan was. For an old guy. Shouldn't a villain have bad teeth or an ugly mole on his face?

"What is the latest update on the king?" Matrix still gripped her wrist.

Sirhaan smirked. "Why don't you ask your girlfriend?"

Rider glanced between the two men. *Girlfriend?*

"I'm asking you." Matrix's voice was low and lethal.

Sirhaan shrugged. "I don't know. The knights in shining forest gear arrived, and I got shut out. And now I'm hiding in a closet."

Matrix ran his fingers through his hair and then grabbed her chin and cheek, pulling her face close to his. "Pay attention, princess. What treatment is your father giving Teo?"

"How would I know? You stepped into my path this morning on my way to find out."

Matrix's eyes narrowed. "I guess we'll find out together."

Rider glared at him, pretending she didn't want to cooperate. If she could get back to Teo's room, then she could let her father, Seth, and Alarick know what was going on. Give them some kind of signal. "There is absolutely no way that I am going to Teo's rooms with you."

Chapter Sixty-Two
Matrix

D ID SHE THINK HIM a fool? Matrix stared at Jenna, her features defiant. He could practically see the wheels turning in her head as she tried to figure out a way to let the others know about him. Her loyalty made his blood boil. After the way Teo had treated her, she was still on his side? The king wasn't worthy of her.

"Don't bother trying to figure out any kind of plan to reveal to them what is going on. I'm not letting you anywhere near your father or the royals without preparations in place." He glanced at Sirhaan. "Where's the armour?"

The man patted one of the boxes he leaned against.

"Open it."

Sirhaan opened the box and pulled out a suit, handing it to him as Matrix shoved Jenna toward his uncle.

Matrix yanked off his hoodie and pulled the armour shirt over his head. It fit like a bodysuit but was resistant to any weapon humankind had devised. He couldn't be burned or pierced. He pulled the chaps on and buckled them in place over his jeans. Then he slid his dagger into the holder on his belt, withdrew the syringes from his jeans, and inserted them into a side pocket on the chaps. *Bioweapon*—the look on Jenna's face had squeezed his chest when he'd mentioned the word. She had nothing to worry about; both needles were full of sedatives. He'd never risk Jenna's life. Didn't she know that? Obviously not, if her glare said anything. He'd have to convince her later when they had time. When this was all over and he was on the throne. He'd show her then that he was the only one deserving of the crown and her.

Grabbing Jenna by the arm, he yanked her out into the hall. Eventually, she'd recognize he was the better man. Until then, he'd have to keep her close.

Sirhaan followed them. "I'm coming too."

Matrix frowned. He wanted Sirhaan to disappear, but that wasn't going to happen. Not yet. Better to keep him close for now, so Matrix could keep an eye on him. His uncle was a loose cannon. Exhaling loudly, Matrix pulled Jenna forward with Sirhaan close on their heels.

Once they neared the king's door, Matrix whispered in her ear, "Tell the guards we've been approved as visitors. They'll believe you."

The guards moved to block the door, but Jenna held up her hand. "They're friends."

When neither appeared to believe her, he and Sirhaan each jabbed a guard in the neck with a needle containing a sedative. Both men dropped to the floor. Jenna covered her mouth with her hand.

The door opened, and Seth peered cautiously out. "Jenna, where have you been?" Before she could answer, Sirhaan shoved his way into the room, knocking the prince backwards. Matrix grabbed Jenna, encircling his arm around her neck. *I hope Dr. Hood's medicine has worked and Teo remembers who she is, or this isn't going to work.*

Eyes sweeping the room, his gaze fell on the king, sitting in a chair, his mouth open. Rising, Teo clenched his fists at his sides. By the looks of things, he'd regained his memory. And his strength. No swaying or staggering today.

The king stepped toward them, holding out a hand. "Let her go. It's me you want."

Seth came up beside his brother, wiping blood from the corner of his mouth. Matrix huffed out a breath. Did they think they could stop him? He pulled the syringe out of his pocket. "Not a chance. She's my insurance." He nodded at his uncle. "My friend, Sirhaan, is talented at making people obey commands they don't want to. He has, shall we say, special skills." Matrix glanced between Jenna and Teo. Would the king take the bait? "I don't want to hurt her, but Sirhaan would take great pleasure in making Jenna sing like a canary or beg for mercy." A sour taste filled his mouth as the words left his lips. He hoped it wouldn't come to that, but he'd choose the crown over a girl if he had to.

Teo held his hands up. "What do you want? I already said I'd go with you."

"Teo, no." Jenna's breathing was shallow next to Matrix's ear.

"Let her go, and I'll come with you in her place." Teo took a tentative step toward him.

"Yes, you will. Let's go." Matrix didn't loosen his grip on Jenna. He'd kill Teo in an instant, but he wasn't about to leave Jenna here. Eventually, Matrix would win her over. If he was patient, she'd come to see the truth that he was the right guy for her.

When Teo took another step, Seth grabbed his brother's arm to stop him, his gaze firmly fixed on Matrix. "Why don't you tell us what you want? Maybe we can make a deal."

"I already told you. The king needs to come with me because he has something of mine I want back."

Teo frowned. "I have nothing of yours."

Matrix leveled his gaze on the king. "I want my kingdom and inheritance back."

Teo's top lip curled up as he shook his head. "I'm sorry. The throne is not up for grabs."

Matrix pulled Jenna closer, leaning into her curls while keeping his eyes on Teo. Matrix sniffed Jenna's hair, her sweet scent filling his nostrils. He smiled at Teo. "You sure about that?" His tone was low, even, but inside his gut churned.

The king's jaw tightened. "What makes you think it's your kingdom? Are you an illegitimate son of my father's?"

"Please don't insult me," Matrix spat. "Your family stole the kingdom from mine."

Teo's eyes widened. "You're Joseph's Haan's relative." He crossed his arms over his chest. "That was resolved long ago. You lost. Get over it."

Matrix tightened his grip on Jenna's throat. "I'm not getting over anything. It's you for Jenna. Surrender would be your best option."

Teo touched a finger to his chin before shaking his head. "I don't think so. Let her go."

Matrix stood his ground. He had his answers. Teo was back to normal; the bioweapon had failed.

He held up a syringe. "Negotiations are over."

Chapter Sixty-Three

Teo

TEO LOCKED EYES WITH the madman whose hold on Jenna made him sick. Much of his memory had come back after the third dose of medicine that morning. All he'd wanted to do was go find Jenna and give her the news, but his brother had convinced him to wait. Teo shouldn't have listened. Thankfully, for the first time in a long time, his mind was clear. *You're right, negotiations* are *over.* Two against two. Sure, Sirhaan and Matrix were bigger, but not by much. As long as the syringe held by Matrix was the only bioweapon they had on them, Teo liked their odds. He glanced at Seth, then lifted his hands, palms facing out. "Let her go and I'll come with you."

There was no way Teo was going to let Matrix leave the room with Jenna. He curled his fingers slightly. Seth stepped closer to the two men.

"Not so fast. You'll both come with us or else..." Matrix didn't sound as though he was bluffing. When he tightened his grip on Jenna's neck and she let out a soft cry, Teo started forward. "Don't hurt her. I'll come." He turned to Seth, who glared at him. "Back off, brother, and let us go."

"Teo—"

"That's an order."

Seth lowered his head, shoulders slumping. Suddenly, he lunged at Sirhaan, ramming the older man's stomach with his head. The distraction caused Matrix to lower the needle slightly, allowing Teo to twirl around and kick it out of his hand. Then he yanked Jenna from Matrix's grasp and shoved her behind him. Matrix came at him, but

Teo was ready for him. When they struggled, Teo channelled every bit of fury coursing through him at the way Matrix had treated Jenna and threw the guy on the ground. Teo slammed his fist into Matrix's jaw, hard, then he flipped him onto his stomach and yanked Matrix's hand behind his back.

Seth lay sprawled on the ground. Was he unconscious? With no one holding him back, Sirhaan jumped Teo, knocking him off Matrix and onto the floor before landing on top of him with an oomph. Teo shoved the older man off him and then attempted to clamber to his feet. Before he could, Matrix jumped him, getting a chokehold on Teo.

Blood rushed to his head, causing his vision to blacken at the edges. He tried prying Matrix's arms off with his fingers, but they were like a vise, blocking out all air. His eyes bulged as blood pounded in his ears.

Suddenly, Matrix's hold slackened, and he fell on top of Teo. Gasping for breath, Teo shoved the guy off him and struggled to his knees, coughing and spluttering.

A steadying hand rested on his arm. "You're okay." Dr. Hood knelt beside him. Teo caught a glimpse of the wide open door to the suite before he shifted his attention to his uncle, who was bent over Seth. Dr. Hood followed Teo's gaze. "He's okay. Just got clocked pretty good."

"Jen—"

"I'm right here."

Teo gulped more air, trying to slow down his respirations, but his whole body felt panicky. Dr. Hood breathed with him, counting the inhalations. Finally, Teo was breathing normally. He glanced around for Jenna, who sat propped against a wall, her face pale. He scrutinized her, searching for injuries, before his eyes landed on the broken piece of pottery in her hand—the top of a vase that no longer had a base.

She looked at it as though she'd forgotten she held it. "It did the trick. Got him to stop choking you. Sorry if it was valuable." She smiled thinly.

A chuckle escaped from his throat, which sent him into a coughing spasm again. He tried to take a few deep breaths as Dr. Hood walked over to his daughter. He gently pulled the broken pottery from her hand, then drew her to her feet, where she collapsed against him.

Teo watched her father gently hold her while she cried, and a wave of jealousy washed over him. After the way he had treated her, the things he had said, would he ever be allowed to hold her like that again?

Chapter
Sixty-Four
Rider

GENERAL SCAR HAD SECURED Sirhaan and Matrix with their hands cuffed behind their backs and leg cuffs around their ankles. Alarick had hit an emergency button as soon as he made sure his nephews were okay, and the general and Wolf Pack came running. Rider figured there were at least half a dozen guards outside the room. The two Matrix and Sirhaan had drugged were at the infirmary, but Dr. Lupine was pretty sure the injection had only been a sedative. So, Matrix had lied about it being a bioweapon.

The Queen Mother had arrived minutes before, looking grim. If looks could kill, the only thing left of Sirhaan would be ashes. She'd hugged each son in a tight embrace.

Teo, Seth, and Alarick stood to one side of the room with the Queen Mother, observing General Scar as he questioned the men. Rider's father had gone to retrieve salves and more medicine for Teo.

"Who else is involved?" General Scar leaned close to the prisoners, a vein throbbing in his forehead. Rider bit her lip. The general was scary when he chose to be, and she hoped to never find herself on the other end of his temper.

Matrix stared straight ahead, but Sirhaan swallowed, his Adam's apple bobbing. Sweat beaded on his top lip.

Scar focused his intense glare on Matrix's uncle, disregarding his personal space. "What do you want to tell us?"

"I—"

Before Sirhaan could say more, Matrix lunged at his partner, head-butting him. Blood spurted from Sirhaan's nose as General Scar and Teo pulled Matrix off the man.

"Shut up!" Matrix screamed.

Rider grimaced at the blood running down the older man's face. Neither the general nor Teo moved to help him.

"Well?" General Scar growled, but Sirhaan's lips thinned, reminding Rider of a zipper closing.

Matrix stared, sullen, at his shoes. Teo moved away from the men, motioning for General Scar to follow. Two Wolf Pack guards hauled Sirhaan and Matrix to their feet and out of the room. The king and the general walked over to Seth, his mother, and Alarick. Rider edged closer, trying to listen in on their conversation.

"How many do you think are involved?" Seth kept his voice low.

"Sirhaan deals in weapons. I'm worried there's an army out there waiting for their signal." Teo propped a shoulder against the wall. He still looked pale, shaken.

"I'm not sure about that. The forest is clear." General Scar scowled. "From what they said, I think they hoped we'd destroy one another."

The thought of the Wolves and Foresters fighting made Rider sick to her stomach. How had they gotten here?

"You might be right, but we still need to send the Wolf Pack to the Lake District and investigate." Teo rubbed his eyes with his thumb and forefinger.

"Do we really want to do that?" Seth cast a glance at his brother before directing his attention to the general. "I mean, Sirhaan's company has amassed a huge stockpile of weapons, and they created the bioweapon too."

General Scar crossed his burly arms over his broad chest. "Since Sirhaan's report, I've been stopping up the gaps he noted. Although there was room for improvement, he did exaggerate how bad it was. The troops are always ready to battle, despite what was reported." He uncrossed his arms and rested his fingers on his sidearm. "We need to show them we mean business, but we're willing to talk peace too."

"I agree." Teo shoved off the wall. "Get a delegation ready, General. Take your best men and show them we're serious, and it's their choice—war or peace."

His mother nodded but remained silent. Perhaps she was learning to trust Teo to lead. Rider could hope.

The general saluted and left the room as Rider hustled to her seat, hoping her eavesdropping had gone unnoticed. The Queen Mother, along with Teo and Seth, moved into an adjacent bedroom. Rider pursed her lips. What was that about? Hopefully the three of them were having the conversation they'd needed to have for a long time.

Suddenly alone, Rider shivered as exhaustion blanketed her body and mind. Would Matrix have harmed her? Rider didn't know, although he had seemed to hope she'd side with him. How crazy was that? He'd basically set up her best friend only to have his partner kill him, and that wasn't even taking into consideration the fact that they were poisoning Teo in an attempt to steal his throne. Matrix was insane if he thought she would suddenly want him and willingly help with his inane plan to crown himself king.

Her dad strode into the room, stopped, looked around. "Where is everyone?"

Rider tilted her head toward the door where the Howell family had disappeared. "Teo, Seth, and the Queen Mother went in there. Private family meeting, I think."

Her dad nodded. "Ah." He sat beside Rider, grabbed her hand. "And how are you, Jenna-girl?" His green eyes bored into her.

"I've been better." Her lips wobbled.

Her dad pulled her against his strong chest and Rider rested there, letting the tears flow down her cheeks.

"It must have been an awful experience to have your friend grab you." Her dad smoothed her hair down her back.

"Dad, he poisoned Teo and tried to take his throne. He's no friend of mine." Still, he was an acquaintance, and it was shocking that he was a part of all the bad things happening in the kingdom. That he'd tricked and threatened her.

"It *was* frightening, especially when I thought he was going to jab me with the bioweapon." She sniffled.

Her dad handed her his hankie and she wiped her nose.

"I'm so thankful you're all right." Her dad kissed the top of her head. They sat in silence, her dad's presence comforting Rider. The people she loved most were all safe—Teo, his family, her dad, and the kingdom. She snuggled up close to her father's warm body, glad for the reprieve. Maybe now things would settle down in Wolf Kingdom, and they could all get on with their lives.

A girl could hope.

Chapter Sixty-Five

Teo

T EO FOLLOWED SETH AND his mother into the bedroom. The large four-poster bed was made, the sheets and bedspread so tight he could have bounced a coin on it. The curtains were drawn back, allowing sunlight to stream in. He sat on the edge of the bed while Seth took a chair nearby. His mother stood before them, her hands clasped tightly in front of her. Not saying anything, she stared at the plush carpet. After a minute more, she released her clenched hands, flexing her fingers. Was she nervous? Teo had few memories, if any, of his mother being nervous when she addressed her sons.

He exchanged a *What's going on* look with Seth, who only shrugged.

As the silence continued, Teo shifted on the bed. "Mother," he prompted.

The Queen Mother inhaled a shaky breath. "Teo, Seth." She swallowed. "I want to tell you how sorry I am." She pressed her fingers to her lips as her eyes glassed over.

Teo stilled, waited. What was happening?

His mother cleared her throat. "Teo, I owe you an apology for not trusting you. You repeatedly said you didn't like Sirhaan; nevertheless, I ignored you. And I did not take your illness nearly seriously enough. I don't know how to apologize for all of that, other than to beg you to please forgive me."

Beg? Teo had never heard his mother beg for anything in his life. The cold, hard ball that had formed in his chest when she had insisted Sirhaan stay in the castle against Teo's wishes or brushed aside the agony he was feeling began to melt. He hadn't believed he would be able to forgive her, but he never would have imagined she would be so broken over what she had done. Deep down, he understood that, even if she had trusted the wrong person, she'd done it because she wanted badly to keep Teo and Wolf Kingdom safe. Could he fault her for that? "Mother, it's okay." In the end, hadn't Teo listened to the man himself? Even if he was being poisoned by a bioweapon, he should have done a better job at keeping the man away from both him and his mother. He was the king, and his failure to assert leadership had nearly cost the entire kingdom.

"No, it's not, Teo. I was infatuated with Sirhaan and all the attention he paid me. It felt so good to be seen after—" she faltered, "well, after the last few years with your father. He was so paranoid and focused on power that, well, it wasn't good for us. I'm sure you noticed."

Both Teo and Seth nodded.

"I'm sorry for that, too. Your father was hard on all of you boys, especially you, Teo. And Bleddyn. I was so angry with Duko for letting him die that I only wanted to forget all the terrible things that had happened. Sirhaan provided a perfect distraction. I didn't want to see the red flags or listen to your warnings." She wiped away a tear from her cheek with her fingers. "Then I almost lost you, Teo, to that bioweapon. How can you forgive me for that?"

"I should have kicked him out. I didn't protect you, either."

His mother huffed a breath. "You tried, but I'm the parent. And I'm the one who allowed that man into the castle. It was my mistake, not yours. I will understand if you can never get past that."

Teo stood and pulled his mother close. As her arms wrapped around him, warmth filled a hollow place in his heart. "I forgive you," he whispered. "I love you, Mom."

She hugged him before stepping back. "I love you too, Son, and I'm so proud of you. You are going to be a great man and a wonderful king." She cupped his chin. "Believe in yourself. I do."

Teo's eyes burned, and he was glad she turned her focus on Seth. Although Teo wasn't sure how he'd make a good king when he'd let himself be duped by Sirhaan. How could he prevent it from happening again? He shoved the thought aside. He didn't want to think about that and ruin this moment, although it was something he and his trusted advisors would need to discuss soon. For now, he focused on his mother and Seth.

The Queen Mother gripped his little brother's forearms. "Seth, I owe you an apology, too. You were the only one who stood by your brother, supporting him. That took a great deal of courage. Thank you for being a good brother and advisor. I'm sorry I didn't believe you either, didn't support you. Will you forgive me?"

Seth was already sweeping her up in an embrace. "I forgive you, Mom."

"I love you, Seth."

Seth squeezed her so hard that she giggled. "Is that an I love you, too?" she laughed.

"Yes, I love you, Mom." He lowered her to the ground.

"I almost lost you both." She bit her lip.

"We're fine. I'm only glad it's over." Teo held his hand out to Seth, who stared at it.

"Seth, thank you for having my back always. You were the only one in the castle who believed me, and you fought for me when I couldn't fight for myself. Thank you." *He'd be a better king.* Although it was the truth, Teo didn't have the luxury of making that choice. He was heir.

Seth swiped at the corner of his eye before grabbing Teo's hand. Teo pulled him into a man hug.

"I love you, little brother."

Seth slapped his back. "If I'm so little, then how come I'm as tall as you now?"

Teo chuckled. "Just remember who's boss, okay?"

"Always. The buck stops with you. As far as I'm concerned, I'm more than okay with that." His face turned serious. "I'll always have your back."

"I know it."

"Bleddyn would have too." His mother smiled sadly. "He would have had both your backs."

"He'll always be with us in our hearts and memories." Teo picked up a photo from the bedside table, of the family taken at some event when the boys were tweens. Although a formal occasion, the brothers were goofing off for the photographer. The deadpan looks on their parents' faces only made it funnier.

"Yeah, he's laughing at Teo's long hair right now." Seth skimmed his hand over Teo's head.

Teo flicked Seth's hand away. "Hey, I like my hair." He placed the photo back on the table.

"I think a certain young lady does as well." His mother tried to smooth down Teo's tousled head, although she couldn't quite reach.

Teo's heart rose in his throat at the mention of Jenna. He still needed to speak with her. He'd been such a jerk to her. What must she think of him? "I'm not so sure. I've treated her horribly. I didn't even remember her." Teo sank onto the bed again, his fingers bunching the gold spread. How could he have ever forgotten her?

"She'll understand." His mother sat beside him and patted his knee. "Give her time."

Teo gave his mother a sidelong look. "Does your change of heart mean that if she does agree to accept me back, the two of us can date?"

His mother lifted her hands, palms up. "She's unselfish and has proven more than once that she loves this kingdom and us Wolves. Her father, too. He saved us from the Lupine flu and now he's brought you back to health. If you want to date her, Teo, you have my blessing."

Teo slipped his arm around his mother's waist, drawing her close. "Thank you." Perhaps things were looking up. There was work to be done, repairing the relations between Wolves and Foresters as well as convincing everyone in the kingdom they were safe now, that the threats of war, bioweapons, and more had been eliminated. His mother and brother were behind him, though. They believed he could lead this kingdom. Did Teo? He still had his doubts.

And Jenna? Maybe she'd forgive him for the way he'd treated her. Really, there was only one way to find out. Inhaling deeply, he stood. He needed to speak with her. Because he didn't want to move into the future without her.

Chapter Sixty-Six
Rider

AT THE SOUND OF the bedroom door opening, Rider sat up, wiping her face with her sleeve. Her father stood as the Queen Mother entered the room, followed by Teo and Seth.

Teo's mom walked over to Rider and her father. She held out her hand to Dr. Hood. "I can't thank you enough for what you've done for my son and this kingdom, Dr. Hood. I'm forever indebted to you. If you ever need anything, don't hesitate to ask."

Her father's eyes widened as he shook her hand, his large one dwarfing her's. "Thank you, Your Majesty."

She faced Rider. "I'm very happy you weren't harmed, Jenna. Again, I can't thank you enough for standing by my son and not giving up. I apologize for being less than accepting of you. You are most welcome here at this palace." The Queen Mother glanced at Teo, whose grin was bigger than a kid who'd just gotten a puppy.

Before Rider could respond, Teo's mother pulled her into a tight embrace. The sweet scent of roses filled Rider's nostrils. The woman stepped back, smiled warmly, then strode from the room, leaving Rider standing slack-jawed. What did that mean? Was there hope for her and Teo? She shoved down the little seed of hope that wanted to sprout.

Seth poured a glass of water and handed it to Teo, who, although still smiling, looked like a wilted plant. He gulped the liquid before sinking onto the couch and leaning his head against the back.

Her father pulled a needle from his bag. Teo closed his eyes, but otherwise didn't react as her father injected him with the meds. "Your Majesty, you've barely had a minute to rest, let alone recover. Please take a nap." Her father gently chided the king.

"I'll rest here on the couch." Teo gripped Dr. Hood's arm. "Thank you, Dr. Hood. For everything."

"It's my privilege to serve you. Now, get some rest. You're too stubborn for your own good." Her father shook his head, but he left the king alone. "He should eat something after he's napped," he said to Seth over his shoulder on his way out. "Salves are on the table if you want to apply them to your mouth."

Seth nodded, rubbing his chin. The blood around his mouth from Sirhaan's large fist was starting to dry. "Thank you, Dr. Hood." He followed her father out of the room, pausing briefly in the doorway to incline his head in Rider's direction. "I'm going to the kitchen for ice. Watch him, okay?"

Rider nodded, her gaze drifting to Teo. He hadn't moved since he'd sunk onto the couch. The door clicked softly, and the men were gone, leaving her and Teo alone in the room. She stood and grabbed a blanket from the back of a chair to drape over his legs. His breaths were deep and even, and she couldn't resist reaching out to swipe his hair out of his eyes. *It's so long.* She squeaked when his long fingers wrapped around her wrist and shoved her hand away from his face. His eyes flew open as he released her. "I'm sorry. I thought..."

She shook her head. "No, I'm sorry. I thought you were asleep. After Matrix held me by my wrist, it caught me off guard when you grabbed me."

"I didn't mean to scare you. Will you sit?" He straightened, his voice raspy from the chokehold. She sat next to him, not touching him but close enough that his body heat warmed her.

"I'm afraid to ask what you think of me. That I fell so easily for Sirhaan's lies..."

Rider frowned. "What? You were drugged. I don't blame you for that. I'm just grateful you're okay."

"The one thing I never wanted to be was my father. These past few days, though, I was worse than him."

Rider rested her hand on his knee. "What are you talking about? You are nothing like Duko."

Teo stared straight ahead, not meeting her eyes. "I am exactly like him. I endangered the whole kingdom. I believed the lies they were telling me. I willingly let in the dark."

"You were under the influence of a bioweapon—"

"Which I never should have allowed near me or my kingdom. I knew there was something about Sirhaan. I should have kicked him out right away. Instead, he was living in the palace!"

"Teo, you're wrong."

"Am I?"

Rider took his chin in her fingers and turned his face to her so he couldn't look away. "Yes, you are."

"No one should have ever gotten that close to me."

"How could you have known? Sirhaan fooled your mother, and Matrix deceived Ethan and others. And he had me second-guessing myself. Besides, letting people into your inner circle is what makes you different than Duko."

He shrugged.

"Hey. I mean it."

A sad smile crossed his lips. "I don't know who to trust anymore. How can I lead when I can't trust people?"

"You have good instincts. You'll know who to trust when the time comes, and if you're unsure, you have Seth and Alarick to advise you. You don't have to lead alone."

Teo pursed his lips as though contemplating that. "My mother and brother just told me that in so many words. My mom apologized for siding with Sirhaan and not me, and I truly believe nothing like that will happen again. So maybe you're right. I do trust them." He rested his forehead against hers. Her heart beat a staccato rhythm in her chest. "I trust you too. And your father."

"You asked what I must think of you now. That hasn't changed. I think you are going to be an amazing Wolf King. You were born for this role at this time. You are going to bring about the changes that need to come. I have no doubt about it."

His eyes darkened, and her stomach flip-flopped as their breaths mingled. He brushed his soft lips against hers. "And us? Do you have any doubts?" His voice was husky and deep, almost a whisper.

She stroked his stubbly cheek, moving on to trace his soft, full lips with her fingers. "No, I don't have any doubts about us. About you." She leaned closer to him, her lips on his once more. His hands moved up her back to her cheeks, and she lost herself in his taste and embrace.

After a moment, he pulled away, his hands cupping her face. "Even if I was under the influence of a powerful drug, I'm so sorry I hurt you. I never want to do that."

"I forgive you, Teo."

He tucked a curl behind her ear. A light rap on the door interrupted them and they pulled apart as Seth walked in, carrying a tray loaded with sandwiches, fruits and veggies, and a bag of ice. He set the tray on a table as Teo laughed.

"Um, did you think you were feeding a multitude, Seth?"

He grinned and shrugged. "I'm famished, so I figured you both would be too." He sat on the floor and picked up a napkin, setting a roast beef sandwich on it along with some veggies.

Teo bent forward to grab a napkin and a tuna sandwich. He offered Rider a plate. "Eat. You must be famished."

Rider didn't reach for it. "I should go. You need to rest and spend some time with your family."

Teo grabbed her hand and tugged on it. "No, you don't have to go. I would like you to stay." He motioned to the plate of food. "We're never going to eat this all by ourselves. Besides, my mom has given her blessing for us to date."

Rider's eyes widened. "Really?" Was that what she'd meant when she'd said Rider was welcome at the palace?

"Yup." Teo grinned and touched her cheek with his finger.

"If you're going to get mushy, please tell me so I can go elsewhere." Seth held a sandwich midway to his mouth.

Teo ignored his brother. "Jenna, whatever we do moving forward, we need your input. If there's one thing I learned from all this, it's that unity is key. We all need equal opportunities and rights so no one gets power-crazy. If true unity is going to happen, we must hear the Foresters' side. We need your voice. So please. I want you to stay."

Seth resumed eating, swallowed. "I agree with Teo, one hundred percent." He filled a plate with veggies and sandwiches and offered it to her.

Rider studied the two of them for a minute before taking the proffered meal. "Did your mom really give her blessing?"

Teo smiled. "She did. After everything that has happened, I'm pretty sure she's going to want you here as much as I do."

Chapter Sixty-Seven

Teo

Six months later

THE PLAID WOOL BLANKET cocooned Teo and Jenna on the porch swing of her house. When she snuggled against his chest, a whiff of honeysuckle tickled his nose. His protection detail was discreetly placed around her father's property. They blended in so adeptly that he and Jenna were mostly able to forget that the men and women were nearby.

The six months since Matrix tried to steal the kingdom had flown by. Teo had regained his strength, and, thanks to Dr. Hood's treatments, his migraines were few and far between. He had talked to a doctor about his fears of becoming like Duko, which had helped him gain clarity about his past and what his future might look like. Instead of fighting to control everything, he decided to empower the people around him, the people of his kingdom. All of them. It had been a small miracle to see Wolves and Foresters talk, debate, and listen. One huge victory was the removal of the documentation to enter the city. The gates were now only patrolled for the safety of all, including the forest. Teo had hosted a bonfire in front of the city gates, where all the Foresters burned their papers. It had turned into a festive party. The memory still made him smile.

"What are you grinning at?" Jenna gazed at him.

Teo kissed the top of her head. "Remembering the bonfire a couple weeks back."

"You were dancing like a crazy Wolf." She snickered. "I didn't realize you had those kinds of moves, Your Majesty."

"Oh baby, you haven't even begun to see my moves." He waggled his eyebrows.

"I'm intrigued."

"It's true. I could show you a few right now." Teo's grin grew wicked as he leaned closer, mere inches from her lips. "Interested?"

"Absolutely," she breathed. He kissed her gently. After almost losing her, he cherished every moment they had to spend together.

She broke the kiss and lifted her shoulders. "Not bad."

"Not bad?" he objected.

She laughed. "Royally good?"

He groaned. "Terrible." He grazed her jawline with his thumb. Her silken skin was creamy, and he had to exercise extreme willpower to not touch her continually. "I love you, Jenna," he whispered.

Her eyes met his.

"I love you, Jenna." Louder this time. "Since that first time you hit me with your bike—"

She punched him in the bicep. He laughed as he rubbed his arm.

"You walked right out—"

Teo kissed her, silencing her protest. "Shh." He placed a finger against her lips. "You are beautiful inside and out. I wouldn't be here without you."

She ran her fingers through his hair, which made the trouble of keeping it on the longer side well worth it. Shivers danced over his scalp.

"I love you too." Her green eyes drew him in.

It was crazy that he felt this way about her. They had once been enemies, but now he would never want to be in a world she wasn't a part of. Whatever the future held, they would weather it together—the good, the bad, and the messy. They might be a Wolf and a Forester, but they weren't enemies.

In fact, Teo knew without a doubt that they were made for each other.

Acknowledgements

Many people came together to make this book a reality.

Sara Davison, my editor extraordinaire. Thank you doesn't seem like enough. I'm so grateful you take on my projects.

My Beta Readers: Trina Jones, Nicole David, Robin Livingston. Your suggestions, thoughtful critiques help me write a more complete story. Your input and feedback is priceless. Thank you.

Thank you, Jenneth Dyke, for another amazing cover. You have a gift and I'm so grateful you've shared it with us.

Thank you, Rachael Ward for the beautiful map of Wolf Kingdom.

Thank you, Mom and Dad, for your constant support and encouragement. You both left this earth so quickly and didn't get to see this one published. I'm so grateful that you encouraged me to chase my dreams and not give up. I love you and miss you.

Marguerite and Peter, my in-laws, thank you for your support over the years. Peter, you also went home to be with Jesus this past year. We love and miss you, too.

Ian, and Ben, you inspire me everyday with your courage, kindness, and big hearts. I'm so glad to call you mine.

Mark, thank you for letting me huddle in my office and do what I love. I wouldn't be here without you. Love you.

To all the amazing Kickstarter backers who took a chance on my campaign. Thank you! (Names are in no particular order): Starr Z. Davies, D.L. Gardner, Gordon Armstrong, Janice Dawson, Sara Davison, Jo Lynn Duck, Aileen Wittich, Lisa Whittaker, Dave Riedinger, Jenni McKinney, Nicole Haarstad, MF Caram, Chiara Heinzl, Brianna Welch-Martin, Alice Hanov, Erin Caldwell, Simon Marwood

About the Author

Jennifer Willcock is a writer, wife, mom and dreamer. She writes clean, contemporary romance and fantasy, with a positive, hope-filled message for the YA genre.

Jennifer believes in the power of #STORY because stories can inspire change in someone's life which can have a domino effect on so many other things and people.

For Jennifer, the power of #STORY is made up of three elements, which she tries to include in her writing:

Be creative—use your imagination. Think outside the box.

Find the beauty—tell beautiful stories even in the ugly. Stories of redemption, second chances and grace.

Share stories—tell your story and listen to others. Community is a big part of the writing journey.

Jennifer loves to dance. She studied ballet for many years but she will dance to any kind of music.

She takes her coffee weak with a lot of milk along with any kind of pastry.

She lives in Ontario, Canada, with her husband and two sons and pet rabbit, Ollie.

Also By Jennifer Willcock

Read the first book Into the Forest: A Retelling of Little Red Riding Hood

What if the Wolf fell in love with Red Riding Hood?

Prince Teowulf, Crown Prince of Wolf Kingdom, believes the lessons of superiority he's learned from childhood until a chance encounter with a despised Forester, Jenna "Rider" Hood. Rider is the daughter of Dr. Hood, the premiere pharmacist of Wolf Kingdom, and she turns Prince Teo's world upside down, making him question everything he's ever believed about the Foresters. When sickness strikes the Wolf clan, Rider and Prince Teo must work together to save lives. But can they get past their own hate and prejudice to help others? Will the sparks between Rider and Teo fizzle or burst into flame?

Be sure to visit Jennifer's website to sign up for her newsletter (get a free story) and check out her other YA novels. Sign up at https://jenniferwillcock.com/

www.ingramcontent.com/pod-product-compliance
Lightning Source LLC
Chambersburg PA
CBHW072048190726
48294CB00005B/1460